I couldn't quite get my head around the idea that my first kiss was going to be with Noah Flynn. My best friend's big brother. The guy who could make me feel the most inexplicable things and drive me crazy in three seconds flat.

I gulped, and it must've been audible because he raised an eyebrow at me. My eyes flitted down to his lips; they looked so soft and kissable. My mind drifted to the memory of Noah in his towel . . . in his football uniform . . .

And I was about to kiss him.

I knew I didn't have to if I didn't want to; nobody could force me to kiss him. And that was the worst part: I knew I had the option to back out, and I couldn't bring myself to do it.

I leaned in as he did.

What if I had cotton candy stuck in my teeth? What if I tasted gross?

Shut up, shut up, shut up!

My first kiss . . .

Beth Reekles penned her novel *The Kissing Booth* when she was fifteen and began uploading it to story-sharing platform Wattpad, where it accumulated over 19 million reads. She was signed by Random House UK at the age of seventeen, and was offered a three-book deal whilst studying for her A Levels. Beth now works in IT, having graduated from Exeter University with a physics degree, and has had three books published with Penguin Random House Children's: *The Kissing Booth, Rolling Dice* and *Out of Tune*.

Beth is still writing and regularly blogs about writing and being a twenty-something. She has been shortlisted for the Women of the Future Young Star Award 2013, the Romantic Novel of the Year Awards 2014 and the Queen of Teen Awards 2014. She was named one of *Time* magazine's 16 Most Influential Teenagers 2013, and in August 2014 she was listed in *The Times* at No. 6 on their 'Top 20 under 25' list.

BETH REEKLES

CORGI BOOKS

CORGI BOOKS

UK I USA I Canada I Ireland I Australia
India I New Zealand I South Africa

Corgi Books is part of the Penguin Random House group of companies
whose addresses can be found at global.penguinrandomhouse.com.

www.penguin.co.uk
www.puffin.co.uk
www.ladybird.co.uk

Penguin
Random House
UK

Published in Great Britain by Corgi Books 2013
Reissued 2018

11

Text copyright © Beth Reeks, 2013

The moral right of the author has been asserted

Typeset in Palatino

Printed and bound in Great Britain by Clays Ltd, Elcograf S.p.A.

A CIP catalogue record for this book is available from the British Library

ISBN: 978–0–552–56881–4

All correspondence to
Corgi Books
Penguin Random House Children's
80 Strand, London WC2R 0RL

In memory of my Nan, who proved to me that no matter what, you can always keep soldiering on.

Chapter 1

'Do you want a drink?' Lee called from the kitchen as I shut the front door.

'No, thanks,' I called back. 'I'll head on up to your room.'

'Sure thing.'

I'd never stop wondering at how big Lee Flynn's house was; it was practically a mansion. There was a room downstairs complete with a fifty-inch TV and surround sound, not to mention the pool table, and the (heated) pool outside.

Even though I treated it like a second home the only place I felt really, really comfortable was in Lee's bedroom.

I opened the door and saw the sunlight spilling in through the open doors leading to his small balcony. Posters of bands covered the walls, his drum kit sat in the corner next to a guitar, and his Apple Mac was proudly displayed on a smart mahogany desk that matched the rest of the furniture.

But, just like any other sixteen-year-old boy's room, the floor was littered with T-shirts and underpants and stinky socks; a half-eaten sandwich festered next to the Apple Mac, and empty cans were strewn over almost every surface.

I launched myself onto Lee's bed, loving the way it bounced.

We'd been best friends since we were born. Our moms both knew each other from college and I only lived a ten-minute walk away now. Lee and I had grown up together. We might as well have been twins: freakishly, we were born on the same day.

He was my best friend. Always had been and always will be. Even if he did annoy the hell out of me sometimes.

He turned up just at that moment, holding two opened bottles of orange soda, knowing I'd have drunk his at some point anyway.

'We need to decide what we're doing for the carnival,' I said.

'I know,' he sighed, messing up his dark brown hair and scrunching up his freckled face. 'Can't we just do a coconut thing? You know, when they throw balls and try to knock the coconuts off?'

I shook my head in wonder. 'That's what I was thinking . . .'

'Of course it is.'

I smirked a little. 'But we can't. It's already taken.'

'Why do we have to come up with a booth anyway? Can't we just manage the whole event and make other people come up with the booths?'

'Hey, you're the one who said being on the school council would look good on our college applications.'

'You're the one who agreed to it.'

'Because I wanted to be on the dance committee,' I pointed out. 'I didn't realize we had to work on the carnival too.'

'This sucks.'

'I know. Oh, hey, what about if we hired one of those, um . . . you know' – I made a swinging gesture with my hands – 'those things with the hammer.'

'Where they test your strength?'

'Yeah. That thing.'

'No, they already ordered one of those.'

I sighed. 'I don't know then. There's not much left – everything's already taken.'

We looked at each other and both said, 'I told you we should've started planning this earlier.'

We laughed, and Lee sat at his computer, spinning around on the chair slowly.

'Haunted house?'

I gave him a deadpan look – well, I tried. It wasn't easy to catch his eye when he was spinning around like that.

'It's *spring*, Lee. Not Halloween.'

'Yeah, so?'

'No. No haunted house.'

'Fine,' he grumbled. 'Then what do you suggest?'

I shrugged. Truth was, I had no idea. We were pretty much screwed. If we didn't come up with a booth, then we'd end up being booted off the council, which would mean we couldn't put it on our college applications next year.

'I don't know. I can't think when it's this hot.'

'Then take off your sweater and come up with something.'

I rolled my eyes, and Lee started surfing Google for ideas for a booth for the Spring Carnival. I tugged my sweater off over my head, and felt the sun on my bare stomach. I tried to wriggle my arms back through so I could pull down the tank top I was wearing underneath . . .

'Lee,' I said, my voice muffled. 'A little help?'

He sniggered at me, and I heard him get up. At that moment the bedroom door was pushed open, and I thought for a minute he'd left me in a tangle, but the next second I heard a different voice.

'Jeez, at least lock the door if you guys are going to do that.'

I froze, my cheeks going bright pink as Lee tugged down my tank top and yanked the sweater off my head, leaving my hair static.

I looked up to see his older brother leaning against the door frame, smirking at me.

'Hey, Shelly,' he greeted me. He knew I hate being called Shelly. I let Lee get away with it, but Noah was another matter entirely. He did it solely to annoy me. Nobody else dared call me 'Shelly', not after I had yelled at Cam for it in the fourth grade. Now everybody called me Elle, short for Rochelle. Just like nobody else dared call him 'Noah', except for Lee and his parents; everyone else called him by his surname, Flynn.

'Hi, Noah,' I shot back with a sweet smile.

His jaw clenched and his dark eyebrows rose a little, like he was daring me to carry on calling him that. I just smiled back and the sexy smirk returned to his face.

Noah was just about the hottest guy to grace this earth; believe me, I'm not exaggerating. He had dark hair that flopped into his electric blue eyes, and he was tall and broad shouldered. His nose was a little crooked from when it was broken in a fight and didn't set quite right – Noah wasn't a stranger to fights, but he'd never been suspended. Aside from the occasional 'scrap', as

5

Lee and I had taken to calling it, he was a model student: his grades never dropped below an A, and he was the star of the football team, too.

I used to have a crush on him when I was twelve or thirteen. It passed pretty quickly though, when I realized he was way out of my league and always would be. And even though he was unbelievably hot, I acted my normal self around him because I knew there wasn't a chance in hell that he'd ever look at me as anything other than his kid brother's best friend.

'I know that I seem to have this effect on ladies, but could you please try and keep your clothes on in my presence?'

I laughed sarcastically. 'Dream on.'

'What're you guys doing, anyway?'

I did wonder for a moment why he was interested, but I shrugged it off. Lee said, 'We have to come up with a stupid booth for the carnival.'

'Sounds . . . crap.'

'No kidding,' I said, rolling my eyes. 'All the good booths are taken. We'll end up with something like – like – like that thing where you hook a duck.'

They both looked at me like I couldn't have come up with a worse idea, and I shrugged.

'Whatever. Anyway, Lee – Mom and Dad are away tonight, so party at eight.'

'Cool.'

'And Elle? Try not to strip off in front of everybody for me tonight.'

'You know I only have eyes for Lee,' I said innocently.

Noah laughed a little, smirking. He was already tapping away at his phone – probably broadcasting the message about a party, just like Lee was. He loped out of the room like a lazy cat or something. I couldn't help but let my eyes drag after his cute butt . . .

'Hey, if you could stop checking out my brother for two seconds,' Lee teased.

I blushed and shoved him. 'Shut up.'

'I thought you were over your crush.'

'I am. That doesn't make him any less hot though.'

Lee rolled his eyes at me. 'Whatever. You're gross sometimes, you know.'

I went to sit at the computer, Lee leaning over my shoulders, his chin resting on the top of my head.

I clicked onto the next page of search results and scrolled down, feeling my eyes glaze over as they scanned the page.

I stopped, something catching my eye just as Lee started to say, 'Hold up.'

We both stared at the screen for a few seconds; then he stood up, and I spun the chair around to face him, identical smiles stretching over our faces.

'Kissing booth,' we both said at the same time, grinning. Lee held his hand up for a high five, and I smacked my palm against his.

This was going to be *so* cool.

Chapter 2

We decided that we'd have a two-dollar fee. Two dollars for a kiss. Whatever booth we'd decided on, the basic stall was already there for us to use at the school, but we'd need a lot of pink and red. I thought we should have black, but Lee told me patronizingly, 'It's not Halloween, Shelly.'

'Fine. We'll stick to pink and red.'

'What are we going to need then? Streamers, crepe paper, ribbon . . . That kind of thing, right?'

'Yeah, I guess. Hey, do you think we'd be able to make a big banner in woodwork?' I didn't want to take woodwork, but it was either that or home ec., and after my cupcake disaster of eighth grade, I've tried to stay away from baking. But maybe it'd come in handy.

'I don't see why not. Mr Preston probably won't have a problem with it.'

I nodded. 'Cool. We could probably get some of the

jocks in on it, and the cheerleaders. We need four, and they can all go in shifts of two.'

'Sounds okay. Who should we ask though?'

'Well . . . Samantha and Lily will definitely do it,' I said thoughtfully. 'And they can rope in some other girls.'

'Sounds good. I'll call some of the guys.'

I pulled out my cell phone, scrolling through for their numbers. Lee and I didn't belong to any particular clique; we just hung out with whoever we wanted, which meant we had pretty much everybody's numbers. Lee was one of those charismatic and likeable people, and we came as a package. We did have a few really close friends, of course – all of them guys.

I got hold of Samantha, who chirpily told me that, sure, she was totally up for it! Lily agreed as well, saying she could, like, just not wait for it and would call every girl she knew.

'Done,' I sighed, flopping back on the bed. I felt it bounce as Lee followed suit, and we grinned at each other.

'Our booth is going to kill.'

'I know. We are scary good sometimes.'

'I know.'

My phone beeped, and I saw a text from Lily telling me that Dana and Karen would do the kissing booth too, so I replied a brief thank you.

'The girls are all sorted,' I said.

'Great. Dave texted to say that he'll fix up the guys for us, so it's all done.'

'Which means . . . we have nothing to do now,' I said brightly. 'So you can come shopping with me.'

Lee groaned. 'Why do you need to go shopping? Don't you have enough clothes?'

'Yes, I do . . . But you're having a party tonight and I'm in a good mood since we've sorted out this booth *at last*. So we're going shopping to buy me something to wear later.'

Lee groaned again. 'You just want a hot dress so you can impress my brother, don't you?'

'No. I just want to go get something to wear. But if I do end up impressing your brother . . . that's just a bonus. Not to mention a freaking miracle. We both know he doesn't even think about me in that way . . .'

Lee sighed. 'Fine, fine, we're going shopping. Stop your moaning.'

I grinned triumphantly; I knew I could convince him. Lee realized I was faking my moaning, but he didn't want to hear it either way.

I picked up my sweater and waited for Lee to grab his wallet and sneakers. I bounced downstairs while he trailed behind me. We got into his car – a '65 Mustang he'd got for a steal at a scrap yard – and Lee turned on the engine.

'Thanks, Lee.'

'The things I do for you,' he sighed, but he was smiling.

We were at the mall in twenty minutes. Lee turned off the engine, leaving my ears ringing slightly from the hip-hop that had been blasting out.

'You know you owe me for dragging me here.'

'I'll buy you a donut.'

Lee wavered. 'And a milkshake.'

'Done.'

He slung his arm around my shoulders and I quickly realized why – when he guided me straight to the food court before I could conveniently forget about his bribe. Once Lee was pacified with snacks, he was quite happy to trail around after me to the shops.

After browsing a few stores, I found the perfect outfit.

It was a coral-colored dress, the skirt not too tight or short, and the neck low enough to be flattering without revealing everything. The soft, sheer material was bunched up down the left-hand side, concealing the long zip.

'Do we have to go shoe shopping now too?' Lee moaned as I announced I was trying it on.

'No, I have shoes, Lee,' I said, rolling my eyes.

'Yeah, well, you have clothes too, but that didn't stop you,' he muttered, following me to the changing rooms. He didn't think twice about wandering into the cubicle with me and lying across the stool. But then again, I didn't give a second thought to changing in front of him.

'Zip me up?'

He sighed wearily, and got to his feet to oblige. I looked in the mirror, smoothing the dress. It looked better on the hanger, I thought doubtfully. It showed an awful lot of leg . . .

Lee let out a low wolf-whistle. 'Nice.'

'Shut up. Do you think it's too short?'

He shrugged and smacked my ass. 'Who cares?'

Playfully, I smacked him across the head in reply. 'I'm serious, Lee. Is it too short?'

'Well. Maybe a little. But it looks good.'

'Are you sure?'

'You think I'd lie to you, Shelly?' he asked sadly, putting on a pained expression and staggering back, hands clutched over his heart.

I gave him a look in the mirror. 'Do you need me to answer that, Lee?'

'No, I guess not,' he laughed. 'So you gonna get it?'

I nodded. 'Yeah, I guess. It's fifty per cent off.'

'Cool.' Then he groaned. 'You're not spending that other fifty per cent on shoes, are you? Please tell me you're not. If you are, then you owe me a soda *and* pizza.'

'I promise I'm not buying shoes, or anything else, okay? We can go home after I buy the dress.' I stepped out of it and put on my jeans and top and sweater: the air-con in the mall made it freezing.

'Aw,' he sighed. 'I wanted pizza.'

I laughed, walking out of the cubicle with him in tow. I walked straight into something – no, some*one*.

'Sorry,' I apologized reflexively. Then I realized who it was. 'Oh, hi, Jaime.'

She looked suspiciously from me to Lee, and a sly smile slipped onto her face. Jaime was the biggest gossip in the school, and while she was really nice, she was one of those people who can annoy you very easily for no reason.

'What're you two doing in here? This is the girls' changing rooms, Lee, you know.'

He shrugged. 'Elle needed a second opinion.'

'Okay,' she said; she actually sounded kind of disappointed, like she'd hoped there was a more gossip-worthy reason. 'Sure thing. Hey, I heard you're having a party tonight. Your brother's going to be there, right?'

Lee rolled his eyes. 'Yeah.'

Jaime smiled brightly. 'Great!'

'Are you dress shopping too?' I asked her, just making small talk.

'No, I need a new pair of jeans. My dog decided that my jeans made a better toy than his squeaky ball.'

I laughed. 'What a nice dog.'

'Tell me about it. Are you wearing that tonight?' She nodded at the dress in my hands.

'Yeah.'

'I'm not sure it's really your color . . .' she said, but I caught the muscle twitch in her cheek, and the expression was one I'd learned to read over the years. Jealousy. I took that as a good sign.

'Hmm, maybe . . . But it's on sale. I can't resist a good bargain.'

She laughed politely. 'Yeah, I guess. Well, see you guys later!'

'Bye, Jaime,' we chorused, and I heard Lee sigh and mumble something about how much she annoyed him.

I paid for the dress and we made another stop by the food court so he could get a slice of pizza before we left. I just had a milkshake.

'Don't spill that in my baby,' he warned when I was slurping it as I got into his car.

'Of course I won't!' I nearly did, though, and, seeing

his threatening look, I didn't dare take another sip till we hit a red light.

As Lee pulled up in his driveway, I checked the time. 'Almost six . . . I'd better head home and get ready,' I said.

'You can be such a girl sometimes, Shelly.'

I laughed. 'Are you only just noticing?'

Lee laughed and headed inside. 'See you later,' he called over his shoulder.

'Bye!'

Nobody was home when I got in, but I wasn't that surprised. My younger brother, Brad, had a soccer tournament today and Dad had probably taken him out for burgers or something after.

I put my iPod into my speakers and let Ke$ha blast out loudly, so that I'd hear it from the shower with the water roaring in my ears.

When I stood in my towel, scrutinizing the dress, doubts about it started creeping into my mind. I'd grown up with Lee, and without a mom, so I wasn't the biggest girly-girl; but that didn't stop me from dressing up for things like this. I shook my head and berated myself. The dress was way longer than some of the girls' *school* skirts, for Pete's sake. It was fine.

So I sat at my dresser, make-up in front of me, my curling iron heating up. I carefully blended foundation over my skin, and perfected my eyeliner to make my brown eyes pop. I took my time to make sure my hair, shiny and coconut-scented after my shower, was cascading down my back in perfect coal-black ringlets.

I felt more than a little self-conscious when I looked at myself in the dress – along with a pair of black wedges with two-inch heels. I knew there would be girls who had their make-up way over the top, dresses way shorter than mine, and heels much higher than mine. But I wavered, wondering if I really did look okay.

But by then it was suddenly thirteen minutes past eight. Where had my two hours gone?

I tore my phone out of its charger, seeing a text from Lee asking where I was.

I walked cautiously around to his house. My heels weren't high, but I always felt more comfortable in flats.

There were people milling around the yard, and the front door was open, letting the bass spill out; it made the grass tremble. I smiled and greeted people on my way through to the kitchen to get myself a drink.

I was looking through the refrigerator, unsurprised that they'd moved all the food out to make space for the drinks people had brought. Lee and Noah tended to do that, after some kids thought it'd be funny to stick slices of ham and turkey to the walls with condiments a few months back.

I grabbed a bottle of orange soda and cracked it open on the kitchen worktop, a trick Lee's dad had shown me.

'Hey, Elle!'

I turned and saw a group of girls waving me over. I smiled to them.

'Hi, guys.'

'Olivia said you and Lee are doing a kissing booth for the carnival,' said Georgia. 'That's so cool!'

'Thanks.' I grinned.

'Nobody's done one of those for years,' said Faith. 'It's such an awesome idea!'

'Well, we are pretty *awesome* people.'

They laughed. 'I will most definitely be stopping by that booth,' Candice said with a sly smile. 'I heard Jon Fletcher's doing it.'

'And Dave Peterson,' Georgia added.

'Jon's doing it?' I asked.

'That's what Dave said.' Candice shrugged.

Faith laughed. 'It's your booth, Elle – you should know.'

I smiled sheepishly. 'Yeah, well . . .'

'Hey, you know who you should've got to do it?' Olivia told me. '*Flynn*.'

For a brief moment I wondered who the hell she was talking about. Then I realized she meant Noah, of course.

'I don't think he'd do it.'

'Well, did you ask?'

'Not exactly . . .'

'Couldn't he do it as a favor to his kid brother, at least?' Georgia said. 'Pull the guilt card – that'd work.'

'But I think we've got our four guys . . .'

'But if you had Flynn, every girl in the *state* would turn up at our carnival,' Olivia said. She, like every other girl, thought she had a chance with Flynn. Well, she kind of did, being head cheerleader, and Noah being on the football team, but Noah never gave her a second glance.

Yet somehow he had a reputation as a player, even though you never saw him pay girls much attention. The weirdest thing was, he almost seemed proud of that status.

'You know, if you got Flynn to do the kissing booth, you'd be a legend,' Faith told me.

'You've got a boyfriend, Faith,' Georgia reminded her with a laugh. 'You can't go to the kissing booth.'

'Why not? It's all for a good cause. What is it this time – saving the dolphins?'

'I think that was last year,' I laughed. 'No, it's for cancer research charities this year.'

'Even better!' Faith exclaimed, making us all laugh. 'Ask him.'

'Yeah, go on,' Olivia urged me.

'Just ask,' Candice pleaded. 'Please, Elle?'

'Well . . . I don't know . . .'

'Look, here he comes,' Candice said suddenly, interrupting me. She gave me a gentle shove. 'Just ask him, at least. If he says no . . . at least you tried.'

'Fine,' I sighed, giving in. I wandered over to intercept Noah on his way to get another beer.

He nodded at me by way of a greeting.

'Will you do the kissing booth for us, for the Spring Carnival? Please? We can't find a fourth guy. It's for charity. Lee and I really need a favor.'

Noah straightened up, cracking open his can. 'Kissing booth, huh?'

'Yeah.'

'That's cool.'

'I know. I'm a cool person.'

'Better than your duck idea.'

'Ha-ha.'

He gave a breath of laugher and a half-smirk that made my heart skitter wildly. 'And you want me to be a kisser? At your kissing booth?'

'It's for a good cause?' I tried.

'Don't think so, Shelly.'

'Please, Noah?' I begged, using the puppy-dog eyes and putting a heavy emphasis on his name.

'Will you go on your knees and beg?'

'No,' I said slowly, 'but every other girl will. Would that do it?'

He laughed a little. 'That's why I'm going to say no, sorry.'

I sighed. 'Well, they can't say I didn't try.'

'Hold on,' he said. 'Did you actually *need* me to do it, or do they just want me to do it?' he asked, jerking his head past me at the girls.

'The latter.'

He nodded. 'Well, sorry. I don't think I can risk my dignity. Plus, imagine how much all the other guys would hate me for stealing all the kisses,' he said with a smirk.

'I was thinking something more along the lines of how much the charity would hate you for putting people off coming to the kissing booth.'

He smirked. '*Touché.*'

'Whatever . . .' I shook my head. 'Forget it.'

I wandered back to the cheerleaders, shrugging with an apologetic smile. 'Sorry, guys. He won't do it.'

'You should've tried harder,' Olivia said. 'Watch and learn.' She thrust her drink at Faith, and sauntered over to Noah, who was talking to a couple of boys. Olivia, in her extremely little black dress, was leaning on Noah's arm, all but throwing herself at him, and it looked like she had something in her eye, the way she was batting her eyelashes.

Then again, maybe I was just being a little too critical. I mean, her technique seemed to turn a few other guys' heads, at least.

Needless to say, he obviously told her no too: she pouted and stalked back to us. 'That guy is so obnoxious.'

'And so hot,' Georgia muttered, sipping her drink.

'Hell yeah,' Olivia agreed with a laugh. The girls all giggled and looked around to check him out.

'Don't you think Flynn's hot, Elle?'

I looked at Faith, blinking. 'Well, yeah. Of course he is.'

'Then why aren't you talking about his fine ass?'

I smiled wryly. 'Because he's so far out of my league there's no point in even trying.'

She gave me a sympathetic look. 'What are you on about? You're really pretty! I mean, I'd kill for hair like yours.'

I shrugged, and blushed a little. 'Thanks, I guess. But whatever, he's just Lee's big brother to me now.'

'Maybe there's something there. You never know.'

I laughed. 'Yeah, right. In my dreams.'

Faith shrugged and Candice started talking to her, so I excused myself and slipped into the lounge, where everybody was dancing. I finished off my soda in a few gulps and set the bottle down before joining in. The atmosphere was contagious; not everybody was drinking alcohol, but that didn't stop them from letting their hair down and going a little crazy.

I hadn't intended to get drunk. I knew I could have a good time without any of that stuff. But I was a complete lightweight, so by the time I'd had two cans of apple cider, I was pretty out of it. Time flew past, and I was dancing around, laughing and chatting to people.

It seemed like everybody had heard about the kissing booth.

And when they asked me if Flynn would be doing it, I told them I'd ask, because that seemed like the easiest option.

It was about eleven o'clock. I'd just joined some boys, mostly seniors, and Lee, Jason and Dixon in the game room. They were doing shots, all lined up on the pool table.

'Can I join in?' I asked, bouncing into the room with a grin.

'Sure,' Dixon said, and poured another shot for me.

'Uh, haven't you had enough to drink, Elle?' Lee asked me warily.

'Who cares?' I chirped. 'Three, two . . .'

Everyone took their shot and slammed the glasses

down again. Dixon poured the vodka out again and again. After the second, I lost track of which round we were on. I didn't even like vodka – it was gross. It burned my throat the whole way down. But I didn't notice.

Everything was bright and out of focus and loud. I giggled helplessly, doubling over in hysterics.

'Elle, you are so wasted,' laughed Chris, walking over and straightening me up.

I giggled again. 'Let's dance. I want to dance. Somebody dance with me. Chris, dance with me?'

'There's no music in here.'

'Oh well. Let's do it anyway.' But then I decided to climb onto the pool table to dance. I giggled a little when I felt the pounding bass from the lounge through the pool table.

I started swishing my hips from side to side in time with the music, my hands in the air, my hair swinging with me. I tried to drag Lee up to dance too, but he wouldn't.

'Why not?' I whined at him.

'I'm not dancing,' he said. 'C'mon, Elle, just get down.'

I stuck my tongue out at him. He tried to grab hold of me and pull me down, but I wriggled away and carried on dancing. He was such a party pooper!

'I'll be right back.'

'Where are you going?' I asked him. He couldn't leave – the party wasn't over yet!

'I'm going to get a drink. Dixon, you want anything?'

'Got all I need right here man,' he replied, and winked at me with a laugh. I blew him a kiss.

It was so hot in the game room, I thought. Had somebody turned up the heating? I was really starting to sweat. Maybe a dip in the pool would cool me down . . .

And suddenly I had the perfect solution. 'Someone come skinny dipping!' I cried enthusiastically, and reached for my zip as I stumbled to the edge of the table, teetering in my wedges.

Suddenly, my feet left the ground and the whole world turned upside down. My legs were in the air and my head was hanging down looking at someone's back.

'Hey!' I cried. 'Put me down! Put me down!'

They didn't put me down though. I watched the stairs stretch out below me as they carried me upstairs. My palm turned clammy. This couldn't be Lee. He hadn't been wearing green – had he? Maybe he had?

No, I was sure he hadn't. Lee was wearing red. I didn't know who was in a green shirt.

But whoever it was was pretty damn strong, given that I was wriggling around like a wild thing.

Eventually I was dropped onto something soft. A mattress! That's what it was.

I sat up straight, folding my legs underneath me as best I could. 'Noah Flynn,' I complained when I saw him giving me a reprimanding look. 'You're such a party pooper! I was having fun!'

'You were about to strip off,' he argued. 'Just take a break for twenty minutes.'

'No!' I cried, pouting. 'Don't be such a downer. I wanted to go skinny dipping!'

He shook his head at me, smirking. 'Tempting as that is, I think you're better off staying here for a little bit – at least till you're more sober.'

I sighed, sinking back down on the pillows. Then I sat up again. 'Are you going to leave me all on my own?'

'No. I don't trust you to stay in the room.'

'You don't trust me? Why not? I'm Lee's best friend. You've known me since *forever*! You should trust me more.'

Noah was shaking his head at me while he went over to push the door shut and turn the key in the lock.

I raised an eyebrow as he wandered back over and straddled a chair facing me.

But, even in my state of mind, I knew the thought was ridiculous.

'Aren't you drunk?' I asked him.

'Not really.'

'Aw, why? It's your party. Go crazy!'

'I think you were being crazy enough for the both of us.'

'I'm sorry,' I said, pouting a little. 'I didn't mean to spoil your fun.'

Noah laughed at me.

I clambered to the edge of the bed and swung my legs back and forth, sitting on my hands. 'Noah . . .'

'Yes.'

'Will you *please* do the kissing booth for us?'

'No.'

'Please?' I begged, bouncing up and down on the springy mattress. Wow. It was like a trampoline or something! Like Lee's bed. 'Please, please, pretty please with a cherry on top?'

'No.'

'Why not?' I whined. 'You're so mean!'

'I don't want to do a kissing booth, simple as.'

'But *why*?'

'I don't want to.'

'Please? It's – I think it's for cancer. Or maybe it's for the dolphins. That's a funny word isn't it, dolphins? Dolphins . . . Dol . . . phins . . . Like dolly-fins.'

'I'm not going to do the kissing booth, no matter who or what it's for.'

27

I got up and moved over to crouch right in front of him, so close that our noses were almost touching. 'Not even for me?'

He shook his head. Then – 'Man, your breath stinks. How much vodka did you have, Elle?'

'I don't know. Dixon poured it.'

He sighed. 'Those guys . . . I swear . . .'

'What?'

'Nothing.'

'Fine, don't tell me then.' I shot back up straight and staggered back, the whole room pitching around me and turning gray and fuzzy around the edges.

'I think I'm gonna be sick.'

Noah was already shoving me into the bathroom, and pushed me over the toilet bowl in time for me to puke my guts up.

Once that was over and I was done dry-heaving, I flopped down on the cold tile floor, my head lolling against the edge of the bathtub. A glass of cold water was pushed against my lips, and he made me drink it up.

'I'm really, really sorry, Noah,' I whimpered. I felt all gross now after throwing up. 'I'm really sorry. I didn't mean to ruin your party.'

'You didn't ruin my party, Elle,' he told me.

I nodded fiercely, but stopped when it made me feel sick again. 'Yes I did. I'm really sorry!'

'It's okay,' he laughed. 'Calm down.'

I scowled, and punched him on the chest. *Wow. That is one solid chest. I bet he has a six-pack too. Maybe even an eight-pack, knowing Noah. Or a ten-pack! Is there even such a thing? Possibly . . .* If there was, Noah would have one.

Halting my internal babble, I said, 'Don't laugh at me.'

He laughed harder, and pulled me to my feet. I half fell, so he wrapped an arm around my waist to support me. After helping me stagger back over to the bed, he let me drop on top of the covers.

'I'll be back in ten minutes to ch—'

I was already asleep.

Chapter 3

Sunlight was trying to filter through the drapes, but it was weak early morning sunshine, and the glow turned the room a dark blue. I closed my eyes again, trying to snuggle my head down into the soft squishy pillow under my head. I curled into a tighter ball under a thick comforter.

I was so cozy and warm. And everything smelled . . . it was something between citrus and woodsy. Whatever it was, it was a really great smell. And I was sure I'd smelled it somewhere before on someone . . .

I gasped suddenly, sitting bolt upright.

My bedroom didn't smell like that. And my bed was not this comfortable. Neither did my room have blue drapes.

So . . . where the hell was I?

I looked around. Everything was sort of familiar . . . But I definitely hadn't been here before. I threw the covers off and saw I was wearing a boy's shirt that was too big on me, just a plain gray shirt. It smelled just like the pillows.

I still had all my underwear on though – that was a good sign.

I climbed out of the bed carefully. What the hell had happened last night? I strained my memory, but came up short. I vaguely recalled dancing on the pool table. Had I really had that much to drink?

There was a disgusting taste in my mouth to match my pounding headache.

I must have thrown up. I remembered someone holding my hair back for me. It must've been Lee; he would've taken care of me.

But where was I?

I tiptoed over to the door of the bedroom and poked my head out. I practically cried in relief to see I was in Lee and Noah's house. It must be Noah's room I crashed in – in all these years I'd never been in his room.

So . . . *why* was I in Noah's room? Why not one of the guest rooms? Or Lee's?

I went back to the bed, my head pounding so hard I didn't think I could stay on my feet much longer, and looked at the alarm clock. It was only half eight in the morning. In the hopes of sleeping off my hangover, I snuggled back under the covers, breathing in Noah's smell.

Just as I was about to drift into unconsciousness

again, the door opened slowly, making the hinges creak.

My eyes flashed back open immediately, and my eyes met Noah's. He was standing in the doorway wearing nothing but a towel around his hips, hung right down low, and his chest and abs were still streaked with droplets of water, his black hair dripping.

My eyebrows shot up. Six-pack. Who'd have thought it?

I couldn't help but blush at how he made my heart race just by looking at me.

'Sorry,' he said quietly. 'I didn't mean to wake you.'

'It's okay,' I said, my voice a little croaky. I cleared my throat, but even that noise hurt my head. 'I just woke up anyway.'

'Right. Hungover, much?'

I grimaced in response, making Noah chuckle. 'You have no idea. I didn't know I'd drunk so much.'

'You had a load of vodka, I know that,' he said, sitting on the end of the bed. My heart went wild. Couldn't he have grabbed a shirt or some jeans before stopping to talk to me?

'What do you mean, *you* know that? When did *you* see me?'

'When you were about to strip off on the pool table in front of a bunch of the guys and then go skinny dipping,' he said casually, looking sideways at me with those bright blue eyes.

I wondered if he could hear my heart racing. Probably. I hoped I wasn't blushing any more, at least. That would just be peachy.

My jaw dropped when his words sank in. 'Oh, God. Tell me I didn't.'

'No, you didn't. I had to carry you out.'

I gaped, my cheeks flaming, and covered my face with my hands, looking through my fingers at him. 'I can't believe I did that.'

'Yeah, well . . .'

'Thanks though. For stopping me. That would've been embarrassing this morning.'

'You don't say,' he said sarcastically, but he smiled. 'You threw up, too. Just FYI.'

'What, in front of people?'

Oh, God, this just gets worse! I thought, mortified.

'No,' he said, shaking his head and flicking water over me. 'In my bathroom. I was trying to make sure you didn't make an idiot of yourself or get hurt.'

I groaned, humiliated. 'Sorry about that. I'm really sorry, Noah, I didn't mean for you to miss the party or anything . . .'

He shrugged. 'It's okay. I didn't mind.'

I scoffed. 'Sure. Whatever. I think we both know it

wasn't exactly the highlight of your night having to take care of me.'

'It wasn't all that bad,' he said after a moment, and smiled again. It wasn't a smirk. It was a real, genuine smile that showed the dimple in his left cheek and made his eyes crease a little at the corners. It was infectious; I had to smile back at him.

'Well, thanks, Noah.' I couldn't help but put a taunting emphasis on his name.

'Any time, Shelly.'

He reached over to ruffle my hair, and when I went to push him away I somehow ended up tumbling off the bed and pulling him down with me.

Noah was really heavy. He didn't have a spare half-pound of fat on him, but he was a hell of a lot of muscle. And he was crushing me.

But I was caught by his bright eyes. He didn't budge, either – just looked back at me.

Before it turned into too much of a staring match, I found my voice again. 'Noah . . .' I breathed.

'Yeah?' he said in just as hushed a voice.

'You're crushing me.'

He blinked a couple of times, like he was jerking himself back to reality. Then he said, 'Oh, right. Shit. Sorry.'

He got to his feet, holding the towel around him – I

don't know what I would've done if he'd dropped the towel.

No, Elle! Don't even go down that road! Shut up! Stop thinking!

He offered me a hand and I got to my feet too. The shirt I was wearing reached barely past my butt, so I felt extremely self-conscious.

'Um, when did I change?' I asked, plucking at the shirt and looking around. I saw my dress draped over a chair.

'Oh, I came back up to check on you and you woke up, and then you started to take off your dress because you didn't want to crease it, you said, so I found you a shirt to wear.' He shrugged, and scratched the back of his neck briefly.

I blinked, my brain trying sluggishly to catch up. 'So . . . you saw me . . . in my underwear . . .' *Please say no, please say no, please—*

His mouth twitched; he was trying so hard not to smirk. 'Uh . . .'

'Oh my God.' I buried my face in my hands.

'I averted my eyes, I swear.'

I laughed it off, saying, 'Don't worry about it,' when truthfully, my pulse was roaring in my ears. Mr Player averting his eyes? Likely story.

'Lee's downstairs cooking breakfast if you want

any,' he told me. His words tumbled out, as though he were trying to change the topic.

My stomach decided to growl in answer to him, making us both laugh. 'Awesome.'

I headed downstairs, closing his bedroom door behind me. I let out a breath I didn't know I'd been holding, and sagged against the door.

'Oh my God,' I breathed, talking to myself. I thought I was totally over Noah. But after those five minutes – with him in a towel and me in his shirt, and him falling on top of me . . . My heart just wouldn't calm down!

It was ridiculous. I knew Noah never saw me as anything other than the annoying girl who was his brother's best friend. To him, I was nothing more than that, I was certain.

But still . . .

I fell backward suddenly, the door behind me disappearing.

Flat on my back, I blinked up at Noah, now wearing a pair of boxer shorts.

I cracked up laughing. 'You wear Superman boxers!'

He looked down at himself, as though he needed visual confirmation of this. I watched pink blossom over his cheeks, and all I could think was, *I made Noah Flynn blush!*

He was smirking like he didn't care, then winked

and said, 'You know you find them irresistible, Shelly.'

Is it that obvious?

'Oh yeah, right,' I scoffed. 'Sure I do.'

I pushed myself to my feet again and pulled the shirt down as far as it would go. Still grinning foolishly at the knowledge I'd made him blush, I headed downstairs to the kitchen.

'Rochelle, Rochelle, Rochelle,' Lee sighed when I collapsed onto a seat at the bar table. 'What am I going to do with you, my stripping, skinny-dipping little friend?'

'Make me some breakfast?' I replied hopefully.

He laughed, and turned back to the stove, throwing some more bacon into the pan. 'The things I do for you.'

Chapter 4

I spent most of the day playing *Mario Kart* with Lee.

'I'm actually pretty surprised Noah took care of me,' I admitted to Lee.

He laughed. 'You're not the only one. I would've, if I'd been there. But I got kind of waylaid . . .'

'Yeah, you told me about Veronica. Was there another girl you kissed, or just the one? You want to watch it – you'll be turning out like your brother.'

Lee rolled his eyes at me. 'Says the stripper. We make a fine pair.'

'I was intoxicated.'

'So was I, a little.'

'Not Noah, apparently.'

'I think he must have been, if he was looking after you like that. He's not usually so . . . so nice.'

I laughed. 'To put it nicely.'

'Indeed. Hey, maybe he's crushing back at you.'

I gave Lee a look. 'Don't be so ridiculous. And I got

over that crush years ago, as you well know.'

Lee wrinkled his nose. 'That'd be weird anyway.'

'Whatever.' I shoved him, making his kart veer off course, and sending Yoshi plummeting over the waterfall while I went into the lead with Luigi.

I got home around five: I had some homework to finish off. I'd made Lee drive me home, since I'd borrowed a pair of his jeans and didn't want to be seen in public. I made a dash for the door, my best friend laughing at me.

'Hey!'

'What?' I yelled, turning back to him.

He threw my dress over to me, and I caught it just before it fell on the ground. 'See you in the morning!'

'Bye, Lee!'

I shut the front door and heard, 'Rochelle, is that you?'

'Yeah! Hi, Dad!'

'Come in the kitchen a sec.'

I sighed, wondering if I was in for a lecture now or not. I dreaded my dad getting angry with me.

He was working on his laptop at the kitchen table, and I heard Brad on the Wii in the lounge.

'Hey,' I said, putting on the coffee maker.

'You can make me a cup too while you're there,' he said.

'Okay.'

'Good party?'

I nodded. 'Yeah, it was great.'

'You didn't get too drunk? Or do anything too stupid?' He shot me a stern look over the rim of his glasses: he was talking about boys.

I'm not sure why he bothered. It was hardly confidential that I'd never had a boyfriend or kissed a guy.

'I, um . . . I wasn't *too* bad . . . only a bit drunk.'

Dad sighed and took off his glasses and rubbed his cheek. 'Rochelle . . . you know what I've said about you drinking.'

'I was fine, honestly. Lee and Noah took care of me anyway.'

'*Noah* did?'

Even my dad was surprised enough to forget about the drinking for a moment.

'Yeah. I thought it was weird too.'

'Mm . . . Anyway, don't change the subject, young lady. You know what I've said about you drinking.'

'I know. I'm sorry.'

'Mm. Next time that happens, you'll be grounded for a month, you hear? And don't think I won't find out.'

'Message received, loud and clear.'

He didn't look entirely convinced, but let it slide. It

wasn't like I went out drinking every other night; it was a once-in-a-while thing.

'So have you and Lee come up with an idea for your booth yet? The carnival's only two weeks away.'

'Yeah. We're doing a kissing booth.'

'That's . . . unusual,' Dad laughed. 'Are you sure you'll be allowed?'

I shrugged, pouring out two mugs of coffee. 'I don't see why not.'

'Well, it's better than throwing balls at coconuts,' he said. 'Anyway, listen, I'm going to need you to watch Brad tomorrow, okay? I'm working late.'

'Yeah, sure.' After adding a ton of milk to my coffee, I gulped it down. 'I'm going to take a shower and do my homework.'

'Okay. Dinner at seven. We've got meatloaf.'

'Cool.'

I hated Mondays. They sucked. There was not one redeeming feature about Monday mornings. I always set my alarm twenty minutes earlier than I needed to, since I hated getting out of bed.

I finally dragged myself up and grabbed my black pants out of the closet. Our school was built in, like, the early 1900s or something like that, and for some stupid reason they kept the tradition of uniform. It wasn't the worst uniform in the world, but I wished we didn't have any.

As if Monday mornings weren't already bad enough, mine was about to get a hell of a lot worse.

Riiiiiiip!

I froze, one leg half in the leg of my pants. Hurriedly, I wriggled out of them and inspected the damage. Last week, it had been a teeny tiny hole in the seam on the inside of the right leg. Now, there was a giant tear down the leg.

'Oh, crap,' I muttered, throwing them down. I wasn't much of a seamstress at the best of times, and there was no way Dad would be able to fix them. I'd have to order some new ones online – they should get here by Thursday, I calculated. But until then, it'd have to be my old skirt.

I hated the regulation school skirt. It was pleated, for one thing, and made of this blue and black striped tartan. You had to wear stockings with it. Not tights. Not bare legs. *Knee-high stockings*. It looked good on some people, and I'd given in and worn it for a while last year before deciding to never touch the thing again.

But I had no choice.

And, worse, it was now a little too short for me.

I sighed again. It'd have to do for now. It's not like I had any other option. I rummaged through a drawer until I found some of the stockings I'd bought to go with it last year. I grimaced at myself in the mirror before heading down to breakfast.

Brad choked on his cereal when I walked into the kitchen. He laughed so hard he sprayed Cheerios everywhere. 'What the hell is that supposed to be?'

'Brad, language,' Dad scolded him. Then he turned to look at me and raised his eyebrows. 'Isn't that a bit . . . inappropriate for school, Elle?'

I huffed, scowling. 'My trousers are ripped.'

'How did you manage that?'

'I forgot to fix the hole in them and . . . I don't know, they just tore.'

Dad sighed. 'You'll have to order some more. I haven't got time to run you to the mall to get any.'

'Yeah, I know.'

I'd barely finished my cereal when I heard Lee beeping the horn impatiently outside. I put my bowl in the sink and said goodbye. I bolted to the car, jumping in before anybody could see me in my skirt.

'You're in a skirt,' Lee commented.

'No shit, Sherlock,' I muttered. 'Let's just go.'

'What's got your panties in a twist?' he teased.

'My trousers ripped.'

'I thought you were fixing them?'

'I forgot.'

'It looks fine, Shelly, don't worry. You really should wear skirts more often.'

I swatted at him, and he grinned and turned up the radio. It wasn't long before we were at school and I told myself to suck it up and, after taking a deep breath, climbed out of the car. We were a little later than usual, and most people had already arrived.

I slammed the car door shut and walked around to sit on the hood with Lee as a bunch of guys wandered over to greet us.

'Hey, looking good,' Dixon said, nodding at me with a wink.

I scowled, folding my arms. 'Shut up.'

'What?' he protested innocently. I knew he was only teasing, but I was in no mood for it.

I decided to go talk to some girls instead, spotting Lisa and May from my chemistry class a few cars down. Someone smacked my butt as I walked past, and I whipped round angrily.

It was one of the soccer players, Thomas, smirking at me.

'Did you just smack my butt?' I asked, clenching my jaw.

'Maybe.'

'Hey, I missed the party on Saturday,' said his friend Adam. I didn't know him too well, but from what I'd

44

seen, he was an arrogant jerk. As if to prove it, he added, 'Do I get a repeat performance?'

A few of the boys laughed and cheered, and Adam started swinging his hips like a girl and pulling his shirt out of his pants like he was going to strip. It would've been funny, but I was so angry at him and his smug little face.

I ground my teeth. 'Oh, grow up already.'

Adam grabbed my wrist and pulled me back over. He probably thought it was all a joke, but I didn't. I tore my arm away and glared at him.

'Hey, back off,' Lee snapped, stepping closer.

'Make me,' Adam shot back, throwing his arms out and daring him.

So I punched him.

Well, I tried to – someone caught my fist before it collided with his jaw.

I wrestled my hand away, but not before a different fist went into Adam's face. Then they slammed him into the old four-by-four next to us, letting go of me.

I looked around. Of course. It *had* to be Noah who'd interfered.

'*Fight! Fight! Fight!*'

Suddenly there was a huge swarm in the middle of the parking lot, everyone either shouting, '*Fight! Fight!*' or giving the appropriate '*Ooh,*' or '*Ouch, that's gotta hurt!'* when required. And I was stuck in the eye of the storm, frozen in place, unable to move.

It took a couple of seconds for reality to bring me back to my senses. I ran forward, trying to drag Noah away from Adam, whose lip was split and bleeding. He couldn't have looked more livid if he'd tried.

'Noah!' I yelled repeatedly, but he wasn't listening. The boys were all yelling and arguing – and now there was a teacher trying to control and assess the situation – but my brain didn't register any of that.

'Lee!' I tried helplessly, tugging on his arm instead. 'Do something!'

'What do you think I'm doing?' he replied sharply. 'Nobody treats my best friend like that and gets away with it.'

'Lee . . .' I sighed, defeated, when he went back to yelling and shoving the mass of guys.

'Dude, if you like her, that's fine,' Thomas scoffed to Noah. 'But I'm sure there's plenty to go around.'

He neatly dodged another punch and looked at Noah, daring him to carry on.

But I stood there glaring. *'What* did you say?'

'You heard me,' he said with a wink.

I grimaced.

'That's it,' Noah growled.

'Flynn!' yelled the teacher, barging through the quickly dispersing crowd.

The other fights all faltered to a stop, and Noah only paused because I stood right in front of him, pushing his chest.

'What is all this about?' demanded the teacher – I recognized Vice Principal Pritchett's voice.

'It's just a big misunderstanding,' I told him. 'Really.'

'All of you,' he said, 'one week's detention. Noah Flynn, Rogers, my office now. You too, Rochelle.'

I gaped. 'What did I do?' I exclaimed.

'Nothing, but I'd like a word with you.'

I sighed dejectedly, and suddenly there was an arm around me. Lee.

'Thanks,' I mumbled. 'But you shouldn't have got involved.'

'Hell yes, I should have. Nobody treats you like that, Shelly.'

'You do it twenty-four/seven.'

'But I'm allowed. We're best friends. Those jerks . . . no way can they talk to you like that and get away with it.'

'Well, thanks,' I said, giving him an awkward side-hug.

He squeezed me back. 'You know,' he murmured in my ear, 'I'm starting to think my big bro has a crush on you, Shelly.'

I scoffed. 'That, or he wanted a fight.'

'Oh, probably the latter then.'

'*Definitely*,' I corrected, making him laugh. The bell rang as we reached the vice principal's office, and Lee sighed.

'I have to get to homeroom.'

'Yeah. Well, I'll just see you later, I guess.'

'Yeah. Good luck,' he added with a grave expression. I laughed, waving as he wandered off, and threw myself down on a chair. Someone took the one next to me – Noah. The vice principal and Thomas went straight into the office. The door shut behind them with an ominous click.

After a few seconds of silence, I said a quiet 'Thanks.'

Out of the corner of my eye I saw Noah sit up. 'Nobody can treat a girl like that and get away with it. Especially if that girl is you.'

I peeked at him sideways, not turning my head. 'Well, thank you. You didn't have to interfere, though. I mean, you could've let me land one punch.'

'It would've been a good punch, I'll give you that.'

'Why did you stop me?' I couldn't help but ask.

He shrugged. 'To be honest . . . I'm not sure.'

'In fact, while I'm at it, why did you need to get involved? Lee and Dixon and Cam would've been fine.'

'Maybe,' he said.

'You're avoiding my question.'

Noah grinned. 'Yeah, I am. I guess . . . I didn't want to see you get in a fight, and I didn't like hearing them talk to you like that . . .' He trailed off, and ran a hand through his hair while my heart raced faster and faster.

Then he said the words that dashed the last tiny shred of hope that had been growing inside me; they spilled out in a tumble: 'I guess you're just like my little sister or something.'

'Oh, yeah,' I said, nodding. 'Of course.'

He nodded too, and then shook his head, like he was trying to clear his mind or something.

I was trying to keep my expression neutral. 'Do you reckon you'll be in much trouble?' I asked casually, pretending to inspect my nails.

'Nah. I never am. Especially not when they find out I was defending your honor,' he added with a smirk.

'Ha-ha,' I snapped back, rolling my eyes. 'I was being serious.'

Noah shook his head. 'I never start fights, I just finish them. You know. In my defense.'

'I don't see why *I* have to be here though.'

'Oh, they'll want a witness, just to verify stuff or something. They usually like that.'

I laughed, looking at Noah and shaking my head.

We sat pretty much in silence for a while, but it was a nice, comfortable silence, which actually surprised me. I realized it was actually the longest period of time I'd ever spent alone with Noah in the past year or so – unless you counted the time I didn't remember because I was drunk.

When Thomas came out and Noah was called in, I mouthed, 'Good luck.' He just smirked and saluted me before closing the vice principal's door. I had nothing to do then but try and get some internet signal on my cell phone, which wasn't easy in this school.

When he came out, he shot me a smile, letting me know that everything was cool.

Vice Principal Pritchett called, 'Rochelle?' and beckoned me in.

I sighed and got to my feet, wandering into his office. I'd never been inside before, only walked past it – and it wasn't a particularly welcoming place. It reeked of rules and punishment.

He asked me what the fight had been about. I told him the truth: that some idiots had been teasing me about something stupid I'd done at a party on Saturday night, and I'd been really offended, so the boys stepped in and a fight ensued.

'I see . . . Well, thank you, Rochelle.'

'I didn't get anybody in trouble, did I? I mean,

nobody got badly hurt or anything . . .' I spoke warily as I stood up and slung my bag over my shoulder.

The vice principal handed me my late pass. 'No, you just confirmed their stories, that's all. Don't worry about it, all right? And stay out of trouble.'

I nodded uneasily. 'Okay . . .'

'Just get off to class now.'

That was a cue to get my butt out of there, so I didn't hesitate a second longer.

Chapter 5

Lunch trays clattered down all around me, and I looked up to find a swarm of girls, both juniors and seniors, clustering.

'So,' Jaime said chirpily, sitting down opposite me with a huge grin. 'Tell us everything!'

'About what?' I frowned in confusion, setting my fork down on the side of my plate of salad.

'About Flynn of course!' Olivia squealed, leaning in to hear better. 'We want to know everything. Are you guys, like, together or something?'

I scoffed. 'God, no.'

'But you call him *Noah*,' one of the other girls said, and I looked over to see Tamara, who'd dropped her voice to whisper his name, like she was scared he'd hear her. 'You don't call him Flynn.'

I shrugged. 'I've always done that, though. He was always there when I was growing up. He even told me I was like his little sister this morning. He's just a good guy.'

'A good guy who always gets in fights?' Georgia raised a skeptical eyebrow. 'Puh-lease. He's protective of you – he always has been.'

My eyes narrowed and I felt my forehead crease again. 'What do you mean, he's *always* been protective of me?'

The girls all looked at each other. Then, finally, Faith said, 'You mean you didn't know?'

'Obviously not,' I exclaimed, getting more and more frustrated by the second. 'What don't I know?'

'Flynn's always told guys to back off of you,' Olivia told me confidentially. 'Told them if they ever did anything to hurt you, they'd be sorry.'

I blinked a couple of times, staring at her, and then burst out laughing. 'You're joking, right?'

The girls looked at each other again, and I sobered up.

'Oh, come on,' I said. 'Look, he's just acting like the protective big brother, all right? That's all it is.'

They looked at each other doubtfully again.

Jaime finally said, 'Well, if you're totally sure . . .'

'A hundred and ten per cent. Ask Lee if you don't believe me.'

'Speaking of, where is your other half?' Tamara asked.

'He's in woodwork,' I said. 'He wanted to get a head

start on our banner. I, on the other hand, wanted some lunch.'

'Fair enough,' Candice said. 'Hey, did you get Flynn to do the booth?'

'He won't. I tried. Believe me, I tried.'

They all sighed. 'I wish he would. I'd pay good money for that booth,' Georgia said, making us all laugh.

'Did he say why he won't?' Karen asked.

I shrugged. 'Not really.'

'Hey,' said Lily suddenly, a gleam in her eyes as she looked from Karen to Dana and Samantha. 'Maybe Flynn will come to the booth, if he's not going to be a part of it.'

They all immediately squealed in excitement.

Not that I blamed them.

'Oh my God! Elle, if you can't persuade him to work the booth, at least persuade him to stop by!'

I wavered. 'I can't make any promises . . .'

'But you'll try?' Dana persisted.

I heard my cell phone bleep, and went to check my pockets before I realized that I had no pockets in this damn skirt. I sighed to myself before reaching down for my bag and rummaging for my cell phone.

Come by woodwork, need some help! read the text.

I put my phone back and stood up, picking up my lunch tray. 'I have to go help Lee. I'm guessing he needs a girl's touch.'

They laughed, and called their goodbyes.

'Oh, Elle?'

I turned back. 'Yeah?'

'*Ask him*,' Samantha told me with a pointed look.

I chuckled and nodded at her, making them all squeal, then shook my head to myself.

And okay, admittedly I wasn't an awful lot better really. But still – I was over my crush. Completely so since he'd told me I was just a sister to him.

But that didn't mean he was any less attractive.

When I got to woodwork, Lee was tapping a pencil really impatiently against a big plank of wood. After just ten seconds, it was already driving me mad – I didn't blame Mr Preston for leaving Lee for the peace of his office in the back.

'Hey,' I said, but Lee didn't notice me until I was right in front of him. I dropped my bag loudly, making him start.

'Oh, I didn't hear you come in,' he said.

'So I see. So what did you need me for?'

He gestured at the board in front of him. 'How big should I make the letters?'

I sighed, then fluffed my hair out before pulling it

back and twisting it into a ponytail. 'All right, big boy, give me the pencil.'

I sketched out the letters for KISSING BOOTH on the huge plank of wood.

'But they're not totally even. That "o" is way narrower than that one. And the "h" is half the height of that "s".'

'I know that. But you can go back over them and measure the lines properly. It doesn't matter if it's not perfect, with what I've got in mind.'

'Pray tell.'

I bit my lip, trying to find the right words to describe the image I had in my mind. It wasn't easy. 'Well, we've got the big main board of the booth, and we'll nail on the letters at odd angles so they overlap and all point different ways, because that'll look cooler than just having flat out "Kissing Booth". Does that make sense?'

Lee nodded, looking at the plank. I could practically hear him piecing together my idea in his mind. 'I see what you mean. It'll look cool.'

'I know,' I told him.

He started drawing the lines out thicker, measuring them all straight and perfect. I sat down on the bench facing him, swinging my legs.

'Hey,' I said, 'did you know that your brother has been warning guys to stay away from me?'

Lee didn't even look up, and merely shrugged. 'Yeah. Everybody knows.'

'Except for *me*. How did I not know that? Why didn't you tell me, more to the point?'

'I don't know – I figured you'd worked it out over the years. Why do you think guys have never asked you out on a date?'

I thought about that for a moment. To be honest, I had never really wondered. I hadn't panicked that there was something wrong with me just because I didn't have a boyfriend. I'd just kind of taken it in my stride that maybe I was more 'one of the guys' from hanging out with Lee, so guys didn't see me as a girl they'd ask on dates.

'You know you're the only one for me, Lee,' I teased. He looked up and winked at me, so I blew him a kiss back. We both laughed and he went back to drawing out the letters properly.

'Seriously, though – you only just heard about it?'

'Yeah. A bunch of the girls told me, since they wanted all the gossip from this morning. Not that there *was* any gossip. I told them Noah just thinks of me like a sister.'

'He's just taken the over-protective-brother role to the extreme,' Lee agreed. 'Though of course I would've done the same. Especially after the way those guys were with you this morning . . .' The pencil snapped in his hand.

'Jeez, calm down,' I said quietly.

Lee tossed the pencil halves aside and pulled another out from behind his ear. 'Sorry. They just really got to me this morning.'

'No kidding.'

'Yeah, well whatever. The point is, Noah's totally right to tell guys to keep away from you. You're so trusting, you'd get hurt real easy.'

'What?' I cried indignantly. 'How am I "too trusting"?'

Lee shrugged again. 'You're just too nice sometimes, Shelly. Not in a bad way. I just mean that . . . well, you know, you're more likely to fall for some jerk who'll hurt you.'

'Oh,' I said. 'I see.'

'I'm just looking out for you. So is Noah.'

'Well, thanks, I guess?'

'You're welcome, I guess?' he mocked, laughing. I launched a rubber band at his arm from the tabletop beside me. He swatted it off and carried on working, while I watched and chatted to him.

I was still wondering why Noah had gone so far as to warn guys off me. Because I realized it was unbeliev-ably unfair. I'd be seventeen in just two months. I'd never been kissed, never had a boyfriend, never been on a date. It was just so, so inconsiderate of Noah. How dare he interfere in my life like that? Sure, it was nice of him to look out for me – but he didn't have to stop guys dating me altogether!

When I asked Lee exactly what Noah had done to scare guys away, he said, 'He told the guys that if they ever did anything to hurt you, they'd have him to deal with.'

I sighed to myself. It seemed clear that Noah just saw me as a vulnerable, too-trusting little sister, but I couldn't help wishing he'd had different reasons for doing it.

Chapter 6

Brad wasn't the most difficult ten-year-old boy to babysit. He mostly just played on video games and yelled at the TV. All I had to do was give him his dinner. Then, at half nine, I had to almost drag him up the stairs until he shouted, 'Fine! I'll go to bed!'

I sighed, relishing the quiet once his bedroom door slammed shut.

I threw myself down in front of the TV and finally settled on some gory movie with Romans or gladiators or whatever.

Just as I was dropping off, my phone rang. I jumped, almost falling off the sofa.

'Hello?' I mumbled into the phone without checking the caller ID. I sounded kind of mad, but I didn't really care. Whoever was on the other end just had to deal with it.

'Um, Elle?'

'Yes?' I snapped irritably.

'It's, uh, it's Adam. Listen, don't hang up, I just wanted to apologize for this morning. I didn't really think it through, I guess, what I was saying. So . . . yeah. Sorry.'

I blinked a few times, trying to clear my mind. Adam? Calling to *apologize*?

I couldn't believe it. Although maybe that was because he sounded like he was trying not to laugh.

'Um . . . Elle? You still there?'

'Y-yeah,' I stammered quickly. 'Sorry, I'm just – just using the stove a sec.' What the hell? Who gets distracted on a phone call because they're using the *stove*? At *ten p.m.*?

'You're calling pretty late, you know,' I said hastily. 'Maybe a little too late for apologies?'

'I know, but I just wanted to say sorry.'

'Well, thanks,' I said curtly. 'I've got to go now, Adam so I'll—'

'Hold on a sec.'

'I don't want to hear it, whatever it is.'

'You don't want to have dinner with me, then?' I could just imagine the smug look on his face from his cocky tone. It made me grind my teeth. 'Give me a chance to really apologize?'

'No. Bye.'

I hung up and threw my phone on the couch before he could utter another syllable. What an ass.

And Lee said I was too nice . . . Ha!

I snorted quietly at that thought, feeling quite satisfied with myself for being so blunt with Adam – though that wasn't what I was thinking about when I went upstairs.

There was only one thing running through my mind. Predictably enough – it was Noah.

For some reason, all I could think about was Sunday morning when we'd fallen off the bed: the look in his eyes – the look I remembered perfectly but couldn't fathom, with his bright eyes shadowed and holding mine.

Because you don't look like that at your substitute little sister, right?

Of course I was being ridiculous; it was just my sleepy thoughts wandering into dreamland. But it made me think maybe there was a different reason he got involved in that fight that morning.

I scoffed at myself, my eyes already drooping shut.

'You're an idiot, Elle,' I muttered. 'A total fool . . .'

School the next day wasn't so bad. There were a couple of joking wolf-whistles and teasing loud comments, but I didn't pay them any attention. And I only heard them when Noah was nowhere near.

Lee was muttering about them and I said, 'Well, it's

kind of my fault. I mean, I did try stripping off to skinny-dip . . .'

He gave me a look, making me trail off. 'What did I say yesterday? *Too nice.*'

'How was that *too nice*?' I demanded.

'It's not like you go parading yourself around, do you? You have some decency. One drunken mistake, and those guys are practically undressing you with their eyes.'

I sighed. 'Come on. I'm not *that* hot.'

'Have you looked in the mirror lately, Miss Thirty-Four C?'

'Lee!' I shouted, smacking his arm. I felt my cheeks go red. 'Don't say it so loud!'

He laughed at me, slinging an arm around my shoulder. 'I can't believe this is the same girl who would've gone skinny-dipping and stripped off for a load of guys—'

'Shut up.'

'Sorry.'

'We have a meeting for the carnival at lunch,' I reminded him as the bell went. While I was a chemistry kid, Lee was biology. It was the only subject we didn't have together.

'Yeah, I know.'

'See you.'

'Bye, Elle.'

I went to take my usual seat in the chemistry lab, but then I heard, 'Hey, Elle! Come sit by me.'

I looked over my shoulder and saw Cody pulling out the chair next to him.

'He's dead,' I heard Dixon mumble behind me.

'And that's not even mentioning what Noah will do,' Cam agreed, and they smiled at me before sitting down. I just shot them back a baffled look, thinking: *Boys.*

'Uh . . . sure, okay,' I said to Cody, and went to sit next to him. I didn't know him too well, but he seemed like a nice enough guy. He had dyed black hair and a tongue piercing, and he was also an amazing classical pianist; I'd seen him play at a school concert once.

'I heard about that fight yesterday,' he said conversationally, doodling squiggles on the corner of his textbook. 'I can't believe they said those things to you.'

'Oh, well, um . . .' I laughed nervously, unsure of what to say to that.

After a few moments he said, 'Is it true you and Lee are doing a kissing booth? For the Spring Carnival?'

I nodded with a grin, grateful for the change in topic. 'Yup! Cool, huh?'

'Yeah,' he agreed with a smile. 'Are you going to be working it then?' He raised an eyebrow, his green-brown eyes flecked with amusement and a suggestive smile on his face – though I could tell that he wasn't entirely serious from the note of laughter in his voice.

'No,' I laughed. 'I'm not.'

'Shame. I was hoping I wouldn't have to embarrass myself here.'

'Oh?'

'You wouldn't want to . . . you know . . . uh, go' – he cleared his throat – 'go see a movie, or something . . . with me . . . sometime?'

I wanted to laugh, just because he was so nervous.

But I managed to stop myself.

Instead I gave a wry smile and said to him, 'Aren't you afraid Noah will break your arm or whatever?'

He shrugged. 'I think I can take a risk for a nice girl like you.'

'Well, when you put it that way,' I said with a smile, 'why not?'

'Really?' His eyes brightened.

'Really, really.'

'Cool. Well, I'll call you sometime.'

I nodded. Then I realized – 'I don't have your number.'

'Here.' He uncapped a biro with his teeth, and grabbed my arm, turning it over. He was pretty skilled to write his number all the way down from my elbow upside-down, I had to admit.

'You could've just put it in my phone.'

'But there's no fun in that.'

I laughed.

Meanwhile the teacher had come in. 'All right, everybody, shut up and settle down. We've got a lot of work today. Now open the textbooks to page one hundred and thirty-seven. Last lesson we looked at the production of ethanol and its commercial uses and social implications . . .'

'Yeah,' some boy – I think it was Oliver – called out jokingly. 'Making Elle strip!'

I blushed, and retorted, 'What would you know? You were passed out by that point, you lightweight!'

'Nice.' Cody laughed appreciatively; the others started jeering at him, but I gave him a smile.

Lee wouldn't mind when I told him I had a date with Cody. He knew Cody a little better than I did, too. It was Noah I worried about.

'Hey,' Cody said, once the bell had gone and I was about to rush out for my meeting about the carnival.

'Yeah?' I said.

'Call me.' He winked, laughing.

I smiled. 'Bye, Cody.'

*

I arrived at the meeting at the same time as Lee. 'Hey, you'll never guess what just happened in my chemistry class.'

'You got asked on a date?'

My grin fell away into a pout. 'How'd you know?'

'Dixon texted me. He said there was someone risking their neck. Cody, right?'

'Yeah,' I said with a big smile. 'Can't you be more excited for me, Lee?' I pushed at his arm playfully. 'I've got a date! Can't you be happy for me?'

Lee laughed. 'I am, Shelly!' He gave me a hug, but that might've been just to stop me bouncing about excitedly. 'Cody's a nice guy. I'm just wondering what my brother will say when someone tells him about it.'

I laughed. 'Don't worry. It'll be fine.'

'If you say so . . .'

'So, Lee and Elle,' said Tyrone, head of the school council, calling the meeting to order with a simple clap of his big hands. He sat at the head of the table, with Gen next to him, pen and paper ready to take minutes. She took her role as the school council's secretary very seriously. Everybody looked up at Tyrone, falling silent instantly. 'I hear you've finally got a booth.'

'Yup,' we said unanimously.

'A kissing booth.'

'Uh-huh,' we chorused.

He gave us a wary look. 'Don't you think that's a bit . . . a bit risky?'

'What? How is it risky? So we just say you can't come to the kissing booth if you've got a head cold. No big deal.'

'No, I mean . . . Well, don't you think it's a bit seedy?' he said. 'Some people aren't too happy about it—'

'But we started the banner!' Lee cried angrily. 'We have kissers to do the kissing booth! Everyone loves the idea!'

'Tyrone,' I said calmly, elbowing Lee sharply. 'Nobody's going to see it that way. Plus, loads of carnivals have a kissing booth. We can always set up a couple of rules. Kind of like height restrictions on a rollercoaster. We can set an age limit if that's what you're worried about.'

'It's a couple of the teachers who're not happy with it,' he said. 'I think it's a great idea. I'm just not entirely sure about it . . .'

'It'll be fine,' I promised him, flashing a big grin.

'Well, if you've got it all sorted out, you really need to get working on your booth. The carnival's next Saturday. It must all be ready by next Friday.'

'Yeah, we know. It'll be ready,' Lee said.

'Awesome. Moving on – Kaitlin, do you have the

number for the cotton candy company with you?'

'Remind me to ask your brother if he'll stop by the booth,' I whispered to Lee. 'The girls haven't stopped going on and on and on at me about it.'

'You know he'll say no.'

'Yeah, but I have to ask anyway.'

'What did I tell you Shelly?' Lee smiled, flicking my nose, and making me scrunch up my face. 'You're just too nice.'

Lee had to go run to the grocery store and pick up a couple of things for his mom, so he dropped me outside his house since we were going to work on a playlist of songs for the kissing booth. I was planning to get a head start on finding some love songs, so I headed on inside.

The door was already unlocked; I saw Noah's car, the one he'd fixed up himself, on the driveway.

'Mom said you need to get some more milk – we're all out,' I heard him call.

'He's already gone,' I called back. 'It's me.'

I walked into the kitchen just as Noah was heading out of it – straight into me; he spilled a glass of water all down my top. It didn't help that it was ice cold, and I gasped, jumping back a mile.

'Noah!' I yelled, plucking at my top. My blouse was

plastered to my skin, and it probably didn't help that I'd worn a pink bra today since all my white ones were in the laundry. I sighed. *Just my luck . . .*

I glared at him. A muscle jumped in his jaw, and his brow knitted together.

'What? What's that look for?' I asked, my temper sparking. When he didn't say anything, I barged past, and stormed into the kitchen to get myself a drink.

'Hey, what's that on your arm?'

I didn't answer him.

'Is it true you got a date with some kid?'

I set the empty glass down on the counter. 'Jeez, Noah! What does it matter? I already heard from Lee I'm too nice – you don't need to be on my case too!'

'You didn't answer my question.'

'You didn't answer mine either.'

'I asked first, Rochelle.'

Oh, dear. He used my full name. Uh-oh. I turned around to face him. 'Yeah, I have a date – with Cody. He's a nice guy.'

'A nice guy?' Noah scowled. 'Elle, are you serious? Do you even know the guy? I mean, really *know* him?'

'Well – well, no, not really. But that's why I'm going on a date. *To get to know him better*. That's what people tend to do, you know? Oh wait – no, sorry, you wouldn't know, Mr Player. You just screw girls and ditch them the next morning. So long as you know their name it's all okay.'

Yeah, he was making me angry. Usually I wouldn't have dared say those things, especially since I didn't know if they were actually true. But he was really, really making my blood boil. Plus, I was still mad at him for warning guys off me like that. I told myself it was anger making my heart race like this.

'He just wants to get in your pants.'

'Since when?' I cried, throwing out my hands. 'How would you know, anyway? You don't even know him?'

'Cody Kennedy. Concert pianist. Takes some AP classes.'

I blinked. Okay, so maybe he did know him.

'Yeah,' Noah said, kind of smugly. 'I know who I'm talking about. And you know something else? He just wants in your pants, like any other guy.'

'So you're telling me that there's not one respectable boy in school who doesn't just want a girl for sex? Or maybe you're trying to say that's all I'd be good for? Do I really have no personality, Noah?'

'I didn't say that. But they're all the same.'

'How would you know? You're the reason I haven't had a date in my entire life! Why would you even do that?'

'You trust people way too easily,' he snapped,

interrupting me. 'A guy would just have to tell you he loved you and he wouldn't be waiting on you much longer.'

I glared. 'Do you really think I'm that easy?'

Noah glared right back at me before he punched the kitchen door. It slammed shut and bounced back off the doorframe.

'Damn it, can't you just listen to me for once in your life? I'm trying to look out for you here!'

'I don't *need* looking out for!' I shouted back at him. 'Can't you just stay out of my life? I think I can handle going on one date, Noah!'

'How would you know? Guys are always checking you out and saying how hot you are – have you never noticed? If one idiot thinks he can date you and then hurt you, he's got another think coming.'

I screamed in frustration. 'Just stay out of my life!'

'You'll end up getting hurt.'

'I won't. In case you haven't noticed, I'm a big girl now. I *can* take care of myself.'

'Which is why you were stripping off in front of everybody on Saturday?'

'I was drunk!'

'And who got stuck looking after you?' he retorted.

'I didn't ask you to! I didn't ask you to tell boys to stay away from me either!' I went to barge past him

72

again, intending to shut myself away in Lee's room.

Noah grabbed my arm, saying, 'Hey! We're not finished here, Rochelle!'

I spun around and pushed at his chest as hard as I could, though it didn't budge him.

'Whoa!' yelled a new voice – Lee. We both looked and saw him standing in the doorway. 'Why are you guys killing each other? What did I miss?'

Neither Noah nor I responded; we were still glaring at each other.

'Nothing,' I said eventually. 'I'll see you upstairs, Lee.'

I heard them both talking quietly in the kitchen. I sighed. Noah was just so . . . so infuriating! Sure, he was incredibly attractive. But hell, why did he have to interfere? How could he just automatically assume a boy couldn't possibly want a date with me because he genuinely liked me?

I threw myself down on Lee's bed and screamed into the pillow, letting all my anger out.

By the time Lee came up to work on the music for the booth, I had calmed down and was already surfing his iTunes library for music.

He didn't ask me any questions except for, 'Found anything yet?'

That is why I loved Lee so much.

*

He waited until we were digging into a Chinese take-away in the lounge to ask me.

'So what went down with you and Noah?'

'I yelled at him for being so overprotective. He yelled at me, trying to say he was only looking out for me. I yelled at him some more. You walked in.'

'He has good reasons though,' Lee said carefully after a moment. 'I tried telling you . . .'

'Yeah, I know you did, Lee. But that's different. I mean, you're my best friend.'

Lee smirked a little. 'Mm . . . yeah, but – but Noah has a point. Not every guy is a nice guy.'

'Yeah, but . . . but I'm not stupid enough to fall for that.'

'I'm looking out for you, Shelly.' He put his hand on my knee and I smiled back at him. See – when Lee put it like that, it was nice. When Noah had said it, I just got mad at him.

'I know you are. It's just Noah I have a problem with. He's just taken it to the extreme. I can survive a date with Cody. You know what Cody's like. He wouldn't try anything like that.'

'Yeah, I know.'

'Noah obviously doesn't.'

'You two were scary earlier, you know. I'm serious.'

'Yeah, I know you are.' But I still had to bite back a laugh.

'Just . . . at least be careful?'

'Oh for God's sake. Hundreds of people go on dates, Lee. You go on dates. It's not like you try and molest a girl on a first date.'

Lee laughed at that. 'Third date, maybe.'

'And that's why Karen wouldn't go to the movies with you.'

He laughed again, since we were just kidding around, but when we both sobered up he said gravely, 'Seriously though, Elle. We don't want you getting hurt.'

'I know.'

'Just be careful.'

'I will. Chill out.'

'Promise?'

'Pinky promise,' I said, wrapping my pinky finger through his and smiling. Lee's protectiveness I could handle. I quite liked it, actually. I didn't mind if Noah was going to act all big-brother and be protective too – but what I didn't like was that he seemed so against me having any dates at all.

What a jerk.

Chapter 7

The rest of the week passed quickly: we were busy trying to compile a playlist for the booth, painting the banner, collecting all the necessary decorations and making signs and posters. Not to mention everyday things like homework.

And I did my very best to avoid Noah when I was over Lee's house.

I was still mad at him, and didn't want another full blown row.

Friday rolled around, and I couldn't sit still all day. I'd be going to the movies with Cody tonight. I was supposed to be meeting him there at seven. I decided I'd aim to show up for five past. You were meant to try and keep a guy waiting a little, right?

I got home to raid my closet. My hands trembled slightly, and my breathing was shallow. Worries and doubts rampaged through my head, but I refused to listen.

I wanted something that looked good but not desperate. It was just a movie, so I couldn't go too fancy, anyway. And since Cody wasn't that much taller than me, heels were out.

I picked out a pair of dark gray jeans. *Okay, good. Progress.*

But I still only had half an outfit.

I hadn't asked any girls for advice: I was too embarrassed to admit I'd never been on a date before and didn't know what to wear to the movies. Sure, I went to movies with guys all the time, but always as friends. This was different. The guys didn't care what I wore, but this . . . Well, Cody was going to notice.

I knew I was panicking over nothing, but I couldn't help it.

At long last, I decided that I'd wear a pale pink jumper with sleeves to my elbows. It had darker pink lace around the neckline, so it was a little nicer than a plain jumper. I threw on a silver necklace and some bangles and decided that looked okay.

But maybe I should've worn something a little more flattering? This sweater didn't really make the best of my boobs – and if you've got it, flaunt it, right? Or not?

I checked the clock.

Crap. It was already five minutes after I should've left.

It'd have to be the jumper.

'Bye!' I called as I ran down the stairs.

'Have fun,' Dad called back. Brad carried on yelling at his video game. I slammed the door on them and saw that Lee's car was already waiting outside. Oops.

I ran around and climbed in the passenger seat.

'Sorry,' I said, slightly breathless. 'But it can't hurt to keep him waiting a little, right?' I laughed nervously, looking sideways. Then I let out a loud groan. 'Noah. What are you doing here?'

'Lee had to finish some chores. Which means I have to be your chauffeur.'

'If you'd told me, I would've got a taxi, or asked my dad to give me a ride. Why didn't Lee text me and let me know?'

'I assumed he did.'

'No.'

'Well, then, I don't know.' Noah twisted round to eye me critically.

I plucked my sweater nervously. 'Does it look okay? I don't know if it's too casual or what . . . Thanks to a certain someone, I've never done this before.'

He smiled dryly. 'It's fine.'

'How's my hair?'

'Okay?' he answered, unsure. He put the car in gear and shrugged at me. 'At least you dressed like normal.'

'What do you mean, *like normal*?'

'Normal for you. I mean, you're not showing too much skin or anything.'

'Wow. I think that was almost a compliment?'

'Not quite. But Elle, if this guy tries anything, and I mean *anything*—'

'Noah. He is a guy. I am a girl. Lots of people kiss on the first date, you know. It's not like he's going to try and get me to sleep with him halfway through the movie. This isn't *you* we're talking about.'

Noah shrugged, scowling a little. 'I'm just saying . . .'

We sat in silence a while.

'I think I've spoken to you more in the past week than in the whole of this last year,' I commented casually.

'Yeah. Weird.'

I rolled my eyes at him. Yup, there was definitely nothing between us, even if I *had* still had that crush on him. He was totally indifferent to me – apart from being all over-protective. All the time I'd wasted crushing on him . . .

Though he was really good looking – especially with his hair falling into his eyes and the dashboard glow shadowing his face like that.

You're going on a date with another guy! Hello! Earth to Elle!

I shook myself mentally. 'Thanks for the ride. You can just stop here.'

'Fine. Are you going to need a ride home?'

'Cody said he'll take me home. If not, I'll call my dad or Lee.'

'Okay.'

I rolled my eyes and got out of the car, walking up to the doors of the cinema.

I looked around. No Cody. Had he stood me up? I checked inside, but he wasn't there either . . . Where was he? My palms started to sweat a little; my stomach was made of butterflies.

After a couple of minutes I texted him to say, *I'm here. Are you inside?*

There. Perfect. It didn't sound too clingy or anything. I sent it and waited for the reply. I waited a full three and a half minutes for one.

Almost there.

Oh, great. Now I was the one waiting around. I leaned against a lamppost, looking at my phone like I was actually doing something. Really, I was clicking on random apps and then going off them again. I hoped I didn't look as worried and nervous as I felt.

'Stood up?'

I jumped out of my skin, and smacked Noah across his incredibly rock-hard chest. 'Don't scare me like that! And no, actually, he's on his way.'

He smirked. 'I thought you said you wanted to keep him waiting.'

'Yeah, well . . .'

'Told you so.'

'Noah, go home. What are you, stalking me?'

'Just enjoying the show,' he smirked. 'You look like you've been stood up, you know.'

'Well, not so much now you're here, really,' I retorted. 'Ha. Don't look so stupid now, do I? Besides, Cody's probably just caught in traffic or something. It's no big deal.'

He nodded dubiously. We stood in silence another endless minute. I kept wondering if I should start conversation, but then I'd remind myself I was mad at him and close my mouth. I must've looked like a fish, opening and closing my mouth like that.

It didn't help that Noah was incredibly distracting: he leaned on the post opposite me, watching me wring my hands nervously.

'Hey!'

I turned and smiled, seeing Cody walk up to me. 'Hi.'

His eyes flitted past me to Noah, who was giving him the coldest look I'd ever seen. Scary. Threatening.

I tried not to grind my teeth. 'Isn't it time you left, Noah?'

He glared a second longer at Cody before shrugging and getting back into his car, leaving without another word. A sigh of relief escaped my lips and I relaxed.

'Sorry, I had to stop for gas. Queues were unbelievable. Sorry. Let's go on in,' Cody said, jerking his head at the doors. I smiled and followed him. 'Do you want to grab some snacks? I'll get the tickets.'

'Sure. Uh, salted popcorn okay?'

'Yeah, that's great.' He shot me a smile, but as I turned away I wondered if it had been a little strained. Huh. Probably just me imagining things. As I ordered the popcorn, I wondered if I should've gone for something less . . . well, something that didn't get stuck in your teeth. If we did end up kissing at all, then . . . I sighed. I was just way too inexperienced when it came to date etiquette.

I thanked the vendor and made my way back to where Cody was waiting, a scowl on his face.

'What was Flynn doing out there?' he asked me. Oh, so *that's* what the frown was for!

'Just . . . being Flynn,' I muttered, shaking my head. 'Forget about it.'

'I didn't know you guys were close.'

'We're not. Lee couldn't give me a ride, so Noah – so Flynn did.'

'Oh. Right.'

We walked into the screen, the adverts already playing. I let Cody lead and pick the seats. He went for some more toward the middle. Not at the back, where the couples would all be making out. I didn't know whether or not that was a good thing.

'Do you want to get something to eat after?' I whispered, plucking up the courage.

'I ate earlier, sorry . . . I didn't know . . . but, I mean, if you're—'

'Oh, no, that's fine,' I said quickly.

'Shh!' somebody hissed behind us.

I rolled my eyes and ducked back down in my seat. The movie came on, and I didn't know what to do. I wondered if Cody would be cheesy and do The Yawn, and put his arm around me. Or if he'd claim the armrest and I'd hold his hand. Or if he'd try and kiss me.

So far, I didn't know whether or not this date had been successful. He'd been late, though he'd been polite enough. He hadn't tried to make a move, but maybe I was blowing things out of proportion. Maybe it was just in books and movies that guys made a move or kissed you on the first date? Maybe he was just as nervous as I was. Probably – he had every right to be nervous about Flynn's threats to any boy who looked at me, let alone dated me.

It was just ridiculous. I hated Noah sometimes.

The movie ended and we walked out. Cody started conversation – first about that movie, then about what kind of movies I liked. He liked sci-fi films and thrillers. I was more of an action or romance person myself. We didn't like many of the same movies.

We didn't have similar tastes in music either, really.

But he was nice, and easy enough to talk to.

We just ... didn't really seem to have much in common.

We talked the whole ride home, and he stopped outside my house. I unbuckled my seatbelt but didn't move. I tried to play it cool, and do it like the movies did. (I always found them to be an excellent source of education. I was so lucky I'd watched *John Tucker Must Die* on the weekend.)

'Well, thanks, Cody,' I said, smiling. 'I had a nice time.'

'Yeah. We should do this again sometime. You still got my number?'

'Well, I haven't lost it since this evening.' I laughed nervously, and he smiled back. I saw him look at my lips and my pulse picked up. Oh gosh. Oh God. He was going to kiss me now, wasn't he? Oh gosh.

He leaned in – yep, definitely going to kiss me.

My first kiss. I'd have my first kiss with Cody Kennedy. He was nice, kind of cute and easy to get along with . . . But honestly, I didn't feel anything for him. But what if I ended up getting stuck on his tongue piercing or something, if he gave me a French kiss? I was so not ready for this. Totally unprepared. But it was happening. He was leaning ever closer . . . *My first kiss!*

I chickened out:

I turned my head and kissed his cheek instead.

And then I got out of the car before I could feel too embarrassed by what I'd done. I smiled and waved, then headed to my front door as fast as I could while trying to look casual. I got inside, shut the door, and leaned against it. I let out a gigantic breath and sank to the floor, putting my head in my hands.

'I'm such an *idiot*.'

Cody probably wouldn't want a second date. Not that I was totally sure *I* wanted one, but I wouldn't have been able to say no, really, if he have asked. After all, one date wasn't really enough to get to know him properly, especially given how nervous I'd been.

Eventually I dragged myself up to bed, ignoring Lee's phone calls for once. I didn't want to deal with that right now. I just wanted to beat myself up about my failure of a first date for a while.

Just as well I'm not working the kissing booth, I thought to myself with a wry smile.

Chapter 8

I gave Lee a rundown of the date, and in return he gave me a sympathetic smile.

'Would you even want another date though? It doesn't sound like you had such a great time . . .'

'Well, not really,' I mumbled, picking at some non-existent fluff on my jeans. 'But I don't know. I probably would've said yes if he asked— Ouch! What was that for?' I exclaimed when Lee smacked my thigh sharply.

'Too nice!' he scolded me. 'You didn't like the guy as more than a friend, obviously. But you would've led him on just trying to be nice.'

'I wouldn't have led him on. Just . . . given him a second chance. It's not like people find their soul mate on the first date or anything.' He raised an eyebrow. 'I wouldn't have led him on!'

'Yes you would. Not intentionally. But because you were being polite.'

I sighed and flopped back so I was lying flat on my back on the grass. 'Am I really that bad?'

'You're not nice to Noah.'

'Yes, but that's Noah. Thanks, by the way,' I added sarcastically, 'for telling me he was giving me a ride.'

'Oh, yeah. My bad. But, hey, you didn't kill each other.'

'I was ready to, believe me. And the look he gave Cody when he showed up! I swear to God, your brother is the most infuriating jackass on the whole planet!'

Lee just laughed at me. I scowled up at the clouds rolling by over my head, cotton wool against the bright blue. I felt my breaths grow more and more even; there was something calming about watching clouds.

'I'm sorry,' Lee said eventually. 'You're funny when you're mad.'

'Whatever.'

'Anyway. Has Cody spoken to you since?'

It was three on a Saturday afternoon. And no, Cody hadn't texted me or called me, and something told me he hadn't had a great time on the date either.

'No,' I answered him. 'He hasn't.'

Lee shrugged. 'He's not interested.'

'What? How would you know? Maybe he's busy. Or maybe he's playing hard to get or something.'

Lee's smile twisted up to one side in sympathy. 'Sorry, Elle, but he's just not interested. Trust me. I'm a guy. I know how the male populous operates when it comes to girls.'

'Fine,' I muttered. 'Maybe he isn't interested anymore. Maybe I should've just sucked it up and kissed him.'

'See, there you go again,' Lee grumbled. 'It's not like you were under any obligation to kiss him. So you guys didn't hit it off – big deal. Move on.'

'I can't quite decide if your advice is helpful or not.'

'I'm not a chick. I'm not going to sit here and dissect your night.'

'You just listened to *me* dissect it,' I muttered.

'Exactly.'

I sighed. 'Fine, I guess you're right. It's going to be awkward in school though, don't you think?'

'Only if you make things awkward.'

'Yeah, I suppose.' I suddenly sat bolt upright, giving myself a head rush. 'Don't tell your brother how badly my date with Cody went, okay?'

'Why would I do that?'

'Just – if he asks. Say it went fine. If you have to say anything, tell him that Cody and I just didn't click. But don't tell him it was as bad as I told you.'

'Okay . . .' he said warily, not questioning me.

I didn't want to even imagine the smug look on Noah's face if he found out how my date with Cody had really gone. Whatever reasons he had for not wanting me to have a boyfriend, Noah was doing a pretty good job of keeping me single.

I sighed to myself quietly, and closed my eyes, the sun warming my cheeks. I felt Lee lie down beside me, and we just stayed like that, basking in the sunshine, too content and relaxed to say anything much.

The whole weekend passed in a lazy way. We couldn't be bothered to do much of anything. We watched some movies and lay around in the sun, dive-bombed in Lee's pool, and tried to get some homework done (we didn't get very far with that one). So Monday rolled around a whole lot faster than I would've liked.

I had chemistry first lesson. With Cody. Who hadn't called or texted me all weekend. I didn't know whether it was just as well he didn't want a second date, or whether I should be worried that he didn't like me.

A few people had already texted or spoken to me asking how the date had gone. I always said, 'Okay.' When they asked if I was going to see him again I said, 'I don't know.' When they asked if we'd kissed, I had to say, 'No.'

But now I'd have to face him and I didn't know how to act.

Yeah, Cody was nice and easy to talk to. But I didn't like him in that way. He obviously felt the same about me, since he hadn't called me. I should've been relieved about that; if the feeling was mutual, it couldn't be too awkward between us, right?

'Aw, no!' I looked up from my locker to see Dixon walking toward me. 'You're wearing trousers again. I miss the skirt. You looked hot.'

'Very funny.'

'I wasn't being funny,' he said with a laugh. I rolled my eyes and carried on trying to find my homework for math. 'Anyway, everybody's talking about your big date with Cody . . .'

'Why? It wasn't that interesting. Really.'

'Yeah, I know that. But he's the first guy to risk asking you out.'

I shrugged, trying not to grind my teeth when I remembered how angry Noah had made me with the whole 'trying to stop me getting hurt' thing.

'Cody told everyone you didn't want to kiss him.'

'It's not that— Wait, he *told* everyone? He actually said that?'

'Well. I say that. It was a couple of guys who pestered him about it, and it got out pretty quick. Just because, you know, your date was such big news. So . . . everyone now thinks you didn't want to kiss him.'

'It's just . . . I don't know . . .'

'Hey, you don't have to justify yourself,' Dixon told me with another big smile. 'It's just that some people are going to talk and ask questions, so be ready for that.'

'Thanks for the warning,' I muttered.

'You're welcome.'

And he was right – people kept coming up to me, saying, 'Is it true you wouldn't kiss Cody? Why didn't you kiss him?'

The first time, I panicked. I didn't want to tell them the real reason, so I babbled something along the lines of, 'I – I didn't feel too great. I didn't know if it was contagious.'

What a lie. I was sure they all knew it, but if they did, not one of them showed it.

I walked into chemistry and Cody was there already. I dithered a second, wondering if I should sit with him or not.

He shot me a smile though, so I went to join him.

'Hey,' I said casually.

'You know, if you were ill on Friday, you should've said,' he commented.

'I know, but I felt okay and I didn't want to cancel.'

I tried not to mumble too much. 'Sorry about that.'

'It's not a problem.'

'So, uh . . . Yeah . . .' I cleared my throat and Cody laughed nervously.

'I don't want to sound too much of a jerk or anything but . . . I was thinking about it and—'

'We're better off as friends?' I filled in, then regretted it when I realized he might not have been saying that. Oh man, what if I'd just dug myself into a grave?

'Uh, yeah,' he said, giving me a nervous smile. 'No offence. We just didn't seem to . . . click.'

'None taken,' I said, smiling. 'I thought exactly the same.' I hoped my relief wasn't too evident. 'So did you do the homework? I didn't get question eight.'

And just like that, my life had snapped back to its (sadly) romance-free ways.

We were working on the banner for the kissing booth. The letters were cut out and Lee had smoothed the edges; we just needed to paint them and then nail them onto the booth itself. We had some decorations back at my house, and the posters were ready too. We also had a couple of boards with the price on.

'Everybody's been asking me all week what happened with you and Cody,' Lee said to me. It was after school on Wednesday afternoon. We needed to hurry our asses up to get everything ready to set the booth up on Friday night.

'You haven't said anything too incriminating?'

'I haven't told them the truth, no,' he laughed, dunking his brush into the pink paint again. 'I don't know why you said you were sick though.'

'It was believable,' I defended myself. 'First thing I thought of.'

'Yeah, I guess. But loads of the guys reckon it's Noah scaring him off.'

'He did look pretty threatening when I was waiting for Cody,' I admitted, printing with my lipstick sponge onto one of the already dry letters.

Lee shrugged. It was a little while before he broke the silence again. 'Shelly . . .'

'Yeah?'

'Does he ever scare you? I mean . . . I know he's not quite the Incredible Hulk or anything, but he can lose his temper kinda quickly.'

'That's just the way he is. I grew up with him around. He couldn't scare me – I know that he's . . . intimidating . . .'

'I guess,' Lee said, nodding. Suddenly he dropped his paintbrush into the pot, splattering me with pastel-pink paint – my face, my blouse, my tie, my hair . . .

'*Lee!*' I screamed.

'Sorry!'

I grabbed a brush and dunked it into the pot of black, totally prepared to flick it over Lee. But something cold and wet landed on my face and neck as he flicked me again, making me jump so much that I dropped my paintbrush, leaving a trail down my front.

Lee spluttered before collapsing into laughter. I scowled at him, waiting for him to stop.

'It's not funny, Lee!'

'Yes it is! You sh-sh-should've s-seen your . . . your face!' He was holding his side now. I glared and grabbed my bag. 'W-where you going?'

'The locker rooms to wash this crap off of my face,' I snapped. 'And stop laughing!'

'I can't help it!' he gasped, bent double. 'Your *face*!'

I stormed out, slamming the door behind me. I thought I had a spare blouse in my locker. We'd be going for a burger later and I did not want to go out looking like a Picasso.

I always thought the locker rooms at school were really weird: a big communal corridor, with notices and stuff pinned up, which led to the 'fitness suite', with its treadmills and weights, and the fields outside. The girls' were on the far left, the boys' on the right.

Just as I came into the corridor, the whole football team poured through the door. I'd already yanked off my tie and undone another button; I hadn't stopped to think I might not be alone.

The boys all slowed down seeing me, and I stopped in my tracks.

And then the laughter broke out, all of them finding me hilarious, apparently.

'What happened?' Jason asked, biting his lip hard to try and keep from laughing.

'We were painting the banner for our booth,' I said. 'Lee had a bucket of paint. Do I need to say anything more?'

He shook his head. Most of the boys started trailing into the locker rooms, still laughing and looking at me. I caught a couple of them shamelessly checking out my semi-unbuttoned shirt and put an arm across my chest.

'Aw, come on,' I said, doing a twirl and giving them a big grin – I'd rather make a joke out of it than be embarrassed. 'Do I look that bad?'

'Well, I'd pay to see you in the art gallery,' said one of the boys, laughing. I rolled my eyes at him and drifted down the corridor toward the girls' changing rooms, calling a goodbye over my shoulder.

A hand caught my arm, making me stumble backward, and then steadied me before I fell.

I turned to see who it was. Then the smile on my face dropped. 'Oh.'

'What're you doing?' hissed Noah. 'You don't walk around half dressed, Elle.'

'I'll walk around however the hell I want, thanks,' I snapped back, jerking my arm away. 'It's no big deal. It's not like I'm prancing around in my underwear, for Pete's sake.'

'Yeah but still . . .' His eyes trailed down me, then he gave me a stern look.

'Leave me alone already!' I exclaimed, glaring at him. 'Honestly, it's bad enough you're being so over-protective, but you don't have to be so . . . extreme!'

'So what happened with you and Cody? I know for a fact the whole "being sick" thing was a lie.'

I gaped. Was he blackmailing me? 'You didn't tell anybody, did you?'

He smirked, giving me a patronizing look. 'I don't gossip. And no, I didn't tell them. Because I figured you had a good reason. So what went down?'

I shrugged. 'Nothing.'

'Something clearly happened – I know you well enough to spot when you're lying. So what's the truth?'

I bit the inside of my cheek, debating whether to tell Noah or just ask him to keep his nose out of it. But I thought maybe if I didn't tell him, he'd jump to the stupid conclusion that Cody had overstepped the line.

While I was debating this, I couldn't help but notice

just how hot Noah looked in his football gear, with the shoulder pads and his helmet tucked under his arm. His hair was a little damp with sweat and he just looked . . . *wow*.

Before he noticed I was checking him out, I finally answered him. 'He was going to kiss me at the end of the night, but I kissed him on the cheek instead. He didn't try to do anything, it was a totally normal situation, and I made a fool of myself by turning my head. It's not a big deal. It got blown out of proportion. It's just embarrassing.'

He studied my face for a moment before saying, 'That's it? You're sure?'

I got the feeling he was trying not to laugh.

I huffed, just about ready to stamp my foot. 'Yeah. Completely sure. Why are you always so dramatic? It's not like any guy in this school is going to make me do anything I don't want to do, anyway.'

He raised an eyebrow, as if to say I was way too naïve. I just shrugged it off.

'Now can I go wash this freaking paint off, or does the Spanish Inquisition have more pointless questions?'

He smirked a little. 'Someone's moody.'

'I'm covered in paint and you're giving me the third degree for nothing! Of course I'm not in a good mood.' I stormed away to the changing rooms.

But when I saw myself in the mirror . . . even I had to laugh. I was such a mess! Paint flecked all through my hair, streaked over my face and dripping down my neck, patterning my blouse . . .

It wasn't so funny when it wouldn't come off, though.

Or when I found no spare clothes in my gym locker.

After about ten minutes of tireless scrubbing, I got some of the paint out of my hair and most of it off my face. It had dripped down under my blouse, so I was stood there in my trousers and bra when the door opened.

Thinking it was Lee, I didn't turn around.

'Hey, Elle? Lee said he's going for some food with the guys, but if you want a ride home . . .' Noah trailed off when he saw me standing there.

I froze, blinking at my reflection in the mirror. I felt my cheeks warm up, and twisted my head around, hoping I wasn't blushing as hard as my reflection was.

'What?' I snapped.

'Nothing.'

'No – what were you saying?'

'Oh. Oh, right, yeah, well, um, Lee's leaving to grab some food with the guys, but he said if you wanted to go straight home, then I have to give you a ride. And considering you still look like some kind of Picasso . . .'

I looked at the flecks of pink paint splattered over my collarbone and laughed, trying to cover my awkwardness at him seeing me in my bra. He'd seen me in a bikini before, but that seemed . . . different, somehow. 'Yeah. Tell Lee to go ahead.'

'Sure. How long are you going to be?'

I shrugged. 'I don't know. Since you're going to take me straight home, I can shower there, so . . .' I pulled on my damp blouse and did the buttons up hastily, then slung my bag onto my shoulder. 'Let's go.'

I wasn't really looking forward to being in the car with Noah – I was half expecting a lecture or something.

'How's the booth coming along?' he asked conversationally as we walked across to the parking lot. I looked at him warily, and he caught my eye, shrugging a little. 'What?' he said. 'I can't talk to you?'

My only reply was to raise my eyebrows skeptically at him.

He shrugged again. 'Whatever. So, are you going to answer me or not?'

I sighed, squeezing my eyes shut for a second. I felt like I should be mad at him, but I couldn't seem to find a legitimate reason *to* be mad at him.

I guess Noah just had a strange effect on me.

Although whether that effect was good or bad, I hadn't figured out yet.

'It's going okay. We still have stuff to do before Friday, but we'll manage – as long as Lee doesn't start painting me instead of the letters again.'

'Well, you made a good piece of Impressionism, I'll give you that.'

I halted in my tracks, making Noah stop a few paces ahead when he realized I wasn't with him. I raised my eyebrows at him.

'What?'

'I think that was a compliment. Noah Flynn just gave someone a compliment. Contact the newspapers, somebody.'

He gave a sarcastic laugh, but I saw the twinkle in his eyes. I smirked back and carried on walking with him.

'Are *you* going to come to the carnival?' I asked him.

'Yeah. I kind of have to. It's one of those things all of the teachers "encourage" to show "school spirit" and shit.'

'Thinking of stopping by the kissing booth?'

He cocked an eyebrow at me, with an obnoxious look on his face. 'Why are you asking, Shelly?'

'All the girls, especially the ones working the booth,

are asking me to persuade you to stop by. The chance to kiss Noah Flynn is just too exciting a prospect for some.'

He smirked wider. 'Ah. You're not asking for yourself then?'

In my dreams.

'No, definitely not.'

'Well, I'm not making any promises. You can tell them I *might* stop by, though, when they ask again. And knowing me, they *will* ask again.'

'You're so full of yourself,' I muttered, shaking my head. I paused, looking around for his car. He'd gotten out a set of keys, but I didn't see it here.

'Where's your car?' I asked, following him.

'I didn't bring it today.'

'So . . . how'd you get here?'

'I took my bike.'

I groaned, lagging behind, then stopped entirely, noticing the sleek red and black motorbike he'd created from the piece of junk he'd had sitting in his shed. It looked awesome, don't get me wrong. But I've never been on a motorbike in my life; it scared the hell out of me just to think about it.

And here I was with no option but to get on a two-wheel death trap. With Noah, no less.

'If I die, it's all your fault.'

'You're not gonna die, Elle. Here. You can even have the helmet.'

'You only have one helmet? But then, what if—?'

'I'll be fine,' he interrupted me. 'I haven't crashed this thing yet.' He patted the handlebars firmly, as if to show how sturdy the thing was.

'But what if *you* fall off? What if *you* crash? You're supposed to wear the helmet for a reason! Do you have some kind of death wish?' My voice got more and more hysterical with every syllable. I had my eyes on the bike the whole time. It seemed more monstrous and intimidating by the second.

'Worried about me, Shelly?' Noah teased.

My eyes narrowed. He was smirking, his eyes sparkling at me, tossing the helmet gently from hand to hand. I snatched it off him.

'You don't have to be scared of the bike,' he said, patting it like it was a loveable pet dog. 'It won't bite.'

'Maybe not, but *you* might,' I muttered under my breath. But he heard me, and chuckled. He tucked his bag into the hollow space underneath the seat, and put my bag in after.

I rammed the helmet onto my head, gritting my teeth. I so did not want to have to do this . . . But I had no choice. I had to get home somehow before I went to join Lee and the guys. Though I'd rather have gone out like this than get on the bike with Noah.

I fumbled with the straps. The helmet was huge and I couldn't see what I was doing. It smelled kind of citrusy. Like Noah's pillow had. It was a nice smell.

I jerked my thoughts back to the matter at hand – getting the helmet on so I wouldn't be so likely to die.

'Here . . .' Noah's hands brushed over mine and fixed the helmet for me. His fingertips tickled my neck, and for some reason I felt all shaky. Weird . . . I shook it off, attributing it to dread at having to get on this so-called vehicle.

'Don't look so scared.' He smiled at me – another real, genuine smile that showed his dimple. It made my heart somersault. I loved seeing that smile.

He slid onto the bike and I cautiously slipped on behind him. *Thank God I'm not in a skirt* was all I could think.

Noah reached behind him and his hands found mine, pulling my arms around his waist. I stiffened a little, and he told me to 'Just relax, Elle.'

With a kick, the bike roared to life and growled beneath me. We hadn't moved half an inch but my arms squeezed him tight around the waist and I pulled myself as close as I could get. My heart pounded, terrified.

I heard his laugh over the rushing blood in my ears and the menacing growl of the engine.

Then we were off.

I wanted to yell at him, and scream, 'Slow down! You're going to kill us!'

Except when I opened my mouth, any sound I might've made was snatched by the wind rushing past us. We were hurtling along the roads, slipping through traffic and zipping past lines of cars and trucks.

My hair was whipped out from under the helmet and my blouse was buffeted against me. I couldn't hear anything except blood rushing in my ears, the roar of the bike, and the wind.

When Noah yanked the bike around and came to a sudden, smooth stop outside my house, I couldn't move.

My arms were still curled tightly around his toned stomach. My legs were as close to him as I could get them.

Noah slowly peeled my arms away, and that jerked me back to life. I slid off the bike, my legs feeling so wobbly they made Jell-O look steady, and my shaky hands fumbled with the helmet.

Noah undid it for me in one swift motion and pulled it off my head.

'Your hair's all static,' he said, and reached up to ruffle it.

I scowled, and my trembling hands smoothed it out – which was impossible. It felt like a bird's nest. It'd take me hours to brush all these knots out. The leftover paint I'd missed wouldn't help much.

'Oh come on,' he said, leaning on his bike casually. 'Don't tell me you didn't enjoy that.'

'I hated it,' I told him truthfully.

'You didn't love the wind in your hair, or the freedom, or the sheer speed of it?'

I shook my head. 'Not a chance. I *hated* it.'

'Even cuddling up to me?' he asked with a cocky smirk. 'Don't tell me you didn't enjoy that.'

'Noah, that was the scariest thing I've ever done in my entire life. I don't care how hot you are, I hated every second of that.'

'You think I'm hot?' His smirk grew wider and I felt my cheeks get warm.

'Oh, shut up. It's not like you don't know you are.'

'True. But it's nice to hear you admit it.'

'You're such a jerk, you know that? And I'm never getting on that bike ever again in my life.'

'But I'm a hot jerk, right?' he teased.

I glowered. 'Shut up already. Just get my bag out. Please,' I added.

He rolled his eyes but handed me my bag.

'Thank you,' I said curtly, and marched up to the door.

'Oh, Elle?'

'What?' I sighed, turning around to give him an exasperated look.

'You have a little paint . . . Just there.' He brushed the side of his face to demonstrate, a giant smirk on his face. I glared and slammed the front door behind me.

'Elle? Is that you?' Dad called. He popped out of the kitchen and did a double take. 'What happened?'

'You don't even want to know.'

Chapter 9

We just about got the booth finished in time. On Friday, we had to work through the whole lunch hour, and stay until six putting it together.

Girls at school kept asking if I knew if Noah would stop by the kissing booth. Every time, I replied the same thing: 'He said he might, but I wouldn't get your hopes up.' And every time, I could see the excitement flash over their face as they got their hopes up.

I hadn't seen Noah since he'd dropped me off on Wednesday. I had a feeling the next time I saw him I'd end up getting teased for letting slip he was hot. He'd make a big deal of it just to humiliate me, I knew it.

Saturday morning, Lee picked me up bright and early, at eight o'clock.

'I hate mornings,' I muttered, climbing out of the car at Starbucks. I was desperate for my half-fat latte with whipped cream. I was still half asleep. I decided to ask for an extra shot of espresso in the hopes of waking myself up.

'Tell me about it,' Lee grumbled in agreement. We stumbled up to the counter and he ordered our coffees, handing over the money.

The carnival started at ten, but we needed to be there at nine to make sure everything was ready. We stayed to drink our coffees and eat brownies. Yes, it was first thing in the morning – but I didn't care. I needed the caffeine and I could definitely do with the sugar rush.

Lee practically inhaled two brownies before I'd even finished my one. We left just in time to be at the school by nine.

'Nice and early, I see. As always,' Tyrone laughed, shaking his head when we turned up at two minutes to nine. 'Your booth is over there, near the cotton candy stand.'

'Awesome,' Lee said, and we both headed over.

We set up four stools inside, and put up the crepe paper decorations. We both put up a bunch of posters advertising our kissing booth around the field.

Everything else looked pretty impressive. Some of the games were awesome. There was even a bouncy castle with a ball pit for the little kids. It was all starting to come together, and I had to say, it was surpassing all my expectations.

I headed back to our booth, where Lee was flirting with Rachel, one of the girls in his biology class. She was one of those girls who're really perky and bright all the time, but not in a bad way. And I knew Lee liked her – he'd barely shut up about her lately. I never saw them together, though – all I could do was hope she liked him back.

That is, until I walked up to the booth. Then I had a pretty good feeling that she did like him back.

'I see the kissing booth is already hard at work,' I teased: Rachel was twirling her hair and leaning close to Lee.

She blushed; he rolled his eyes at me.

'Lee was just asking me to go see a movie, actually,' Rachel told me.

'Aw!' I said, smiling brightly. 'Well, you kids have fun. When are you going?'

'Tomorrow night.'

'Awesome,' I said. She had this smile on her face that was bordering on goofy, and there was a twinkle in her eye. I glanced at Lee and gave him a barely perceptible nod. Rachel was most definitely into him.

Lee hadn't had a girlfriend for months. I just hoped that this time, his new girlfriend didn't get fed up with us being attached at the hip. That's why they usually broke up: his girlfriend got sick of Lee spending so much time with me, and Lee got sick of her complaining about me, and then – *bam* – they're both moving on.

So I left him talking with Rachel, and wandered off to meet the girls and boys who'd showed up now, a quarter of an hour before the carnival was due to start.

'Hey!' I said, smiling at Samantha and Lily. Jason and Dave were already waiting, deep in conversation about a Mets game, and then Jon arrived too.

'Who're we waiting on?' Dave asked, seeing me.

'Karen, Dana and Ash,' I told him. 'But they should be here soon.'

'Shall we head on over?' Lily asked.

'Give it a few minutes,' I said. 'Lee's flirting with Rachel and probably putting the booth to good use already.'

They laughed. Samantha said, 'They're going out now? At last! Rachel hasn't shut up about Lee for weeks!'

'Oh, God, don't even bring that up,' Lily agreed. 'I'm on the next table to her and the other day I just wanted to yell at them to go on a date already!'

'Oh, by the way, guys – you'll all be doing thirty-minute shifts. Is that okay? That way you all get a decent break.'

'Yeah.'

'Sure.'

'That's fine.'

'Totally fine.'

'Cool.'

Then I heard, 'Hey, hey!' and saw Dana and Karen half running, half skipping over to us. They, like the other girls, were in cute pink or red summer dresses. The guys wore jeans and a fitted shirt that showed their jock muscles.

Well, they all looked a lot better than me in my cut-offs and black camisole.

'Oh, shoot!' Karen cried, rummaging frantically through her purse. 'I forgot my lipstick!'

'I have some, don't worry,' Lily told her.

Karen breathed out in relief. 'Thank gosh.'

'All right, folks – I'm here, panic over,' announced a voice. I turned around to see Ash strolling over.

'Hey, great,' I said. 'Okay – so, Ash and Dave, you guys are up first. And Lily and Karen. Then we'll text the rest of you at ten twenty-five to remind you to head on back to the booth to switch over.'

They all nodded in agreement.

The nine of us made our way across the field, everybody checking out the other colorful, bright booths and stands at the carnival with interest. Rachel had disappeared by the time we got back, and Lee was putting up a dividing rope, cutting the booth in half so the girls could queue one side and the boys on the other.

'All ready?' I asked, when we heard Tyrone calling out that we only had a couple of minutes till the gates opened for the public.

'Yup, all set,' they chorused.

I looked at Lee, and we grinned at each other.

People started flooding in, and within twenty minutes there was a huge queue at our kissing booth.

Lee and I had to stay on hand to collect the money and make sure there weren't any guys – or girls, for that matter – trying to get more than a quick peck.

We made almost two hundred bucks in the first hour.

'This is insane!' I exclaimed to Lee when we were finished counting and closed the box again.

'Tell me about it! I'm so going to win my bet with Joel.'

'What bet?'

'I bet him thirty bucks our kissing booth would make more than his water balloon one.'

'Oh, yeah, I remember.' Joel and Francis had set up a booth where you had to throw darts at water balloons. You had to pop three to win one of those giant teddies. We could see it from where we stood.

'I don't know,' I said warily. 'They seem to be pretty busy . . .'

'Yeah, but I bet they haven't made two hundred dollars,' he said smugly, tapping our metal moneybox.

I grinned back. We had our carefully constructed playlist blasting out of the speakers and when you looked around, it was clear that everyone was having a great time.

Shrieks of laughter filled the air; the smell of sugar alone made you feel hyper, and the whole place was buzzing.

Lee and I wandered off for twenty minutes, leaving Tyrone to watch over things; we got some hot dogs, sodas, and then headed back with giant cotton candies – on the house, of course, since it was Rachel working that stand.

I had to drag Lee away. 'You guys are cute together,' I told him. 'Apparently she's been crushing on you for weeks.'

'Really?' He grinned, looking at me with wide eyes.

'Yup.'

'Cool.'

'I'm glad you asked her out. You've been single for ages.'

'Were you getting sick of my company?' he teased, nudging my ribs.

'No,' I laughed. 'I'm just happy for you, that's all!'

'Yeah, me too. I like her.'

'I know. You've said so enough times.'

He laughed, and slung an arm around my shoulders as we headed back to the booth. 'Now we just have to find a guy brave enough to risk my wrath and ask you out – not to mention brave enough to face Noah's threats.'

I laughed dryly. 'That'll never happen. I'll die an old maid if he doesn't back off.'

'Oh, come on. Forty-year-old virgin maybe—'

I elbowed him and bit into my cotton candy. 'Shut up,' I told him, mouth full.

He laughed. 'I'm only teasing, you know that.'

'Yeah, I know.'

Karen, Lily, Dave and Ash had turned up again a few minutes ago. Lee and I went to the back of our booth, collecting up the cash and putting it safely in our box. The queue was getting pretty big now. Excited girls topped up their lip gloss to kiss the jocks, and boys tried to work out which of the girls they'd be kissing, comparing them.

Lee and I waited to one side, watching everybody strolling past.

Suddenly Karen came rushing out of the booth, looking terrified.

'What happened? Are you okay? What's up?' we asked frantically. I thought maybe some guy had tried something on with her.

'I can't,' she said hysterically. 'I can't do it! *He's* out there!'

'Who?'

'Your ex?' Lee guessed, frowning.

She looked from me to him, and then nodded, gnawing on her lip. 'Yeah . . . Sure, let's go with that.'

'But – but we can't just . . . just let Lily do it on her own till he's gone,' I stammered.

I was suddenly shoved between the shoulders. 'Get on the booth!' Lee hissed at me. 'At least until Karen's ex is gone.'

'But – but—'

I couldn't work the kissing booth! I'd never kissed a guy in my life!

'You have to – we haven't got any choice!' he told me pleadingly.

First I find myself riding a motorbike – with Noah, of all people. Now I find myself working a kissing booth. Remind me why I ever thought this was such a good idea?

'It'll be good practise!' he joked as I left him in a daze.

I walked over to Karen's vacant stool in a daze, and picked up the lipstick on the counter, putting a little on.

It was bright red – not really something I'd go for. I wasn't even dressed to work the booth.

I looked at the line of guys in front of me. Lily shot me an encouraging smile before calling, 'Next?'

Then I saw him.

I twisted around sharply to give Karen and Lee a frantically wide-eyed look.

It wasn't Karen's ex waiting in line.

'*Flynn?*' I hissed, gaping at her. My heart was trying to break through my ribs, my eyes bulging out of their sockets.

I couldn't believe it! After all the times they'd asked me to persuade Noah to turn up, she bailed – and she had a crush on him! How lame was that?

'Sorry!' she mouthed, biting her lip.

'Next?' Lily called again. Crap. He was up next. I gulped. Lily gave me a look that told me to get on with it.

So I swallowed, cleared my throat and said a shaky, 'Next?'

Noah walked up to the booth, and sat down opposite me.

'Since when were you working the kissing booth?' he asked.

'Since you turned up and Karen wimped out,' I mumbled as he looked me up and down. 'What? I didn't dress for this, okay?'

'No, you look fine.'

'Oh.' I blinked, taken aback. That was almost like him telling me I looked nice. 'Thanks . . . I didn't think you were going to show up here.'

He shrugged. 'I didn't pay to talk to you, you know,' he told me, pushing his two dollars over the counter pointedly. 'I paid to get a kiss.'

He's just joking around . . . right?

He's just teasing me, playing a prank.

He raised an eyebrow and looked at me, waiting.

Oh, God, he really isn't joking. I have to kiss him.

I couldn't quite get my head around the idea that my first kiss was going to be with Noah Flynn. My best friend's big brother. The guy who could make me feel the most inexplicable things and drive me crazy in three seconds flat.

I gulped, and it must've been audible because he raised an eyebrow at me. My eyes flitted down to his lips; they looked so soft and kissable. My mind drifted to the memory of Noah in his towel . . . in his football uniform . . .

And I was about to kiss him.

I knew I didn't have to if I didn't want to; nobody could *force* me to kiss him. And that was the worst part: I knew I had the option to back out, and I couldn't bring myself to do it.

I leaned in as he did.

What if I had cotton candy stuck in my teeth? What if I tasted gross?

Shut up, shut up, shut up!

My first kiss . . .

Chapter 10

When my lips touched his, he tasted of spearmint and cotton candy, which wasn't as bad as it might sound. I kissed him back and forgot everything for a moment – forgot this was a kissing booth, forgot we were in public, forgot that it was Noah, who I was supposed to hate so much for being so interfering. For a second, I even forgot that this was my first kiss.

I just kissed him back, following his lead. And when I felt his tongue touch the tip of mine, I opened my mouth a little wider, letting him deepen the kiss. I kissed him back harder. I didn't have the slightest clue what I was doing; I just followed his lead.

We broke apart at the same time, but he stayed there, his forehead resting on mine. Both of us were breathing hard.

'Damn,' he said; a smirk played at the corners of his lips and his eyes sparkled at me. I couldn't tell if that was a good 'damn' or a 'damn, I just kissed my little brother's best friend'.

'Yeah,' I whispered back anyway, making him chuckle.

There were a few wolf-whistles from the crowd. I barely noticed them.

Someone tapped my shoulder, making me jump.

'Uh – I'll take over now, if you want,' said Karen, giving me a knowing smile. Still feeling dazed from the kiss, I nodded and stood up, letting her take my place. I walked out of the booth slowly, feeling totally surreal. This must have been a dream. I did *not* just make out with Noah Flynn! And not in front of so many people!

After the almost-stripping not so long ago, that probably didn't do much for my reputation. I fought the urge to bury my head in my hands.

My lips felt all tingly – in a good way, though. It was weird. I could still taste spearmint and cotton candy, and feel his slightly scratchy stubble on my cheek.

It was surreal.

I'd had my first kiss. And it hadn't been any old kiss; not a peck on the lips, or anything like that – more like a full-on make-out session.

The chances of me having my first kiss on a kissing booth with Noah Flynn were so slim . . . I was starting to think that it had never happened.

'See, that wasn't so bad.'

I jumped at Lee's voice.

'What?' he asked, oblivious, looking up from his cell phone.

'I – I think . . . I think I just made out with your brother,' I stammered quietly, disbelievingly.

His eyebrows shot up. 'How the hell did I miss that? Not that I wanted to see it. You and my brother? Weird. Just plain weird. But seriously, how did I not notice that?'

'Are you texting Rachel?'

'Yeah.'

'That's why you missed it.'

He laughed and shook his head at me. 'Okay, you're right. Hey, um, would you mind if I took Rachel to the movies tonight? After the carnival's over.'

'Sure,' I said. 'No problem. I can find another ride.'

'Maybe your dad can take you. He's brought Brad, right?'

'Yeah. They're here somewhere.'

Suddenly, in the blink of an eye, I was surrounded. There were at least a dozen girls wanting to know if it was true – had I just made out with Flynn at the kissing booth? Like, seriously?

They wanted every last detail. With a sigh, I explained that Karen had bailed . . . Um, yes, there was tongue . . . What? . . . No, I didn't know if I liked him that way or not . . . Maybe? I don't know.

And yeah, it had been my first kiss.

They were all undeniably jealous of course. But they wanted to know if I was getting together with Flynn. Of course, none of them really wanted Flynn to be taken. They wanted a single Flynn they could flirt with and drool over (probably at the same time).

But everybody wanted to know.

Word travelled fast – texts, phone calls, and given that everyone was at the carnival anyway . . . My popularity had just shot through the roof, and I was helplessly lost.

Some sophomore kids walked past and a girl pointed at me. *'That's* the one who made out with Flynn.'

At first I grimaced. But then again, there were worse things to be known for.

'Do you want to be with him?' Lee asked when we were finally alone, after the carnival had finished. The student council and a few others were still clearing up their booths and counting the cash. 'I mean, I thought you were over him.'

'I am. I don't know. It's *Noah*. You know?'

'Not really. For one thing, he's my brother. For another, I'm a guy.'

'I guess. But you know what I mean . . . I kind of hate him, I kind of like him.'

'Well, if you're not sure, then don't do anything. Should you talk to him or something?'

I ignored the last part. 'I don't know that I would anyway. If I did get together with him, which is totally unlikely anyway, and it ended messily, then it might damage our friendship. I don't want that.'

'How cheesy of you.'

'Shut up.'

'But I was thinking the same ... Five hundred and fifty,' he muttered, setting the pile aside. 'If you guys *did* get together then had a messy breakup, you might not want to be around me so much. And I'd miss you.'

'I'd miss you too. Just a little.'

'Thanks,' he said sarcastically, and we both laughed.

'It's going to be so awkward when I see him now.'

'Yup.'

'How comforting, Lee,' I said sarcastically. I smacked his arm. 'You can't be a little more sympathetic?'

He shrugged. 'I don't think you should get together with my brother anyway. It's weird. And kind of gross.'

'For you.'

'Yup.'

I shook my head at him. 'Lee, there's only five hundred and forty-nine here.'

'Oh, damn.' He passed me another dollar bill and I

added it to the pile. It was just as well I was double checking everything he counted.

'So is your dad giving you a ride home?'

I shook my head. 'He had to taxi Brad's friends to the movies straight after they left so he can't. I'll just hitch a ride with someone. Since you're *ditching* me for your new *girlfriend*.'

'I'm not ditching you! You said it was okay! I asked you first!'

I laughed. 'Calm down, I'm just messing with you.'

Lee rolled his eyes at me.

In the end we counted up six hundred and fourteen dollars. Our booth raised the most, which was pretty impressive. That might've been because we didn't have to buy a load of giant teddy bears, or hot dogs and buns, but whatever. Lee left with Rachel, while I stayed to help clean up some of the litter with Joel, who was still grumbling about losing his bet with Lee.

'It's your fault, you know. Really, *you* owe *me* thirty bucks.'

'Why?'

'If you hadn't made it a smooch booth, guys wouldn't have been queuing up in the hope of a quick French kiss,' he said, his face and tone innocent. 'So hand over my thirty bucks.'

I laughed, bumping against his shoulder. 'Not

happening. And it wasn't my fault. Or do you, like, ohmygosh, totally *need* to know every single detail of my first kiss?'

I put on a hysterically excited tone, and Joel feigned a look of pure horror. He laughed and bumped me back with his hip. 'Okay, okay, keep your money! Spare me, please.'

There was a cough behind us and we both looked around to see Noah raising an eyebrow at me; his quick look at Joel told him to back off. Joel turned to pick up some cotton-candy sticks and hot-dog wrappers.

Crap. What do I do now?

What was he even *doing* here?

Noah jerked his head, and Joel gave me a little shove to follow him. I shot him a helpless look, but he was already heading over to join some of the others.

I followed Noah towards the parking lot. There were wrappers and labels strewn everywhere, along with bits of food that the seagulls hadn't picked up yet.

'Lee said you were stuck for a ride so I should come pick you up.'

Why? Why was my best friend such a guy some-times? Of course, he probably thought he was doing me a favor somehow. But seriously? He'd just ignored my mini freak-out earlier and told Noah to give me a ride?

'Sure.' What else was I supposed to say? He hadn't

mentioned the kiss yet. Was that a good thing or not?

'Wait – you haven't got your bike, have you?'

'No,' he chuckled. 'I took my car since you hated the bike so much.'

'Thank God,' I breathed, and heard him chuckle again. Suddenly my heart went all weird, flip-flopping and somersaulting. Probably just nerves. I *almost* wished he had brought his bike – just so there wouldn't have been any chances for an awkward silence to settle.

He led me out through the mostly empty lot to his car, and we both got in. The tension was almost unbearable. I didn't know what to say or how to act now. I'd *kissed* him. And it had been a pretty intense kiss too. Not even a drunken one. What was I meant to do now?

'Do you mind if I stop by my house on the way?' he asked. 'My dad bought a video game he thought Brad would like. I'm supposed to give it to you.'

'Oh, sure,' I said, nodding. 'No problem.'

'Okay.'

After another couple of minutes he asked, 'So how much did your booth raise in the end?'

'Six hundred and fourteen bucks.'

He gave a low whistle. 'Wow.'

'I know. We made even more than the hot-dog stand.'

He nodded, and then the silence returned. I nudged

the radio volume up a little in an attempt to diffuse the tension. It didn't really work.

Everything just felt so weird. Strained.

I stole a peek at Noah from the corner of my eye. His head was bobbing slightly in time to the music and the sun hit the left side of his face, throwing shadows over the side closest to me.

The kiss probably didn't mean anything to him, I tried telling myself. He was a player, so what was one kiss to him? It was only a kiss. I was probably imagining all the awkwardness and tension in the air, making a big deal out of this because it had been my first kiss.

Although . . . He was the one who'd turned it into a French kiss. And afterward he'd looked just as dazed as me. But maybe it was because I was a terrible kisser and he didn't say anything to save me the embarrassment?

My mind was going a mile a minute. I was confused, I was worried, I wanted to kiss him again—

No. That's not going to happen. You won't be kissing Noah again, Rochelle, because he's Noah. *He's Lee's big brother. He's the jerk who's responsible for your non-existent love life and who told you he only sees you as a sister. Remember, you're supposed to be mad at him for being so overprotective and annoying and interfering? You're not*

*meant to be thinking about kissing him. You're mad at him
. . . right?*

It didn't really help, telling myself that.

I still wanted to kiss him again.

The car journey stretched on for what seemed like
an eternity – and we weren't even halfway yet. I sighed.
I felt him glance over at me, but I was too busy with my
internal battle to pay him any attention.

I wanted to kiss him again – to reassure myself there
hadn't been any fireworks, I told myself. I shouldn't do
it, though. I bet he still thought of me as his kid
brother's friend, the little girl he grew up with . . . But
what about that time after his and Lee's party, when we
fell off the bed? I was sure there had been something
between us; but maybe I was deluding myself.

And I was also probably deluding myself that he
had been checking me out when he'd walked in on me
in my bra.

But maybe there was something between us and we
just didn't know it yet. Maybe just one more kiss – to
prove myself wrong. Or right. Would that really be so
bad?

No. I couldn't kiss him again. I couldn't do it . . .

Could I?

I sighed again as we drove up his street. *What was I
going to do?*

We finally pulled up at his house.

'I'll come in and get the game for Brad,' I said. 'I'll walk from here.'

The truth was, I didn't want to spend any longer with him in this car than I had to.

'Sure, whatever.'

We got out and I followed him into the kitchen and hung around near the doorway while he rifled through a pile of papers on the counter, biting my lip nervously.

He turned around with a new Mario game, and handed it to me. He wasn't even a whole foot away from me. A couple of inches of air separated us.

Before I knew what I was doing, I went up on tiptoe and pressed my lips against Noah's.

Immediately I realized what a fool I was being and stepped back, my cheeks burning and my heart racing.

Noah looked at me, blinking in shock, it seemed. He stared at me, his expression unreadable.

'Oh God,' I babbled hastily, feeling beyond humiliated, 'I'm sorry. It's just – I mean, I just – Oh man, I—'

Noah took a stride forward and shut me up very effectively by crushing his lips against mine. Any resistance and tension went gushing out of my body (whether from shock or something else, I wasn't sure), and my arms curled around Noah's neck.

I forgot what a fool I'd just made of myself and kissed him back. His hands were on my back and in my hair, squashing me against him so it seemed like every inch of our bodies was touching.

And for the record – there were definitely fireworks of some kind going on.

Hands on my hips, he lifted me up onto the kitchen counter so my legs were either side of him. He moved on to kissing my neck, and that was when my head began to clear a little, and I realized just exactly what we were doing here.

'Noah, we – we can't do this,' I said breathlessly, shakily.

He sighed, stepping back and running his hand through his hair. I had no idea what he was thinking; his expression was indefinable.

He met my eyes again, and I got the feeling he wanted an explanation.

'I – I'm not going to just be another girl you sleep with and don't call back in the morning,' I said, sticking my chin out. 'I'm not risking my friendship with Lee just for that.'

Noah looked at me for a long moment. 'That's what you think I'd do, really?'

'W-well . . .' I trailed off. Wasn't it?

He came closer, so there were only a couple of inches

between us. If I could have moved back, I would've, but I was still sat on the counter.

'Let's get something straight here,' he said quietly and firmly. 'Two things. First off: do you have any idea how many girls I'll kiss at a party who, the next day, claim they've slept with me? And second: despite what all those girls think, they never actually want to date me. They say they do, but think about it. Who wants a serious relationship with someone who has a reputation for getting into fights, or just a fling?'

I studied his face and quickly decided he was totally serious.

Noah could be a jerk, sure – but he was never big on lying.

I saw his point. Even if girls didn't want anything long-term, they might not mind just having a fling with a hot guy with a history of violence. I had always thought it kind of weird how so many girls said they'd slept with him when it had looked like he'd spent the night alone; Lee and I had never really wanted to question it too much, though.

'You see my point, right?'

I nodded. 'Yeah. But – but you'd never do something to a girl. You're not like that.'

'Yes, but that doesn't seem to factor into it for them.'

'So hang on – what are you trying to say here?' I

said, putting my hands up, palm out, and feeling more than a little confused. 'It's not your fault you're a player? Or, at least, that you've got a reputation as one?'

'Right.'

'And . . . ?' I prompted.

He bit his lip. Did Noah Flynn actually look . . . *nervous*? No, I had to be imagining it. The only time I'd seen him looking like this was when I caught him in those Superman boxers and made him blush.

'I just mean,' he said slowly, looking down at the counter rather than at me, 'that I wouldn't treat you like dirt, as you seem to think I would.'

'I still don't know what you're trying to say, Noah.'

'I don't either,' he said with a sudden chuckle, rubbing a hand over his face. 'But . . .' He came closer still. Now there was about an inch between us, and his hands were resting on my thighs. My breathing suddenly turned shallow, my heart pounding in my ribcage. 'I *do* know I want to kiss you again.'

Part of me wanted to say no, to push him firmly away. I wasn't going to risk my friendship with Lee just to carry on kissing Noah. Besides, I couldn't really see us as a couple.

Not to mention, I was hardly the kind of girl to be randomly kissing boys. I was the hopeless romantic.

Or I thought I was, anyway.

But when Noah lowered his head slowly to mine, giving me plenty of time to shove him away, I didn't. Instead, I let him put his lips against mine, kissing him for the third time today. I was making out with Noah Flynn, of all people. Just this morning, I'd never even kissed a boy.

Noah wrapped my legs around his waist, and I put my arms around his neck, toying with the hair at the nape of his neck. I suddenly couldn't get enough of him – his taste, his touch. I couldn't understand why he had such an effect on me.

He lifted me off the counter, carrying me out of the kitchen. I really wasn't sure if this was a good idea, but the feeling of his lips on mine clouded my mind, and I couldn't focus long enough to think it through. It wasn't until we both fell onto something soft and springy – a mattress – that my dormant consciousness seemed to wake up.

'Noah,' I said, trying to pull away. I knew where this was leading now. 'Noah . . .'

'Yeah?' he murmured, and started nibbling on my earlobe. It sent sparks all through my body and for a second I forgot what I was saying.

'We can't . . . I'm not . . .'

'Hmm?' He drew back only far enough to look me in the eye. I still couldn't remember what I was about to say. He seemed to understand, though, since his eyes went wide and he said, 'Oh, no, I didn't mean for . . . you know . . . I wasn't . . .'

'I – I can't do this,' I stammered. I wriggled away, standing up, making my way to the bedroom door and straightening my top. I couldn't think straight when I was that close to him. I had to get out of here, think it through properly.

A hand on my arm pulled me back, and another hand moved past my head to shut the door. Noah was pressed right against me. I had no space at all – the door at my back, the handle digging into me, and Noah in front of me.

'Noah,' I said firmly. 'I'm not going to do this. Nothing is going to happen between us because we just don't *go* together. All we do is argue. You scare guys away from me. And I'm not some – some plaything you can just use when it's convenient. Got that?'

Noah sighed softly, his breath blowing on my face. It still smelled and tasted of spearmint and cotton candy.

'I never thought you were something to use when it's convenient,' he mumbled, looking me in the eye.

'Okay. But tell me honestly – would you date me, Mr Player?'

He sighed again, leaning his forehead against mine. 'You tell me.'

I groaned in frustration. 'You're not making this any easier, Noah! We argue and you're such a jerk, not to mention you're Lee's big brother, but—'

'But . . . ?'

Humiliating as it was, I blurted, 'But I felt something when we kissed. I don't know what the hell to do – but I'm not going to make out with you if we're just hooking up.'

'You want the truth then, Elle?' Noah was starting to sound really frustrated now, and his eyes were level with mine. 'You're the one girl who is herself around me, and I like that. But the fact that you don't want me back is sending me crazy. You're the only girl who didn't fall at my feet and it is driving me *insane*. I haven't so much as looked at anyone else because of you – did you know that? You're all I can think about.'

Whoa.

Okay.

So it wasn't like he'd just confessed he loved me and had done for years . . . But *hell*! Who would have guessed that I, Rochelle Evans, the girl with no experience whatsoever in the boy department, would be the one to drive Noah Flynn crazy?

I was stunned. 'And how long have you felt like this? Just out of curiosity.'

He shrugged. 'A couple of months.'

I nodded, trying desperately to appear steady and collected. 'I thought you said you saw me as a little sister.'

'That was until you grew up,' he said simply. Then, 'I made you blush.'

I ignored him. 'If that's true, why did you tell me I was like a sister to you?'

He averted his eyes. 'You didn't want me back. I'm not the kind of guy to tell someone what I'm actually feeling. You know that. You know this whole conversation is torture to me?'

I smirked slightly, then blurted, 'I wanted you, believe me.'

He looked like he'd just won a million dollars or something. He tilted his head so his lips brushed against mine. 'Just . . . I don't . . . I don't want you to think that I'm only interested in one thing here, okay? I'm not. I'm not. That's one of the things I like about you. You're sweet, and innocent. Different. It's cute.'

'You think I'm cute now too?' I raised an eyebrow and he smirked against my lips. 'And here I was thinking I was just your kid brother's annoying best friend.'

'Well, that too.'

I giggled and traced a finger across his chest.

Then he said again, 'I'm not just interested in you for *that*, okay?'

'If you were, I'd seriously question your judgment,' I mumbled, making him chuckle. But I suddenly felt warm inside.

He placed a finger under my chin, tilting my face up. The look on his face, the crease in his forehead . . . he looked cautious more than anything else.

I wouldn't think of him as Lee's brother, or as that jerk who could be too protective of me. I refused to let all the horrible repercussions of this situation enter my mind – plenty of time for those later.

Right now, he was just Noah. And I leaned up to kiss him.

And, naturally, with me being so inexperienced, I clashed teeth with him. I never thought people actually did that. Go figure I would manage it. 'Sorry,' I muttered, biting the inside of my cheek.

His lips tweaked up against mine. I felt his chest reverberating with suppressed chuckles under my hand. 'Practise makes perfect.' And that time, we didn't knock teeth.

We stayed on his bed making out for ages. We talked a little about school, about where he was applying to college (he was thinking of going to San Diego, since it was closest), and had a minor argument about how All Time Low were so much better than Linkin Park. (Noah was a big fan of Linkin Park's newer music, while I hated them.) I found I was actually enjoying being with Noah even when we weren't making out. I actually liked his company – even when we argued over music.

But we didn't talk for more than a few minutes at a time before he started kissing me again. And when that happened, I forgot what we'd just been talking about; forgot that I really should've left by now. I just got caught up in the way his kisses made my stomach fill with wild butterflies.

It was just that he was a good kisser, I told myself. I mean, it's not like we had a 'connection' or anything. We were far too different for that. There was no guarantee that he'd still want to be with me in a week or so, when he'd never been in a long-term relationship.

'So what exactly,' he said after a while, propping his elbows behind his head and looking me in the eye, 'are we doing here?'

'I'm not just going to hook up with you,' I replied firmly.

'I told you,' he sighed, touching my knee, 'that's not all I'm interested in.'

I shouldn't like him. I *couldn't* like him. We were too different; this was too wrong. Not to mention how I could ever face up to Lee and tell him I was with his brother.

But . . . I enjoyed being with him like this. I liked the

way it felt to kiss him; the feel of his arms around me; the smile in his eyes when we argued over bands. It felt *nice* to be like this with Noah. Like it was natural.

Was that worth hurting Lee for, though? I couldn't do that to him, could I? He'd already made it clear that it'd be weird for him; that it could potentially damage our friendship – and nothing could be worth that. Right?

'I . . . I don't know,' I admitted after a while. 'It's just . . . we shouldn't, and – and Lee . . .'

'I see.' Noah was quiet for a moment. His fingertip traced circles on my knee, and I watched the movement, waiting.

He spoke haltingly. 'Well . . . maybe Lee doesn't have to know.'

I let that sink in a moment. 'You mean I should lie to him?'

'Maybe just not tell him the whole truth . . .' His mouth twisted a little, like he was struggling to word it properly. 'Until we figure out what to do.'

I nodded. If Lee didn't know, it couldn't hurt him. If things didn't work out between Noah and me, then Lee would be none the wiser, and things could stay as they were between us. And if things *did* work out with Noah . . . then I'd cross that bridge and tell Lee when I came to it.

I heard him sigh, and I looked up. He gave me a wry

smile. 'I told you girls didn't want to be with a guy who's got a history of punching things.'

I shoved his arm lightly. 'It's not that. And besides, I know you'd never lay a finger on a girl. You're not like that.'

And before I could think about it any more, I said, 'Okay.'

'Okay?'

'But just promise me you won't let Lee find out.'

Noah nodded. 'Of course I won't.' Then he sat up and leaned forward far enough to kiss my nose. Smiling, I moved my head so I could kiss him on the lips instead. I felt his lips curve up against mine, and when we pulled apart, there was that dimple in his left cheek that only appeared when he smiled.

Then I looked past him and saw the time, glaring at me in red from his digital alarm clock. I gasped; I had to be home for dinner in twenty minutes. Where had the afternoon gone?

'I should get going,' I said urgently.

'Oh . . .' If I didn't know better, I might have thought he was disappointed. 'Do you need a ride home?'

I turned to raise my eyebrows at him. 'I can walk. I have legs. Two of them, actually.'

He smirked. 'Have it your way, then. I was just trying to be nice . . .'

'It's okay. Really.' I wanted to clear my head a little, and this would not happen if Noah was with me.

'You're cute when you look like that,' I told him, nodding at his expression.

He grimaced. 'Don't call me cute. Please.'

'Aw, how cute,' I teased, laughing. I shoved at his shoulder playfully, a gesture which he returned with an eye-roll.

I went to pick up my cell phone from the dresser next to his bed, and blurted out a question before I could help myself.

'Why do you hate people calling you Noah?' I asked.

'Noah's not exactly the coolest name in the book. You can't imagine some guy running in terror at the name Noah. Flynn's just—'

'It suits you.'

'Exactly. So why do you always call me by my first name?'

''Cause I grew up with you. Then I did it to annoy you. But it's kind of hot.'

The words had come out before I realized what I was saying. My mouth snapped shut and my cheeks flamed as I held a hand over my mouth. I couldn't believe I'd just said that! I mean, I *did* think Noah was a hot name – maybe not on some people, but Noah Flynn pulled it off. He made it sexy. I just couldn't believe I'd *told* him that!

He smirked, pulling my hand away from my undoubtedly beetroot-colored face. 'Well, when you put it like that, it doesn't seem so bad.'

I gave an embarrassed laugh and he gave me a quick peck on the lips before letting my hand go. I needed to get going now. And if someone came home unexpectedly, it was bound to look more than a little suspicious that I was here with Noah. They'd hardly believe we were just 'hanging out'.

I detoured to the kitchen on my way out to grab my purse and the video game for Brad.

When I turned around and saw Noah leaning in the open doorway, it made me jump. He hadn't made a sound; I'd had no idea he was there.

'Are you free tomorrow?' he asked me.

'I don't think so . . . I have a ton of homework I have to do, so . . .'

Only after I'd said that did I think maybe I should've tried to be more mysterious – ask what he had in mind, tell him I might or might not be available. But I waved away the notion immediately – as if *I* could pull that off.

'That sucks.'

I waited for him to expand on that, but he didn't. He

just gave me that infamous trademark smirk and his bright eyes bored into mine. I wondered if that meant he wanted to meet up with me. But he didn't say anything more.

'Um,' I said quietly.

He grinned. 'I'll find somewhere out of the way to meet you, don't worry.'

I smiled back at him. In just one day I'd gone from having no love life to what I could only call sneaking around with the most desirable guy in school, all because of that damn kissing booth.

'Bye,' I said quietly, brushing past him to get to the front door.

'Hey, hold up,' he said, tugging me back by the belt hook of my jeans. 'I want my goodbye kiss.'

'Hmm, no.'

Wow, that may just have been the flirtiest thing I've said today. Go me.

'No?' He raised his dark eyebrows challengingly.

He bent to kiss me anyway, and I was going to kiss him back – but he pulled away after barely brushing his lips to mine. He gave me an innocent look, at which I rolled my eyes.

'Bye, Shelly,' he called teasingly after me.

'Bye, Noah,' I replied in the same tone, smiling to myself.

I didn't stop smiling the whole way home.

That night, I lay in bed thinking about it all. I had no way of knowing for sure how long this would last; I'd always thought of myself as the kind of girl who would be in more long-term, committed relationships. From what I'd heard, Noah's longest relationship had been maybe a week. But I couldn't help it. I didn't want to hurt Lee, but I felt an attraction to Noah that wasn't only something physical—

Not that I would do anything so stupid as to fall for him.

Nope. No way.

If anything could damage my relationship with Lee, it was that. It wouldn't happen. It couldn't happen. I wouldn't let it.

I just had to try and deal with this whole thing the best way I could. And if that meant hiding the fact that Noah and I were together, then so be it. I didn't want to not be with him; just the thought of this afternoon made me feel warm inside.

I'm pretty sure I fell asleep smiling.

Chapter 11

Monday morning came way, way too soon. I was all set to tell the girls about my kiss with Noah, because I knew they would want every detail. I was ready for the jealous looks I'd be getting. I was also prepared to wave aside any assumptions they might make about us getting together.

Noah and I had both been too busy to meet up the day before; but we'd texted. I still felt light and bubbly inside remembering his last text when I said I was going to sleep: *Sweet dreams.*

It had been very unlike Noah, but I'd still liked it.

A car pulled up outside my house, so I hurried downstairs and yelled goodbye over my shoulder.

'Hey,' I said to Lee, smiling as I climbed into the passenger seat.

'Hey! What are you looking so happy about? I thought you were dreading today, after the whole kissing-booth situation.'

I shrugged. 'I don't know. Why can't I be in a good mood?'

'Well, for one thing, it's a Monday. For another, you are not a morning person. Believe me, I know.'

I shrugged. 'Don't complain. I'm in a good mood – let's leave it at that.'

Lee laughed. 'Okay, then . . .'

Once we got to school, I had barely stepped out of the car before I was surrounded by squeals and questions. It seemed like every single girl wanted me to describe the kiss.

'Give her some space, guys!' I heard Lee laughing.

'Ooh, you're so lucky. I wish I'd been there. I would *kill* to kiss Flynn. I cannot believe you chickened out, Karen.'

'I don't blame you. It must've been terrifying when you realized you had to kiss Flynn!'

'I wish it had been me.'

'I can't believe you got to kiss Flynn.'

'Isn't it really awkward though, with Lee?'

'No,' I scoffed. 'Of course it's not! Lee's my best friend.'

'Yeah, but it is his *brother* you made out with. And I saw – that wasn't just a quick kiss,' Candice added, waggling her eyebrows suggestively.

'Yeah, but it's *Lee*.'

'Have you spoken to Flynn since?'

'Do you like him, Elle?' Faith was suddenly right in my face. 'Don't you have a crush on him?'

'I can hardly form a full sentence around him,' laughed someone else.

'You're not the only one!'

'Elle's the only girl who can talk to him.'

'I don't see how you can act so normal around him,' Georgia said.

I shrugged. 'I grew up with him, because I was always with Lee. And I don't know, Faith,' I said, turning to her. 'He's just Noah.'

'*Just Noah?*' they all cried out in shock. I bit my cheeks. I really needed to start thinking before I blurted out stuff like that. 'This is Flynn we're talking about! How can you say that?'

'Look, I'm going to go talk to some of the guys. I kissed Noah – yeah, it was great. But can we all just move on now? I'm kind of sick of talking about it.'

I felt mean, and I tried not to storm across the parking lot too angrily.

When I finally reached Lee and the other boys, I let out a huge sigh of relief.

'That looked like fun,' Lee said casually.

I elbowed him in the ribs.

'Oh my gosh! You, like, *totally* have to tell us

everything! Oh my *gosh*! I cannot believe you made out with *Flynn*! Like, *oh my gosh*!' Cam said in a falsetto voice. The boys cracked up and I rolled my eyes.

'Don't even start. Please, I'm begging you.'

'Don't worry, we're not going to ask,' Dixon told me. 'But seriously, you're not dating?'

'No.'

He nodded. 'Cool.'

'Why – you interested?' I batted my eyes flirtatiously.

'Maybe,' he joked. Then he added, 'Nah, just – you know, rumors.'

'I'll let Noah know next time I see him,' I said seriously, making all the boys laugh and push Dixon around playfully. 'Have an ambulance on standby.'

'*Touché*.'

'Oh, hey,' Warren said suddenly. 'I forgot. My parents are out next Friday, so you know what that means, right?'

'House party!' Lee yelled, high-fiving him. 'Awesome.'

'Don't go spreading the word, though. I don't want things getting too crazy.'

'Sure, no problem,' they all agreed.

'You in, Elle?' Warren asked me, since I hadn't commented yet.

'Sure thing. But I'm sticking to the alcohol-free stuff at this one – I do not want another near-miss of the skinny-dipping episode.'

'Damn it, Elle, my dreams are crushed,' Cameron muttered, and laughed.

Lee looked at me doubtfully. 'Don't worry, Shelly, I'll keep an eye on you.'

'No you won't, you'll be too busy making out with Rachel,' Oliver said, making everyone laugh.

The bell went then, and we all filed into the school for assembly.

Lee and I got a special commendation from the principal for raising so much money on our booth. That's not the only thing I got, though.

There were so many comments and whistles from boys passing by about me and Flynn. It was really starting to bug me. Nothing as offensive as what had been said after Lee and Noah's party. But the way they said it was really making my blood boil.

By Thursday all the excitement had mostly died down. New rumors and gossip came onto the scene, sidelining me.

I couldn't have been happier.

I was so sick of talking about kissing Flynn at the carnival. I was so sick of hearing the girls tell me how jealous they were. I was so sick of having boys look at me differently in the corridors because now I wasn't quite as innocent any more.

And then, to top my week off, I got to Lee's on Thursday afternoon, like we'd arranged, to find he wasn't there.

'I'm heading out to the store,' his mom told me. 'But if you want to stay and hang around for a bit, you're more than welcome.'

'Okay, I'll see how long he's going to be. Thanks, June.'

'Bye, Elle!' she said cheerfully before leaving. I sighed and texted Lee to find out where he was.

Over Rachel's. Sorry! :-(I didn't know you were coming over.

He'd clearly forgotten that we'd arranged to hang out. That was so unlike him.

No problem, I'll head on home. I added a smiley face to let him know I wasn't mad at him – even though I *was* a little annoyed. Lee never blew me off for other girls without at least giving me advance notice.

He must really like Rachel, I thought.

I was heading for the door when I heard movement at the top of the stairs and looked up.

'Oh, hey,' said Noah. 'Lee's not here.'

'Yeah, your mom just said. She's gone to the store, by the way.'

'Oh, right.'

150

I rocked back and forth on my heels while he just looked at me as he came down the stairs. I didn't know whether to leave or not . . . I didn't want to now I knew Noah was here.

All week, whenever I saw him in the corridors or on the field at lunch, I remembered the feeling of his lips on mine, and I ached to kiss him again.

He was just wearing a pair of threadbare sweatpants with old oil stains on, and a white T-shirt. Nothing special. So why did he manage to look like a freaking male model? He was so out of my league.

I'd been starting to convince myself that whatever had happened with Noah on the weekend was just a closed chapter in my life, and that he'd forgotten all about it. That I just had to get over it and move on.

Then he kissed me. Taken by surprise at finding him there, I let him back me up two steps to the wall, and then I put everything I had into kissing him back.

Apparently, my worries and doubts had been entirely irrational.

When we finally broke apart for air, he stayed so close that when one of us spoke, our lips moved against each other.

He said quietly, 'I've been waiting to do that all week.'

I felt a thrill of excitement run through me. I willed

my cheeks not to color and tried to keep my cool, so he didn't see how relieved and happy I was.

Not that I should be getting too attached to him, I told myself; I had to be careful. For Lee's sake.

Attempting to be the flirty, confident girl I really wasn't, I replied, 'Sorry to have kept you waiting.'

He shrugged. 'It was worth it.'

Now, *that* I couldn't help but blush over.

'How long do you reckon we've got?' he asked me.

'Hmm . . . half an hour, at least,' I mused, and there was a laugh in my voice.

Noah's blue eyes looked even brighter than usual, if that was possible. He gave me another quick kiss, and then took my hand, leading me upstairs.

'Are you going to Warren's party next week?' he asked me suddenly.

'Yeah,' I answered. 'Are you?'

He nodded. 'Just don't go wearing anything too revealing, all right?'

'Why not?' I asked curiously. He'd never said anything about that for previous parties.

'You wouldn't believe what guys have been saying about you all week,' he said angrily, a muscle jumping in his jaw.

'I think I would,' I muttered under my breath without thinking.

'What have you heard?' he snapped, even angrier now – though the anger wasn't directed at me.

Resisting the urge to roll my eyes, I shrugged. I really, *really* needed to keep my mouth shut more. 'Just comments about the kissing booth, really.'

'Like . . . ?' he prompted. I could tell he was starting to get mad. I knew all the warning signs after all these years – that muscle in his jaw; the cracking knuckles; the line creasing his forehead just above his eyebrows; his legs shifting into a fighter's stance.

His fingers were flexing, the muscle in his jaw was going . . .

Oh, and there went the legs.

'They've just been saying stupid things,' I sighed, falling onto the bed. I couldn't even enjoy the bouncy mattress – that's how tense things were. 'Making comments about me kissing you, asking if the two-dollar fee was still standing . . . It's fine, nothing happened,' I assured him quickly.

Noah was shaking his head. 'You're sure nobody tried anything? At all?'

I sighed. 'Positive. Calm down already.'

'I'm serious, Rochelle,' he said, frowning. *Way to kill the mood*, I thought bitterly. 'Anyone comes near you and—'

'I'm a big girl, I can look out for myself. You don't

need to be so . . . so . . . so damn controlling all the time! Calm down.'

'I'm not being controlling!'

'Yes you are!' I yelled back, sitting up now to scowl at him. 'I'll wear whatever the hell I want to that party next week. I don't need you telling me who I can date or what I can wear or who I can talk to!'

'I'm trying to stop you getting hurt,' he shouted at me.

'I'm not going to get hurt! Not everybody's a jerk like—'

'Like me?' he finished for me.

'Yeah! Yeah, like you!'

By now I was standing right in front of Noah, trying to look him in the eye. It wasn't easy when he was about four inches taller than me, but I did my best to glare back at him.

'You don't seem to understand just how bad some of these guys are,' he argued. 'You act normal, but they think it's flirting and take it the wrong way. They'll try something and you might not think you've led them on but you sure as hell have.'

'I'm not leading anyone on!' I cried in outrage.

'That's exactly what I'm talking about! You don't mean to, and you don't know it, but when you act like yourself and joke around, some guys take that the wrong way – they think you're flirting. And if you're not careful, you'll end up getting hurt.'

'Fine! But I don't need you making my every move for me!' I jabbed him sharply in the chest, and he grabbed my hand before bringing his lips down on mine.

The kiss tasted strangely sweet, fuelled by an anger that melted into passion. It was weird how the situation flipped from a really heated argument to a really heated make-out session.

Noah's hands knotted in my hair, keeping me as close as possible while he pulled me down onto the bed. I couldn't think straight when he was kissing me. He sent my head spinning and banished every rational thought.

We broke apart for air, and I noticed his eyes were roaming over my body while I was trying to get my thoughts together. I was fully clothed, but I had never felt more incredibly self-conscious.

Noah pulled me back down, holding me tenderly, and placed a soft, lingering kiss on my lips. 'You're gorgeous, Elle, you know that?'

Gorgeous.

Not hot. Not sexy. *Gorgeous.*

It's one thing for Lee to say that when I'm picking at my clothes, asking if I look okay. It was one thing for my dad to say that when I went to the Winter Dance a few months back. It's a totally different thing coming from Noah Flynn's mouth.

I smiled and kissed him back.

'I don't mean to be so controlling,' he murmured, not quite meeting my eyes; he toyed with the ends of my hair, wrapping it around his fingertips. 'I just . . . it gets me really mad hearing guys talk about you like that. I don't want to see you get hurt. I – I care about you too much.'

I was certain he didn't mean that he 'cared for me too much' in a romantic sense; we'd grown up together, so of course he cared about me. But it still made my heart skip a beat.

I smiled. 'That's nice to hear.'

'Even if I'm a total jerk?'

I laughed. 'Even if you're a total jerk.'

'Not to mention a hot jerk,' he smirked.

'Mm, debatable.'

He raised an eyebrow, and suddenly flipped me so I was pinned underneath him, my arms held above my head.

'You want to try that again?' he asked, his voice a low growl in my ear, his mouth brushing the skin under my jaw. I squirmed, because it tickled.

'Okay,' I giggled, 'maybe you are a little hot . . .'

'Try again, Shelly,' he said quietly, threateningly; but I heard laughter in his voice. He moved to kiss my neck, right where he knew it tickled most, and I laughed, wriggling about.

'Okay, okay,' I said shakily, weakening. 'You're really, really hot.'

'I know.' He brought his lips down on mine and let go of my hands. My fingers tangled in his dark hair.

We were still making out, oblivious to everything else, when a car door slammed outside.

'Damn it,' Noah exclaimed quietly as I scrambled up. He jumped up to look out of the window.

'Who is it?'

'My mom – she's back from the store already . . .' He trailed off, seeing the time on his clock. She had been gone for a nearly an hour now. Why did time always fly when we were together?

'I'll go help her unload the groceries,' he said. 'You sneak out the back door.'

I nodded. 'Okay.'

He paused by the doorway, his eyes sparkling with amusement.

'What?'

'This is kind of fun, sneaking around,' he said. 'Don't you think?'

'Noah? I'm back!' June called up to him. 'Can you give me a hand unloading the car?'

'Sure, Mom, whatever,' he called down, then smiled at me, showing his dimple. I grinned back. 'Come on. You can make a run for it when she's out at the car.'

I snuck to the top of the stairs, and waited until Noah followed his mom out of the front door. He jerked his head urgently, and I sprinted for the kitchen to escape out the back door. I waited until I heard bags rustling into the house before hurrying out through the side gate and down the street.

I found myself thinking that Noah was right. It was kind of exciting, sneaking around.

I just wondered how long we'd last together.

Chapter 12

I was still debating over what to wear at seven o'clock.
Lee would be arriving in forty-five minutes. I'd been
getting ready for two hours, and I'd changed my outfit,
like, fifty times already.

The past week had gone by way too fast; it was
already Warren's party.

I stood with my hands on my hips in front of my
closet, critically looking over all my clothes again. 'You
know what,' I said to myself. 'I'll be going in my underwear at this rate.'

I didn't really want to wear a dress or skirt – mostly
because I'd forgotten to shave my legs – and that lim-
ited my 'party wardrobe' considerably.

What I really wanted to wear was a sheer black top
that was basically backless, with thin crisscrossing
straps. The neckline was cut straight across my collarbone, so it was far from low cut; I just didn't know if it
was party wear.

I sighed, rubbing a hand across my collarbone (I didn't want to mess up my make-up). Did I really care if I wasn't dressed up too much?

I knew why I *really* wanted to look good.

I wanted to look good for Noah.

But that was silly. To hell with it. I was going to wear the black top, and if I looked out of place, then so what?

I snatched up my jeans. They were pale blue denim, artfully torn in the legs. I pulled on the top too and sat down at my dresser to finish my hair. I still wasn't really in the party mood, and pulled it up into a pony-tail on the top of my head.

I topped up my mascara; I had a few minutes to kill before Lee got here.

Then I got a phone call.

'Lee, what's up?' I asked, immediately sensing something was wrong. Why else would he call?

'Listen, um . . . I'm really sorry, but do you mind if . . . well . . .'

'Spit it out already,' I laughed.

'Well, Rachel just asked if I could give her a ride because her friend bailed and . . .'

'You want to know if you can bail on me to take your girlfriend, like the amazing best friend you are?' I said dryly, but I was smiling and he probably knew it.

'Actually, I was just going to ask if you'd mind if we

took Rachel too. I wouldn't ditch you! Give me some credit.'

'Well, I'll ask my dad to give me a lift,' I said. 'I'll let you and Rachel be alone.'

'You don't have to do that, Shelly! Don't be silly.'

'No, it's okay, Lee, I really don't mind,' I told him honestly. 'It's okay.'

Before, his relationships had ended because he and I were too close, and his girlfriends didn't like not being the number-one woman in his life. I didn't want to spoil things with him and Rachel.

He thought for a moment. 'Well, I can ask Noah to take you. He hasn't left yet.'

I heard him shout to his brother as I was saying, 'No, Lee, don't – it's fine, really—' I broke off with a sigh.

'Elle? Shelly, you still there? Hello?'

'Huh?' I'd totally spaced out, not even hearing Lee talking to me.

'Noah said he'd give you a ride there, no problem. He'll be at yours in about twenty minutes.'

'B-but . . .' I protested quietly, weakly.

'Thanks, Elle. I owe you big time. See you later!'

'Bye . . .'

I sighed, letting my cell phone slide out of my hands and onto my bed and burying my face in my hands.

Standing up, I looked myself over critically in my mirror.

I'd kept my make-up simple, except for the dark burgundy lipstick. My jeans hugged my figure; my top emphasized my curves and bared almost my whole back. I felt good. Noah would most likely try to find something inappropriate with my look though.

But that wasn't why I was worried; I was more worried about the gossip and rumors that would start when people saw us turn up together.

Just then, the doorbell went. I put my cell in my back pocket and went downstairs as I heard Dad call my name.

He opened the door and I saw him do a double take. 'Noah.'

'Hey, is Elle ready yet?' Noah asked, shockingly polite for him.

'Uh . . .' My dad turned to call me again, and saw me. He looked confused. 'One second, Noah.'

He pulled me into the kitchen. 'What's he doing here?' he asked me quietly.

'Lee took his girlfriend and got Noah to drop me there instead.'

'Oh, good. For a minute there I thought you two were dating.'

I forced a laugh. 'Yeah, right.'

162

'Be careful, though. I'm still not sure whether I trust that boy – what with the fights he gets into . . . and that motorbike . . .'

'Yeah, I know, Dad. But Noah's fine. Don't worry about it.' I gave him a quick kiss on the cheek. 'Bye!'

'No alcohol!' he yelled after me.

I went back to the front door, closing it behind me. I smiled casually at Noah. 'Ready to go?'

He looked me up and down, very slowly. Instead of blushing, I sighed internally. *Here we go.* I wondered how angry he'd be. Though the look in his eyes made my heart race.

'You really don't listen to a word I say, do you?'

'Nope.' I smiled easily again and started off toward the car.

'Honestly, Elle – do you have to dress so . . . so . . .'

'So *what*, Noah?' I asked tightly, but a part of me was eager to hear what he really thought of me.

'Well, look at you!' he sputtered angrily, his jaw clenching. 'Can't you wear something a little less . . . sexy?'

I couldn't help but grin. Who'd have thought there would be a day when *Flynn* said *I* looked sexy? I felt giddy – though it wasn't as good as the feeling when he'd told me I was gorgeous.

'It's not funny,' he snapped at me.

'Oh, calm down. I could've worn something much more revealing. It's a party. I'm not changing, Noah. I'll walk there if I have to, but there's nothing you can do about it. If you want me to change, then I'll go back in and come out wearing the shortest skirt and the tightest top in my closet.'

We had a brief glaring match.

Then, with a sigh, he got in the car and slammed the door behind him.

I did the same, and crossed my arms over my chest. But I felt a little smug inside that I won *that* argument.

Then he said, 'You look really hot when you're angry.'

I raised an eyebrow at him. Was he mocking me?

He just winked, catching my eye.

Yeah, I was pretty sure he was mocking me.

'Oh come on,' he said. Placing a hand on my thigh, he leaned in closer to whisper, 'You know you can't stay mad at me forever, Shelly.'

'Watch me.'

He chuckled and moved away, pulling off my drive and down the street toward Warren's.

'I still don't see why you have such a problem all of a sudden with what I'm wearing to parties,' I said. 'What about all the other parties I've been to in clothes that were far more revealing than this.'

He shrugged. 'That was different. Guys weren't so brave then, and they wouldn't dare go near you. But since that Cody kid asked you on a date, they all think I've backed off a little and they have a shot with you. Plus our little display at the carnival definitely didn't help.'

I bit the inside of my cheek, feeling a blush rise. 'Whatever.'

He just reached over to squeeze my thigh lightly, and chuckled.

We pulled up at the end of Warren's street, around the corner.

Nobody seemed to notice we'd come together.

I was immediately grabbed aside by some of the girls, who were chatting about all kinds of things, from how hot Jon Fletcher looked, to how tacky Hannah Davies' shoes were, to how much they *loved* this song!

After a while I found Lee out the back, but he was pretty busy making out with Rachel. I took another swig from my can of Coke, feeling buzzed off the atmosphere alone, and headed back inside.

I found myself in the lounge, which was cleared of all furniture and had been turned into a dance floor. The lights were down, except for some cool green and blue lights someone had set up, flickering like strobes.

It was so cool: the colors made everything look almost underwater. It was so weird. I joined in the dancing, swishing my hips back and forth in time with the beat, and throwing my hands in the air.

Someone put their hands on my waist to dance with me, and I turned around. I blinked a few times and saw it was Patrick, a senior on the soccer team.

'Patrick!' I said, smiling. 'I haven't seen you all night.'

He laughed, staggering sideways into a chair. 'Oops! How're things, Elle?'

'Good, yeah . . .'

'Awesome. Hey, come on,' he said, and grabbed my hand.

'Where are we going?'

'For some fresh air. It's really crowded in here.'

'Okay.'

The night air was cool compared to the heat indoors.

'Oh my gosh, it's freezing,' I said, rubbing my arms.

'Here.' Patrick hugged me from behind, his body heat thawing out my back a little.

I laughed and shook my head at him, but before I could step away and tell him not to be silly, I felt a kiss on my shoulder. I stood there in shock for a moment, my brain sluggish to process what had just happened. Then he kissed my neck a little further up, his hands on my waist.

I turned to push him away, but Patrick clearly thought I was turning toward him, and his hands locked around my back. Before he could try and kiss me, I pushed his face sideways with the palm of my hand and wriggled away. It would've been more effective to just knee him in the crotch, but that didn't occur to me.

He stumbled when I pushed him (he was drunk, and not all that steady on his feet), but it was somebody else that sent him sprawling on the grass and put a firm hand on my arm.

'Dude, you always spoil the fun like that!' Patrick slurred, struggling to his feet. 'You're such a killjoy, Flynn – why you gotta be so tough all the time?' He must've been pretty damn drunk, because he was just asking for a fight – and Patrick was a pretty smart guy; he'd never have done something as stupid as that sober.

He was thrown backward with a punch to the gut, and landed on the ground again, groaning a little.

'Anybody else?' Noah asked loudly and clearly, calmly looking around the crowd I hadn't seen forming in the garden. Most people quickly went back in, especially once they saw the fight was over.

'Come on.' He jerked my arm, leading me around the side of Warren's house.

'Ouch! Noah!' I protested. His legs were longer than

mine and his strides were quicker; I stumbled to keep up. 'Noah!' I tried again. 'You're hurting me.'

That seemed to get his attention. He loosened his grip considerably, and grabbed my hand instead to march me down the street.

I started to get angry at him. Who did he think he was? It was barely half ten – the party still had a few hours of life in it yet. I didn't want to go home. Up until the little episode with Patrick I'd been having a good time.

Most of all, though, I didn't want to explain to my dad why I'd left so early.

When we finally reached Noah's car, he unlocked it and I stood by the passenger door, my arms crossed firmly over my chest and my eyes narrowed at him.

Noah rubbed his fingertips over his eyes. 'Would you please just get in the car.'

'I'm not going anywhere with you. Are you some kind of violence junkie? I'm not getting in that car with you behind the wheel after you've had a drink, no matter how much alcohol you say you can take.'

'I haven't had *anything* to drink, Rochelle! Do you think I'm an idiot? And – what? *Violence junkie?*'

I shrugged. 'Still. You can't make me leave. I don't have to go anywhere with you. I'm going to stay here.'

I saw his jaw clench in the dim light. Shadows were

cast over his face, which made his controlled anger look a little scary. 'You're leaving before some other drunk jackass tries anything on with you.' His voice was clipped, tense.

I carried on glaring at him. 'I had it under control. It wasn't that bad.'

He let out something between a snort and a bark of derisive laughter, which only made me feel angrier. '*It wasn't that bad?*' he repeated, eyebrow up. 'You—'

'You're overreacting,' I snapped back at him, 'You're being a controlling, obnoxious jerk, like always, and if you think I'm going anywhere with you, then—'

'Just get in the damn car,' he snapped suddenly, slamming his hand palm down on the roof. The sudden bang made me jump. But I gritted my teeth and stood my ground.

'Please,' he finally added after a while.

I got in the car.

As Noah slid into the driver's seat, he sighed, 'Thank you.'

I nodded. 'You didn't need to yell so much.'

After a second he said, 'I know. I'm sorry.'

I sat there, fiddling with the frayed rips in my jeans. 'Patrick didn't do anything, you know.'

'He would've.'

'We just went out for some fresh air. Is that a crime?'

'Is that what he said?'

'W-well, yeah . . .' I faltered.

Noah sighed heavily, leaning his head against the steering wheel in exasperation before he sat up and looked me in the eye. He looked a lot calmer now, if a bit hopeless.

'And you really thought he meant you were going out for fresh air?'

'At first I did.'

'Elle, this is exactly what I've been trying to say to you. You're so naïve when it comes to guys.'

'And whose fault is that?' I retorted, twisting in my seat to frown at him. 'If you hadn't been so freaking protective and let guys ask me out, I wouldn't be so naïve and so innocent and so damn freaking nice! You're the biggest hypocrite in the book, Noah Flynn.'

Noah stared at me for the briefest second before his lips came down on mine. It was only a short kiss, though, and he pulled away first.

'Well, that's one way to win an argument,' he said with a smirk.

'No fair. You cheated. And you didn't win.'

'Oh, really?' He checked the mirrors before pulling out. I hated the way Noah drove at the very edge of the speed limit. He didn't just cruise along – he pushed the car as fast as he could get away with.

'Yes, really. That wasn't fair.'

'Then go ahead and finish your argument, Elle. Be my guest.'

I opened my mouth, ready to snap at him again, but . . . I fell short. What had I been saying? His kisses were too intoxicating. I couldn't remember my train of thought now.

He smirked again, triumphant. 'I win.'

'You just wait, Noah,' I muttered. 'I'll get you back for that.'

'I'm looking forward to it.' He caught my eye and winked. I felt a blush creeping over my cheeks and hoped it was too dark for him to see.

We drove around for about twenty minutes. I had the window down, the cool night breeze on my face. Neither of us spoke, but it wasn't a bad kind of silence.

When he finally pulled up, I unbuckled my seatbelt and got out of the car. I did a double take when I realized that he hadn't come to my house.

'Why are we here?' I asked, looking around to see him get out of the car too.

He shrugged. 'Party's not over yet, Elle.'

The way he said it made me blush again, and I tried to shake my head clear. 'But – but where are your parents?'

'They have a seminar downstate tomorrow so they

171

went up earlier to save travelling in the morning.'

I thought for a moment that maybe I should just head on home, but it was pretty cold out. And dark. There could be all sorts of shady people lurking around at this time of night.

At least, that's what I told myself as I followed him inside.

But really?

I just wanted to stay with Noah a while longer.

First, though, I went into the kitchen for a drink, feeling parched.

'Are you okay?' he asked from the doorway as I set down the empty glass. I nodded at him, rubbing my face. 'Not going to throw up or anything?'

'I didn't drink, actually. After the last party I figured it would be best to lay off for a while.'

'Oh.' Suddenly, his arms were around me, and he kissed the top of my head. 'Okay, so maybe you don't need me there to look out for you all the time.'

I laughed. 'I kind of like you looking out for me. What I don't like is when you act like a jerk about it.'

He chuckled quietly, kissing my head again, his fingers toying with my ponytail. 'Do you want to go home?' he asked.

I shook my head against his shoulder, then looked up at him. 'I'd rather stay for a while.'

'You can crash in the spare room if you want. If you don't want to go home.'

I shrugged, unsure. It depended on how fast time flew when I was with Noah.

Then we were kissing again, and stumbling up the stairs. After a while I was pulling at his top and, before I could second-guess myself, tugging mine off too.

His hands caught mine and, holding me still, he broke the kiss but didn't move back. His forehead rested against mine, our noses pressed together. I could feel the bumps where his nose had been broken. I looked into his electric-blue eyes, so bright in the darkness.

'Rochelle,' he said quietly, 'we don't have to. We can wait. I'll wait.'

Any doubts I had about this washed away completely at those words. It wasn't like I'd planned on this happening, especially so soon: I'd always thought that this would only happen once I was in a committed relationship with a guy I loved. But everything felt so good – so *right* – with Noah, that I didn't care.

And maybe I wouldn't have gone all the way if he hadn't told me, in that soft voice, that he'd wait. But that was it. I knew he cared.

So I replied, my voice as quiet as his, 'I know. But I want to.'

Chapter 13

When I woke up, the citrusy scent that was becoming more and more familiar to me teased my nostrils, and the weirdly calming sound of spring rain pattering on the window was muffled as if by cotton wool.

The hard, smooth surface beneath my head was rising and falling slowly, and the arms curled around me were so warm and safe. If I really listened, I could hear a steady thud of a heartbeat under my ear.

I blinked my sleepy eyes open a few times, my body unwilling to wake up. It was just so cozy and peaceful here . . .

When Noah's messy room came into view, the weak daylight trying to push through the drapes, I woke right up.

And then I realized exactly what I'd done, and my pulse picked up in a panic.

I'd slept with Lee's big brother. With Noah.

I was too confused to know what I really felt

about this. All I knew for certain was that if Lee ever found out, it would kill him. I was a horrible, horrible person.

I tried to stay as still as possible so I didn't wake him up. I needed to sort my mind out, before he—

He moved underneath me, stretching out before dropping his arms back around me again. 'Morning,' he said casually.

'I – I really should get going,' I stammered, already pushing his arm away. 'If Lee sees me here—'

'I don't think he came home last night, actually,' Noah said, and yawned.

I wanted to go to the window and check for his car. If Lee really *was* here, then I'd have to make sure he didn't see me leaving. But if he wasn't here . . .

'I should go,' I said again, and scrambled to my feet. I picked up my underwear, pulling it all on quickly and very, very self-consciously.

Oh man, what had I been *thinking* last night? Hiding a few kisses from my best friend was not such a big deal – but *this*? Surely he'd know that something was different? And if he found out . . .

I hadn't been thinking of Lee last night. I should have done. But I'd only thought about Noah – it hadn't once entered my mind that this was some kind of horrible betrayal of my best friend.

'Why are you in such a rush?' Noah asked, stretching out lazily again.

I looked down at him, stepping into my jeans now. Where I'd thrown off the covers, he hadn't bothered to pull them back over himself. 'I – I just – it's . . .'

Noah frowned, a little confused, and pulled himself up to be closer to me, now that I'd sat down on the bed to untangle my foot from the leg of my jeans. I cursed myself for rushing so much; it was only slowing me down.

'Elle?' He brushed my hair over my shoulder, but I didn't look at him. 'What's up?'

'N-nothing!' *Damn; I stammered. That would've been convincing otherwise.* I tried again. 'Nothing.'

'Elle . . .' He touched my shoulder, turning me a little so I could look into those amazing blue eyes boring into mine from under all that dark hair.

'I have to go,' I said again. I went to stand, but he pulled me back down.

'Not until you tell me what your problem is. Why am I getting a bad vibe here, like you regret this?'

I nearly exploded with the truth, but I managed to stop myself. 'I – I don't.'

'Come on, Shelly, I know when you're lying to me.' He sighed. 'I should've known you'd be like this.'

'Like what?' I questioned, immediately defensive.

'Like this,' he said, gesturing at me like it explained everything. 'You're acting all weird with me now – like you regret it. Because you *do* regret it: I can see in your face.' He closed his eyes for a moment. He looked almost . . . upset.

'I don't . . . It's not that I regret it so much as . . . I'm just scared. In case Lee finds out. He'll hate me. I mean it was – amazing, but—' I broke off and bit the inside of my cheek as I blushed. 'I'm sorry.'

'What? God, no, don't apologize,' he said quietly, sweeping my hair all over my right shoulder. 'I feel like I should be the one to say sorry. Look, I told you, I wasn't in this for sex, and I'm still not, if you decide you don't want to. Okay? I just don't want to give this up. Whatever "this" is.' He kissed my temple. He looked so – so torn up about it. 'You know I hate all that emotional crap. Please don't put me through all that torture.'

I definitely didn't regret last night. And as long as Lee didn't know, it couldn't hurt him. So I just had to make sure he didn't find out.

It would've been smart to end things before I got in too deep to dig myself out. It would've been smart to back out before I did something stupid – like fall for him. Because I wasn't falling for him. Of course not. No way. And I wouldn't.

I nodded once, as though I was reassuring myself of that fact.

I would just have to be careful not to fall for him. And, stupid as it was, I wasn't going to end this relationship. I didn't want to.

Then I leaned forward to give Noah a soft kiss on the lips; where his hand touched the back of my neck, my skin felt tingly.

'I really should get going,' I said to him. Not so much because I wanted to get out of there, but because I didn't want Lee to suspect anything when he got home, and because my dad would wonder where I was.

But this time Noah didn't argue. He just nodded and kissed me again. 'Okay.'

And this time, I actually did leave.

I found out that Lee hadn't actually gone home with Rachel like I'd first assumed; he'd just crashed on Warren's sofa because he was too tipsy to drive himself home. I only spoke to him on the phone though, afraid he'd see something was different about me. I knew I didn't *look* any different after last night, but I was worried that he would notice anything shifty about my behavior.

'Is everything okay?' I jumped. We were on the

phone, but I still tried not to look too flustered. 'I mean, I know there was that thing with Patrick, then Noah dragging you off after, but . . . you sure you're okay about it?'

'Yeah,' I said. At least I could answer that honestly. 'Yeah, I'm fine, Lee, seriously. It was no big deal, really.'

I wasn't looking forward to school though. All the questions people would ask about me leaving early . . . They'd probably wonder about me and Patrick, and me and Noah . . . I could come up with an innocent answer easily enough, but I hated having to lie. I was dreading it all.

That's not why I was wide awake at three in the morning though, staring at my ceiling and willing sleep to find me. No – I was awake because I couldn't stop thinking about Noah.

I wanted to confide in Lee, but I couldn't. Not just because he'd hate me for lying to him and it'd kill him to find out, but also because it would be downright *weird* to tell him I'd slept with his brother.

Times like this, I wished my mom was still around. But wishing wasn't going to bring her back, so I just rolled over onto my side and stared blankly ahead.

I missed having Mom around. But she died in a car accident when I was much younger, and when Brad was around three. I grew up through all those important stages – like getting my first period and buying my first bra – without having her around. It's just times like this . . . Well, I was hardly going to confide in my dad, was I? And Lee was out of the equation completely.

So I'd have to keep it to myself and hope nobody found out.

I sighed and ran my hands over my face. My eyes were drooping but I couldn't fall asleep. My mind was too restless.

Stupid Noah. Everything was his fault, I thought, but a drowsy smile played on my lips.

Everything.

Chapter 14

On Monday morning, not even Lee noticed anything different about me – thankfully. But that was probably because he was too enraptured in his loved-up world. I couldn't have been more grateful to have him talking non-stop about how funny, how pretty, how cute, how smart, and how sweet Rachel was.

Up until we got to school, everything was all hunky-dory.

'Why did you leave Warren's early?' Jaime asked me, first thing.

'Oh, well, um . . .'

'Was it Flynn? Did Patrick really kiss you? He says he didn't, but you never know. I heard Flynn was really, really mad.'

'Oh, yeah, he was furious!' Olivia appeared out of nowhere beside Jaime. 'I saw the whole thing. He beat Patrick up and everything.'

'He didn't kiss me though,' I said. 'Patrick, I mean.'

'So what did Flynn do?'

'I heard he broke Patrick's rib.' Candice turned up out of the blue too, startling me. Jeez, where were these girls coming from?

'What?' I exclaimed.

'I said, what did Flynn do?' Jaime repeated.

I gaped at Candice. 'Are you serious? Is Patrick okay?'

'I don't know,' she said. 'He said he thought it was broken and a couple of guys said it was, after he went to hospital.'

'Oh my God,' I breathed. He *couldn't* have broken Patrick's rib. Not just because Patrick was drunk and was going to kiss me. No way.

'Hey! Hey – Earth to Elle!' It wasn't until Jaime snapped her fingers sharply right in front of my nose that I realized they were still talking to me.

'Huh?'

'Did Flynn take you home or what?' Karen asked. When had she turned up? 'I saw him drag you off.'

'Oh, that. Yeah. He took me home and I think he went back to the party?' I hoped it didn't sound too much of a lie. I didn't think I was too great at lying; until this situation with Noah, I hadn't ever done much of it.

'No, I don't think he did,' Olivia said thoughtfully. 'I'm sure he didn't.'

'Weird . . .' I said with a shrug. 'I'll be back in a minute, I need to find out about Patrick.'

I walked off before they could pull me back into another conversation.

I grabbed Joel's arm, since he was the first guy I saw.

'Oh, hey,' he said, smiling. 'What happened on Saturday? I heard Flynn dragged you home after that thing with Patrick.'

'Did Patrick really have a broken rib?' I demanded.

'Uh . . . someone told me he might,' he said. 'He's not in hospital, though – he's coming into school.'

'That must've been some punch Flynn packed.'

'Glad I wasn't on the other end of it,' laughed Cam.

'Hell yeah,' Joel agreed.

'Do you know if he's here yet?' I asked.

'Who, Flynn? No idea,' Cam told me.

'No – no . . . *Patrick*,' I clarified, tripping over my words with impatience.

He shrugged. 'I haven't seen him.'

'Okay, thanks.'

'Wait,' Joel called. 'Where're you going, Elle?'

'To find Noah,' I snapped, loud enough for them to hear me. I stormed off to where Noah usually parked: in the far corner of the lot, under the big tree. And sure enough, there were the telltale signs he was there – freshmen girls giggling over him and trying to hide behind other cars; others lounging on their cars and trying to catch Flynn's eye; and the drifting smoke.

I stormed over to the lazy figures around the tree. There were a couple of stoner kids huddled under one tree, some huge guys off the wrestling team under another. Noah had a cigarette sticking out of his mouth right now, and was leaning against a massive sycamore tree. He was doing something on his phone, looking busy and bored all at once.

It was always hard to pin down Noah's friends. He'd hang around with the guys on the football team, or he might be with guys from his classes. He was a bit of a drifter though. Not a loner or an outcast, but he wasn't friends with practically everybody like Lee and me either. He was probably a little too intimidating for that.

'Noah!' I yelled, ignoring the glares and astonished stares – from both girls spying on Noah, and from the mass of people who wondered what the hell I was doing.

He looked up and, seeing how angry I was, heaved himself away from the tree.

'I cannot believe you!' I shouted at him.

He strolled up to me, dropping his cigarette in the progress and stomping it out under the black boots he usually wore. He slid his phone into his back pocket.

'What?' he said innocently.

I shoved him in the chest as hard as I could over and over, one shove for every word: 'You – broke – his – ribs!'

'What are you on about?'

My shoving had no effect whatsoever on Noah's muscly body, but I could tell it was getting on his nerves a little. Like a fly buzzing around your head.

'Patrick! Everyone's saying you broke his rib! He had to go to hospital!'

Noah smirked. He didn't even raise his eyebrows or look remotely guilty. He just smirked a little. 'Yeah, I heard about that.'

'He could press charges,' I hissed.

'Yeah, but we both know he won't.'

'He didn't even *do* anything! And you don't have to look so happy about it!' I yelled, shoving him again. 'You broke his rib – for no reason!'

'The hell I did!' he yelled back. 'The guy was all over you. Anyone could see you were trying to push him off.'

'He was *drunk*!'

'I don't care if he was drunk, high, or just twisted,' Noah said, all up in my face. 'I'm looking out for you here, Rochelle, and the guy deserved what he got.'

'A broken rib? He probably won't be able to play soccer for weeks now!'

'Then he shouldn't have tried anything with you,' Noah said firmly. 'If he got his rib broken, that's not my problem. Why do you even care?'

'You hurt him over something stupid! You – you stupid violence junkie!'

I punched his chest with both hands, and Noah caught my wrists tightly. I glared at him and tried to snatch my hands back, but I couldn't; his hold was too tight.

We'd gathered quite an audience with all the yelling.

Someone pulled gently on my shoulder. 'Shelly, come on,' Lee said quietly. 'Just calm down. *Both* of you.'

Noah rolled his eyes at him.

'Calm down?' I exclaimed to Lee. 'Your brother beat up someone over a drunken mistake and *broke his rib*! How can you not see there's something wrong with that?'

'I didn't say there was nothing wrong with it,' he said calmly. 'But calm down about it.'

I clenched my jaw before realizing Lee was right, as usual. I yanked my hands away from Noah, and this time he let go. I didn't quit my glaring match with him though.

'I cannot believe you,' I said.

Noah just shrugged.

'I hate you sometimes – you know that, right?'

'Yeah, I know,' he said casually, his eyes twinkling at me – with something else that made my heart somersault.

No! Don't let him do this to you! Stay mad at him. You're mad at him, Rochelle, remember? He hurt someone for no good reason. Don't just stop being mad at him because he's giving you that look and you want to kiss him.

Before I gave in and did something stupid, I grabbed Lee and stormed off. I didn't even need to barge through people. They parted for me, before coming together again to share the gossip.

'I thought you were going to kill him,' Lee told me, failing to hide the laughter in his voice.

'Not quite,' I muttered. 'Ugh, he just makes me so *mad* sometimes! I mean, seriously, there was no need for him to break Patrick's rib!'

'Look, I know it's what everyone's saying, but you of all people should know there's a chance they're blowing it out of proportion. It might not be that bad. And it's Noah – you know what he's like. I don't know why you got so mad about it.'

'I can't do anything without him looking over my shoulder! And don't you start on about me being too nice or any of that crap. I'm getting a little sick of everyone looking out for me.'

So maybe I'd needed Noah's help at his party a while back. And I was grateful he'd been there to stop Patrick. But it was the way he acted – like he just assumed I'd do as he said.

Lee sighed in defeat but smiled at me when he threw up his hands in surrender. 'Look, I know you're mad at him, but don't take it out on me. And I see what you're saying. I'll try and talk to him, how about that? Ask him to lay off a little?'

I didn't know why I'd overreacted so much to Noah like that. I figured it was because I was so on edge that Lee might find out what I'd done after the party.

So I said, 'I doubt it'd have any effect.'

'I know it wouldn't.'

'But thanks for offering.'

'No problem. So have you done the English home-work, or not? Because I didn't get a chance to do the conclusion and I'm stuck.'

I smiled. Lee always made me feel better. I loved my best friend, I really did. And his optimism was too infectious for me to stay mad about anything for very long.

The total opposite to his brother, of course. His stupid, sexy brother.

*

Call me a coward, but I hid out in the library over lunch. I couldn't bear to face any more questions about why I'd been so mad at Flynn, how I could even speak to him like that . . . I was half considering going home and skipping school for the afternoon, I was so sick of everyone, but I couldn't bring myself to actually walk out.

Lee kept me company of course, but eventually we had to leave.

I was half expecting to bump into Noah – or, worse, one of the girls – on my way to classes. I didn't. My karma must have done a sudden one-eighty since that morning.

When the last bell finally rang – I'd been watching the snail-like second hand move around the clock in chemistry – I couldn't have been happier. I just wanted to get out of there.

Lee had biology though, so I had to wait for him at the front of the school, lounging on his car.

'Hey, Elle.'

I turned around, looking up from playing solitaire on my cell phone. I smiled, but it felt a little forced. 'Patrick. Hey. How's, um . . . How's your rib?'

He gave a half-smile. 'Well, it's not as bad as everyone's been saying. It's just some bruising, but my mom made me go get it checked out because she got all paranoid I'd broken something, is all.' He said it quite light-heartedly, and I felt a weight lift from my shoulders.

'Oh, that's great! Well, no, it's not – but, I mean, everyone was saying it was broken so . . . I'm so sorry, Patrick, honestly. This is all my fault – I didn't mean for you to get hurt or—'

'No, it's *my* fault,' he said quickly. 'I came over to apologize. I didn't see you at lunch.'

'You don't need to apologize,' I insisted.

'No, I do, and I'm sorry. I shouldn't have tried anything like that with you, and all the beer was no excuse.'

'Really, it's okay,' I told him fervently. 'I'm so sorry Noah went all . . .'

'Yeah, well, don't worry. It was just Flynn being Flynn. It's not your fault, Elle, so don't worry about it.' He smiled. I gave him a smile back.

A throat was cleared, and we both turned around to see a glowering Noah.

I ignored him and looked back at Patrick, who was trying his best to look like he didn't want to flee to safety. 'Well, I hope you get better soon.'

'Thanks, Elle. And seriously, I'm so sorry.'

'Don't worry about it. See you.'

'Bye,' he said, already walking off.

I shot Noah a glare and went back to playing solitaire. I could still feel he was there, watching me.

'What did he want?' he said after a while.

'To apologize.'

'What, and that's it? He just wanted to say sorry?'

I quit the game and shoved my cell phone in my pocket, whipping around to glare at Noah. 'Yeah, even though it's you who should be apologizing to him for hurting him! He had to go to hospital because of you!' I figured I'd guilt-trip him a little, so I didn't add that he'd only gone to hospital at his mom's paranoid request.

'Don't start this again . . .' He'd taken a couple of steps closer, and now he half turned away from me, tugging at his hair.

'Start what, Noah?' I snapped.

'You're really hot when you're mad at me, you know,' he commented in a husky voice.

My mind blanked momentarily and my breath caught in my throat. Why did he have this effect on me? 'Shut *up*, Noah. Go away.'

Where was Lee anyway? He shouldn't be taking *this* long . . .

I looked around. Most of the other students had left by now, and a few stragglers were looking curiously over at me and Noah. Finally I spotted Lee and Rachel standing by her car, talking and looking all cute and loved-up.

Damn it. I wished he'd hurry up already.

'You can always get a ride home with me, you know,' Noah said conversationally. I refused to answer. 'Elle . . . ?'

Eventually I had to look back at him, and when I did, he was smirking victoriously, thinking he'd won the argument.

'Do you want the ride or not?' he asked. 'Lee's going to be ages, we both know it. My offer stands for the next thirty seconds. Time is ticking.'

I really *did* just want to go home. By the time Lee turned up, I would probably have run down my cell and be dying of boredom . . .

'Tick-tock,' Noah teased.

'Bike or car?'

'Bike.'

'No.'

He laughed. 'You know you didn't really hate it, Shelly. And it gives you an excuse to cling onto me.'

'Um, no.'

He got this weird look on his face then – like he was confused; like he was annoyed by my reaction. I'd honestly hated my last experience on his bike and was in no rush to repeat it unless I absolutely had to. Like, if a horde of monkey-ninjas were chasing me, and Noah's bike was my last hope of escape.

Then he let out a sigh and briefly touched my cheek, turning me to look at him. 'Elle, come on. Don't be mad at me.'

He wasn't talking about Patrick anymore, I realized.

'I'm not mad at you. Well. I am, about you punching Patrick. But other than that – I'm not, you know, mad about the whole, um . . . the other night.'

'Oh, come on. You've been avoiding me all day and now you're acting weird.'

'I'm not acting weird.'

'Yes you are. You aren't arguing with me like you usually would, and you aren't being your normal bubbly self either. You're mad at me.'

I sighed. 'I'm not mad – it's just that . . .'

'What?'

Oh, gosh, don't say anything! Make something up! Anything but the truth!

And, as per usual, my mouth seemed to be working away regardless of my brain.

'I'm worried because of Lee, and . . . I just don't want you to forget all about me now we . . . you know. Did it.'

Oh, dear God. I said 'did it'.

Way to go, Elle. You complete and utter fool.

Noah didn't seem to notice anything, though; he simply replied, 'Elle, I thought I put myself through this torture with you the other morning. I told you I was *not* just playing you for sex.'

I could see from his face that he was completely sincere. His wide eyes were pleading and honest, and there wasn't a hint of a smirk.

So I nodded. 'Alright.'

He let out a tiny sigh of relief. 'So . . . ride home? I'll even drop you straight to your place if you want.'

Now the smirk was back, because he was so sure I wouldn't be able to resist the opportunity to make out with him again. And I was tempted . . . but then I remembered he had his bike.

'Noah, there is no way in hell I am riding that bike.'

He held up his hands in surrender. 'Okay, okay – your loss . . .'

Then I frowned. 'I'm still mad at you for almost breaking Patrick's rib. It's a big deal because you lost your temper and you were stupid,' I added before he could argue.

He sighed. 'I know.'

I looked him in the eye, and the only reply I could come up with was to nod. He gave me an apologetic half-smile that made him look absolutely adorable; but I kept my expression neutral.

'I am sorry.'

I nodded again. 'You should probably get going.'

'Mm.' He didn't sound like he totally agreed with me.

'Goodbye, Noah,' I said, my voice level.

He lingered a moment before walking away, and I swear I heard him chuckling under his breath.

Well . . . that could've gone worse.

There was a little voice somewhere in the back of my mind that told me I wouldn't be in this whole mess in the first place if we hadn't done the damn kissing booth.

Chapter 15

At last the school week was over. I hadn't seen much of Noah, unless you counted the times when we passed each other at lunch or in the corridors on the way to class, or when I saw him when I hung out with Lee.

It was Friday night. The sun was just setting, staining the sky pink and red before it turned inky black and starry. It looked so picturesque and pretty.

The boys were dive-bombing into the pool, challenging each other to make the biggest splash, to do the wildest stunt, and all the other stupid things boys will do. I was lying back on one of the sun loungers with Rachel and Cam's girlfriend, Lisa, from one of my classes. They were talking about going shopping, but I was perfectly happy just to lie there and close my eyes, completely relaxed, bopping one of my feet in time to the song that was coming from the speakers on the decking.

It was still mild enough for me to feel comfortable

in my bikini. It wasn't quite the weather for sunbathing, especially at nine in the evening, but it was nice to just lie there.

'Hey, you girls coming in?' I opened my eyes lazily to look at Oliver, who flicked his dripping hair off his face as he leaned on the edge of the pool.

'Maybe in a minute,' I said.

'Um, maybe,' Lisa said. 'I don't know . . .'

'Yeah, I don't really want to get my hair wet,' Rachel admitted with a sheepish smile. Oliver rolled his eyes but I smiled.

'Isn't it really cold?' Lisa asked dubiously.

'See for yourself,' Warren challenged, surfacing next to Oliver.

'No thanks,' Rachel laughed. 'We're good.'

Warren looked at me expectantly. 'You coming in, Elle?'

'Maybe . . .' I replied lazily, letting my eyes droop shut again.

'Elle, what's going on with you and Flynn? I mean, *really*?' Rachel asked quietly. I heard a chair creak as Lisa leaned toward me too.

I shrugged. 'Nothing.'

'But you act so . . . I don't know. It's strange. You're so normal around him.'

'Yeah, but that's hardly surprising,' I pointed out. 'I

grew up with Lee, and Noah was always around. That's why I don't call him Flynn. But also because I know it gets on his nerves when I call him Noah.'

I heard Lisa laughing a little and I smiled. Rachel said, 'He's just so protective of you I thought maybe there was something . . . you know . . .'

I shook my head slightly. 'No. That's just how he is. It's not that big a deal.' It wasn't exactly a lie . . .

'I guess,' Rachel said.

'I think you'd be quite cute together,' Lisa commented. 'You're so opposite it'd be, like, a perfect match, don't you think?'

I couldn't help but snort dubiously. 'We argue constantly. If we were ever like that – not that we would be: God, no – we'd end up killing each other.'

They both laughed, and then started talking about some new movie. I tuned out, too content and drowsy to be distracted for long.

After a few moments of peace, I felt something grab my ankle. Another something snatched up my other leg, and my arms were pinned at my sides. The sun lounger disappeared from under me too, all in the space of a second.

My eyes flashed open, and I saw Lee, Dixon, Warren and Joel all grinning and laughing down at my horrified expression.

I started thrashing around as they carried me off. 'Let me go! Put me down!'

They just kept laughing. Lee said, 'No can do, Shelly!'

'Put me down! You're going to drop me! *Put me down!*'

'If you say so . . .' Joel said mischievously. The boys swung me back and forth, once, twice . . .

I screamed out, laughing helplessly. 'Don't!'

Too late – they'd already launched me.

I landed with a huge splash in the middle of the pool, hearing everybody laughing as I smacked down through the surface. I felt more than heard it when the boys bombed in after me.

The water was freezing! I broke the surface gasping for air, my hair plastered to my face and neck. My teeth chattered slightly. 'I hate you guys!' I yelled, but I was laughing.

They laughed, and I looked at the girls, who were both giggling helplessly.

'It won't be so funny when they throw you in next,' I told them, and they laughed even harder.

I made to swim for the ladder so I could get out again.

'No! You just got in – you can't get out already!' Warren protested, and dived at me, trying to pull me away from the ladder. I laughed and scrambled to get out, but it was like trying to run through treacle: I felt Warren pulling me back again.

'What's all the screaming?'

I yanked myself up the ladder just as Warren made a grab at me. My bikini top came away in his hand, and everyone was silent as Noah looked at me with a disapproving frown.

I threw my arms around my bare chest, cheeks burning.

Oh, God.

How humiliating was this!

My cheeks were burning, even though the rest of my body trembled with cold.

Then I heard someone spluttering with laughter. Lee. I recognized that laugh all too well. And once he had broken the awkward and embarrassing silence, everyone else started laughing too.

'Warren, I officially *hate* you!' I said, turning to glare at him when I'd made sure I was completely covered.

He grinned sheepishly, then said, 'I'm sorry, I didn't mean to grab it . . . I wasn't intending to pull it off.'

'You complete idiot,' I giggled.

'Do you want it back, or . . . ? I mean, I'm not complaining if you don't,' he teased, and I laughed sarcastically.

'I haven't exactly got any hands free to get it back,' I told him flatly.

'Oh yeah.' He laughed again and tossed my bikini top at me; with a wet slap, it landed on the ground. Oliver swam over and dunked the unsuspecting Warren, keeping him under for a few seconds before letting him back up for air.

I laughed along with everyone else. 'Got him for ya!' Oliver told me proudly with a thumbs-up.

'Just wait till I get my hands on him, then he'll be sorry,' I threatened, but I was still laughing too much for anybody to take me seriously.

'Wait till Flynn gets his hands on him, more like,' I heard Dixon mutter, and when I turned around, I saw Noah looking at us with a frown on his face.

I sighed. *Here we go . . .*

'Don't,' I hissed at him sharply, stalking past him and into the house. Luckily, Lee's parents had gone out for dinner since Lee had invited us all over, and they still weren't back. If they'd been here, it would've been just plain embarrassing to go in to find one of Lee's T-shirts with my arms wrapped around me to cover my bare chest. I had clothes by the pool, of course, but I had no free hands to collect them.

I rummaged through Lee's drawers, and found a T-shirt from a concert we'd been to a couple of years ago, then tugged it on awkwardly over my damp body. It was a little big for me, but not by too much.

I heard a throat being cleared behind me. The noise made me jump a mile; I hadn't even heard anybody come up.

Noah was leaning against the doorframe with his arms crossed over his chest, and a look on his face that made my palms turn a little clammy. His expression was pretty neutral, but it was the shadow in his bright eyes that made me anxious.

'What, did you nearly break Warren's rib too?' I snapped at him, covering my nervousness with irritation.

'No,' he said, his brow knitting together.

'Oh, what then – his leg? An arm, maybe?'

He took a couple of steps toward me. 'No. I think he got the message to back off just from the look I gave him,' he said smugly. 'I scared the shit out of him.'

'But you ... you didn't actually *say* anything to Warren? Or *do* anything? Oh my God, I must have stepped into some parallel universe.'

He laughed sarcastically. 'I didn't have to do anything. He already got the message.'

I shook my head slightly to myself, still reeling from the shock.

'Besides, even I could see it was an accident,' he muttered grudgingly.

'It's not like anybody saw anything.'

'Except me.'

'Well, yeah, but . . . I mean, you've . . . You know what I mean.'

He smirked at my red cheeks and my confusion.

'You're the one who wears Superman boxers anyway.' I could see the band peeking over the top of his jeans. I remembered how I'd actually made him blush when I saw him in them.

'Whatever,' he said dismissively – though he couldn't meet my eye. I grinned triumphantly, knowing I'd managed to embarrass him.

As I strolled out of Lee's room, brushing past Noah, I said casually, 'Imagine what everybody would say if they found out that bad-ass Flynn wore Superman boxers—'

'You wouldn't.'

I looked over my shoulder with an innocent smile, biting my lip as if daring him to try me.

When he tried to grab me, I gasped and made a dash for the closest room, which just happened to be his.

I couldn't decide whether to say thank you or curse my luck, but I was now stuck in Noah's room and he closed the door behind him, grinning at me.

I backed up, but he took a step closer to match each one of mine.

When my back hit the wall and I had nowhere left to turn, Noah seized his advantage and was suddenly pressed right up against me, his hot breath tickling my face.

'Sometimes, Elle,' he breathed, his lips brushing against mine ever so lightly, 'you are too irresistible for your own good.'

A small thrill ran through me.

He dragged his lips over my jaw, making my pulse go manic and my breathing catch in my throat. When I couldn't stand his teasing anymore, I grabbed his face and kissed him. This time, I didn't clash teeth. A hell of a lot of practise had seen to *that*.

He pulled away when I was totally breathless, and my eyes opened very slowly to meet his. Noah brushed a piece of still-wet hair off my face and let his hand linger on my cheek tenderly.

'You're so gorgeous, Elle, you know that?' he said softly, his thumb brushing over my cheek. I saw him smirk when I blushed. It was so weird. The girls had told me a couple of times that I was pretty and I'd get teased by the guys that I was hot – but when Noah said it, my heart did those weird flip-flop things.

'I love making you blush.' I could hear the laugh in his voice.

'Shut up,' I muttered, pushing against his chest weakly.

'You should go back,' he murmured, 'before they start to wonder what's taking you so long.'

'Or before Lee thinks we've murdered each other.'

Noah chuckled. 'Yeah, that's more likely.'

But he didn't step back. I could've walked away if I really wanted to, but we both stayed exactly where we were, and Noah's thumb kept stroking my cheek. My eyes trailed over the lines of his cheekbones, his jaw, the bumps in his crooked nose, the length of his eyelashes, the barely-there freckles on the bridge of his nose – little things I'd never really noticed before.

'Noah . . .'

'Yeah?'

'I really need to go.'

I said it reluctantly – my voice gave away my true feelings – but he sighed and stepped away, dropping his hand. The atmosphere was thick enough to choke me. All I wanted to do was stay here with Noah, but I knew I couldn't, and I turned and headed downstairs.

My cheek tingled where his hand had been; I could still taste his lips on mine. I had to stop for a moment and compose my expression so nobody would notice anything was up. The hardest part was having to rein in my smile.

'Flynn seemed pretty tetchy,' Rachel said quietly when I joined her again. 'What did he say?'

'I didn't see him,' I lied – I hated how easy it was to lie to her.

'You should've seen Warren's face,' Lisa giggled. She picked up her cell phone, tapped some buttons and handed it to me. A picture of Warren's face filled the screen; he was white as a sheet, eyes bulging, mouth hanging open gormlessly.

I laughed. 'Oh my God, that's fantastic!' And that was that.

I sighed internally, relief washing over me. It didn't look like anybody suspected Noah and I were together.

I was determined to shove all thoughts of him to the back of my mind and enjoy the rest of my Friday night with my friends.

Chapter 16

Between classes and the homework the teachers were piling onto us, the next two weeks went by before I could blink. If I wasn't hanging out with Lee, then I was sneaking around with Noah. We went to a movie, and there were a few chances – if my dad was out and Brad wasn't home, or if his house was empty – when we could meet up.

I think both of us were surprised to find we could actually hang out, not just make out. After the movie, we'd sat in his car for at least half an hour just talking. We'd play video games or just sit and watch TV and it was . . . well, it was *nice*.

Not that we didn't still argue and disagree over almost everything, even over what to watch on TV.

I still wasn't over the thrill that came with sneaking around though. But I hated the guilt that came with it – lying to my best friend, my dad, and everyone else . . .

On a humid Sunday night I was sat on a workbench

in the garage, and Noah was tinkering with the two wheeled death-trap he called a bike. The door was cracked open a little, but not so that anyone could see us.

'I cannot believe,' I said, 'that you think the second *Transformers* film was better. Nothing beat the first one, I swear.'

'Come on – those twin cars? They were hilarious.'

I scoffed. 'But the first one was just . . . epic!'

'The second one's better, Elle, I'm telling you. Hey, pass me that wrench a second?'

'Where is it?' I stood up, looking around. I didn't speak mechanic, but I did at least know what a wrench was. I may not have had a clue what Noah was doing, but he looked hot doing it.

'It's on the shelf above your head.'

I clambered up onto the workbench I'd been sat on, my fingers gripping the shelf, looking for a wrench. I scrunched up my nose at the cobwebs I saw there, hoping there weren't any gross spiders lurking right by my head.

'Um . . .' I spotted it then, and picked it up. As I turned to step down, I bumped my head on the shelf. 'Ouch!' I yelped automatically, dropping the wrench to clutch my head. Reacting like that threw me off balance, and my foot slipped off the bench.

With a thud and another yelp, I crashed onto the floor. Dazed, I blinked a few times, clearing the bright spots from my vision until the room came back into focus. A wave of pain hit me.

'Oh, shit,' I heard Noah say.

'*Ow*,' I moaned, clutching my cheek. I tasted blood; I must've bitten my tongue.

Noah had dropped the screwdriver and rag he'd been holding and was now crouching beside me, one hand on my back and the other pushing my hair out of my eyes. 'Are you all right? Elle?'

I touched a fingertip gently to my cheek, and winced, because *man, that hurt!*

'Does it look bad?' I asked, sounding like a little kid.

He chuckled. 'No. It's just a graze. You might get a bit of a bruise though . . . Actually, we should probably clean it. Knowing you, it'll get infected, and *then* it's gonna look bad.'

I didn't laugh. I just pouted at him for mocking me.

But he was right: I should clean it up – there were all kinds of things – dirt and oil and cobwebs – around the garage.

I got to my feet, Noah's hand on my back steadying me. I was fine to stand on my own, but I didn't shake him off. I liked it. It felt nice, having Noah's arm around me. Like it belonged there.

Man, I really have got to stop reading so many of those cheesy romance books!

I winced.

'What? What's wrong?'

'I'm fine,' I said, waving him off. 'It feels like I've broken my butt, but I'm fine. It's nothing.'

Slowly, I straightened out again. There. Everything was okay. Noah regarded me for a long moment, then shrugged.

We went back into the house through the door connecting the games room and the garage. Noah glanced down the hall before pulling me up the stairs and into his room. He kicked the door shut, and I sat on the edge of his bed as he went into his bathroom.

I wriggled a bit; my butt hurt.

'You're such a klutz,' Noah chuckled, suddenly two steps away from me.

I rolled my eyes. 'Not always.'

'No. Only half the time.'

He crouched in front of me. After shooting me a sorry smile, he took my chin between his index finger and thumb – oh, so gently – and turned my face slightly. I just sat there, doing my best not to wince as he wiped my cheek with a damp washcloth, then put some sanitizer cream on, which really stung.

'Sorry,' he said when I winced for the fourth time.

'It's okay. It's not your fault.'

'I shouldn't have told you to pass me the wrench.' He sounded annoyed – but he wasn't angry at me, I knew. 'That was a stupid thing to do.'

'It's fine. Really. It was an accident, and my fault anyway. No biggie.'

He didn't say anything; though he looked like he wanted to.

'Since when were you such a doctor?' I said teasingly after a moment, trying to distract both of us – myself from the throbbing pain in my left cheek, and Noah from whatever his train of thought was; he didn't look very happy.

'Since I kept on getting into fights.' His face was impassive and I couldn't decipher his expression. 'You kind of learn to take care of yourself when that happens.'

'Oh.'

'Go ahead, say it.'

'Say what?'

'That I'm a stupid violence junkie. It's what you always say.'

'You are, though,' I said simply. 'I mean, why do you even get into all those fights? I've seen you fighting, Noah: it's not a good thing, and—'

His deep sigh cut me off midsentence. Then he said,

'Fine, okay. I'm an idiot and I pick fights just for the hell of it. You win.'

He said it all kind of fast – ever since we were little he'd hated to admit he was in the wrong. Everybody knew it.

But now he'd just admitted he was wrong – and that I was right.

Okay, so it wasn't something I liked being right about, but . . . I felt kind of smug. I wondered if Noah always felt like this when he won our little bickering matches.

'You just admitted I won . . .' I couldn't help the jeering, sing-song tone that crept into my voice.

Noah rolled his eyes. 'Yes, I did. All right, you had your moment of glory.'

'I was being serious though,' I told him. 'About you, you know . . . seeming to get off on fighting.'

He sat back, his eyes still level with mine. There was none of the teasing or joking in the air now.

'I know you were. And I know I am. I can't help it. Remember that summer when you and Lee went to soccer camp? You were thirteen or something. You came back raving about how nice cheesecake was.'

'Yeah . . . ?' Where was he going with this?

Then I thought, *He remembered when I went to soccer camp? I* hardly remembered that. It was just a blurry few weeks of fun. I'd forgotten all about the cheesecake thing.

'Well, that was the summer after I'd started getting into fights at school and shit: my parents sent me to see a couple of counselors. They were trying to help, I know that. But the thing is . . .' He sighed a little. 'They tried, but they failed miserably. I'm a bad boy and always will be. Guess it's just the way my brain's wired up.' He shrugged like he couldn't care less.

I really liked these rare conversations where I saw the Noah behind the sexy smirk; when he let me see his vulnerable side. I never knew he'd been to see counselors – maybe Lee didn't even know about it.

'You're cute when you look all embarrassed like that,' I teased, lightening the mood.

'One, I'm not embarrassed,' he said, knowing I was joking. 'And two' – he bumped his knee against mine – 'don't call me cute.'

I laughed now, and he gave me a smile, one that flashed the dimple in his left cheek. My smile started making my cheek hurt, and I groaned, putting a hand to my aching face.

Pulling my hand away, Noah leaned forward and gave me a light kiss there. I felt all fuzzy inside; I guess kissing the boo-boo better doesn't only work on five-year-olds.

I jolted, though. I shouldn't be feeling all fuzzy and happy. I was being careful and cautious with my feelings for Noah.

We were probably closer now he'd confided in me like that – but that was *bad*. We shouldn't be getting closer. I couldn't let myself have feelings for Noah; if I did, when things ended up messy, everything would spiral out of control. Lee would hate me, and I wouldn't have Noah to fall back on, and I'd be a total mess.

But looking into his eyes, suppressing a giggle as he tenderly kissed my sore cheek, all I could think about was him. How much I liked being with him. How amazing it felt even when he just had his arm around me. How bright and blue his eyes were . . .

'Elle—' he started to say, looking grave, but I'd already started talking.

'I think I hurt my lips too,' I told him quietly, pointing at them.

He laughed almost inaudibly, shaking his head at me but leaning in closer—

The door, which hadn't been closed properly, was pushed open before we could move apart.

'What's going on?'

Noah shot to his feet and turned around while I stayed numbly on the edge of the bed.

A whole string of curses I'd never say aloud ran

through my mind when I saw Lee standing in the doorway.

'I said, what's going on?' he repeated, his eyes narrowing suspiciously as he looked from me to Noah. Then his eyes flashed back to me and his jaw dropped. 'Jesus! Shelly, what happened to your face?'

'Thanks,' I mumbled sarcastically, but it didn't have the right amount of enthusiasm to lighten the mood.

Lee was in front of me in a second, looking at my hurt cheek. He whirled around to glare at his brother. 'Did you do that to her?'

'What?' Noah asked tightly. 'What did you say?'

'What, are you deaf?' Lee muttered. Then, much louder, he said, 'I said, did you do that to her? Did you hit Elle?'

Noah's jaw clenched so tight you could see all the muscles up the side of his face straining. 'You really think . . . I'd hit Elle?'

'Yeah, well, I wouldn't put it past you!' Lee snapped angrily. 'Then how the fuck did it happen? What the hell were you doing?'

Lee only ever swore like that when he got really, really mad. I knew things were getting bad, but I was frozen in place, numb.

Noah retorted carelessly, 'I don't have to answer to you, little bro.'

Lee's fists clenched and unclenched at the sneering tone Noah used. 'Then what happened to Elle?'

'It's nothing,' I said timidly, and both of them turned to look at me harshly. I dipped my head, my hair hiding my face as I peeked up at them again. 'It's fine, I'm okay . . .'

'The hell you are,' Lee muttered darkly. He thrust a finger in my direction and almost yelled at Noah, 'What happened?'

'She came looking for you and tripped in the garage. It's not that big a deal. Calm down already. She's fine.'

It was the flippant tone that was getting Lee really riled up, and I bet Noah knew it. It would've got me really angry too.

'It's not his fault . . .' I tried; they both ignored me.

'And you just let her fall over? I bet it was your crap lying around that made her trip in the first place.'

'It's not like I have some kind of divine power to control her klutziness.'

Gee, thanks, Noah.

'But it *was* your fault, then? I knew it,' Lee scoffed, his head shaking back and forth. He was biting the inside of one cheek in anger. I was sure he knew Noah wasn't really to blame, but he was mad enough at him that he'd blame him anyway.

'It was an accident,' Noah said through gritted teeth, his eyes blazing blue with anger.

Lee just shrugged, winding Noah up even more. 'I wouldn't have put it past you to actually *do* that to her.'

'That's it,' Noah growled, flying at Lee, who'd already taken a swing.

I jumped off the bed, pushing myself between them before they actually killed each other. I shoved Noah's chest as hard as I could, with no effect. But at least, now that I was in the middle, they'd stopped trying to hit each other.

'Noah,' I said quietly. 'Noah, look at me. Noah.'

He stopped looking daggers at Lee and turned, his expression a little softer. 'You know I wouldn't hit you, Elle. If I could've, I would've stopped you falling. I wouldn't hit you – you know that, right?'

I nodded patiently. 'Yes, I know. But you don't have to pick a fight with Lee, all right? He's just worried about me.'

'*I wouldn't hit you,*' Noah said fiercely, his jaw clenching again.

'I know,' I said, making my voice as soothing as I could. I placed a hand on his chest, which rose and fell rapidly with his shallow breaths. 'I know, alright? Just calm down already. Please. I know you wouldn't. Calm down, please.'

He held my gaze a few more seconds before stepping back, running his fingers through his hair. I turned around and grabbed Lee's hand, tugging him out of the room and into his bedroom.

When he shut the door behind us he said, 'Wow. I have never seen anybody calm him down like that before. That was . . . weird. And you're usually yelling at each other.'

'Look, just forget it. At least you're not trying to attack each other any more,' I sighed, and threw myself onto his bouncy mattress. He plopped down beside me, then reached over to touch my cheek. I sucked in a sharp breath, cringing away.

'Sorry,' he said instantly. 'So tell me what happened.'

What had been Noah's story? I'd gone looking for Lee . . .

So I mumbled something about coming over and hearing someone in the garage, but it was Noah. I'd gone through to the games room to find Lee, but I'd fallen over and hit my face.

My stomach was twisting around and I felt ready to puke. Most likely from guilt, I decided. I hated having to lie to Lee. But I could hardly tell him the truth, especially now, when he was still angry at Noah, even if he was calming down.

So I was just hanging in your garage, flirting with Noah,

making out with him a little before he went back to messing with his bike, and then I fell flat on my face. Oh, and by the way, I've been sneaking around with him for the past few weeks, so it's no big deal. We do this kind of thing on a regular basis – just without me falling over all the time.

Yeah, that'd go down *great*.

It wasn't the right time, I told myself. I couldn't tell him.

Not that there was anything to tell – it's not like I had any feelings for Noah in that way – and even if there had been, it wasn't the right time.

'Fine, so it wasn't his fault,' he grumbled. 'But he—'

I didn't let him finish; there was something I was desperate to ask him. But the truth was, I was scared of what he'd answer.

But now I blurted, 'Did you *really* think he'd hit me?'

Lee looked at me for a long moment, then dropped his gaze. 'I know, I know, he's my brother. But just for a second I thought he'd seriously blown his top and you were just in the wrong place at the wrong time, or you guys had been arguing again . . . I hate to think he would, but—'

'He wouldn't hit me,' I said quietly, fiddling with my T-shirt. There was a rip in it; it must've happened when I fell off the workbench. 'Even Noah knows where to draw the line.'

'I hope so,' Lee muttered.

'I *know* so.'

'One minute you're at each other's throats, the next you're defending him?' It wasn't an accusation, just a statement.

'You flipped out pretty quickly yourself,' I pointed out. 'What's up?'

He sighed, mussing his hair. 'I'm just on edge. Failed my history test, remember? My parents said maybe I'm spending too much time with Rachel. I'm just stressed.'

I reached for his hand, linking my fingers through his. He squeezed my hand back tightly, and took a deep breath.

'Anyway, don't change the subject, missy. Since when were you two so buddy-buddy, anyway? You and Noah looked pretty close when I came in.'

My heart raced. I didn't think he'd seen anything – Lee was never the kind to beat around the bush – he'd have already asked me straight out if he suspected anything was up.

Now isn't the right time. Not right now. You can tell him some other time, but not now . . .

My stomach twisted around. I should just tell him. I mean . . . he was bound to find out at some point, so why not just tell him now, before he found out from someone else? I should just *tell him*.

I didn't want to. He was going to hate me.

But he'd hate me less now than if he found out later.

'Lee, please don't hate—'

'Elle?' came a voice from the doorway.

I broke off with a sigh, flopping back onto Lee's bed. Noah had the worst possible timing in the world. Not now, when I was just about to tell Lee. Not now.

'What the hell do you want?' Lee snapped at him, when I didn't say anything.

Noah shot him a glare, but said, 'Elle, can I talk to you a sec?'

'Sure.' I squeezed Lee's hand once more before letting go and pushing myself up off the bed. I gave Lee what I hoped was a reassuring smile, and shut the bedroom door as I left.

Noah was scratching at the back of his neck, his jaw tight. It took me a while to read his expression: he was thinking about something pretty hard. He opened his mouth, closed it, then dragged me after him to his room again. This time, he shut the door properly.

'I get it if – if, you know, you don't . . . if you want to stop . . . you know, whatever we've been doing. If you don't want to see me any more.'

I frowned a little. Where was this coming from all of a sudden? 'Why would I want to do that?'

He shrugged. 'I get it if you do. You were saying

earlier about me being violent, and then there was that stuff Lee said about – about me hitting you, and I just . . . I get it.'

I kept on frowning.

'*Violence junkie* isn't exactly on anyone's list of top five qualities in a guy, huh?' He gave a bitter smile. 'I'd never do something like what Lee said, though – you know that, right? I'm serious. I'd never hurt you, Elle, I swear.'

I nodded. 'I know, okay? I *know*.'

'But I still understand if you don't want to . . . keep this up. Whatever we're doing. If you want to stop—'

'I don't. I mean,' I went on hastily when his face fell, 'I don't want to stop.'

He smiled, and gave a breathy chuckle, pulling me forward and resting his forehead on mine. 'I'm such a bad influence on you. Letting you make stupid decisions like this.'

'Like what?'

'Like staying with me.' He gave me a quick kiss on the lips, then stepped back and said, 'Go on – before he thinks you've pushed me out of the window or something.'

I laughed, and shook my head at him as I walked out. Lee was waiting outside his bedroom – but he wasn't eavesdropping. Just waiting.

'What was that about?'

I said something about Noah telling me he wouldn't hit me, waving a hand around dismissively like it didn't matter. But my heart was hammering in my chest, waiting for Lee to nod and accept my lie.

'Is this the part where you tell me my best friend and my big brother are madly in love?'

I snorted, burst out laughing. 'Lee, you do come up with some trash,' I told him.

In love? Me, in love with Noah Flynn?

Yeah. Right.

My dad just sighed and told me to be more careful when I told him I'd fallen in the garage at Lee's.

'Honestly,' he said. 'You're worse than your mom ever was. You remember that time she tripped on the escalator at the mall? Almost had to have stitches in her foot.' He shook his head, smiling nostalgically at the memory.

Nobody at school doubted my story that I'd fallen in Lee's garage either. And why should they? It wasn't a lie – for once. Lying seemed to go hand in hand with my relationship with Noah, and I hated that.

But I seemed to be getting better and better at it every day. Not that it was something I was proud of.

At lunch I was waiting for Lee and the guys to finish

loading their plates when the entire table suddenly filled with the girls.

'So I was thinking,' Jaime announced, looking right at me, 'about Flynn.'

'Ooh, spill,' Tamara said eagerly.

'Is he with anyone?' she asked me bluntly.

Everyone knew Flynn was single, that he didn't have girlfriends, just flings. So why did she suddenly think he was 'with' someone? Had we slipped up? Had she seen us? Was that why she directed that question at me?

I swallowed, flexing my fingers into my clammy palms. I went for an easy answer. 'I'm not exactly clued in on what Noah's doing all the time.'

'You're more clued in than any of us,' Olivia muttered. 'Lucky bitch.' But she winked at me with a big smile and I laughed, feeling a little relieved.

'Why are you asking?' I said to Jaime.

She shrugged. 'We just had this theory.'

'Theory?' I repeated. Jaime nodded, and Candice leaned in closer, dropping her voice to a whisper. Casually, like my pulse wasn't racing wildly, I picked up a forkful of my pasta salad.

'We think Flynn's got some mystery girlfriend.'

I very nearly dropped my fork. I only just kept from dropping my jaw too.

Samantha snorted. 'I doubt it. This is Flynn we're talking about. He's such a player, I *cannot* picture him going long-term with anyone . . .'

'Well, maybe if he met the right girl,' Karen laughed, pointing to herself.

'Think about it though,' Candice went on. 'I haven't seen him with anybody – and I mean *anybody* – in weeks. Usually you'll see him making out with some lucky girl at parties, but—'

'Ohmigosh!' Tamara squealed. 'You're so right! There hasn't been any girl with him for weeks. But you all saw that hickey he had a couple of weeks ago, right?'

'Who could miss it?' Olivia laughed.

I was trying so hard not to blush or look too guilty or worried. These girls noticed more than I gave them credit for.

'Have you seen him with anyone, Elle? You know when you're around his place, hanging out with Lee?'

I shook my head. 'No, I haven't seen him with anyone.'

'I wonder who it is . . .'

'*If* there is anyone,' Faith put in.

Then I said, oh so very casually, 'Maybe he's gay.'

There was silence for a little while, and I carried on calmly eating my pasta salad. Everyone was gawking at me.

'No way.'

'He can't be.'

'You don't think he *really* is, do you?'

'No, there's no way!'

I couldn't hold it back any longer; I burst out laughing. 'I'm kidding! You should've seen your faces just then . . . I wish I'd had a camera . . .'

Candice swatted my arm, scowling. 'That wasn't very nice, Elle.'

'I'm sorry,' I giggled. 'I couldn't resist.'

But it had distracted them from the subject of Noah Flynn's supposed mystery girlfriend, and *I* was completely off the radar. I breathed an inaudible sigh of relief, listening to them discussing boys. I heard enough Flynn-related gossip when I wasn't involved in it; I don't know how I'd ever survive if they found out that innocent little Rochelle had been fooling around with bad-ass Flynn.

Hell, that would be about as believable as if I told them I'd gone out and bought a motorbike.

Chapter 17

Way too soon, it was the middle of May.

As if I wasn't already preoccupied enough with everything going on in my life – not to mention finals coming up – I had the school council to deal with, too.

'Well, the Summer Dance is going to be at the beginning of June,' Tyrone announced to us.

'What? But that gives us hardly any time!' someone protested loudly.

Tyrone threw his hands up in surrender, and everyone hushed up. 'I don't choose the date, sorry. This is the only time we could get the ballroom at the Royale.'

'You got us the Royale?' Kaitlin shrieked, voicing what most of us girls were thinking. The Royale was a totally extravagant hotel, all white and gold and marble.

Tyrone nodded. 'Yup. The budget managed to swing

it, but we'll be tight pressed on the decorations and the band, unless we bump tickets up a little.'

'Well, we can do that,' I said. 'It's the Royale. Nobody will care if they have to pay a little more to go there.'

'True,' he said, and everyone nodded to show they agreed with me. 'Well, anyway, we really need to figure out food, a band, the tickets and—'

'We need a theme,' one of the girls said, planting her hands down on the table.

Faith jumped in her seat excitedly. 'We should totally do, like, medieval! I saw this show where they had a medieval theme and it was awesome!'

'No,' all the boys said, almost simultaneously. I giggled at the horrified look on Lee's face.

'How about black and white?'

'That's hardly summery.'

'Vintage? Like, the sixties or something? Or, no – we should do, like, the Roaring Twenties! The guys would all turn up like gangsters in flashy suits, and you know they had those – oh, what do you call them? – the flapper dresses. It'd be so cool,' Bridget suggested excitedly.

'Um, no,' someone said flatly.

'Do I get to take a gun,' Tony joked, 'if I'm Al Capone?'

'That would totally work,' one of the boys said sarcastically. It was Max, from my English class. 'Prohibition era? At a school dance? Because nobody's going to try and smuggle in alcohol and get school dances banned.'

'Well, we could have a masquerade—'

'Yeah! Oh my God, yes! That's awesome!'

I groaned and banged my head down on the table before sitting back up. 'Oh, come on! Don't you think that's just so overdone? *Everybody* has a masquerade these days. It's even all over TV. There's got to be *something* else . . .'

'We already had that stupid Hollywood theme or whatever the hell you called it for the Winter Dance,' Eric grumbled. 'At least the masquerade thing is kind of cool.'

'But it's been done so many times!'

'I agree,' Lee said.

'Of course you do,' I heard Tyrone mutter as he shook his head at us.

'Hey, we could always have a mini carnival,' said Lily with a gleam in her eyes. 'You know, with a fortune teller, cotton candy . . . another kissing booth.'

'So long as Elle's running it I'm all for that,' laughed Tony, one of the seniors, winking at me. I just rolled my eyes and hoped I wasn't blushing. All this time, and they were still bringing up how I'd made out with Flynn at the kissing booth.

'No, we're not doing that,' Lee said, sounding so much like Noah I did a double take.

'Well, anyway,' Tyrone said, clearly getting impatient now. 'Everyone in favor of a masquerade?'

Everyone bar Lee and I raised their hands.

'Then it's settled. Lee, Elle, can I count on you guys to do the posters and the tickets?'

'Sure,' we sighed at the same time. While Tyrone basically dictated what we were to make, without giving us a particular design, everyone else split up the rest of the duties between them.

Don't get me wrong – I was really looking forward to the Summer Dance. It would be amazing – especially since the venue was the Royale. But I hated the prospect of having to get a date.

The dances at our school were for juniors and seniors. The Winter and Summer Dances were huge events here. For the Winter Dance I'd just gone with Lee as friends, since he didn't have a girlfriend at the time.

But now he'd ask Rachel.

And that meant he wouldn't be going with me – so I had to get a date. There was no way I was going alone.

So . . .

Who would I go with?

I knew who I *wanted* to go with – but then I thought of the rumors and gossip that would spread like a virus if I turned up with Noah Flynn . . . even the thought of that made me feel nauseous.

And I could hardly turn up without explaining it all to Lee first: he'd hate me if I sprang it on him; but when would I get a chance to tell him? And summon the courage to tell him . . . ?

I couldn't exactly see guys queuing up to ask me, thanks to Noah.

On the bright side – if I turned up alone and it was a masquerade, maybe nobody would know it was me?

I held out a wild hope that Noah would ask me, though. I wondered if I should drop a few hints, and the opportunity rolled around a couple of days later.

We were doing some mock-ups of posters and tickets on Lee's computer when his phone rang.

'Hey, Dixon . . . What? Are you serious? Oh, man! I'll be right there!'

Lee leaped up, grabbing his sneakers and looking like a five-year-old on Christmas morning.

'What's going on?'

'He's at the food court in the mall with some of the guys, and guess who's there? Buying *donuts*?'

'Uh . . .'

'Matt Cain. From the San Francisco Giants. You know – the baseball player? He's a pitcher?'

'Oh, right, cool. So you're off then.'

'Hell yeah!' he laughed. 'Hey, do you know where my baseball cap is?'

'In the closet,' I said, pointing. I rifled through his messy desk before finding a Sharpie, which I handed over my shoulder as he ran out of the room.

'Later!' he yelled, the front door slamming behind him.

I laughed. I'd heard of Matt Cain, but I wasn't much of a baseball fanatic. Sure, it was great to play and fun to watch. I'd been to a couple of games with my dad and Brad, and with Lee. Personally, I preferred watching football.

Especially if it's Noah playing . . .

They had another game coming up Friday, I remembered. It was, like, the quarterfinals or semi-finals. I'd probably end up going with some of the guys.

I saved what we'd done so far on the computer and got up to head on home. Lee wouldn't be back for ages and I didn't really want to stay here alone.

I made my way outside and heard noises coming from the garage. I wandered around, pulling the front door closed behind me, and saw the door half open. I heard the clank of metal and the slight crackle of a radio interfering with the music playing.

I ducked under the door. 'Noah?' I asked, looking around the empty garage, even though I knew it was him.

There was a rattle, and he suddenly appeared from under his car lying on a skateboard, oil stains on his face and arms and shirt, and some kind of tool in his hand.

'Oh, hey,' he said. 'I think I just heard Lee leave.'

'Yeah, there's some baseball player at the mall so he ran off. We were working on posters for the dance.'

Noah groaned. 'I hate all these crappy school spirit events.'

'It's optional, you know.'

'Yeah, not so much for the football team,' he muttered. 'It's like with the Carnival. It's "strongly encouraged", but we all know that we'll end up having to sit on the sidelines for a game if we don't make an appearance.'

I laughed. 'I can't believe they'd actually do that.'

'They're all about image, this damn school,' he muttered.

'Which is why you're still there?'

He smirked. 'Hello, have you met me? Perfect grades, great footballer . . . They overlook a couple of fights for that. Especially when I never actually *start* the fights.'

I just rolled my eyes at him.

'So are you and Lee going to the dance again?' he asked as he slid back under the car. I didn't bother to ask what he was doing; I wouldn't understand anyway.

'No. He'll go with Rachel.'

Noah slid back out again to give me a concerned look. 'Then who are you going with?'

'I don't know,' I admitted.

The look on his face told me he'd probably threaten to beat up the first guy to ask me, but I pretended not to notice.

'It's a masquerade, by the way,' I said.

'It is?'

'Yup.'

He nodded and went back under the car. That was one thing that annoyed me about Noah – most of the time I couldn't even guess at what he was thinking. Whereas with Lee, we could finish each other's sentences and tell exactly what the other was thinking – well, except for this whole Noah situation. That was just a lucky fluke . . . or he was choosing to ignore any signs of something going on.

But Noah . . . Noah was like a Rubik's Cube. An impossible puzzle, but one I didn't want to give up on just yet because it was too compelling, too enticing.

'Well, if someone asks you, say no.'

'I'm sorry?'

'I don't want you going with any idiot who's gonna try something, got that?' His voice was a little muffled, what with the music and the metallic clanking, but I could hear the command in his voice. 'If someone like that Dixon guy asks you – *as a friend* – then fine, if you want to, say yes, but—'

'You can't tell me who I can and can't go with,' I protested. I knew he'd do this, but it was the way he just *expected* me to accept what he said that made me mad.

'Elle—'

'I'll go to the dance with whomsoever I choose – *got that*? Whether or not they ask me to go as a friend.'

Noah slid back out, setting down his spanner. 'Listen, Elle. I'm trying to look out for you here and you're not making it easy. It's a dance – guys are bound to try something. I mean, look what happened at that party. And if it's a masquerade, and there's a chance they won't get caught stealing a kiss, then they'll try it.'

Alright, maybe he had a good point about the masquerade bit. So what?

'Not everybody's a jerk like that, Noah.'

'A hell of a lot of guys are.'

'Maybe I don't care,' I snapped. I *did* care, really, but I wasn't going to agree with Noah without putting up a fight first. Even if he was right about it. 'Maybe I want some guy to kiss me during the slow dance.'

'*I* sure as hell care,' he told me firmly, but he wasn't shouting or anything. He stood towering over me. I hated being so much smaller than him when I was trying to stare him down.

'Why? Why do you even care?' I snapped, narrowing my eyes. I had a feeling I knew the answer, but I didn't care. I was mad at him.

'Because I want that slow dance with you all to myself,' he retorted.

He probably thought that cheesy line would soften me up – with me being such a romantic at heart – and it kind of did. Because when he kissed me then, I kissed him back, my heart racing, sparks dancing through me.

'I hate you,' I mumbled against his lips, smiling.

'I know,' he said, and I felt him smile back.

The sneaking around with Noah, the thrill that we might get caught together, made the whole thing so exhilarating. I knew we couldn't keep it up forever, but I'd sure as hell enjoy it while it lasted.

'Did you really mean that?' I asked, slightly breathless, after a few minutes. 'About having that slow dance?'

He nodded. 'Yeah, I did. In fact, I want the whole night.'

'Oh, do you, now?'

'Yep.' He kissed my lips again quickly.

'Is that you asking me to the dance?'

'Not quite,' he chuckled, kissing me again. 'But almost.'

'I'll take what I can get.'

He gave me another kiss before moving away to carry on fixing his car. In the shiny hood of the car I could see that there were oil smudges on my face and neck now. I'd have to try and clean those off before I got home.

'This is it,' I said quietly, a smile spreading across my face. 'This is the one.'

'You said that about the last five dresses,' Lee complained. He sounded a lot like Brad when he was given vegetables with his dinner.

'Yeah, but I'm sure about this one.'

'How sure? You were sure with the others. I liked the pink one.'

'That's just because it practically had my boobs falling out.' I rolled my eyes in the mirror and Lee laughed. 'Can you imagine what your brother would say if I wore that?'

'He wouldn't be able to keep his hands off you.' For a second he sounded so serious, my stomach dropped and my eyes bulged with panic. But then he laughed. 'Or, you know, he'd stand there batting guys away from you with a stick. You're sure about this one though?'

I nodded, grinning. 'Positive.'

'How much is it?'

'It's on sale. Sixty bucks.'

Lee nodded. 'Cool.'

I smoothed out the skirt again, admiring myself in the mirror. The dress was a dark apple green, just about hitting my knees. The skirt flared out and swung when I moved, and the dress was completely backless, right down to my hips. It had straps that tied behind my neck, and a V-neck that didn't go too low. Tiny silver beads adorned the neckline, sparkling brightly when the light caught them. I loved it.

'Are you sure it's the one?' Lee checked again.

'Yeah,' I said. 'It looks okay, right? Before I buy it?'

'Yes, Shelly, you look beautiful.'

'You said that about the blue one. And the black one.'

'Well, you looked lovely in all of them,' he said with such honesty that I had to laugh. Lee was great for occasions like this. He would give me an honest opinion – he didn't just say 'You look great,' and 'No, you don't look fat.' He'd tell me straight out if my butt looked big, or if my legs looked stumpy.

I went back into my little cubicle to put my shorts and shirt back on.

I really did love the dress. Lee had a tux already, from the Winter Dance. Boys were lucky like that – it's not like I could wear the long-sleeved blue dress I got on sale for the previous Winter Dance without it being recognized. But besides, it'd be way too warm. Girls had it so much harder!

I'd get shoes while we were still at the mall, but that would be easy, I thought as we left the shop. I already had my eye on some silver heels nearby. We just needed to find some masks—

Oh, man.

'What?' Lee asked when I groaned as we left the dress shop. 'What now?'

'We need masks.'

'No shit, Sherlock!' he gasped dramatically.

I hit him with my free hand. 'Thank you, Sergeant Sarcasm. But we need masks that *match our outfits*. Which means you need a purple one like your tie, and I need to find a freaking *apple-green* one that'll match this dress . . . Or, no, ooh, maybe I could get silver . . .'

'Should've gone for the pink dress,' Lee said in a sing-song voice.

'Oh, shut up.'

We managed to find a fancy dress shop that had a small selection of masks at the back. Lee instantly picked up a big bird mask with a giant beak and green feathers, thrusting it at my face.

'How's that?'

'Oh, grow up.' But I was laughing too. There was a mirror straight ahead of me and the mask looked hilarious.

We weren't really taking this very seriously. Lee wanted to buy a purple horror mask, some kind of zombie thing. I found a mangled cyborg one that was silver so would kind of match my dress.

Eventually, though, after the manager gave us a few stern warnings, we managed to settle on our masks.

Lee found a purple mask that only covered his eyes and was all superhero style. It was pretty cool actually. My mask was a little more elaborate, covering my face all the way down to the bottom of my nose. It was almost the exact shade of my dress, only slightly darker, and had silver beads and sequins around the edges. It was perfect – if a little too expensive. But I rationalized that since the dress hadn't been full price, I could afford to pay a little extra for the mask.

'Now you just need a date and you're all set,' Lee said.

I stopped in my tracks with another groan. 'Damn.'

How was I going to explain when I turned up with Noah? Someone was bound to recognize me, or Flynn, surely . . . Especially Lee. *Definitely* Lee.

I was screwed.

I'd have to come up with a really good excuse.

Or you could just, you know, tell him the truth . . .

I sighed and shook my head. 'Never mind.'

'You've still got a week,' he said brightly. 'That's plenty of time for guys to ask you—'

'Guys have asked me,' I said. 'Three of them. I counted. So did you. But Noah said no before I had a chance to respond. He's just there, hanging over my shoulder, at the most inappropriate moments, I swear.'

Lee laughed. Then he said, 'Hey! Maybe you could go with Noah!'

I gave him a look, hoping he wasn't aware of my racing pulse. But there was so much innocence in his smiley, open face I knew instantly that he didn't suspect anything. 'Why?'

'Because he won't have a date, and he won't let you have one. Just make the best of you both being loners.'

I rolled my eyes. But actually . . . maybe I'd use that. If that's what Lee thought we were doing when we turned up together . . . then why not?

Or you could tell him the truth.

If Lee told people that's what we were doing, they'd all believe him.

Or you could just tell. Him. The. Truth!

I'd think about that. It seemed like a pretty good idea.

Lee trailed around after me while I bought some shoes, and then we went to the food court for giant ice-cream sundaes and sodas.

'I can't believe there's only one week till the dance,' he said.

'Hey, and only, like, two and a bit weeks till our birthday!' I exclaimed.

'I know!' He grinned. 'Do you know what you're getting?'

'I think I'm getting a car, but I don't know yet. My dad won't tell me.'

'So it's a surprise but not really a surprise?'

'Pretty much,' I laughed. 'I've seen all the car brochures he's failed to hide. How about you?'

'Nothing special.' He shrugged, mouth full of ice cream. 'I think I might get a new computer – pitch in some of my savings for it or something. My model's kind of old now. Plus, it's slow – and I mean, slower than those computers in the library.'

'I know. You've complained about it enough times. I still think you have a virus from playing those online racing games against Dutch people.'

'Hey, now, that game is awesome.'

'You don't even understand what's going on. It's in *Dutch*.'

'So?'

I laughed, but it felt and even sounded half-hearted. 'Okay.'

'All right, Shelly,' he said, putting his spoon down. Everyone knew that if Lee stopped eating, things were getting serious, so he had my attention straight away. 'What's going on?'

'Huh?'

'Don't be all "Huh?" with me. Something's on your mind. Now, are you going to tell me what it is?'

'Honestly, don't worry, it's nothing.'

'It's Noah, isn't it?'

I did a double take, worried that he'd finally caught me. It had been almost two months now; I'd been starting to doubt our good luck with the whole sneaking-around thing.

But he hadn't seemed suspicious or anything earlier . . . So what was he saying?

All I could think was, *Huh?*

'I knew it.'

'Lee, just – don't . . .' I stammered helplessly, feeling flustered. My palms had turned clammy, my stomach had dropped away. Suddenly my toffee ice cream with the strawberries didn't look so appetizing.

'Don't let him get to you, Elle,' Lee said gently, putting his hand on mine and smiling at me warmly, comfortingly. 'He's looking out for you, and I know it's a bit too extreme, but . . . just bear with it, all right? Just another couple of weeks, then he'll have left school, yeah? Things won't be so bad next year. And he's just trying to keep you from getting hurt.'

I was lost for words.

He didn't know I'd been sneaking around with Noah. He didn't know that there was something between me and his brother. He thought I was worrying about how overprotective Noah was, and how he wouldn't let me have a date for the Summer Dance.

I didn't know whether to be grateful and relieved or sick with guilt. It was a weird mixture of both.

I forced a smile at Lee. He was just so sweet sometimes. 'Thanks,' I mumbled. 'And yeah, you're right. I forgot Noah was leaving for college in September. Do you know where he's going yet?'

Lee shook his head. 'I know he wanted to go to San Diego, but I don't think he's decided yet. He applied to a couple of Ivy League places too.'

'Really?' Lee nodded, shovelling more ice cream into his mouth. 'Oh, right. That'll be weird if he's not there all the time.'

'I know what you mean. At least things will be a little quieter. And then I will officially be the hottest guy in school,' Lee added with a cocky smirk that was weirdly similar to his brother's. The resemblance to Noah was marked: they both had dark hair and bright blue eyes and strong jaws. Their noses used to be the same before Noah got his broken. Noah was a bit taller though, and way more muscled. Not that Lee was too bad – a few summers spent in the gym had seen to that, and all the swimming.

I laughed. 'In your dreams, Lee.'

'Just because you have a crush on my brother . . .' he teased.

'Shut up! I do not!'

He laughed again, taking another giant mouthful of his ice cream. I rolled my eyes before going back to mine.

But part of me was still thinking about Noah going away to college.

I kind of wanted him to stay close to home so he'd still be around. I didn't want to think of him leaving. It'd be so weird. And I'd definitely miss his kisses . . .

And, I realized, I'd miss those times when we just hung out.

But there was another voice that said it would be a good thing if he went to college further away. Then I could have a fresh start at school without him threatening every guy who might ask me on a date. I still hadn't had an actual date since that disastrous one with Cody, unless you counted the secret ones with Noah.

I sighed. My life was getting so messed up.

Chapter 18

'So, um . . .' Warren leaned against the lockers next to mine.

'Yes?' I prompted, when he trailed off.

'Do you have a date for the dance yet?'

I shook my head. 'Noah scared them all off.'

He laughed nervously. 'Yeah, right . . . Well, I was thinking . . . Do you want to maybe go with me?'

'As friends or . . . ?'

'I was thinking as more of a date than friends,' he admitted, not quite meeting my eyes.

I smiled at him easily, wondering at how nervous he was. He was usually a pretty confident guy.

'I don't know, Warren . . .'

'Well, we could always go as friends?'

'How about if you haven't managed to find someone who hasn't already got a date, I'll go with you then? But I'm sure there are plenty of girls who'll go with you.' I smiled again.

He looked a little disappointed but smiled back. 'I'll hold you to that.'

'Okay,' I laughed. 'Good luck.'

'I'm going to need it,' he said. 'Everybody rushed to get their dates as soon as the flyers went up. There's barely a week to go.'

'I know. It's ridiculous. I only just got my dress on Saturday.'

'Really?'

I nodded.

'Well, I'm going to go see if I can get myself a date. See you later, Elle.'

I closed my locker and turned around. I jumped when I saw that Thomas was suddenly stood right there. He was smiling at me – well, actually, he was smirking at me. 'Hey, Elle.'

'Um, hi . . .' I wanted to storm off, or tell him where to go. But I couldn't summon the courage to do that. Then it hit me what Noah had meant about me being too nice. Guess this was one of those times.

'So why'd you turn him down?' he asked me, jerking a head towards Warren.

'None of your business,' I snapped. 'If you'll excuse me . . .' I tried sidestepping, but he blocked my path. I went the other way, but he moved again. Just as I was about to look up and glare, he stepped forward, forcing me back into the lockers.

'Then what do you say to going with me?'

'No, thanks.'

'Aw, come on, Elle, why not?' he asked, still looking obnoxious and confident. 'You don't have a date, and neither do I. Why not?'

'I don't *want* to go with you. All right?'

He was about to argue when someone slammed him sideways into the lockers, making me jump violently, my heart skittering.

'Back off,' Noah said menacingly.

Thomas scowled, shoving Noah away. He glared at him and stalked off. Before I could respond, Noah grabbed my hand and started dragging me off.

'Where are we going?'

He pulled me into one of the small study rooms, with its computers and bookshelves and couches and an old out-of-order coffee machine. He shut the door behind us, and luckily (or maybe unluckily), the room was empty. The bell rang at that moment, signaling we should be getting to class. I had a free study period, but that was irrelevant. Neither of us moved.

'How many guys is that today? Four? Or five?'

I huffed. 'Two, actually. And Warren doesn't really count. So only one.'

'See what I mean, though?'

I rolled my eyes.

'I heard you say you bought a dress,' he continued. 'What's it like?'

'It's tiny and low cut and extremely tight,' I said sarcastically. He raised an eyebrow and I rolled my eyes, sighing. 'It's down to my knees and green, and the skirt's really swishy. It's really nice, actually.'

He nodded. 'It sounds nice. I'm sure you'll look great.' Then he lowered his voice. 'And, uh, since we're already late . . .'

He took a couple of steps closer and I smiled, going on tiptoe so that I could kiss him. I knew I should've made an excuse to go – but I really didn't want to. His arms curled around my waist, warm and secure, and I smiled against his lips.

'Hey, Elle? Noah? Are you—' Lee's voice cut off.

I sprang away from Noah, tripping over my own feet and staggering to regain my balance. My entire body had turned to Jell-O, and suddenly I was finding it hard to breathe. I glanced over at Noah, who was frozen in place, his eyes fixed on his brother, his expression indefinable.

The hustle and bustle of stragglers getting to their classes died down outside, until the three of us were surrounded by silence.

Lee closed his mouth, which had been hanging open the entire time, and took a breath as if he were about to say something. Except no words came out.

I was speechless too. He *had* to understand – I couldn't lose him. He was never supposed to find out like this. Now he'd hate me for ever. I had to say something.

But I didn't know what to say that wouldn't just make this worse than it already was.

I looked over at Noah, who gave me an almost imperceptible shrug; he didn't know how to fix this any more than I did.

'Noah?' Lee choked out eventually, his eyes fixed on me. They weren't just sad, or angry – they were distraught. 'Noah? Please, Shelly, tell me this isn't what it looks like. Tell me right now that there's a reasonable explanation.'

'I – Lee, I – you have to believe me, I didn't – we—'

'Rochelle,' Lee said, his voice taut. 'Tell me this isn't what it looks like.' His eyes bored into mine hopefully. I knew he didn't believe in that shred of hope for a single second, though, not really. He walked toward me, his footfalls heavy, and slow, but stopped a few feet away, like something was holding him back. The next word to leave his mouth was a desperate plea, one that broke my heart to hear.

'Please.'

And I had only one reply, one which I was sure would hurt him even more.

'I'm sorry, Lee, I'm so sorry . . .' I tried to hold his hand, tell him with my eyes how I'd never meant for any of this to happen. But he reeled backward, moving away like he was physically repulsed by me. Tears welled up in my eyes and a lump rose in my throat. I wouldn't let myself cry, though; Lee might just think I was pathetic.

'Please, Lee, it's not like – like I was . . .'

'Not like you were what?' he snapped, but no matter how angry he tried to sound, I heard the pain of betrayal underneath it all. 'Lying to me so you could go screw my brother?'

'Lee!'

'When were you planning on telling me this, exactly? Or did you think you could hide it from me for ever? You think I hadn't notice the so-called *curling iron burns*' – he used the phrase mockingly – 'and how jittery you were when you got a text? You think I hadn't noticed that something was going on?'

'I – I didn't . . .' I drew in a deep breath, trying to collect my thoughts. 'If you knew, why didn't you say anything?'

'I was waiting for you to tell me, Elle!' he yelled.

'We've been best friends our entire lives, and there you were, keeping a secret from me! We've always told each other everything. I figured that whatever it was, you must've had a good reason for not telling me, but you would do eventually.'

Before I could find any sort of a reply, he let out a bark of bitter laughter. 'And this is what you were keeping from me. This is what you lied to me about all this time. And you let me find out like this.'

'You were never meant to find out like this!' I burst out, desperate. He had to listen, he had to understand – he had to forgive me.

'Then you should've told me in the first place,' he shouted back.

I couldn't remember the last time Lee and I had had a proper fight. We'd argued now and again; that wasn't unusual in any type of relationship. But never like this. We'd never yelled at each other.

'Oh, c'mon, Lee. It's not like it's all Elle's fault,' Noah pitched in, his tone flippant and cool, when neither Lee nor I said anything more for a few seconds. 'Lay off her already. You—'

'You,' Lee said, so angry his voice was more like a growl. 'Don't you dare even get me started on you. How hypocritical can you get, huh? Telling guys to keep away from Elle, not to hurt her – and there you are, treating her like some slut you picked up in a club!'

The muscle in Noah's jaw began to jump, and I saw his fingers flexing into fists. 'You have no idea what you're talking about.'

'Are you trying to tell me you two haven't slept together?' Lee's eyebrows went up and he looked between us accusingly. When neither of us replied, it was answer enough. He scoffed, and tugged at his hair. 'I knew it. So you really were just screwing my brother. Lying to me. Choosing him – some guy – over me, your best friend. If you were stood here trying to tell me how madly in love the two of you are, I might've thought differently, but—'

'No, Lee, it wasn't like that, I swear. It was just the one time.'

He was silent for a second, before asking, 'When?' He'd spoken so quietly that, for a moment, I thought I heard him wrong. Surely when it happened wasn't the most important issue here?

'Sorry?'

'When did it happen?' he repeated, looking right into my eyes – but I couldn't look at him. I was too ashamed. 'Rochelle.'

'About two months ago,' I mumbled, still looking at the floor. 'After Warren's party.'

'What, like . . . like straight after you guys left early?'

I nod.

'When she was drunk?' Lee yelled, turning on his brother. 'You slept with her when she was drunk? After all the shit you've sprouted about—'

'I wasn't drunk,' I snapped. 'I'm not that stupid.'

'Oh, really?' Lee retorted. 'Right now, I'd beg to differ.'

At that point, whatever was keeping Noah back finally gave way, and he strode forward, grabbing the collar of Lee's polo shirt in his fist and slamming him back into the wall. 'You really think I'd treat her like that? You think I don't have any respect for her?'

'You had her lying to me for *months*.'

'That was her choice,' Noah spat out, pushing his brother into the wall again. I saw Lee's eyes flit past Noah to me, and all I could do was look back at him mournfully. Yes – it had been my choice.

I chewed my lip for a moment, watching my best friend's face warily. For the first time ever, I had no idea what was going through his mind. His eyes were shadowed, his expression neutral, and his stance calm. In a scary kind of way, he was just like his brother for that moment.

But instead of reacting to me, Lee swung a fist and clipped Noah right on the jaw, hard enough to make him loosen his grip so that Lee could shove him away.

He looked at me one last time, his expression so incredibly disappointed, and then he was out of the room, storming down the corridor.

Noah rubbed at his jaw. 'Not a bad swing, actually.'

I gaped at him before jolting back to my senses. This was no time to argue with Noah. Right now, the most important thing was making sure I didn't lose Lee.

And in a split second, I was running after him, hurtling down the corridor and yelling his name, trying to catch up with him as he escaped down the staircase and out of the building towards the parking lot. I heard Noah chasing after me, but didn't pay him any attention. Lee was all that mattered.

'Lee, would you please just stop for a second?' I yelled, clutching at the stitch in my side. I was totally out of breath.

Lee was just about the biggest person in my life. Except for the whole Noah thing, he knew everything about me. He knew my bra size. He knew I hated the smell of jojoba in the shampoo he used to use. Hell, he even knew I had a birthmark shaped like a strawberry on my butt. He was my other half. I couldn't lose him. We were supposed to be best friends until the day we died – and we'd probably even do that together too. We were born just minutes apart.

Some people say you'll fall in love, and that's the

person you'll spend forever with; the person who'll know your deepest and darkest secrets and still love you even then, the person who'll know exactly the right thing to say to make you laugh or smile or feel better. They'll be the person who, no matter what, you can't live without.

I couldn't have cared less about whoever I fell in love with, to be honest. I just cared about losing Lee.

Lee stopped in his tracks, his back to me. I could see the tension knotting the muscles of his back, and he was breathing hard. What felt like eons later, he turned around to look at me, just as Noah jogged up and slowed to a stop behind me.

Lee's hands were balled into fists, but they still trembled. His jaw quivered too; he was fighting so hard not to cry.

'Please,' I said quietly. 'It's not like you think.'

'Then what the hell *is* it like?' he snapped back. 'I can't believe you, Elle. Lying to me for months and going behind my back to be with my brother, of all people. Do you have any idea how that feels, knowing my best friend picked my brother over me, just for sex?'

'I wasn't – I didn't, I mean – I didn't pick. No, wait, I mean, it – it wasn't for . . .' I shook my head, trying to get out some words that made sense. 'I didn't know what else to do! I knew you'd react like this if I told you, but I – I couldn't . . . I thought I was doing what was best for you, I—'

'You know what, Rochelle? Save it for someone who gives a damn.'

He climbed into his car. He put the engine in gear, reversed out of the space, and left.

And I wasn't sure if he'd ever come back.

Chapter 19

I stood looking at the empty space that Lee's car had just vacated. The growl of its engine and the screech of rubber on tarmac rang in my ears.

I crumpled to the ground, only now there was nobody to catch me.

Noah walked up slowly, cautiously, behind me. I heard his footsteps, and his shadow fell in front of me, but I didn't look at him. I couldn't bear to.

He stopped just behind me. My limbs stiff and reluctant, I pushed myself to my feet and dusted myself off.

Lee had left me. He was my best friend, my twin, my other half. And he'd left me.

He hated me. I'd ruined everything.

If only I'd told him sooner; if only we hadn't been stupid enough to kiss in school, or—

Or I'd just never been with Noah in the first place.

I sighed and ran my fingers through my hair. What

if Lee never talked to me again? What if I'd lost him, not just for a little while until he came around, but for ever?

Noah laid a hand softly on my shoulder. 'Elle,' he started quietly, but I shrugged his hand off and turned away. If it weren't for Noah and that stupid kissing booth, none of this would ever have happened.

'Elle,' he said again as I began to walk away.

'Just leave me alone,' I told him. My voice sounded defeated, but didn't even begin to reflect how bad I felt inside. Noah didn't try to follow me. I headed back to school, alone.

I couldn't concentrate on any of my classes for the rest of the day. Lee didn't show up; when people asked me, I said he'd gone home sick. I avoided Noah, and tried to act as though nothing was wrong.

I got Dixon to give me a ride home, after ignoring Noah's texts and voicemails.

'You sure everything's okay, Elle? You look like you're going to throw up,' Cam said.

Dixon slammed on the brakes. 'If you're going to upchuck, please do so outside the car.'

I shook my head, attempting to laugh it off. 'I'm not going to throw up, don't worry. I just ... I think I must've caught whatever Lee's got.'

'Big surprise there,' Cam laughed. 'You two can't even get sick alone, huh?'

'Guess not,' I mumbled.

When I got home, Dad's car was on the drive already. I'd forgotten that Brad's soccer practise had been cancelled today – the one day I could've done with being at home alone, I thought with a sigh as I opened the front door.

'Elle? That you?' Dad called from the kitchen.

'Yeah, hi.' I wandered in to see him, and smiled. 'Busy?'

He nodded. 'The whole team's trying to get a deal closed by Wednesday, so it's pretty stressful. I have a conference call later, at five thirty. It should take about an hour or so. Will you fix Brad's dinner? There's lasagna in the freezer.'

'Sure,' I told him. 'No problem.'

I made us both coffee and took mine into the lounge, leaving my dad to get on with work. Brad was splayed over the floor, surrounded by papers and his math book. But there was the faint, tinny sound of the Super Mario Bros. theme, and he jumped when I entered the room.

'Hand it over,' I instructed.

'Hand what over? My math homework? Here, help yourself. We're working on angles.'

I laughed sarcastically. 'Funny. Hand over the console.'

My brother glared stubbornly at me. I could see the red plastic of his Nintendo DS console in the crook of his arm.

'Well,' I said airily, 'I guess I'll just have to do some extra vegetables with your dinner. Broccoli, I'm thinking.'

His eyes narrowed. 'You wouldn't dare.'

'Try me.'

'Ugh, fine! God, Elle, you're so annoying!' He slid the console across the floor to me, going back to his math homework – which I noticed he hadn't even started yet. I settled down on the couch with the poetry book we were currently working on in English Lit, drinking my coffee and trying very hard not to worry about Lee and Noah.

Trying to analyse Larkin didn't help stop my mind wandering, though. What would happen when Noah got home? Would he and Lee have a fight?

I didn't want to talk to Noah. All I needed was Lee, and he wouldn't even pick up the phone if I called him. So I had no way of knowing what was going on with the Flynn brothers. I badly wanted to go over to their house, but the rain outside was torrential; there was no way Dad would let me walk over there in this weather, and if Lee wouldn't let me in to talk to him, I'd have to tell my dad everything.

It wasn't that I thought he wouldn't understand, exactly . . . I just didn't even know where to start. It wasn't like I could just swan into the kitchen and announce that, 'Hey, did you know I've been sneaking around with Noah Flynn, and now Lee knows and he hates me? Oh, and would you like another coffee while I'm here?'

Yeah, right.

That'd go down a treat.

It wasn't until about eight o'clock that evening when the phone rang that I knew anything.

'Hello?' Dad answered. 'Oh, hi, June, how are you?'

I could tell that she was almost hysterical, but I couldn't quite hear what she was saying. Dad looked at Brad and me before taking the conversation out into the hall, where we couldn't hear.

'What's that all about?' Brad asked.

'How should I know?' I snapped back at him.

'*How should I know?*' he mimicked, and I tossed a cushion at his head in reply, trying to hear what Dad was saying. I felt sick to my stomach. What was going on?

Dad finally came back into the room, staring down at the phone in his hand.

'Noah's gone.'

My heart skipped a beat. 'What do you mean, Noah's *gone*? Gone where?'

'He and Lee had a big argument, and June said he packed a bag and left. Didn't tell them where he was going, or how long he planned on being gone. He won't answer his cell phone, so Matthew's out trying to find him now.' Dad shook his head hopelessly.

'Well . . . I mean . . . He – he can't have gone too far, right?' I stammered.

'I don't know. He left about twenty minutes ago.'

My stomach dropped away, like it would on a roller-coaster. I gulped. 'Did – did June say what – what they were arguing about?'

My dad looked me in the eye before saying, 'Brad, why don't you go take a shower and get ready for bed?'

'What? That's not fair, it's not even nine o'clock yet!'

'Brad.'

'Fine,' my brother grumbled, and stomped upstairs. His bedroom door slammed behind him. My dad sighed before sitting down in the armchair, and I took that to mean I ought to sit down too.

'Apparently,' my dad said, clasping his hands, 'they had a fight about you. Anything you'd like to tell me, Elle?'

I gulped, feeling sick all over again. 'What did June say?'

'Don't avoid the question, young lady.'

I looked at my knees. 'I – I've kind of . . . kind of been seeing Noah.'

'What do you mean, "kind of been seeing" him?'

'Well, we – at the kissing booth we did for the carnival, he kissed me, and then – we, um, we've been . . . I guess you could call it dating in secret.'

'You've been dating him.'

'Not exactly, though. It's complicated.'

'Better start talking, then.'

Was there any way to word this situation without disappointing my dad? I knew well enough that he didn't exactly approve of Noah – how he got in fights, that he had a motorbike . . . It had never been a problem – until now. Because there was no way he'd be happy with me dating Noah.

'We've been seeing each other in secret because I didn't want Lee to find out. Noah and I argue all the time, and I didn't think it would really work out between us but I wanted it to – which is why we carried on, and then Lee did find out, and now everything's ruined and my life is over.' I sucked in a breath when I was done.

My dad looked . . . well, I guess shell-shocked is the

only word to describe the look on his face. Like he couldn't believe the words that had just come out of my mouth. Like he didn't want to believe it. I dropped my eyes to the floor again.

'How long has this been going on, exactly, Rochelle?'

'About two months. Since the carnival.'

Dad removed his glasses, pushing them onto his forehead and rubbing at his eyes like he did when he was really stressed out. 'And all that time, you didn't tell Lee?'

'I thought I was protecting him,' I explained.

Dad shook his head. 'Funny way of doing things. But – Noah? Of all the boys out there? He's not exactly . . . the most stable, when it comes to relationships.'

'I know, I know, it's not some sort of match made in heaven, or anything, but—'

'Are you in love with him, or something?'

'What? N-no!' I exclaimed. 'No, of course not!'

All my dad did was sigh again. I carried on, trying to repair at least a bit of the damage. 'He makes me happy, Dad.'

He looked at me again, brow furrowed. 'You sure about that, Elle?'

I nodded. 'Yeah.' My voice was hushed, and for some reason I found it hard to restrain a smile. Shaking my head in an attempt to clear it, I stood up. 'So what happened with Lee and Noah? What did June say?'

'They were eating dinner,' my dad told me, 'and all of a sudden Lee flipped out. Started shouting at Noah, and then they were fighting, and then Noah went upstairs, packed a bag, and stormed out.'

The phone rang again, and we both looked at it, lit up, on the coffee table. Dad answered, and I sat on tenterhooks listening to his half of the conversation. 'Hey. Mm-hmm. Yeah, I just spoke to her about it now. What? No, no, I didn't have any idea . . .' He sighed again, then listened for a while.

Then he handed the phone to me. 'She wants to talk to you.'

My hand trembled as I took the phone. 'Hello?'

'Oh, Elle, hi. Look, do you have any idea at all where Noah might've gone? He won't answer his calls, and Matthew can't find him, and . . . we don't know where else to look for him.'

'I – I'm sorry, I really have no idea.' She began to sigh, so I added, 'He's impulsive, you know that. He's probably just gone for a drive to blow off some steam. He'll come back home, don't worry.'

'Well,' she replied, her voice slightly wry, 'I guess you know him better than any of us, don't you, Elle?'

'I – I don't mean . . .' But I couldn't formulate a proper reply; I was lost for words.

'It's okay. I kind of suspected there was a girl in his life lately. He's been acting different. I just never expected you to be that girl.'

Again, I didn't have any reply except for, 'Um . . .'

'Look, just . . . if you hear from him, can you please, *please*, just let me know that he's okay?'

'Of course.' Then, before she could say thank you and goodbye, I blurted out, 'Is Lee there? Can I talk to him?'

'I . . .' She halted. 'I don't think that's the best idea right now, Elle. I'm sorry.'

'He doesn't want to see me, does he?'

'No,' she said, somewhat reluctantly. 'Would you mind putting your dad back on the line, please?'

'Sure. Bye.'

'Bye, Elle.'

I handed the phone back to my dad. The conversation didn't last much longer; all I got from my dad's end of the call was 'Mm-hmm, I know, yeah . . . No, I understand . . . Yeah, of course.'

We didn't talk much more the rest of the evening. I thought that maybe I should call Noah, in case he answered, just so I could give his mom some peace of mind. But I couldn't even pick up my cell phone to do that.

I knew Dad was disappointed in me. It might've

been better if he'd shouted, or shown that he was angry or upset or something – *anything* – but the muted discomfort that clung to the air around us.

It was twenty-three minutes past nine when I couldn't stand it any longer. 'I'm going to bed,' I announced, standing.

Dad didn't respond until I was almost out of the lounge. 'I can understand that you wouldn't tell me about it – but Lee? Elle, you've gotta talk to him. He'll come around. You've been friends far too long to let this come between you.'

All I could do was nod. 'I hope you're right, Dad. I really, really hope you're right.'

Chapter 20

I couldn't get to sleep, no matter how hard I tried; it was impossible to relax when I was worrying so much. I was worried about Noah, of course, but most of all I worried about Lee. Noah could take care of himself – he'd be alright. But Lee? He couldn't just stick a Band-Aid on this and be all okay.

It got to midnight before my willpower ran out and I couldn't stand it any longer. I grabbed my cell phone and speed-dialed number two.

It rang. And rang, and rang, and rang. And, when it was on the verge of going to voicemail, he picked up.

'Shelly?'

I let out a huge gush of air; I hadn't known I was holding my breath. 'Lee.'

Seconds of silence passed between us, the sound of each other's breathing the only reassurance that we were still both there. I broke first.

'How are you?'

'Honestly? I don't know.'

I nodded, even though he couldn't see. 'I'm so sorry, Lee. I never meant for this all to happen. Not like this.'

He sighed. 'Yeah, but you still let it happen.'

'I know, I know. I screwed up.'

'That's the understatement of the century,' he snorted, but I heard the chuckle in his voice he tried so hard to disguise as a cough. I let out a breath of laughter too.

'I know. I'm sorry. I just . . . It seemed like the best option, not telling you. I knew it'd kill you to think I was going behind your back to hook up with your brother – it was so stupid of me . . . I kept meaning to end it, and I hated lying to you, but I didn't end it, and I let it all carry on, and . . .' I trailed off helplessly. 'I thought I was doing the right thing by not telling you: it might not have worked out, and I didn't want you to get caught up in any of it. I thought I was . . . protecting you.'

He didn't say anything for a long while. I knew he was still there; he was breathing down the phone.

'I'm sorry, Lee. I'm so sorry.'

It didn't surprise me to find that my eyes were brimming with tears. I sniffed, trying not to cry. Lee would know if I was crying, even without being able to see me.

'Do you hate me?' I had to ask him. I couldn't bear not knowing, especially when he wasn't responding to me. 'Lee?'

'I don't . . . hate you,' he replied hesitantly. 'But I sure as hell don't like you an awful lot at this moment. I can't believe you kept that from me all this time! And Noah too, when I thought you guys couldn't go five seconds in the same room without arguing.'

Now I was silent. I was too afraid of making things worse.

I stifled a yawn.

'Get some sleep, Elle,' Lee sighed, his voice gentle, caring. 'I'll see you in the morning.'

'You mean you're still taking me to school?'

'Of course I am. When have I ever not?'

That was when I did start crying – but these were tears of relief. I wiped the back of my hand across my cheeks. I didn't want Lee to hear and think I was being pathetic.

'I'll see you in the morning,' he repeated. ''Night, Elle.'

''Night,' I replied. But just before he could hang up, I blurted, 'Lee?'

'Yeah?'

'You know I love you, right?'

I heard the smile in his voice when he said, 'Yeah, I

know. I love you too. Although that doesn't mean I have to like you all the time.'

I was smiling now. 'I know.'

They say if you love something, you set it free. Well, there was no chance in hell I would've let my best friend free without putting up a fight.

Then we hung up. Within seconds, I was asleep.

The next morning, I stood in front of the mirror layering concealer over the bags under my eyes. I didn't want anybody to suspect that anything was wrong; I couldn't let it get out about Noah and me – and it wouldn't exactly make Lee feel any better.

The giveaway noise of two short bursts of a car horn outside made me spring back from the mirror. My huge grin spread from ear to ear. I snatched up my satchel and barreled down the stairs.

'See you later!' I called.

'Is Lee there?' my dad asked.

'Yeah. Bye!'

I slid into the passenger seat of the Mustang and threw my arms around Lee. The handbrake stuck into my stomach and I hit my elbow on the steering wheel, but I didn't care. I still had Lee. That's what mattered.

He chuckled, hugging me back tight. 'Nice to see you too.'

'I'll do anything to make this up to you, I swear. Honestly, I really am sorry.'

'I know you are,' he said. 'And I'll hold you to that.'

'Anything within reason,' I added. 'So no lifetime supplies of milkshakes. I do have to save up for college, you know.'

He paused, hand hovering over the gear stick, and looked me in the eye. 'Fair enough. Then how 'bout a kiss?'

I blinked. 'Excuse me?'

'You heard.' There was a twinkle in his eye, but I still wasn't entirely sure if he was joking or not.

'Is this the part where my best friend tells me he's madly in love with me?' I tried to joke, laughing nervously.

Lee looked away shiftily, clearing his throat and putting the car in gear. I think my heart actually stopped.

'Well . . .' He cleared his throat again and shifted around in his seat, tugging at the seatbelt.

My jaw dropped for a split second before he chuckled. I gave a weak smile, laughing too now. I swatted his arm with the back of my hand and he waved me off.

'I'm kidding,' he laughed. 'No way. I just couldn't resist. Did you actually think I was serious? C'mon, Shelly, that'd just be way too weird.'

I smiled. 'Yeah, you got that right.'

He pulled away from the sidewalk, and we sat in silence for a few seconds before I asked tentatively, 'Have you, um . . . Have you spoken to your brother since last night?'

Lee's hands gripped the steering wheel tighter; his knuckles turned white. 'No,' he told me through clenched teeth. 'And you know what I say? Good riddance to him. If he can't deal with the mess he's made, then he really is just a coward. I know you're not innocent in all of this, but he shouldn't have treated you like that. You deserve better.'

I shook my head. I couldn't agree with that.

'He's never going to change, Elle. He's always going to be a self-centered player.'

'You can't honestly believe that.' Neither of us had ever been entirely sure the whole 'player' thing was a hundred per cent true, but here Lee was, buying into it.

Lee shrugged. 'It's Noah.' As though that were answer enough to everything.

Shame it didn't seem to feel like the right answer; the answer I wanted to solve all this.

I'd woken up unusually early that morning and hadn't been able to go back to sleep. I was too preoccupied thinking about Noah and our relationship – whatever kind of relationship it was. I was happy with

Noah, sure – but Lee was still the most important person in my life, and I couldn't risk losing him again. And if that meant I had to sacrifice being with Noah, then I'd do it in a heartbeat.

But I didn't know what Noah would think of all this. Did he still want to be together? Maybe this was just a short-term thing for him, something until he left for college in the fall. Something that had caused far too much hassle.

'What?' Lee asked.

'Nothing. Never mind.'

For once, he didn't push it.

At school, nobody seemed to think anything had happened; there weren't even any rumors going around. Everything was totally, completely normal. The way it should be.

I stole a glance at Lee as we were talking to the guys. He caught my eye and gave me a half-hearted smile, shrugging one shoulder. He was just as uncomfortable acting like everything was fine as I was.

Things weren't too bad until we were on our way to homeroom and I heard my name being called over the noise of students moving though the school.

'Elle! Hold up a second! Elle!'

My head snapped up. It was Noah's voice. I grasped

Lee's arm, looking at him with wild eyes. What was I supposed to do now?

'Elle!' He was getting closer. I didn't want to deal with this right now. 'Elle, hang on!'

I yanked Lee's arm and tugged him after me as I diverted down the nearest corridor. We stopped just outside the classroom.

'I can't deal with him right now,' I explained to Lee quietly, finally letting go of his arm.

'Yeah, I don't blame you.' He gave me a smile. 'Forget about him.'

'You say that like it's so easy. I can't avoid him for the rest of my life. He's your brother, for Pete's sake.'

'Thanks for the reminder,' he muttered irritably. Then he sighed, running a hand back and forth through his hair and making it stick up even more. 'Never mind. Guess you're right, though. It's gonna be pretty awkward between you two now.'

'Thanks for the support,' I mumbled sarcastically.

'Come on.' He led the way into our homeroom, and that was the end of the conversation.

I managed to avoid Noah until lunchtime.

I sat down next to Rachel and Lee, who were hanging out under a cluster of trees near the football field.

'Very healthy,' Rachel commented, nodding at my can of orange soda and candy bar.

'Yup. You know me – ever the health freak.'

'So I heard about the whole Flynn – I mean, Noah – thing,' she said quietly, offering a sympathetic smile. Promptly, Lee climbed to his feet, then bent to give Rachel a quick kiss. 'I'm gonna go join the guys playing football. See you in a bit.'

'Still a bit of a sensitive topic,' I mumbled. 'At least, more so for Lee.'

'Yeah . . . but I thought you could maybe use some girl talk.'

'You're absolutely right.'

'So . . .' She wriggled so that she was half lying down, propped up on her elbows, and I moved around to sit in the same position beside her. 'Did you really like him? Or was it just for sex?'

I blushed. 'That was only the one time. I was too scared of getting caught after that.' I exhaled through my nose, searching for the right words. 'He doesn't exactly have a lot of redeeming qualities. He can be overprotective, he gets in fights, he's impulsive—'

'Aside from his undeniable hotness,' she argued. 'Don't tell me that's not a redeeming quality.'

I laughed. 'Careful – that's practically your brother-in-law you're talking about there.'

She shrugged, and we both laughed again. I wanted to change the subject, but couldn't think of any subtle way to do so.

It was Rachel who carried on talking. 'Lee's going to be pretty torn up if you do get back with his brother. I can see how it's weird for him; and if you get hurt, you might not want to see Lee any more – he'd miss you and I know he'd hate to lose his brother too, and . . .' She trailed off, biting her lip and looking away.

'Did Lee say all that?'

She smiled guiltily. 'You know, he sounded ready to cry when he called me yesterday. He doesn't want to lose you. You guys are practically twins.'

I broke off a blade of grass and twirled it around my index finger. 'Most of his other girlfriends have been threatened by how close we are. They've always said they're suspicious that, you know, it's one of those things where you fall for your best friend. Which is just ridiculous and way more than a little weird, you know? Anyway. My point is, I'm glad you're not like that.' I laughed wryly. 'I think you're actually the first of his girlfriends who hasn't hated me.'

'You're peas in a pod. I couldn't imagine you guys being in a relationship like that.'

'Finally,' I exclaimed, 'someone who sees that other than Cam and Dixon.'

'Although … the way you're talking, it is a little unnerving how many girlfriends he's had.'

'Not that many actually,' I said. 'But I'll tell you a secret.'

'Ooh, I'm listening,' she said, making both of us giggle. 'Shoot.'

'You're the first girl he's ever ditched me for. So it must be pretty serious with you two.'

'I hope so,' she said. 'I really, really like him.'

'You'd better! Have you seen the way he looks at you?'

Her whole face brightened up. 'It's not just my imagination then?'

I shook my head. 'You guys are so cute together.'

'Thanks.'

We sat in silence a little while, watching the boys throw the ball around in front of us.

'So what do you think you're going to do about Flynn? I mean, Noah. God. Lee keeps telling me to just call him Noah, but it's so weird, you know?'

I sighed. I thought I'd managed to steer her away from that topic. 'I don't know. I shouldn't do anything, but I want to, and … I'm *confused*. And Lee …' I sighed again. 'I don't know.'

'Well, you'd better figure out quick.'

'Why?'

'He's coming over here right now.'

I sat bolt upright, spilling my soda in the grass. 'Shit,' I muttered, clambering to my feet before it spilled onto my pants too. I dusted myself off and looked up to see Noah striding across the football field, coming straight toward me with a purposeful expression. All eyes were on him – or me, in the case of some extremely jealous girls.

'Elle! Where are you going?' Rachel cried after me.

I ran off to the girls' bathroom like I was running from fire. I locked myself in a cubicle and despite several girls – Rachel, Lisa, Olivia, Jaime, Karen – trying to get me to come back out, I refused.

I didn't come out until someone started bashing the door in and I heard Lee shouting, 'Shelly, get your ass out here now.'

I threw open the door. 'You can't come in here! This is the girls' room!'

'Who gives a shit. Now come on. Get yourself together.'

'Lee Flynn! What on earth do you think you are doing in here?' cried a teacher, suddenly appearing from nowhere – Miss Harris, one of the math teachers.

'Uh . . . women's troubles? Really bad cramps, you know.'

'Get out of here right now, young man, before I give you two weeks' detention!'

He rolled his eyes and grabbed my wrist before I could do or say anything. I didn't want him getting in trouble so I let him drag me out. Luck was on my side for a moment though: the bell rang and we had to go to class. As I sat down in English, I checked my cell phone. Another text from Noah.

I deleted it before I even read it.

Chapter 21

Noah didn't turn up back home at all on Tuesday, or Wednesday. His parents still hadn't heard from him, but were satisfied that Lee had seen him at school and he was alive and well. I carried on ignoring his voice-mails and texts, and avoiding him in school. He called the landline at my house Wednesday night, and my dad picked up. He hung up on Noah almost straight away.

Thursday morning, my luck ran out.

I stopped by the bathrooms before homeroom, and on my way out, I walked right into something – no, wait. Some*one*.

'Oh, ouch, sorry,' I said automatically. I'd been in such a daze I wouldn't have been surprised if I'd just apologized to a brick wall. It sure as hell felt like—

Ah. Close enough.

'Oh.' I tried sidestepping him, but a hand on my arm stopped me.

Noah looked . . . well, to be blunt, totally awful.

He had bags under his eyes from what I assumed to be several sleepless nights, and he smelled faintly of smoke.

Hey, this was Flynn, after all – I shouldn't be so surprised. Who's to say he wasn't drunk too?

'We've got to talk,' he said, his voice a little croaky. Without waiting for me to answer, he pulled me into the nearest empty classroom, closing the door behind us.

I sat on the edge of the desk at the front while he stayed by the door.

'How are you?' he asked abruptly, looking me dead in the eyes.

I frowned in confusion, more than a little taken aback. 'Much better now that Lee's forgiven me, if that's what you're asking?'

'That makes one of us,' he muttered, running both hands over his face. 'Too late to go back on it all now. Cat's out of the bag.'

I felt like he was accusing me, and bristled. 'Hey, look, I didn't exactly want to tell him like that—'

'I wasn't blaming you, Elle,' he said quickly. 'I . . . Look, I need to talk to you, and . . .'

'Then talk,' I said, sounding way calmer and more confident than I felt. Not that I was complaining. I was glad he (hopefully) couldn't tell how anxiety made my pulse go wild, how my palms were all clammy, how my stomach twisted.

'I . . .' He gulped, his Adam's apple bobbing up and down. 'I'm sorry. I took advantage of you, and I hated seeing you get hurt when Lee found out. We should've just told him from the start. I shouldn't have let you lie to him like that. It was my fault too. I messed up. And I'm sorry.'

He said it all so rapidly, like he was trying to get the words out before he could take them back, that I thought I'd heard him wrong. And – and he sounded like he meant every word. As though he were really torn up about this.

'I know,' he said slowly, 'you probably never wanted to see my face again, and I get it, but . . .'

'Can I ask you something?'

'Uh . . . sure?'

'Where have you been the last few days?'

He gave a bitter smile, and looked up from his boots to my face again. 'I was staying in a motel. I didn't want to make things worse for you with Lee. I've been trying to forget about you. I haven't been able to sleep, so I've been driving around. I can't stop thinking about you,' he added quietly.

That wasn't quite the answer I'd expected.

But I knew Noah. He wasn't one to lie.

He moved closer to me – so close that I got off the desk to avoid being trapped by him as he towered over me, his body brushing against mine.

'I don't know what the hell it is about you, Elle, but I can't . . . I don't . . .'

'What?'

'You drive me insane,' was all he said then, his voice quiet, soft – intimate. 'Absolutely insane. I need you back.'

My racing heart stopped, and then flip-flopped wildly. What was he saying? It wasn't anything else. It wasn't like he was in l—

Lee had just forgiven me. Maybe not moved on, but forgiven me, at least.

And now Noah just wanted to . . . to carry on where we'd left off? Was he crazy to think I could just do that?

After coming so close to losing my best friend, I wanted to finish this year in peace. Was that too much to ask? Besides, Noah was leaving soon for college.

I couldn't get back with him. I *couldn't*. It wouldn't be right.

So . . . why was it so hard to convince myself that it was wrong?

'Elle,' he said, stroking my hair back off my face. 'Shelly . . .'

I shook my head, putting my foot down. 'No. It's not happening. I can't . . .'

'Elle,' he said, those electric-blue eyes darkening as he backed me up a step. 'You're killing me here.'

'Are you drunk?'

'No. I'm completely sober, and this is all true. I *need* you back.'

I shook my head again, retreating until I felt the wall at my back. Noah stepped forward, hands on either side of my head, his body pinning me there. His breath tickled my face.

'Elle,' he said again. I looked into his eyes. I knew he was telling the truth, but I didn't want to believe it. I wanted to be able to put my foot down, close the door, lock this all away. I didn't want to go back to the firework feeling of his touch and his kisses because I knew I'd never want to leave him. If I didn't do this now, I never would – at least not until it was too late.

And I managed one word: 'No.'

His palm slammed into the display board behind me, making the wall rattle and a loosely tacked poster fall down.

I shook my head, closing my eyes as if not looking at him would help steady me. It didn't. 'No.'

His hands dropped onto my shoulders then, and when I opened my eyes, his were pleading with me.

'Get off me,' I said, trying to push him off. I prayed he wouldn't kiss me now – because I knew I'd end up kissing him back.

'I can do it right this time,' he said. 'No sneaking around.'

'I'm not dating you,' I said feebly.

He sighed, leaning his head forward so it rested against mine. I stiffened. I wasn't scared of him, though. I was scared of myself.

He almost had his arms around me. All I wanted to do right now was let him hold me, kiss me.

I couldn't. I couldn't go back to that. I'd never get back out. I couldn't do that to Lee.

'Noah, please, just . . . don't.'

'I can't help it,' he said tightly, the muscle in his jaw jumping when he pulled back to look at me. 'I tried, believe me. What is it about you? You're driving me crazy here, you're killing me. I need you back.'

'I said *no*.' I shoved him hard in the chest, and slipped out under his arm to the other side of the class-room. 'Noah, I can't do it. I'm sorry, but I can't.'

'Why?'

'I – I just . . . I can't.'

I was saved by the bell: the hallways filled with people going to their first period class. Noah didn't move, and I found I couldn't either.

'I . . . I have to go,' I managed to say, and I fled, barging my way through people and not caring when I stood on someone's toes. I just had to get away.

Not because I was afraid of Noah.

I was afraid of my feelings for him.

'Are you telling me that for your seventeenth birthday – oh, wait, I'm sorry, *our* seventeenth birthday – you have no idea what kind of party you want?'

I laughed. 'I haven't really thought about it lately. But we need to sort something out really soon. We have, like, a week.'

Lee sighed melodramatically. 'And you say *I* procrastinate! So what are we going to do? Tiny gathering of close friends and family?'

'Close friends? You've got to be joking. That's half our grade, and then there's the seniors.'

'True. Then a *large* gathering of close friends and family? Huh? Yeah? Yeah? My parents said before we could rent out a club for the night.'

'That'd be kind of cool . . . but it'd be so expensive . . .'

'All right. House party at my place?'

'I guess so. There's not exactly much else we can do, is there?' I said.

Lee and I had decided months ago that we wanted to do something so cool, so epic, that nobody would be able to top it. And since our birthday fell just after school let out, recently our party had been the big end-of-year celebration. With all the seniors we hung out with leaving now, we wanted to do something even bigger and better than just any old party.

I knew that Lee wanted a big party, and I owed him. I'd been selfish over the whole Noah situation, not telling him about it, sneaking around behind his back. I owed him. I had to come up with something awesome for him.

Then it hit me.

'Remember in sixth grade – we had that costume party at the kiddie place that shut down? It had a ball-pit and everything.'

'Yeah. And I was the Cat in the Hat. And you went as some Disney princess.'

'Yeah.'

'What about it? Oh, God, no. No way. No way.'

'Yes way.'

'No.'

'Why not? It'd be so fun!'

'Shelly, do you realize how childish that sounds?' he laughed, grinning at me and making his eyes crinkle at the corners.

'I know, that's what makes it so cool! We're, like, the

only people who can pull this off and make it epic. Trust me.'

'And you're sure about this?'

'Uh-huh.'

'We're going to shake on this before you change your mind.'

I nodded, smiling easily and sticking my fist out to him.

Lee grinned, laughing, and pounded his fist with mine. We both made identical explosion noises.

'We haven't done that since the sixth grade.'

'It seemed appropriate, given the party,' I laughed.

'We're really going to have a costume party?'

'Hell yeah. And we're going as the Olsen twins.'

He biffed me across the head, laughing. I rolled out of the way, ending up on the grass. I sat up, crossing my legs underneath me and grinning up at him.

'Thing One and Thing Two,' he told me.

'I'm not dying my hair blue,' I protested. Then I smirked. 'But I'm sure Rachel would love to see you in a snug red jumpsuit . . .'

'I take it back,' he exclaimed, shaking his head wildly and waving his hands around. I laughed harder.

Then he said, 'Shall we do it next Friday? After the graduation ceremony?'

'Yeah, we may as well. I mean, our birthday is on the Sunday so . . . And if I get drunk, I—'

'I don't want to be hungover on my birthday,' he finished for me.

'Same.'

'Of course. So shall I start sending the message around right now?'

'Well, I was thinking—'

'Careful, don't hurt yourself.'

I laughed but still managed to frown at him and say a sarcastic 'Ha-ha. I was about to say "the same thing" before you so rudely interrupted m—'

His phone started ringing and he held up a finger. 'Hold that thought,' he said, deliberately interrupting me again. I just laughed as he fished his iPhone out of his pocket and tapped away at it, broadcasting the message to about fifty of our friends. We figured we could always invite more people if we wanted, but it was harder to uninvite them.

My cell phone buzzed in my pocket, and I took it out.

'Who is it?' Lee asked.

'Noah.'

His head snapped up from his cell. 'What the hell does he want now? He didn't harass you enough earlier?'

I pressed the 'busy' button, ignoring Noah's call. 'He didn't harass me, Lee . . .'

'Mm. Maybe. I just don't think he's good for you, Elle, that's all. I'm trying to look out for you. I know my brother.'

'You think I don't know him? He never treated me badly, Lee.'

'But he never treated you the way you deserved, either,' he argued. Then, sighing, he said, 'Never mind. I don't want to argue about that any more. So. Costume for our party.'

'Oh, don't you worry about that.' I grinned mischievously. 'I have the perfect solution.'

Chapter 22

Friday, when I wasn't in class, I was running to and fro calling people to ensure all the finishing touches were in place for the Summer Dance the next day. It was more than enough stress to keep my mind away from any thoughts of Noah.

Rachel, May, Lisa and I were all planning on going to this little spa on Saturday to get our nails and hair done; Lisa's mom worked there, so she got us a discount.

I felt so out of the loop though – all the girls were gushing constantly about their dates; how his tie matched her dress just perfectly, how their crush had asked them to save a dance, how he looked so hot in his tux . . .

And there was me, dateless. I'd be showing up alone. I couldn't ask any of the guys to go as friends because they all had dates. I must've been about the only person in the school who didn't have one.

'We can all go as friends, though, right?' Lisa said Friday lunchtime, when I had a twelve-minute break to grab some lunch. She was going with Cam. Dixon and May were going. Warren was taking a girl from his history class who I didn't really know too well.

'Yeah,' Lee agreed. 'That way you won't show up alone.'

'It works out fine, Elle, see?' Dixon tried convincing me.

'Well . . . you did turn down a lot of offers,' Cam said tentatively.

'I didn't, actually. *He* turned them down for me just about every time.' I didn't need to clarify who I was talking about, of course.

'Hey, speaking of, is your brother going to the dance, Lee?' Rachel asked him.

'I don't know. I couldn't care less if he does or not.'

Rachel and I exchanged a look, both knowing that Lee did care. But neither one of us said anything.

Even though we were all renting out the limo together and going together as a group, I'd still be alone.

I kneaded my forehead. I could try blaming Noah, try being mad at myself for letting him tell everyone who asked that I wasn't going with them.

But I knew why I hadn't put up a fight. I knew why

perfectly well – because I'd assumed I'd be with him, given that it was a masquerade. I'd hoped he could be my date. He'd even asked me, that afternoon in the garage – not in so many words, but in his own way.

But no, that was not going to happen now, no way. And what were the chances of anybody asking me now, when the dance was tomorrow?

Zero.

My hair was blow dried and straightened to perfection, soft and sleek and shiny. My nails were done in the most immaculate French manicure. I'd spent the last half-hour on my make-up, following the 'professional's guide' I'd found online.

Not that there was an awful lot of point: my mask covered half of my face. It was only for the sake of it, really.

My dress looked wonderful now I was dressed up properly. The dark apple-green color seemed to make my skin glow and my brown eyes sparkle from under the mask. The material swished gently when I moved, floating around my thighs. My silver kitten heels matched the beading on the dress and mask perfectly.

I looked great. Hell, I *felt* great!

I hadn't felt so normal in ages. It was almost as though the entire Noah situation had never happened.

Well, if I'm going to show up alone, I'll look pretty damn awesome doing it, I thought firmly. Then I remembered what usually happened at the Summer Dance: yes, I was sharing the limo with the others, but I wouldn't get a photo in the ballroom with my date, I wouldn't have my dad taking embarrassing photos of us . . .

I might have looked the part, but suddenly I didn't quite feel it.

I sighed and the doorbell rang. I picked up my silver clutch and checked myself one last time in the mirror. They were early, but at least I was ready.

'Elle, they're here,' Dad called up as he went to answer the door.

'Yeah,' I answered.

I went downstairs to meet them all and get into the limo. On the landing, I stuck my head in Brad's room. 'See you later, then.'

He paused his game to look at me. 'Wow. Took you long enough.'

'Long enough to what?'

'To go from troll-butt-ugly to not half bad.' But he smiled in his sweet ten-year-old way with his missing tooth, and I had to smile, ruffling his hair.

'Ugh, get off! God! You're so annoying!'

I laughed again, and said goodbye.

I stopped in my tracks at the top of the stairs.

'. . . want to speak to her.'

'She doesn't want to speak to you. I think you'd better leave now.'

'Not until I speak to her.'

'No. Now get the hell off my porch before I call the police.'

Noah pushed his way in anyway, and as my dad started shoving him back out, I let out a strange noise – it wasn't even a word, just a weird squeak that made them both pause and look up at me.

'What are you doing here?' I hissed at Noah, scurrying down the stairs while gripping the banister so I didn't trip in my tiny heels. 'Noah, what the hell are you doing here?'

'He's leaving . . .' It was said with all the threat of an angry father. It actually made Noah shift from one foot to the other; he was intimidated or, at the very least, uncomfortable.

I just looked at Noah, waiting for him to answer. Then I *really* looked at him.

He was wearing a white dress shirt and a slim green tie that was a little haphazardly slung around his neck. He had a black tux, but had paired it with his trademark black boots which he somehow managed to pull off as sexy. His dark hair almost fell into his eyes and looked a little windswept and disheveled.

He scratched the back of his neck nervously. 'I came to talk to you.'

I sighed and half turned to Dad. 'Can you give us a minute?'

'Fine,' he said after a long pause. He pointed a finger threateningly at Noah. 'But you lay one finger on her, and I swear—'

'Dad!' I hissed pointedly, jerking my head at the kitchen. He glared at Noah again and then walked into the kitchen. I could hear Brad's music still playing; he was totally oblivious to what was going on down here.

I looked over at Noah, who was stepping out of the front door. 'What are you doing? I thought you wanted to talk.'

'I told you, Elle. I'm going to do this right.'

And with that, he pulled the front door shut behind him. I stared at it in confusion for almost a full minute, feeling beyond lost, and then the doorbell rang.

Still baffled, I opened it.

And there was Noah, of course. Holding a white calla lily corsage. On one knee.

'What are you doing?' I said, laughing nervously.

'Elle Evans, will you be my date to the Summer Dance?'

I couldn't help it – I honestly couldn't. I burst out

laughing. I saw him scowling at me, so I sobered up and bit my lip hard.

Seriously? Who'd have ever imagined Noah Flynn, of all people, the bad-ass (supposed) player and violence junkie, bending down on one knee on a girl's porch to ask her to the dance? It was just so surreal, it was hilarious.

'Are you serious?'

'Yeah. So are you going to be my date?'

I wavered. I wanted to say yes, and it was such a sweet gesture too. But I knew I shouldn't. It would be such a terrible decision to say yes. I'd hate myself for it. And I'd hate myself for saying no . . .

He stood up then, and looked at me with a little smile, one of those wonderfully rare, infectious smiles that showed his dimple in his left cheek.

'Come on, Shelly, cut me some slack here. I'm trying, aren't I? I know I was a complete jerk and I hurt you, and I've done and said a lot of things that I regret, and . . . I'm trying to make up for that here. Please come with me to the dance?'

He held out the corsage to me, and I looked down at the gorgeous, sweet-scented flower and back up to his face. He still had that smile, and a hopeful spark in his blue eyes. I couldn't say no to that face, could I?

'I . . . I don't know . . .' It came out as a whisper. 'I don't think it's a good idea.'

'Forget what everyone else thinks and what anybody else will say. What do *you* want?'

'I shouldn't – I mean, we *can't*—'

'Screw what's the right thing to do. What do you *want?*'

I looked at him. Ah, hell, I knew what I wanted to do. My head was just fighting it. I knew what I should do, what was the right thing, what everyone else wanted me to do.

'Shelly?' he prompted me, holding the corsage out again.

I took a deep breath, closing my eyes for a moment. This was it. Do or die. Now or never.

It'd be doing everything against my better instinct and every piece of sense screaming at me . . .

I held out my wrist. 'Yes, Noah, I'll go to the dance with you.'

He gave a breath of laughter. 'Seriously?'

I nodded, looking him right in the eyes. He grinned wider that I've ever seen him smile, and pinned the corsage onto my wrist.

Refusing to listen to those stubbornly sensible thoughts, I blurted, 'Have you even got a mask? It *is* a masquerade.'

'Yeah.' He rolled his eyes with a slight smirk, as if to say, *Duh*.

'Oh, okay.'

He smiled at me again, and all I could do was smile back. 'I must be a complete fool agreeing to go to the dance with you.'

He nodded. 'Yup. So you ready to go?'

'Uh, one sec,' I said, and went to the kitchen, leaving Noah on the doorstep. I slipped inside – Dad had clearly just rushed back to his seat and grabbed the TV guide to make it seem like he hadn't been eavesdropping.

'Don't be mad,' I said quietly, hoping he wasn't too disappointed in me.

'I'm not mad, exactly . . . I just don't think it's a good choice,' he said, shaking his head at me. 'After everything you went through with Lee—'

'I know,' I said patiently, 'but . . .'

Dad sighed heavily, taking off his glasses and pressing his fingers to closed eyelids. 'There's a "but". Great. And just when I thought—'

'He got down on one knee to ask me,' I said. 'I think he's really sorry.'

'Mm.' Dad clearly thought otherwise. 'That, or he's only interested in one thing.'

'Dad. Come on. It's just a dance,' I said quietly. 'This

doesn't mean I'm like . . . I don't know, back together with him, or whatever.'

'The fact you agreed to go speaks volumes, Elle. Look, do what feels right, but just be careful. I don't want you getting hurt. Or pregnant, for that matter,' he added sternly.

'Yes, Dad,' I said, ever the impatient teenage daughter.

'I'm serious, bud. You do what you want – do what feels like the right thing. I can't stop you. But I really don't think this *is* right for you.'

'I don't know what to do.' I sighed and felt like I was seven years old again, not almost seventeen. So I did what any vulnerable little old girl would do – I hugged my dad. 'I don't know what to do.'

He hugged me back. 'You'll figure it out.'

'I damn well hope so.'

He chuckled and pulled me up to my feet. 'Look at you, Elle. When did my little girl grow up?'

I gave him a little smile.

'You look gorgeous. And you'll figure this all out, I know you will.'

'He really does make me happy, Dad.'

He gave me a weary smile – one that suddenly made him look so much older.

I gave another half-smile in return and went back

303

into the hallway, where Noah was waiting for me, looking a little nervous. I didn't even realize Dad had followed me out until he spoke.

'All right – well, I suppose if you're taking my little girl to this dance I have to have some photos.' He picked up the camera again and motioned for me to stand by Noah.

Feeling more than a little awkward, I shuffled over. Noah pulled me in close to his side, his arms going around me. I felt at ease in an instant. It was familiar. Nice.

Dad took a couple of photos and then said, 'Now listen up. I'm not happy with this at all, but if it's what Elle wants, then I'll put up with it – *for now*. But you do anything – and I mean *anything at all* – to hurt her, and boy, you'll wish you never stepped foot in here tonight. You got that?'

'Yes, sir,' answered Noah, sounding surprisingly sincere and polite.

'All right then. You kids have fun.'

'Bye, Dad,' I said. I shot him an encouraging smile and he gave me a dubious shrug in return. I pulled the door closed, and Noah, his arm still around my waist from the photos, guided me down the driveway.

'Wait,' I said, stopping. 'Does Lee know about this? Did you tell him?'

'No. Why? Does it really matter that much? Tell him later.' But he looked down at the ground when he said that last part.

'Well, they're all supposed to stop by, like, right now, with the limo . . .'

'Text them and tell them you've gone ahead. Or something went wrong and you'll meet them there later. I don't know. Tell them you're with me if you really want.'

'I'll say I had a make-up malfunction,' I'd already decided, and texted Lee.

They've just left Dixon's. Thanks for the heads up. Meet you there.

That was the wonderful thing about my best friend being a boy: no condolences and no worried messages asking if I needed help or what was wrong. He just accepted it without question.

I felt horrible for lying to him, even if it was only via text. I had a horrible, ominous sensation in my gut that it was all starting again – the lying, the sneaking around, the backstabbing . . . And the worst part was that I was doing it all so willingly, without a second thought.

But I could hardly text him saying, *Don't worry about collecting me, I'm going to the dance with Noah instead now.* Yeah, right.

I had to tell Lee to his face. Make him understand. Explain everything. That was the only way. No more lying. That was the least I could do now. He deserved more than a text, or even a phone call.

I wondered for a moment what Noah was doing when he went to the passenger side of the car. Surely he wasn't going to let me drive? He barely let anybody touch his car without permission. Lee was almost as bad – he never let me drive his car either. (Seriously – one teeny tiny scratch on my dad's car from a mailbox and I'm branded for life.)

But instead, he held the door open for me. It was such a gentlemanly gesture that I wondered if my eyes were working properly.

'Thanks . . .' I said, unsure, sliding into his car. He shut the door behind me before getting in himself, then pulling away and heading to the Royale. It was a twenty-minute drive maybe, and I had no idea how to fill that time without things being awkward between us.

I did have one question I needed to ask, though.

'What do we do, then? Just turn up there together and let everyone know we're . . . we're . . . whatever we are?' I didn't want to say 'dating' in case he didn't think we were.

Noah sighed. 'Look, I'm going to just lay it all down

here, Elle. Cards up. I like being with you. I really care about you – more than I probably should. So . . . I don't want to lose you again. I'm trying to make things up to you here, but I get it if you want this to stay . . . you know, casual or whatever.'

'So . . . ?'

'So, what I'm trying to say here is . . . I guess it's up to you.'

My heart was pounding so hard, I hardly heard the rest of what he said.

'If you, you know . . . want to date . . . be a couple . . .'

I stared at him – from his eyes, which were focused on the stop sign in front, to his fingers, flexed around the steering wheel. He looked . . . well, there was no other word for it: vulnerable.

He'd told me why he never had girlfriends, only flings – because they didn't want to date a guy who gets into fights. And I didn't blame any of those girls. But . . . there was no denying it: Noah had a really, really sweet and caring side. Like showing up at my door tonight, and holding the car door open for me.

Lee is going to hate me for this . . .

But what I said was, 'I have to talk to Lee first. I can't just drop this on him.'

I didn't say anything in so many words, but even so, Noah's eyes brightened when he looked over at me. A smile – not a smirk, a smile – was tugging at the corners of his lips. 'Really?'

I laughed. 'Really, really.'

We both knew what my answer really was. But I needed to make sure I wasn't going to lose my best friend over this. No guy, not even Noah, was worth that. And he understood I'd said I had to tell Lee first.

I didn't get a chance to say any more, because he leaned in quickly to give me a quick kiss on the lips before the lights changed. It was way too quick for my liking, but it still made my heart go wild.

He reached over and his hand found mine, our fingers linking together. It felt so natural and easy, like we fit perfectly – even if everything about our personalities and habits would've suggested otherwise.

The rest of the ride passed mostly in silence. Except it wasn't an awkward kind of silence, one where I wondered if I should make conversation. It was the nice kind of silence. The one where you just enjoy the company.

We weren't too far from the Royale now. There was a little traffic, thanks to the fire truck, the two police cars, a bunch of limos, the town cars and the Rolls-Royce, and the two or three horse-drawn carriages – not to mention the people who'd turned up with their normal everyday cars.

'The limos I understand,' Noah said. 'But the carriages? That's just madness. It's not like MTV are gonna be here. It's a total waste of money.'

I laughed at that, having thought pretty much the same thing.

I smoothed out my dress and then took out a compact to touch up my lipstick. Feeling his eyes on me, I glanced over at Noah. 'What?'

'Nothing.'

'No, seriously, what is it?' I persisted, checking myself in my too-small mirror, wondering if maybe there was lipstick on my teeth now.

'Nothing. You look great.'

'Oh. Thanks. Hey, it's weird how your tie matches my dress.'

He looked down at his tie, like he needed visual confirmation. 'Well, yeah. I remembered you telling me your dress was green, and this was the only green tie I could find at the mall that wasn't covered in palm trees.'

My reflection grinned back at me as I continued to check my make-up.

'Honestly, Elle, put it away. You look gorgeous enough already.'

Gorgeous . . . I couldn't stop smiling. 'Really?'

'Really, really,' he chuckled. The traffic started

moving, now that the limos had begun to disperse, and we crawled forward another few yards. 'Oh, hey, look – there's your limo.'

I craned my neck, looking over to where he pointed. A black stretch SUV limo was parked outside the Royale doors, and I recognized Lee instantly, with Rachel on his arm, and the others all climbing out after them.

With everybody in their masks, it was actually quite hard to tell who people were. You could easily mistake them for someone else. Plus, a lot of the boys wore plain masks that all looked really similar.

Maybe nobody (except Lee, of course) would recognize me and Noah together. Maybe I wouldn't be surrounded by hordes of girls wanting to know why I'd turned up with Noah Flynn.

I kind of hoped we wouldn't be recognized. It would make this night a whole lot easier.

We drew up to the hotel, where a valet was waiting to park the car. I got out, but not before Noah had rushed around to open the door for me. I hadn't even noticed him put his mask on; it was a black one with gray metal studs on the top edge, and it covered at least half his face.

The valet took the keys from Noah while Noah put an arm around my waist and guided me up to the doors. I could feel people looking at us already, trying to figure out who we were. And we weren't even inside the ballroom yet.

There was a knot in the pit of my stomach and I could hear my breathing getting a shallower.

'Calm down,' Noah whispered in my ear, his breath tickling my cheek. 'It'll be fine, I swear.'

'Oh, I really hope you're right . . .'

Chapter 23

A small queue of people lined up with their dates, waiting to have their photo taken under the magnificent flower archway against the wall of the ballroom. Noah guided me into the queue, and I shot him a smile. Looked like I would be getting photos with my date after all.

The delicate crystal chandeliers gave the room a warm glow, throwing sparkles off the gold that lined the walls, the pillars, the ceiling. The marble floor was splashed with shadows of dancing people. The ceiling went up in a high dome, and there was a bar against one wall. Small round tables with white tablecloths and flower arrangements stood around the sides of the ballroom, and the band was set up on a low platform at the far end.

In short, it was perfect. Unbelievably, flawlessly beautiful. I was pretty proud of myself for suggesting the flower arch for the photos, since it looked so romantic.

'It's amazing, don't you think?' I said to Noah with a grin.

'Yeah,' he agreed, looking around like I was.

'Next?' the photographer said, and we moved into his spotlight. I stood there a little awkwardly, aware of people looking at us. Of course, they were really only watching because we were having our photo taken. In thirty seconds the focus would be on the next couple. But right now, I was just waiting for someone to cry, 'Oh my gosh! Elle and Flynn?'

'Hey, relax,' he breathed in my ear, making me jump a little.

'Sorry, I'm just a little . . . on edge.'

He smirked that gorgeously sexy smirk. It relaxed me a little. So I turned to face the photographer, and Noah stood behind me, both arms wrapped around my waist and my arms wrapped over his. I smiled into the lens and the flash was almost blinding, then—

'Next?'

And we were no longer the center of attention, just like that.

'You thirsty?'

'Uh, y-yeah.'

'I'll go grab some drinks.'

'Okay.'

He'd barely left my side for a full four seconds when

the other Flynn brother was right in front of me.

Crap. Had he just noticed me with Noah? Had someone seen us come in together? I mean, he didn't look mad, but . . .

He slid my mask up off my face. 'Shelly, you're here.'

I smiled. 'Hey, Lee.'

'Make-up malfunction all sorted?'

I breathed a sigh of relief inside. He hadn't noticed . . . 'Yeah, thanks. Everything's great now.'

'Awesome. So, uh, are you going to come sit at our table or stand here on your lonesome?'

I wavered. 'Lee, I kind of need to tell—'

'Is that Elle?' Someone spun my shoulder around and a masked blonde girl grinned at me. 'I thought it was you! Nice dress, by the way. Hi, Lee. Listen, Elle, there's a problem with the food, and Tyrone asked me to come find you. Something to do with the vegetarian option and a nut roast . . . ?'

'No, no, we said no nut roast because Jon Fletcher's got a nut allergy.'

'Yeah, I know. But Tyrone said to come find you.'

'I wasn't in charge of the food, though.' I hadn't been; I just helped out a little.

'I know,' she said. I was almost sure it was Kaitlin I was talking to, since her voice was a little nasal. She sounded even more nasal now that she was irritated.

Yep, definitely Kaitlin, I decided. 'But Tyrone asked me to find you because Gen's freaking out.'

I sighed. 'Sure. Okay.'

'Great! Okay, go through that side door near where the band is playing, and there's a door to the kitchens about halfway down the corridor.'

'Lee, I'll be back in a sec. Don't disappear, though – I have to tell you something,' I said.

'Sure thing.' And he disappeared into the crowd.

I followed Kaitlin's directions and, after a couple of wrong doors, found the kitchen, where Tyrone and Gen were arguing partly with the chef, but mostly with each other.

'You should've specified if there were nut allergies . . .' the man was saying angrily.

'We did!' Gen practically screamed.

'Are you totally sure, Gen?' Tyrone's mask was pushed up on top of his head and his nostrils flared.

'I'm sure! I wouldn't have forgotten to tell them, Ty!' She spun around to face me, her eyes wild, desperate. 'Elle, tell them!'

I sighed, and looked past her to the chef. 'Can't you just make one vegetarian meal that isn't a nut roast? Just the one?'

He was far from impressed, but eventually we

managed to talk him around – and with no extra charge for Jon's meal.

By the time I made it out of the kitchen, I had no idea where any of my friends were. Or my date, for that matter. Everyone was dancing, or standing in crowds around the table.

With the guys in tuxes, and masks hiding their faces, there was hardly any distinction between them. I searched for Lee for a full five minutes before giving up. I knew Rachel had a floor-length lilac dress with a violet bow on, but I couldn't even find her.

I went over to lean against a wall where there was some breathing space and sighed. Dinner would be served in forty minutes and I was not planning on spending all that time alone. Why did we have masquerade again? Forget cool and chic and fun. It was *annoying*.

Someone sidled up next to me. 'Here, you look like you could use this.' Whoever it was held out a small glass of fruit punch to me.

'Thanks . . .' I frowned, trying to work out who it was. The music was just loud enough that their voice wasn't entirely distinguishable.

My rescuer pulled the mask off his face just enough for me to say, 'Cam!' before he put it back on.

'Who did you think it was?' he laughed.

'Peter Parker. Well, that's who I was hoping for.'

'Maguire or Garfield?'

'Garfield.'

'Sorry to disappoint. I only noticed you because I saw you talking to Lee earlier. You look really nice.'

'Oh, thanks.' I grinned. 'So do you. How're you?'

'I'm good. Anyway, did I see you coming in with somebody?'

'No . . . I don't think so . . .'

I hate lying.

'Oh. Must've been someone else, then. Well, anyway, we better go find the others. I only went to get a drink, but you looked pretty lonely over here. Plus, I couldn't find anyone with these damn masks.'

'I said it was stupid.'

'What're you doing by yourself anyway?'

'I couldn't find anyone,' I laughed, defending myself.

'Excuses, excuses . . . Come on. I *think* they're all over here still.' I followed Cam through the crowds of dancing masked teenagers, holding onto his arm so I didn't lose him. The whole time, I kept an eye out, but I didn't have a clue where Noah had gone.

We soon found the others. The girls all looked beautiful, of course, and the guys looked pretty good too. Lee had matched his tie perfectly to Rachel's dress, but the other boys had mostly just gone for black. Cam, however, had made the effort to try and match Lisa's dress – except he'd gone for scarlet when Lisa wore burgundy.

Lee and Rachel were just so cute together.

'You're not too upset, Elle, are you? You know, because you're here on your own,' said Warren. It was a little insensitive, but that was Warren, so I didn't think anything of it.

'No,' I said. 'I'm fine.'

'I swear I saw you come in with someone and have a photo,' said Bridget, Warren's date.

'No, that wasn't her, I asked,' Cam answered for me.

'Oh. That's weird. See, everyone in these stupid masks and I can hardly tell anybody apart!'

Conversation moved into easy chatter then. I kept looking around for Noah but couldn't see him any-where. I went up and danced with the girls for a while, and danced with Cam and Lee too. Then Cody came over, tapping Lee's shoulder.

I only recognized him by the tongue piercing that caught the light when he said, 'Can I cut in?'

'Be my guest,' Lee said. He gave me an elaborate, sweeping bow, then went to where the others were dancing. The music had just switched to something slower – an acoustic cover of some pop song.

'Hi, Cody.'

'Hey, Elle.' He smiled. 'Hope you don't mind me stealing this dance, by the way.'

I laughed. 'Don't worry about it.'

'You look really pretty tonight,' he said. 'Sorry to hear you didn't get a date.'

I groaned dramatically. 'Does everyone know?'

He shrugged, laughing with me. 'Don't worry. It's just 'cause Flynn scared guys off, right? But nobody's seen him anyway – you'll be dancing all night, stealing some other girl's date.'

'Who did you come with again?'

'Amy. Amy Johnson.'

I nodded. 'Cool. She doesn't mind you dancing with me, though?'

'Nah. Don't worry about it. How've you been, anyway? I don't see you much outside of chemistry.'

'Good, I guess. You?'

'Same old, same old.'

We laughed at the awkward lapse in conversation that followed, and chatted easily about the band and how everything looked until the end of the song, when I begged off Jason's offer of a dance to go 'find Lee'. What I really intended to do was find Noah.

I might've found him – if everyone hadn't suddenly

started to take their seats for dinner. I went up on my tiptoes, craning my neck to look for him.

'Elle! Elle!' I looked around. 'Over here!' Lee waved his hand, gesturing for me to join him.

I smiled, though it felt more like a grimace, and squeezed through the crowd to take my seat.

The table was left with one empty seat, of course: it sat five couples, and we had Warren, Dixon, Lee and Cam with their dates, and then me with an empty seat beside me.

I prayed really hard that Noah would see me and come sit by me.

'Flynn! Space here, man . . .' I heard the strong Brooklyn accent of Andy, one of the football players, beckoning Noah over to their table. It was a mixture of girls and guys over there – nobody really sat with their dates, and there was just one seat left.

He started over to them, and I noticed that his mask was in his hand now. He opened his mouth to say something, but one of the girls jumped up excitedly and started pulling him over. His eyes were flitting around the room, and then they caught mine as he was being pulled to his seat.

Both of us shot the other a helpless kind of look: one that said we were kind of stuck with these tables. I supposed it was lucky in a way, since I hadn't told Lee yet . . . I was going to, though. I wouldn't let it be like the last time.

If I hadn't had the food crisis to help out with, or I hadn't been asked to dance . . . And now Noah was being forced to sit down, but not next to me. And I still hadn't told Lee.

The odds were against us; but I wasn't going to let that stop me, not this time.

I pushed all these thoughts to the back of my mind. I could deal with that later. Right now, I'd just enjoy being with my friends.

That was easier said than done, of course: it was hard not to turn around and look at Noah, and I was distracted.

It didn't go unnoticed.

Fingers snapped in front of my face, making me jump and drop my fork.

'Earth to Elle! What's up with you?'

'Nothing,' I told Lee as innocently as possible. I forced a smile too. 'Nothing's up.'

'Something is. Oh, that reminds me! What was it you wanted to tell me about earlier? You know, before you got dragged off?'

I gulped. 'Uh, n-nothing much . . .'

'Oh, right, okay. Excuse us a minute, guys.' Lee got up, pulling me with him.

My heart began ramming its way free from my ribcage, and my palms turned sweaty.

'Elle, what's going on?' asked Rachel.

'N-nothing . . .' I mumbled to her, and she gave me a concerned look.

Lee pulled me out of the door near our table into the hotel lobby.

'Seriously,' he said, folding his arms sternly. 'What is it?'

I gulped, fiddling with the corsage strap on my wrist. 'Well . . . Just promise me you'll hear me out, okay? Don't freak out or get mad. Just hear me out. Please?'

'Okay,' he said warily, and it looked like he was bracing himself for bad news.

'I didn't have a make-up malfunction earlier,' I started, and he decided to interrupt me with a relieved laugh.

'That's it? What, did you just not want to be the only one in the limo who was alone? Man, for a minute there I thought you were going to tell me you were hooking up with Noah again.'

I bit my lip. 'He turned up. Earlier, he turned up at my front door. That's why I told you I had a make-up malfunction.'

Lee scowled. 'What did he want?'

'He . . .' I heard footsteps behind him, and glanced up. Noah looked right back at me. I grabbed Lee's elbow. I didn't want him to turn around and start making a scene over nothing. 'Don't get mad, Lee, promise me. But he – he said he was trying to make it up to me, and . . . and . . .'

'Hey, guys, what's up?'

I could've killed Noah at that point. Couldn't he just have let me tell Lee without interfering? Now Lee was bound to overreact, or Noah would twist things around just to wind him up, and . . .

'What were you doing, turning up at Elle's earlier?' Lee demanded. 'You don't think you've already done enough?'

'That's why I was there,' he said, those blue eyes piercing into mine. 'Trying to make it up to her.'

'Lee, he had a corsage and everything,' I put in.

'I don't care,' he exclaimed, turning to face me. 'Elle, he was a jerk to you. Left you in the lurch when I found out, and couldn't have been less supportive.'

'It's not like that,' Noah put in, scowling. 'And you know it. I tried calling, and—'

'It makes no difference, Noah,' Lee spat. 'The fact is, you weren't there when she really needed you. You didn't try and talk things through properly. You left her to deal with everything while you bailed and went off on that damn motorbike of yours. You had her lying to me, lying to her dad, and for what? A bit of fun? Some action?'

'Lee . . .'

'Why don't we ask her, huh? Why don't we see,' Noah said, the muscle in his jaw jumping, 'what Elle wants?'

They looked at me. They waited.

I looked at Noah. All I had to do was look at him, and Lee sighed in defeat.

'Elle, seriously, do you really think that's the best thing to—'

'Noah,' I interrupted, 'do you think you could give us a minute?'

He shrugged. 'Sure.' He walked a couple of yards away from us, and leaned against the wall.

I turned to Lee again, dropping my voice to a whisper. 'I know you think it's stupid and reckless, but . . . I want to be with him. It *feels* like the right thing to do.'

Lee's mouth twisted sideways thoughtfully. I could see the cogs turning in his mind. 'If you guys are just hooking up . . . I mean, you always seemed so be the kind of girl for commitment rather than a fling. I worry about you, Shelly.'

I smiled calmly, reaching for his hand and squeezing

it. 'I know you do. And we're doing it right this time,' I echoed Noah's words from earlier.

'As in . . . ?'

'She means we're dating,' Noah said, and his voice carried so that we could hear him. I blushed, looking at my toes before turning back to Lee, whose eyebrows were raised as high as they could possibly go.

'With your approval,' I added. 'Only if you're okay with it.'

'Wait, this is for real? Seriously?'

I nodded. Noah, who had wandered back toward us, said, 'Yeah. Why? You got a problem with that, little bro?'

Lee wasn't looking at him; his eyes were trained on me, and they creased at the corners with the hint of a smile. 'If any girl was gonna change him . . .' His voice sounded slightly strained. He wasn't happy with this. But he was accepting it.

'I'm going to head back in before things start looking suspicious. See you later, Elle.' Noah nodded at me before going back inside. I took a deep breath, unsure of what Lee might say now that Noah wasn't within earshot.

'And you said he was never going to change,' I said jokingly, pushing his arm lightly.

He didn't laugh. Instead, he sighed heavily and

pinched the bridge of his nose for a second before speaking. He always did that when he was upset – like at his granddad's funeral, and when his dog, Patches, died when we were ten.

'Are you really happy, though, Shelly? I know what Noah's like. Are you sure he didn't just sweet-talk you into this? You know what he's like too. You're *really* happy with him?'

'I am,' I told him. 'I know you'll call me silly and cheesy and corny for saying this, but he makes me feel good inside. It's like – it doesn't matter what's going on in my life, because when I am with him, I can forget about all that. I can just enjoy being there with him, and I'm happy. I'm happy, Lee. And I know it's stupid, because we'll probably just end it when he goes to college, but . . .'

I trailed off, not knowing what else to say. I couldn't find the words to explain how I felt about Noah; I just hoped that Lee would at least try to understand.

Well, the heart wants what the heart wants.

Except this wasn't a matter of the heart. Because I didn't love him. Of course I didn't. *That* would just be ridiculous. No. I definitely didn't love him.

'So . . . what, are you trying to tell me you're in love with him?'

'No! No – no way,' I insisted. I should've known

he'd jump to that conclusion. If I was in love with Noah, then it would be a reasonable explanation for getting back with him, but I wasn't. Most definitely not.

'Oh.' There was a kind of pitying look in his face that I didn't quite understand. Like he knew something I didn't.

'Lee, what—'

'Look, I don't agree with this, Shelly. He hurt you really badly, and I don't think this is going to end well. It's just not the right thing for you. But if it's what you really want . . . I'll be there to pick up the pieces after, okay?'

I smiled. It wasn't a big smile, but it was a genuine one, mirroring Lee's perfectly. 'Seriously? You're not mad at me?'

'No, Shelly . . .' He grinned, 'If it's what you want, I'll be here for you at the end of it. I'll always be here for you.'

I hugged my best friend tight and whispered, 'Thanks, Lee.'

He squeezed me back. 'I told you you'd started making me talk like a chick.'

I laughed and said quietly, 'I love you.'

'Yeah, I love you too.' He stepped back and gave me another smile. 'Come on. We don't want to miss dessert. I want my cheesecake – if I'm not there, I know Dixon will steal it.'

Laughing, I followed him as he marched back toward our table.

'Everything all right with you guys?' Cam was looking at me with concern.

'You sure you're okay, Elle?' Dixon asked.

I caught Rachel mouthing to Lee, 'Your brother?' and he nodded in response, offering her a helpless sort of look. Understanding dawned on her face and she smiled encouragingly at me.

I turned around and looked over to Noah's table. He was laughing at something one of the guys had said, but he was looking over at me. He caught my eye and winked before turning back.

'Yeah,' I said with a smile. 'Everything's great.'

And at that moment, it really, truly was.

Chapter 24

'Uh, can I have your attention please, everyone?'

Silence fell instantly on the mix of dancing bodies. I'd been dancing with the girls for the past twenty minutes, but no matter how many times I tried excusing myself, I couldn't seem to get free. They just kept wanting to dance some more, or started up an interesting conversation. The one time I got out to 'grab a drink', I hadn't seen Noah anywhere.

And now he was up on the platform, in front of the microphone in the place of the lead singer.

And everybody was silent. All eyes on him.

'Uh, can I have your attention please, everyone?'

I couldn't explain why, but my heart started racing and I could hardly breathe. I didn't have a clue what Noah was doing up there in front of everyone, but my body reacted with anxiety, like it knew what was about to happen before I did.

He pulled his mask up off his face, so that there was no doubt about who it was.

I gulped. What the hell was he doing?

'Now, the only reason I'm up here tonight is because I'm trying to show someone that I'm sorry. See, there's this girl. I can't get her out of my mind. And I did some pretty crappy things to her and I'm making up for it. So . . . Elle? Where are you?'

Everybody just turned, almost as one, to look at me. Even with my mask on, they all knew where to find me. I fiddled with the folds in the material of my dress, shooting Noah a glare through my mask.

'Can we get a spotlight over here?' he called out, pointing, and I heard the teasing tone in his voice.

Somehow, somebody found a spotlight to blind me with. I squinted, holding a hand up over my eyes.

'Great, thanks. So, uh, Elle. This is me saying sorry. Guys?' At the last word, he turned and gestured to the band, who started playing. It wasn't a slow song – it was pretty upbeat. And I recognized it instantly.

I Really Want You by the Plain White T's. It was one of my favorite songs. It was hardly Noah's way of romantically confessing his love for me . . . Hell, he didn't even sing it himself; the band did.

He jumped off the stage, microphone in hand, and bee-lined through the crowd, who'd parted to

330

make a path for him, stopping right in front of me.

'There goes your reputation,' I said quietly, laughing.

'You think I care?'

I bit my lip. 'But—' Before I could ask why, he interrupted me, speaking into the microphone while there was a little bit of instrumental.

'Will you be my girlfriend, Elle?'

I blushed under my mask.

Up until now, I hadn't even noticed the other people in the room. I hadn't heard the whispers while Noah was up on the stage. But right now their voices hit me like a confetti cannon at a pep rally.

'Say yes!'

'Oh my gosh, that's so sweet!'

'I can't believe *Flynn's* doing this . . .'

'She's so lucky!'

'Look at him. This is so cute!'

'Say yes, Elle!'

Everybody was egging me on. My eyes drifted back from the crowd to Noah, who just looked at me calmly, with a hint of a smirk at how much he was embarrassing me here.

'So? Will you be my girlfriend, Elle Evans?'

I bit my lip, but there was no way I could suppress the beaming smile that took over my face. 'Oh, hell yeah.'

He chuckled quietly, but that was the only sound I heard – none of the cheering or whooping or whistles or catcalls or 'aw' noises. Just his chuckle.

Noah tossed the microphone to someone, who handed it back along the crowd to the stage, but I wasn't paying attention. The music switched to a slow song, and couples soon started dancing again. Whoever was manning the spotlight shut it off.

Noah pulled me into his arms, and I hooked my hands around his neck.

'That was cute,' I said, knowing he'd hate being linked to the word 'cute'.

He promptly grimaced. 'Ugh. Please don't call me cute.'

'I'm sorry. I meant sexy. Very macho.'

He smirked at that. 'I just made a fool of myself for you, Shelly. I hope you know that.'

'Oh, yeah, I know,' I laughed. 'You really didn't have to, though.'

'I know, but I wanted to. I told you I'm going to do things right this time. And I've got a lot to make up for.' He twirled me around, making me laugh giddily, then pulled me in even closer than before. My skin was tingling where we touched and I could have stayed like that in his arms for hours.

'And anyway, now that we're, you know, official, I

can tell you something without sounding like a complete fool.'

'Oh?'

My heart raced wildly and he leaned in close to whisper in my ear.

Don't say it don't say it don't say it

Say it say it say it.

Don't say it don't say it don't—

'I really like you, Shelly.'

Something washed over me – relief, I'm sure. Not disappointment. Definitely not disappointment.

I smiled at him. 'I like you too.'

He leaned forward slowly to kiss me. It wasn't the heated kiss we usually shared. Nothing close. But even though it was a soft, intimate kiss, it still had all the fireworks and the intensity.

I pulled away first. 'Noah . . . everyone's staring,' I mumbled, my face burning.

'So?'

I bit the insides of my cheeks. 'It's . . . weird. Plus, some of these girls might burn a hole in my head the way they're looking at me.'

'Tell me about it. Some of the guys look ready to rip my head off.'

'What?'

He looked at me like I was stupid. 'I'm here with the

333

most gorgeous girl there is. Don't you think they're just a little bit jealous?'

I blushed all over again. 'I don't know . . .'

'Seriously, Elle, trust me on this. You're beautiful.'

A smile spread over my face along with a blush this time. I would never, ever have imagined Noah Flynn using the word 'beautiful' to describe a girl. It sounded so strange coming out of his mouth, but in a good way – the best way.

'I made you blush . . .' he teased in a sing-song voice, his lips brushing over my cheek.

I swatted his back. 'Shut up. At least I don't wear Superman underwear.'

'Ha-ha,' he said sarcastically. 'Come on.'

He grabbed my arm and pulled me out of the ball-room into the lobby, and then into a small alcove with a large potted fern. He pulled me behind the fern and pinned me to the wall, a hand on either side of my head.

'I have been waiting all night to do this,' he whispered, and his lips came down onto mine.

When we finally went back in, Noah was immediately swept away by a couple of the jocks to grab a drink with them – and the girls had me surrounded.

'Oh my God, Elle! Why didn't you tell us?'

'How long has this been going on, anyway? You should've said something!'

'Ooh, you're so lucky, Elle! I can't believe it. Flynn has an actual girlfriend?'

'You have to tell us everything!' Jaime shrieked, gripping both my wrists and making me sit down at a table. 'When did this all start, then?'

'Uh . . . It's complicated . . .'

'What, were you dating before, or something?'

'No, but . . .'

'Ugh, you're, like, the luckiest girl ever, you know that? Do you know how jealous we all are of you? I mean . . . it's *Flynn*!'

'Hey . . . so, Elle,' said Dixon, suddenly appearing and planting a hand on my shoulder. 'The guys are wondering . . . just how long have you been off the market?'

I laughed, blushing. 'Why?'

'They want to work out how badly Flynn might beat them up for talking about you.'

I laughed again. 'Uh, since this evening.' *Officially*, I added silently.

'I see . . . So nobody's in too much danger of broken arms,' he laughed. 'Well, you know . . . congrats. I think that's appropriate. Who'd have thought it?'

'Tell me about it . . .'

'Hey, Elle!' I looked over and saw Rachel pushing her way to my side. I smiled, sighing in relief. I stood up, brutally ignoring the girls wanting to talk to me about Noah, and grabbed her arm, dragging her away.

'So you guys worked things out?' she said.

I nodded. 'It looks like it. But—'

'Oh no, oh no, no, no,' she said frantically. 'There's a "but". This does not bode well.'

'It's not a bad but! It's just a . . . I-don't-know-how-this-is-gonna-end-up but.'

She nodded slowly. 'I see . . .'

'What?' I asked. 'What is it?'

'It's . . . well, are you sure this is really the right thing? I know you like him and stuff, but still. Everyone knows what he's like . . .'

I shrugged. 'I know, but . . . I really don't care any more.'

She looked at me a long moment, then something clicked and she nodded like she understood.

When the band announced that they'd start slowing things down after the next song, Rachel got a distracted look on her face. 'Well, whatever floats your boat, Elle. I totally get it. Listen, I have to head off . . .'

'Lee?'

'Yeah,' she laughed guiltily. 'Yeah. Sorry.'

'Go ahead, Rach. I've got to find Noah anyway.'

'Right. Find Noah.' She winked elaborately before hurrying off.

Someone grabbed my arm in a strong grip I recognized instantly, and tugged me out onto the dance floor before I could protest.

'You didn't give me the first dance,' Noah said, giving me the sweetest smile in the world, 'but I'm sure as hell taking the last.'

He'd got us a room at the Royale for the night too. When I saw it, I realized why he'd disappeared earlier.

I giggled when he tugged me out of the elevator. 'You didn't have to do—'

'I know, I know, but I've told you a billion times tonight. I'm trying to make things up to you, so I am being a stupidly perfect and unrealistic boyfriend just to show you how seriously I'm taking this.'

'Oh, this is you being serious?' I said skeptically.

'Hey, cut me some slack, I'm trying here!'

I laughed. 'Okay, okay, I'm sorry, I'll shut up.'

He laughed too as we stopped outside a room on the seventh floor. He pulled out a key card and swiped open the door.

'After you,' he said, and made a grand sweeping gesture for me to go in first.

I'll be honest: I'd expected to come in and see the

floor scattered with rose petals and candles everywhere, and maybe even the sappy mood music – the kind of scene you see in films, like on Valentine's Day or when the guy's madly in love and about to propose.

Because when Noah had said he was being a 'stupidly perfect and unrealistic' boyfriend, I'd kind of thought maybe he'd gone all out here – made a huge display to try and impress me.

So when he opened the door and ushered me inside, I was relieved to find there were no candles, no music, no dimmed lighting. Nothing sappy, or cheesy, or romantic. It was just a regular suite, with a plush white lounge, soft white carpets, and an open doorway leading through to what must've been the master bedroom and en-suite bathroom.

It would've been just so artificial if he'd gone all out. This was Noah Flynn – violent and crude and totally unromantic. Even his 'romantic gesture' at the dance wasn't exactly him serenading his love to me. It was typical Noah – and I'd loved it.

'So much for stupidly perfect and unrealistic,' I said jokingly, turning around to smile as he shut the door behind us.

'Oh, believe me, you haven't even seen that yet. Come on.'

He grabbed my hand, tugging me into the bedroom.

Now *this* – this *was* stupidly perfect and unrealistic. Well, almost. It was close enough for Noah's standards.

'Now you know where I disappeared to earlier,' he said. 'Do you have any idea how long it takes to spell things out with petals? It's impossible. I gave up in the end. I was going to write "sorry", but . . .'

'I can see,' I laughed.

Deep red flower petals were scattered over the bed and the floor.

I went up on my toes to kiss his cheek. 'You didn't have to do that.'

'Yeah, I know. But I'm trying, right? I told you I was going to try. And I know how much of a romantic you are at heart.'

I smiled sheepishly.

'I am kind of surprised you gave me another chance so easily, though,' he said, pulling me down onto the bed and taking me in his arms. 'I was expecting you to put up more of a fight.'

'Are you asking for another argument, Noah?' I asked.

He tugged at my hair playfully. 'No, I'm just saying. I'm not complaining. There is a difference.'

'Barely.'

He chuckled, and I felt it reverberating through his chest. He kissed me softly. I was about to return the gesture, but at that moment my cell phone decided to ring.

I felt more than heard Noah sigh, and he took his arms away almost grudgingly as I pushed myself up to go find my purse.

I sighed when I saw the caller ID, wandering into the bathroom with my purse, my cell already at my ear. *May as well check my make-up if I'm stepping out for a moment*, I thought.

'Hi, Dad,' I said, hoping my irritation at being interrupted didn't show in my voice too much. I leaned toward the mirror to clean up a little smudged eyeliner.

'How was the dance?'

'Good.'

He cleared his throat. 'Did you figure out what you're going to do about him?'

I bit the insides of my cheeks before answering. 'Yeah. Yeah, I made up my mind.'

Dad sighed. 'You're going to stay with him, aren't you.' It was more of a statement than a question; he already knew.

'Yeah,' I admitted quietly. 'I have to go now. I'll see you tomorrow, okay?'

'All right.'

I took a few breaths just to calm myself down. I turned my cell off so we wouldn't have any more interruptions. Then I dabbed on a little lip balm and fluffed my hair out before I went back into the bedroom.

Noah was lounging on the bed, his arms behind his head and one leg slightly bent. It wasn't a pose, really, but right then he looked like a male model. He had his eyes half closed, totally relaxed. I didn't think he'd noticed me come back.

I looked him up and down. He was so handsome, with his tousled dark hair and the tux – even his crooked nose. He was tall enough to make me feel dainty. And I loved his eyes, so bright and blue and piercing – and now they were wide open, looking me up and down in such a way that I blushed.

'Beautiful as you look tonight in that dress, Elle, I have to say I prefer you without it.'

'Oh really? And what makes you think that's going to happen?'

He smirked. 'I don't think it'll be a problem.'

I smiled flirtatiously back at him as he swung himself up off the bed and strolled toward me. I raised an eyebrow, wondering exactly what his plan was.

But he suddenly stopped short of me. 'Come here,' he said in a surprisingly soft voice, then pulled me into his arms and walked backward until he was sitting on the bed, with me on his lap. When he wrapped his arms around me tight, I snaked mine around his shoulders. It was such a tender, intimate moment.

'We don't have to do anything, you know. If you want to take things slow now, just say the word. I didn't get this room for that. I just wanted to be alone with you – even if you choose to go home later.'

I was stunned – here I was, certain the one reason he'd booked us this suite was so we could have sex, and now he was saying he wouldn't rush me if I didn't want to. Flynn, giving up sex for me.

Jeez.

First he got down on one knee to ask me to the dance, then the whole song dedication, then the petals on the bed – now this?

Man. He really *had* changed.

'I heard you saying to Lee earlier you thought we'd rushed into it before,' he said then. 'And we're doing it right this time, so I thought . . .'

I did say that to Lee, because I could be brutally honest with him now and not feel so judged. I hadn't even imagined Noah might've been there to hear though . . . Lately I had been worrying that we'd rushed into it, that I hadn't been thinking straight, too caught up in the thrill of sneaking around.

This was how my first time *should've* been, I thought, looking at the suite, the flower petals; Noah . . .

I shook my head against his. 'No, I want to.'

If this was a cheesy romance, now would be the time for us to say *I love you*.

As it was, he mumbled something I didn't catch, and kissed me full on the lips, making me melt in his arms. He helped me pull off his jacket, and while I worked on his shirt buttons, he yanked at his tie, pulling away from me just long enough to tug it over his head.

I giggled helplessly when, in his haste, he managed to get the tie stuck in his mouth.

'Don't even,' he threatened, a mouthful of tie muffling his words. I giggled even more, but he soon shut me up by kissing me. At that point I let myself stop thinking completely. There was no conscious thought behind any of my actions. Tonight was just . . . just *us*.

Chapter 25

Blinking my eyes open, I yawned and rolled over, and found myself nose-to-nose with Noah. His lips were slightly parted, and his eyelashes looked unusually long lying against his cheek like that. He looked so peaceful, so innocent.

I wriggled in closer to him, and watched him sleep. I'd always wondered why people in relationships did that – why they just stared at someone who wasn't even doing anything. But now I understood. It was like seeing them in their most vulnerable state.

After a while, though, when he still hadn't moved and I was too wide awake to even think about going back to sleep, I decided to wake him up.

'Noah,' I said softly, close to his ear. 'Noah . . . Wake up . . .'

He grumbled incoherently, and put an arm around me, pulling me in closer, but he didn't open his eyes.

'Noah,' I said again.

No response.

I leaned forward and pressed my lips gently against his, and then he rubbed his eyes and ran his hands through his hair.

'If that's how you're going to wake me up, I wouldn't mind spending the night with you more often,' Noah told me with a gleam in his eyes.

'Ha-ha,' I replied sarcastically, but I was smiling. I brushed some hair out of my face. 'Good morning.'

He kissed the tip of my nose. 'Good morning to you too.' He stretched, and then tugged me back against him. Our legs wrapped together.

Immediately, I jerked my right leg away from him. 'What?'

'Your feet are really cold,' I explained, and he laughed, rolling his eyes. Slowly, I eased my leg back to where it had been a moment ago, avoiding Noah's feet.

We didn't get up for at least an hour; we stayed wrapped around each other in bed, speaking in soft voices and exchanging kisses.

I couldn't have been happier.

I got Noah to drop me at my house. I'd stop by to see Lee later. I was desperate to know if he'd finally said 'I love you' to Rachel (because even if *he* didn't realize yet, I knew he was in love).

But he still wasn't entirely comfortable with me and his big brother being together. And showing up with the remnants of last night's make-up and my crinkled dress on would just be rubbing his face in it.

I would much rather face my father's disapproving sigh at how I'd spent my night than face Lee looking like this.

'Elle?' Dad called out as I shut the door as silently as possible behind me.

I sighed. I'd have been a terrible rebellious child. I couldn't sneak in or out of the house if my life depended on it. So I called back, 'Yeah, it's me!'

'How was the dance?' he asked, and with a sigh I smoothed my dress out and went into the lounge. Brad was hanging upside down, his feet up on the top of the couch, his head brushing the floor. He glanced over from the Nintendo and went back to playing his game.

'The dance was great,' I answered. 'Except there was a bit of drama involving nuts in the vegetarian dish, and one of the guys is allergic to nuts . . .'

'Boring,' Brad said loudly in a sing-song voice, irritating me as only a little brother could.

'Did you go to the after-party?' my dad asked.

'No . . .' I said cautiously. 'We, um – Noah booked us a room for the night . . .' My voice faded into a mumble before trailing off completely.

'Is that so.' My dad's words swelled with disapproval.

'Nothing happened,' I said quickly, not able to keep my cheeks from burning. Talk about embarrassing . . .

It was Brad who spoke: *'Noah and Elle, sitting in a tree, doing things they shouldn't be . . .'* he sang mockingly.

'Whatever,' was my witty comeback, mimicking his voice. He scowled over the top of his Nintendo and I poked my tongue out at him.

'Is it too late to take back what I said last night about my little girl being so grown up, Elle?' Dad laughed, shaking his head at us. I gave him a sheepish smile. 'So you had a good time at the dance.'

'Yup. And you know what Noah did? He actually got the band to dedicate a song to me so he could ask me to be his girlfriend in front of everybody. That's how serious he is about this. About me,' I amended.

'Aw, is ickle Ellie-belly in *luuurve*?' Brad said in a soppy voice, making kissing sounds and pulling faces at me.

'No!' I said quickly. 'No! Most definitely not.'

Dad could only look at me like he was torn between acceptance and disappointment. I was starting to shrug it off when the doorbell rang.

'I'll get it,' I said quickly, shooting up to open the door.

'I heard on the grapevine that you were back,' Lee said, leaning on the porch fence and grinning at me. The smile went out of his eyes for a moment when he saw me – it was blatantly clear what I'd been up to last night – but he recovered quickly.

'Plus I had to get out of the house,' he went on. 'My parents are going crazy at Noah.'

'Why?'

'Well, for starters, he's been, quote, "God knows where doing God knows what this past week," and he's – again I quote – "going to get kicked out of college before he's even started if he keeps acting as stupid and reckless as this".'

I sighed, and ran a hand through my hair. Lee added, 'It'll blow over. But I'd rather not be around.'

'How was the after-party?'

'You missed some serious shit,' he told me gravely, then cracked another huge smile. 'It was freaking hilarious. Warren got wasted and was doing some major karaoke, complete with dancing and telling everyone he loved them. Funniest thing *ever*. No fights or anything though.'

'That's because there was no Noah,' I said.

He laughed. 'True, true . . .' He cleared his throat. 'Um, I'd ask how your night went and tease you to "tell me every single detail, *girlfriend*"' – he put on a falsetto voice and pretended to flip his hair – 'but I don't really want to know all about you doing the nasty with my brother.'

I smiled. 'I didn't think you'd want to know, to be honest. But on that note, my chum, did you and Rachel . . . ?'

'No, we did not,' he said, rather proudly, sticking his chin out.

'Really? I thought you guys would've by now.'

'So did I . . .' He shrugged. 'But she said she wasn't ready, so, I don't know, we'll just wait till she is.'

'Aw!' I cooed. I tweaked his nose. 'You're whipped, my friend.'

Lee didn't even argue. He just rolled his eyes at me. And he blushed under all his freckles. I giggled, but not in a mean way.

'Does Rachel know how whipped you are?'

'Well, uh . . .'

'Oh my God! You said it, didn't you? You totally did! *You said you loved her!* When did you say it? Was it when you were slow dancing? Were you under the stars at the after-party?'

Lee laughed, putting his hands firmly on my shoulders. 'Calm down, Miss Romantic. If you give me the chance, I'll tell you how it happened.' I mimed zipping my lips shut. 'When we were slow dancing, I just kind of blurted it out really quietly. She didn't hear and said, "What?" so I had to say it louder, but she still didn't get it, so I had to say it really loud, and then a few people looked over and she started blushing like crazy . . .' He smiled and laughed. 'It was really cute actually, 'cause then she said it back with this bright red blush – honestly, she was like a beetroot, and—'

I smacked his arm. 'That's so mean!'

'It's not mean, it was cute, I *said* it was cute! And stop interrupting! Anyway. She said it back, looking like a really *cute* beetroot,' he said pointedly, 'and I said, "What? I can't hear you," so she had to say it really loud too.'

I smiled. 'Aw, that *is* cute.'

'You're rubbing off on me,' he said, pushing my shoulder. 'I'm turning all mushy, hanging around with you all these years.'

'Did you kiss her then? After you guys said it?'

'Duh.'

'Aw . . .'

'Are you going to stand here gushing and cooing all day or are we going to watch some *Judge Judy*? After you take a shower, of course. Your mascara is all smudged.' He poked me under the eyes and then all but skipped past me into the house.

All I could do was laugh and shake my head as Lee

350

made himself at home talking to Brad and my dad while I headed upstairs to clean up and change.

There was something nagging at my mind though: my stupid little brother teasing me about – about being in . . . in love with Noah . . .

I couldn't be.

I mean, I knew at the start it wasn't . . . well, it wasn't anything serious until last night, officially. And even before last night, I couldn't be . . . I wasn't . . .

Was I?

Chapter 26

Lee and I were lounging in my back garden; the sun was shining and the weather was too nice to stay inside. We generally spent days like this relaxing around Lee's pool. His garden was nicer than mine too: we had one of those swinging chairs with a canopy, but it was so old it creaked whenever it moved. And half the grass had died – Dad had been too busy lately to fix it up, and too stubborn to hire a gardener.

I had suggested we go to Lee's, pointing out that the pool would be great right now. But Lee had wanted to wait a bit.

'Shelly, my dad said he'd text me when it was safe to go back. Meaning when either Noah's stormed off or they're done arguing and telling him off for everything. And I haven't heard anything yet.'

'Was it really that bad?'

'Trust me, you don't even want to know.'

Just then, his cell phone rang and he fished it out of

his pocket. He frowned and didn't answer straight away, as I'd expected.

'Who is it?' I asked, getting up to see the screen.

'Noah,' he muttered as I saw the caller ID. 'What the hell does he want?'

'Here's a thought: answer it and find out.'

He gave me a mock glare and clicked to answer. 'What?'

I heard Noah's voice on the other end, sounding equally unhappy, but I couldn't make out what he was saying.

'Sure,' Lee said, then handed the phone to me. 'Your cell's still off. He wants to talk to you.'

'Oh.' I took the phone, and found I was smiling, even at the prospect of talking to him over the phone. And he hadn't even said anything yet. What was up with me lately? 'Hi.'

But I knew exactly why that was. It was the same reason I'd said I'd go to the dance with him – however much I tried to find a reason to prove otherwise.

'I've been trying to get hold of you for ages.'

' "Ages" being how long exactly?'

'Um, the last four minutes? I tried you *twice*.'

I laughed. 'Oh yeah, that's really "ages", Mr Impatient. What did you want, anyway?'

'Listen, Elle . . .' Noah sounded kind of weird, like

he was finding it hard to speak. I could imagine him tugging at his hair, rubbing a hand over his cheek. I frowned a little, wondering what was up.

Then he said it. Those fatal words.

I knew I should have stopped things with Noah a long time ago – hell, I shouldn't have even started. But it was too late now. I knew I was in too deep, because the next words he said made me stop breathing for a moment.

He sighed into the phone. 'We need to talk.'

We were going to meet at the Starbucks on the edge of town. That was all I got out of the conversation. I hadn't been able to say a word other than stammering out, 'Okay.'

'What's up?' Lee asked me, looking concerned. 'You look really freaked out.'

'I – he – we're . . . Starbucks . . .'

'What? Shelly, take a breath then tell me what he said. But first of all – are you okay?'

I nodded, then shook my head. 'Well . . . I – I don't know. He . . . we . . .' I took a breath. 'He said that *we need to talk*.'

Lee winced, sucking in a breath. 'Ouch. But – wait, are you serious? Are you *sure* that's what he said?'

I nodded. 'We're meeting at Starbucks at eight o'clock.'

'That's in, like, an hour.'

I nodded. 'I have to go get ready . . .' Numbly, my legs feeling wooden, I went up to my room, feeling in that dream-like, dazed state. Dad was busy working in the lounge, and Brad had gone to the local park with some of his friends. Lee jogged up the stairs after me.

'Hold on, what do you think is going on?'

'He's breaking up with me, isn't he? I mean, we only just started going out officially . . . and now he's going to end it, right? That's what people say when they want to break up. They say, "We need to talk," and then they say, "It's not you, it's me," and—'

Lee snapped his fingers right in front of my face, making me jump since I hadn't expected it. 'Calm down.'

'Sorry . . .'

'Look, maybe he just . . . wants to talk. Maybe he's not going to break up with you. I don't see why he would.'

'But – but then he'd have told me, wouldn't he? He'd have said, "Don't worry, we're not breaking up." Oh, God, what do you wear for someone to break up with you?'

I started rifling through my closet and drawers, looking for something to wear. I was serious – should I wear something really cute and make him think twice about dumping me? Should I wear what I already had on – my old denim shorts and purple tank top – so it looked like I didn't care that he was breaking up with me?

I decided not to get changed but to put on a bit of make-up.

'Elle, chill – he probably doesn't want to break up. He's crazy if he does.'

'Thanks, Lee, that's really reassuring.' I picked up my eyeliner, but my hand was shaking too much, so instead, I threw myself down on my bed, covered my face with my hands, and gave a cry of frustration.

I knew I'd gotten too close to Noah. I just hadn't wanted to believe it. I'd thought that by telling myself it wasn't possible, that would make it true. That by telling myself I wasn't getting in too deep, it would mean I hadn't . . . hadn't fallen for . . .

I wondered just how long I'd felt this way about him. Now – now, when I finally realized, he was about to break up with me.

Even Brad had known before I did. And Lee . . . he knew. That's why he kept giving me those weird looks. My dad and Rachel had guessed it too; those looks on their faces made sense now. Was I really the last one to realize how I felt?

I'd known, though, deep down; I was just too scared to admit it to myself.

Logic told me he definitely didn't reciprocate; he was about to break up with me. *We need to talk.* . . I gnawed on my lip.

I felt Lee's hand on my knee; when I opened my eyes, he was leaning right over me, his nose an inch from mine, his big blue eyes staring straight into mine. I stared right back.

'Lee . . .'

'Mm?'

'We have a problem.'

'Mm?'

'I think . . .' I gulped, looking him right in the eyes. 'I think I might have fallen for him.'

'At *last*. Jeez, I would've thought that was obvious when you agreed to go to the dance with him. No one in their right mind would've agreed. I was waiting for you to tell me when you'd said he was your date to the dance.'

'Wait – you knew, and you didn't tell me?'

'I thought you had to figure it out for yourself . . . Okay, okay,' he admitted, seeing my skeptical look. 'I thought you wouldn't admit it.'

'How did you know before I did?' I said stupidly.

'I'm your other half. The Ashley to your Mary Kate, the Thing One to your Thing Two,' he added with a smirk.

357

'Lee, what am I going to do? He's going to break up with me . . .'

Lee shrugged. 'I don't know what to tell you, Shelly. Except that it'll be okay. And you know why? Because you've got me. I told you – whatever happens, I'm here for you. Whether you get heartbroken or – or pregnant, or what.'

I smiled. 'Well, so long as I've got you . . .'

He laughed. 'Consolation prize, eh?'

'Don't be silly. You're not the consolation prize. You're my best friend.'

He gave me a small, sad smile. 'But I'm not as important to you as he is. I can't compete with the guy you're in love with. Whether he's my brother or not.'

'Lee, don't be stupid. You will always, always, always be the biggest man in my life. Except for my dad. But you're pretty close.' I smiled. 'Noah or no Noah. No guy is ever going to come between us. Ever. Got that?'

'No girl, either,' he told me. 'Best buds.'

'We'll grow old together and everything.'

'Can't imagine playing knock-knock-ginger without you in your wheelchair beside me trying to whiz away at high speed.'

I laughed, and gave him a big hug. He squeezed me back tight enough to force all the air out of me.

'You're really worried about losing me, huh?' I teased.

'Was I that obvious?'

'I don't want to lose you either.'

He grinned and winked at me. 'Hey, you ever wonder if things would've worked out if we'd . . . you know, ever got together?'

I raised my eyebrows slightly.

'I'm not suggesting we should've tried it!' he added quickly. 'I'm just saying.'

'Everyone expected us to end up together.'

'God only knows why. Too many chick flicks and cheesy novels, I say.'

I laughed. 'We would've sucked as a couple.'

'Damn straight. Would've messed us up royally.'

I laughed in agreement. I don't know how I would've handled it if Lee had told me he loved me romantically. We would only ever be best friends. 'Besides, you're all loved up with Rachel.'

'And you are with Noah.'

'For now at least . . . Thanks for reminding me.'

'Damn. I was doing a pretty good job of keeping your mind off it, wasn't I?'

'You were, with your big sappy moment there. Now move – you're blocking my light and I need to do my make-up.'

He laughed, shifting to let me get to my dresser. At least my hand wasn't shaking now so I could actually do my eyeliner without stabbing myself in the eye.

'Do you want a ride? You kind of need to be leaving soon, if you don't want to hit traffic . . .'

'Yes, please,' I said, shoving a couple of five-dollar bills into my pocket. Lee eventually found his car keys in his pocket after hunting through gum wrappers and dimes.

'All right, let's go get heartbroken,' I said with a wry smile.

He smacked my back – a little too hard. Almost like he thought it'd knock some sense into me. I stumbled forward and had to grab the banister to stop myself from crashing down the rest of the stairs.

'Calm down. It'll be fine.'

Funny thing was, though, I didn't really believe him.

We got to Starbucks soon after eight, since there was a little traffic. I could see Noah's bike parked outside. I made a mental note to call Lee to come pick me up before accepting a ride back from Noah – if he even offered . . .

'Just send me a text if you want me to come get you, okay?' Lee told me softly as we walked up to the door. I nodded and went inside, my eyes raking the room nervously. I saw a hand go up: Noah was at a table toward the back, tucked in by the window.

Lee squeezed my arm. 'You'll be fine, Shelly. Besides . . . he doesn't deserve you.'

I laughed, but it sounded forced. 'I'll talk to you later, Lee.'

He gave me a military salute and I turned to face Noah, walking over with my chin held high.

He looked even more handsome than usual. Maybe it was because I realized how I felt about him, or maybe it was because I was on the verge of being dumped by him. His hair was windswept, and he was wearing dark-wash jeans and a plain white T-shirt, his beaten old leather jacket on top. He actually stood up when I reached him, which surprised me.

I could almost hear Lee saying, 'Ooh, look who turned Noah into a gentleman!' with a nudge in the ribs.

'Hey,' Noah said, sounding a little flustered and breathless. 'Uh, sit down.'

So I sat down. We both started speaking at the same moment, then stopped, then started again.

'You go first,' we said unanimously. He cracked a half-smile, half-smirk, and I let out a breath of laughter.

Then a waiter bustled up, some guy in his midtwenties looking like he was on a caffeine buzz to keep him going through another shift. 'What can I get you guys?'

'Uh . . .' Were we even staying that long? Or was Noah just going to cut me loose and ride off on his two-wheel death-trap?

'I'll have a regular coffee,' he told the guy. Then he pointed a finger at me and said, 'And she'll have a half-fat latte with whipped cream on top.'

The guy scribbled on his pad, nodding away, and said, 'Great. I'll get those for you right away.'

Once he was gone, all I could say was, 'How do you know my coffee order?'

'You had one before. It was a weird order – I guess that's why I remembered it.'

'Oh.' I was shocked – but shocked in a good way. This guy couldn't be about to break up with me, could he?

I so, so badly wanted to believe Lee had been right; that his brother really was whipped. But . . .

But.

There was always a 'but'.

I didn't say anything, and neither did Noah. We just waited silently until our coffees came, and then he just took a sip and leaned back in his chair, one leg crossed up on his knee, an arm slung over the back of the chair.

I didn't bother sipping my latte yet; it would only

scald my tongue. I wasn't willing to burn all my taste buds off my tongue, even if there was an awkward silence.

Then, at last, he decided to speak. 'Look, we need to talk.'

'Are you breaking up with me?' I blurted, unable to hold the question in any longer.

He sighed, and my heart dropped away. I felt deflated, seeing the look on his face.

'Listen, Elle, I want you to hear me out, okay?'

I nodded – what else could I do?

'I've been offered a place at Harvard. On the Computer Science course there.'

'Harvard . . . like, Harvard in Massachusetts?'

He nodded. 'Yeah.'

'That's great – congratulations.' Except my voice didn't have the right amount of enthusiasm in it. I tried again. 'That's fantastic, Noah.'

'I know. But . . .'

There it was again. That horrible, horrible word.

Only this time, a part of me liked hearing it.

'Whoa, wait, no buts. You can't *not* go to Harvard.'

'It's in Massachusetts. On the other side of the country, Elle. I got into the University of California in San Diego. It's not that far away, even, and they have a good engineering course—'

'Noah, why would you even consider giving up Harvard? You can't do that.'

'I don't know,' he sighed. He sounded so confused and helpless. 'My parents want me to go, but I don't know if it's just because they want to ship me off so they haven't got to deal with me anymore. I've accepted the offer, but I don't know if it's the right thing to do.'

'I'm sure your parents are just happy for you. It's amazing. It's a great opportunity. Of course they want you to go.'

'They were so mad at me,' he said with a small humorless laugh, watching his finger run around the rim of his mug. 'Especially over everything with you . . . They just want me gone.'

'They don't want you gone. They're only worried about you.'

'Whatever,' he said, sounding so defeated I didn't even bother trying to argue.

I ran my index finger around the side of my mug and looked down at the steam rising from my latte, and said, 'I'm happy for you.'

He reached over and cupped my face in his hand, gently brushing his thumb over my cheek. My heart skipped a beat. 'There's this whole thing with you now, and I don't know what I want to do.'

I gulped. He wasn't going to say it. Lee was wrong. I was just fooling myself. I was ridiculous to think he'd ever, ever say that to me.

He looked into my eyes for the longest moment, then leaned over and kissed me incredibly softly, sending shivers up and down my spine.

His lips lingered on mine for a long, long time; then he sat back in his chair. I couldn't quite make out his expression, but there was a deep line creasing his forehead.

'Elle, I know I – I was a complete asshole, and I said I'd try and make things up to you, but . . . thing is, I just . . .' He sighed, ran a hand back and forth through his hair, making it stick up at all kinds of angles. 'Elle, I'm going to be going to college in the fall, and I don't know how things are going to work out and I don't want to lose you. I don't want to break up with you, but—'

'Noah,' I tried interrupting.

Then he said, 'No, forget it. It can wait. Look, finish your coffee and we'll get going. I want to take you someplace.'

'Where?'

'I can't tell you, that'd ruin the surprise. But you're going to like it, trust me. It's not far away but we need to go soon if we're to get there in time.'

I wanted to ask, 'Get where?' but I knew he

wouldn't tell me so I stayed silent, sipping my coffee. Noah pretty much downed his, and I wondered at how it didn't burn his throat.

When I put my mug back down, Noah chuckled.

'What?'

He reached over and brushed his finger over the tip of my nose before wiping it with a napkin. 'You had some cream on it.' My cheeks flamed, but he laughed. 'It was cute. Now come on . . .'

'Okay, okay!' I laughed. 'Why are you so impatient today?'

Then I realized something: 'Oh, God, no, I'm not going *anywhere* with you.'

'What? Why not?'

'You have your bike. I saw it outside. I'm not going on that thing ever again. Once was bad enough.'

'Aw, come on, everyone deserves a second chance. You gave *me* one. Don't hate the bike.'

I laughed, momentarily forgetting the nausea and worry of potentially losing Noah. Besides, right now, I felt a lot more confident. I honestly didn't think he was breaking up with me; he'd even said he didn't want to lose me.

'I'm sorry, I can't do it. I can't get on that thing, it's horrible.'

'But you can snuggle up to me,' he said teasingly.

'Come on, it's seriously not half as bad as you make out.'

'It's awful,' I told him sternly. 'I'm sorry, I can't do it. I cannot get on that bike with you.'

'Well, you don't have a choice. I'm taking you to this place even if I have to tie you up.'

I frowned.

'I'm kidding. But it'll be worth it, I promise.'

'No.'

He leaned over and gave me a quick peck on the lips. 'Please? I swear, it'll be completely worth it. I'll be your slave for life if you don't like it.'

How could I say no to that face?

So I said, with a suspicious frown, 'For life?'

'Yup.'

'Okay, okay, but just this once. And you owe me – big time. Even if I *do* like it.'

'Whatever you say, Shelly. But you're going to love it. And the bike won't be half bad either.'

'I highly doubt that. I hate you sometimes, Noah Flynn.'

Chapter 27

He put the helmet on for me, clipping it in place. I had a sense of déjà vu of when I'd first ridden the bike, and smiled at the memory. Then he swung himself over the motorbike, which looked even more monstrous and intimidating than I remembered, and gave me a hand. I put my arms around his waist cautiously. My palms were sweating. I could hear my heartbeat echoing in my ears.

Wherever we were going, it had better be worth it.

Was it too late to back out? Tell him we'd go another time?

'Noah, I changed my mind, I really don't—'

He revved the engine, the bike roaring to life all of a sudden. I jumped, let out a little squeak, and held on as tight as I could. I felt his body rumble with a chuckle, and before I could tell him again I'd changed my mind, he sped off down the street.

I didn't even open my eyes.

The wind slapped my bare arms and legs; I knew I'd have goosebumps all over when we got off. At least my hair was all tucked inside the helmet so it wouldn't be a total mess when I took it off.

But I didn't want to look at everything blurring past. I heard a horn blare, most likely at us, but I still kept my eyes squeezed tight shut and clung to Noah.

I hate this I hate this I hate this.

I love him I love him I love him.

I hardly even noticed when we stopped. Everything suddenly went silent, and it was only when Noah unhooked my arms from around him that I dared to open my eyes.

We were at the bottom of a hill by a park outside of town. I used to come to the park in the summer with Lee, since they had a public pool here that was open in the summer; it made a nice change of scenery from his back yard.

Noah got off the bike first, and then pulled my helmet off gently. I just glared at him, and he chuckled.

'It wasn't that bad – come on, admit it,' he said, smoothing down my flyaway hair.

'I think I might throw up.' I wasn't even exaggerating – much.

He laughed again, steadying me as I climbed off the damn thing. My legs felt like Jell-O and almost gave way beneath me. Linking his fingers through mine, Noah opened up the seat of the bike, taking out a big blanket, the kind you'd have for a picnic. He tossed it over his shoulder and spoke before I could ask what the blanket was for.

Surely – surely, I thought, we weren't on the verge of a break-up. It didn't make sense.

'Come on. We don't want to be late.'

'Where are we going?' I asked.

He was already walking up the hill, towing me along too.

'Noah! Where are we going?'

'Now who's the impatient one?' he laughed, squeezing my hand.

It didn't take us long to reach the top. And when we did, he let go of my hand and spread the blanket out on the grass underneath a big oak tree that leaned over at an angle, its branches hanging down low enough that the leaves grazed the top of my head.

He sat on the blanket, patting the space next to him. 'Come on, then.'

Frowning a little in confusion, I slowly sat down next to him.

Then I saw what we'd come for.

This place overlooked half the city, and you could see the beaches and the ocean. The view of the city alone was pretty astounding, with its twinkling lights. But with the sunset, the sky was stained red, and the thin bands of cloud were pink and silver. It was beautiful. The sunset reflected in the sea too, turning the dark blue water red and yellow and pink. It was breathtaking: the sun looked so big, dipping down behind the skyline of the city. It was quiet, too – there was no noise from the city, or from the surf on the beach. Just the breeze rustling the leaves over our heads.

'Wow,' I breathed. There really wasn't any other word for it – just *wow*.

'I know. Told you you'd like it.' Noah bumped my shoulder, and when I tore my eyes away from the landscape to look at him, he was smiling at me, one of his real smiles that showed his dimple and made his eyes light up even more.

'It's amazing,' I said quietly.

'Yeah, you are,' Noah murmured.

I was silent for a second before I laughed. 'You're so cheesy.'

'You love it really,' he teased, bumping my shoulder again.

'I can't believe you actually brought me here to watch the sunset. It's so . . . so romantic.'

'I told you, Elle, I'm going to do things right this time. And I knew you'd like it. You're just that kind of girl. And it's not even over yet. Give it fifteen, twenty minutes,' he said after checking his watch.

'What happens then?'

He chuckled, avoiding answering, and with his free hand tilted my face to kiss me. It started out as another soft kiss that made my heart melt, but soon enough I had my fingers knotted in his hair, and his hands were on my back, holding me tight.

I don't know how long we stayed like that, but at some point he lay me down and was half on top of me, still kissing me. There were sparks dancing through me like crazy and my head felt ready to explode. I was kissing him like a drowning person, like he was my air; and he was kissing me back in just the same way. It was like this should be a thing of fairy tales, but it wasn't. This was real, and it was all happening to me.

Hell, even the fireworks between us when we kissed seemed real. Like they were exploding right over my head—

I broke the kiss, and Noah sat up slightly, both of us looking out at the view. The sky was darker now – not pitch black or even inky blue, but it was still dark enough. The glittering rainbows of fireworks were just disappearing, fading away.

Another few went up, exploding and whistling, then

bursting out into a pattern of green and gold, and blue and pink.

'Oh my gosh,' I breathed.

'There's a display down on the beach,' he told me. 'I forget what it was for, but there was some event, and . . . yeah.'

'Wow. First the sunset, now this?' Another few fireworks went off, splashing over the sky in a hypnotic burst of color. 'What's the occasion? For all the cute gestures, I mean . . .'

'Elle. Don't call me cute. Please.'

I rolled my eyes. 'Just answer the question.'

He shrugged. 'I don't know. I just . . . well, I mean . . . Taking you to the dance and stuff like that was me trying to say sorry. But sometimes, saying sorry doesn't really mean a lot. And you deserve a hell of a lot better than that; than me. And man, I hate all this emotional shit, but I'm gonna say it all anyway because you deserve that much.'

He gulped, and I lifted my head off his shoulder to look at him.

'Noah . . .' I whispered, but I don't think he even heard me properly.

'No, just let me say this, Elle.' But he chewed on his lower lip, looking more like a scared little boy than bad-ass Flynn. The next second, his lips crashed down on mine so suddenly and so roughly it knocked the breath out of me. I was too surprised to kiss him back, only recovering when he decided to pull away.

The fireworks were still crackling in the background, throwing colored flashes of light across his face.

'I love you, Elle,' he told me, brushing some hair off my face.

I could only breathe. I couldn't say anything, and my mind went entirely blank for a moment; my heart alternated between doing somersaults and skipping a beat. *Breathe*, I told myself. *Breathe*.

Noah blinked at me. 'Say something, Elle. I just laid everything on the line, dignity included, and you're not saying anything.'

I laughed, and practically tackled him, throwing my arms around his neck and kissing him. He hugged me back, his lips responding and his tongue slipping inside my mouth.

When we broke apart a minute or so later, he just leaned his forehead on mine, those captivating eyes boring into mine. A bright purple firework exploded across the sky behind him.

'I love you,' I whispered.

He chuckled, and I heard the relief in his voice. 'Well, thank God for that. I thought I'd scared you off for a minute.'

I laughed, shaking my head against his. 'Nope. Still here.'

'Good.' He gave me a brief peck on the lips.

Then he wrapped his arms around me, and I rested my head on his shoulder again. The firework display from the beach carried on, lighting up the darkening sky, while I was happy sitting on the top of a hill in Noah's arms.

He said he loved me. He loves me. *He* loves *me. I'm in love with my best friend's older brother . . . and he loves me back.*

He loves me.

'Noah?'

'Yeah?'

'What are we going to do? With you going off to college, I mean.'

He sighed and rested his head on top of mine. His fingers played with the ends of my hair.

'I don't know, Elle. I don't want to leave you either. But . . . it's Harvard, you know? *Harvard.*'

'I know.'

'I love you,' he murmured. 'I don't know what I'm going to do.'

'Do your parents know about us now?' I asked, curious.

He nodded. 'Yeah. I told them once they'd calmed down.' Then he sighed again. 'You should've seen how mad they were at me. Even Lee got out of the house. Remember what they were like to you two after you guys started that food fight in the eighth grade? Imagine that, just a thousand times worse.'

'Mm . . .' I didn't really know what to say. I'd never imagined Noah would tell me all this stuff. Hell, I never would have imagined Noah even *thought* about this stuff.

Don't get me wrong, I know Noah loves his family. He and Lee have always been really close too; when it comes down to it, they've always been there for each other. But I would never have thought he'd be so sensitive about half of this stuff.

'My mom softened up a lot once I told her the lengths I'd gone to, to win your heart back.' He smirked; although he ran a hand over his face, so I let it drop. He didn't want to talk about it anymore, so I changed the topic.

'I'm assuming you're going to be Superman for our party next week? I mean, you've already got the underpants for it . . .' I bit my lip when I saw the look he gave me – but he was clearly embarrassed.

I opened my mouth and he clasped a hand over my lips. 'Don't you dare.'

'What?' I tried to say, but his hand muffled it.

'You were going to say it's cute, I know you were.'

I laughed sheepishly. Actually, I *had* been about to say that ... 'Whatever. So who *are* you going to go as?'

'I think James Bond is a little overdone, don't you?' He tweaked my nose. 'You'll just have to wait and see, Shelly. No – hold up, I have just had a stroke of genius. You should dress as a giant seashell.'

'Oh, yeah, that'd be a fantastic outfit. Totally doable.'

He just smiled rather than smirking. I couldn't keep the sarcastic glare on my face anymore; I grinned back and laughed along with him until we lapsed into silence.

We sat like that, not talking, for a few moments, our thoughts elsewhere, before I spoke again.

I wanted to tell him that he couldn't go to Harvard, and I could see him half waiting for me to say that. But I just couldn't.

'You really want to go, don't you?' I said quietly. I don't know why I bothered asking – I already knew what his answer was.

He leaned forward and hooked his arms around his knees, looking out at the night sky and the last few fireworks.

I sat up too, crossing my legs underneath me and

watching him. His expression was totally unreadable, his face in shadow.

Then, after a while, he nodded. 'Yeah. Yeah, I want to go. I don't want to leave you, though,' he told me quietly, still looking ahead. 'After everything that's happened between us, and . . . I just don't want to leave you, Elle.'

'I don't want you to leave me either,' I admitted, scooting over and holding his forearm with its strong, defined muscles, resting my head on his shoulder again. 'But you'd only regret it if you passed up the opportunity, and we both know it.'

'Yeah, I know.' He slid his arm around me. His hand traced circles on my lower back and I felt my whole body relax at his touch.

'You have to go,' I told him in a whisper.

After a pause, he kissed my temple, and left his lips pressed there as he said, 'I love you.'

'I love you too.' Suddenly, I found myself laughing. 'What happened to the bad-ass player?'

'He fell in love,' he told me simply, planting a kiss on my cheek. 'Talk about a cliché.'

Chapter 28

The next day Lee and I went to the mall to buy each other's birthday presents and pick up the costumes we'd reserved for our party. After grabbing lunch, we split up, and I scoured the mall for things to buy him. In the end, I got him a new wallet, a CD he said he wanted, and the coolest T-shirt I could ever imagine. He'd *love* it.

'I told you so,' Lee said for the billionth time that day when we met back at his car. 'Didn't I tell you he was whipped? Huh? Didn't I?'

I laughed. 'Yes, all right, I get it! You were right.'

He sighed contentedly, slinging his shopping bags into the trunk. 'I will never get sick of hearing you say that, Elle.'

I rolled my eyes and climbed into the car. As he slid into the driver's seat beside me, he said, yet again, 'I still can't believe you're okay with him going to Harvard.'

My smile faded. 'I'm not okay with it, Lee. Like, at all. I don't want him to go. But I can't exactly keep him here – tell him to go to San Diego or something. I can't do that. He has to go. He *wants* to.'

'So are you guys going to try long-distance?'

'Yeah. At least, we think so. For now. I don't know, Lee – we could both change our minds by the end of summer. But we said we'd try.'

'Just remember what I told you, alright? If it doesn't work out, I'm here to pick up the pieces.'

I reached over and squeezed his hand. He squeezed mine back.

I was glad that school was out for the summer. It meant that I didn't have to constantly deal with questions about me and Noah. Of course, the girls called, and I spoke to them, told them the sort of details they wanted to know. I expected to get sick of it, but I didn't – I was happy to talk about Noah. I was happy because I loved him.

Although there was another very pressing matter that everybody was talking about: our costume party.

I was on a three-way call with Karen and Olivia discussing the party.

'If you have to,' I told them, laughing, 'just throw on a dress and call yourself a Bond girl.'

'I may have to do that,' Olivia said. 'I ordered my

costume the other day and it still hasn't been shipped yet.'

'What're you and Lee going as, anyway?' Karen asked. 'I know you told us at some point, but I can't remember. My internet's been playing up all week.'

'Robin,' I told her, smiling.

'Robin as in Batman and Robin?'

'Yup. Lee's Batman.'

'I guessed that much,' Karen laughed.

My cell started to vibrate in my hand, and I pulled it away from my ear to look at it. 'Sorry, guys, I gotta go.'

'Which one is it?' Olivia asked.

'Sorry?'

'Which Flynn brother?' Karen clarified. 'It's got to be one of them.'

I chuckled. 'It's Noah.'

They both chorused, 'Oo-ooh!' down the phone at me, and I laughed before saying goodbye to them. Then I nestled against the pillows on my bed and a smile spread over my face when I heard Noah's voice. We didn't talk about anything in particular, but that didn't matter; as long as I was talking to him, I was happy.

So this is what love does to people, I thought as Noah told me about the football program at Harvard. *It really does turn people into saps.*

Because quite honestly, I couldn't have given a damn

about anything football-related; but Noah sounded so excited, I found myself hanging on his every word, wanting him to tell me more.

Love had turned me into even more of a fool than I already was.

But you know what? I thought, a smile spreading over my face. *I don't even care.*

'Wow,' I said, getting up from my seat. 'I can't actually believe this year's over.'

'Tell me about it. Even weirder, though' – Lee elbowed me and jerked his head toward the platform, where the teachers were clearing the chairs – 'next year, that'll be us graduating.'

'Now that *is* weird.'

'Seems like only yesterday we were just little kids, huh? Going to soccer camp, baseball camp . . . The costume parties . . .'

I laughed. 'Yeah, well, we're kids at heart.' I looked around, peering through the swarm of dark blue robes for the familiar dark hair and crooked nose. Lee and Noah's parents had already gone off to find Noah and congratulate him on graduating.

'I'm just glad he made it here,' their mom had sighed as we'd sat down. 'I thought he'd be expelled before we saw him graduate. And now Harvard next year . . .'

There was no denying the pride in her voice as she said that though.

And I was pleased for him. Really, I was.

But it made my stomach twist a little to think of him leaving. I didn't want to see him go.

It's not fair.

Childish as it was of me to even think it, I couldn't help it. Why did Harvard have to be on the other side of the country? Why did I have to choose *now* to fall in love with him?

'And you kids turning seventeen,' she was still saying. 'Gosh. Seventeen! Just think. Next year you'll be going off to college and . . .'

'Mom,' Lee said before his dad could, 'don't start crying.'

'I'm not!' June protested, but her voice cracked a little.

And now we were standing in the midst of grinning teenagers in their graduation gowns and proud families. I craned my neck, trying to spot Noah. From the corner of my eye, I saw Lee steal a glance behind me, and started turning to look over my shoulder and—

'Boo!'

I jumped out of my skin, practically leaping a foot into the air, and even gave a little scream, which earned me plenty of strange looks from the crowd. Lee just laughed again, his brother chuckling at me too, flashing me one of his rare real grins.

I smacked him across the chest, glaring, my heart still pounding. 'You're so childish, Noah Flynn, I swear to God!' I snapped.

He gave me that infamous smirk of his. 'You should've seen your face.'

'Shut up.'

That just made him laugh harder.

'Hey,' Lee said, 'congratulations. You actually made it.'

Noah laughed. 'Yeah, tell me about it. But you're carrying on the Flynn legacy, you know. Get in as much trouble as possible and narrowly avoid being suspended.'

Lee laughed. 'Sure, I can see that happening.'

Noah shrugged. 'Your choice.' He slung an arm around my shoulders. 'All right, Elle?'

I scowled at him briefly, but that smile that showed his dimple made it impossible to even pretend to stay annoyed at him; I let out a sigh.

'Nothing to say about me actually graduating high school, then?' Noah asked, nudging my hip with his. 'No congratulations? Not even a little one?'

'Depends,' I said teasingly.

'Saving that for tonight, huh?' He waggled his

eyebrows at me and my face flamed at his words; his expression didn't help either. I worried for a moment that Lee must feel awkward about what Noah had just said, and stole a glance at him. But he was giving a melodramatic grimace, complete with gagging noises.

'Ugh, please, stop!' he cried, shaking his head.

So I smiled and said to Noah, 'Congratulations.'

'Thank you.'

'College, now.'

'Yeah . . .'

Silence filled the lapse in conversation quickly, and it wasn't the easy kind of silence. Lee said hastily, 'Got your outfit for tonight then, bro?'

Noah clicked his tongue, raising a finger to point at Lee. 'That is a good point . . . No.'

'You haven't got . . . ? Noah!' I cried in exasperation.

'Hey, I barely remembered to fill up on gas so I could get to the school for graduation,' he defended himself. 'You think I can remember to get clothes for a party?'

'Flynn! Come on, man, they're doing photos!' someone yelled over, before I even had the chance to roll my eyes at him.

'Be there now!' he shouted in reply. He gave me a quick peck on the lips. 'I'll see you tonight, Elle. See ya,' he added to Lee, and then left to go for the photos with the rest of the graduating seniors.

'Ew,' Lee commented. 'Cooties!'

I laughed. 'Shut up . . .'

'Shall we away to the Batmobile, Robin?' He put on a deep, husky voice.

'Let's,' I said, taking his arm. We exchanged a grin before heading to his car, arm in arm, and I couldn't have felt happier: after all the drama that had come from my relationship with Noah, I still had my best friend.

Chapter 29

'Is that you, Elle?' I heard June say when I walked into Lee's house.

'Yeah!'

She came out of the office, and smiled at me. 'I'm just locking away some of the ornaments,' she explained. 'So they don't get destroyed.'

I laughed. 'Good idea. I'm just going to head on upstairs and get ready.'

'Sure thing, hon.'

She and Matthew were going out to some theatre show with my dad tonight – they got a night out, and they were out of the way for the party too. Brad had a soccer tourney tomorrow, and was staying over at a friend's anyway, so Dad was tagging along with Lee's parents.

'Lee said the boys are going to turn up earlier to help move some furniture, by the way.'

'Oh, are they? Cool.'

'Do you want anything to drink?'

'I'll grab something out of the fridge, thanks.' I smiled again as she went into the lounge to get the rest of the ornaments, and grabbed two cans of orange soda from the fridge to take upstairs.

Lee's door was open, and he was hanging upside down off his bed with his earphones in. 'Long time no see.'

'I come bearing drinks.'

'Awesome.' He rolled off the bed and landed in a heap on the floor before scrambling to his feet again to take the can.

'Cam and Dixon are going to drop by at seven to help move the couches and stuff, and set up the speakers.'

'Yeah, your mom said.'

I set down my drink on Lee's desk and pulled my costume out of the bag. I stood up, holding the dress against me, and pulled a face. 'Maybe it'll look all right on . . .' I thought aloud.

There was a slit in the skirt that went too high for my liking, and the top seemed too small in the wrong places. The dress was a flimsy kind of material in metallic shades; the skirt and cape were emerald green, the top of the dress was ruby red. There was a mustard-colored belt to go around my hips.

'Try it on,' Lee said, his voice sounding somewhat hollow.

I looked up, frowning curiously at his voice, and laughed at the Batman mask he wore. He threw the cape over his head like a veil.

'I'm not looking, I swear.'

I laughed. 'You look like an idiot.'

'Sure you're not just looking in the mirror, Shelly?'

'Ha ha ha,' I retorted sarcastically, rolling my eyes. I tugged off my shorts and tank top, and stepped into the dress. Lee came over to zip me up, except that wasn't too easy. It was too tight around my boobs, and I heard a couple of stitches rip as Lee yanked the zip the rest of the way. I fastened the belt around my waist.

'Jeez, did it have a built-in push-up bra?'

'No,' I huffed. It was actually kind of hard to breathe. But the slit was not as high as I'd expected, and the skirt was actually a decent length.

'It doesn't look that bad.'

'You sure?'

'Positive. Besides, there'll be girls there looking like hookers. It'll be fine.'

'You sure?'

He laughed. 'No, I was lying. Seriously, though, there's nothing you can do now. Unless you want to turn up in your underwear and say you're a Playboy model?'

'No, thanks. I think I'll stick with this.'

'Shelly, it'll be fine. You'll be the belle of the ball.'

Almost an hour later, my hair was clipped back and cascaded in dark curls over my left shoulder, and I was ready. Lee made an awesome Batman, and despite the breathing constrictions, I liked the Robin outfit.

Lee's parents left when my dad arrived and, not two minutes later, the doorbell rang.

Cam and Dixon must have coordinated; those costumes weren't a coincidence.

Cam had a posh old-timey white wig and a naval hat that matched his uniform. And then Dixon was there in full Captain Jack Sparrow gear – from a wash-off tattoo to the tricorne hat to a plastic sword and pistol.

'Commodore Norrington, at your service, ma'am,' Cam said, sweeping off his hat in an elaborate bow and kissing the back of my hand. I bit back a laugh as he straightened up and put his hat back on.

'Cool costumes,' I said.

'Very authentic,' Lee added.

'Thanks,' they both said unanimously, and laughed.

Dixon said, 'My brother hooked us up with a

discount, since he knows some guy who owns a costume warehouse.'

I went to swipe a finger across Dixon's cheek as I said, 'Is that fake tan?'

'Don't touch!' He batted my finger away. 'Do you have any idea how hard it is to get three gallons of cocoa powder on your face like this?'

'It's cocoa powder?' Lee snorted. 'Like the stuff you use to make hot chocolate with?'

'My sister uses it as bronzer when she runs out. She said it'd work.'

The three of us just laughed at him. Not in a mean way – it was just the fact that Dixon was taking beauty advice from his fourteen-year-old sister.

'Shut up,' he said, mock-glaring at us all.

'Okay, okay, we're sorry,' Lee chuckled. 'It looks cool though.'

'I should hope so,' he muttered. 'Anyway – furniture?'

'I'll sort out the speakers,' Cam said.

'I'll help Cam,' I volunteered.

'Yeah, wouldn't want you to break a nail now, would we, Shelly?' Lee teased.

'I was thinking more along the lines of I might mess up my hair.'

'Dude,' Dixon said to him, 'your sidekick sucks.'

I rolled my eyes at them and went off with Cam. Lee

and Noah had purchased several sets of speakers that we could hook up to the big docking station in the lounge, but they were in a closet with a tangled mess of wires.

It didn't take too long to set them up, though, and Dixon and Lee pushed all the furniture to the edges of the lounge and the game room, and the kitchen was cleared as much as possible. There was plenty of space for a crazy house party – all we were missing was the guests.

And they arrived thick and fast, right on time.

Soon enough, the Flynn household had music pounding through it, and swarms of teenagers – no, not teenagers: more like a menagerie of movie characters.

There were Disney princesses, fairies, and Candice made an amazing zombie version of Alice in Wonderland. Her boyfriend had turned up as the Mad Hatter, à la Johnny Depp (what was it with everyone dressing up as him? I think there was an Edward Scissorhands somewhere too). Karen embraced her ginger hair and was Ginny from *Harry Potter*.

There were both male and female versions of super-heroes, from Spider-Man to Wonder Woman to Captain America. Warren had come as Dumbledore, a tacky beard half hanging off where he hadn't stuck it on properly. *Harry Potter* characters seemed like the default

– I'd thought we'd be swarming with 007s, not half of Hogwarts.

My favorites had to be Tyrone and Jason.

Lee and I had opened the door to Tyrone. He stood there, topless, in a pair of denim cut-offs that looked like they'd been jeans before he hacked at them with scissors. I got who he was straight away – he had the short dark hair and the dark skin to pull off the character.

'Happy birthday for Sunday, guys,' he smiled.

'Thanks. But, uh, what are you meant to be? A Calvin Klein model?' asked Lee.

'He's the werewolf from *Twilight*,' I told him in a 'duh' tone of voice.

On cue, Tyrone turned to show us the tail duct-taped to the butt of his jeans. 'I cut it off my sister's old stuffed dog,' he told us.

'Right . . .'

Then there was a, 'Hey guys! Happy birthday!' and Jason came into the porch, wearing a pale blue shirt – unbuttoned to show his jock's abs; his light brown hair stood up straight, and he was covered in glitter.

'Who are you, the Glitter Monster?' Tyrone jeered at him.

'You're one to talk,' Jason scoffed. 'I mean, what *are* you?'

'I'm a werewolf.'

'Yeah?' he scoffed. 'Well, I'm a vampire. *The* vampire.'

'Dude . . . that costume *sucks*,' Lee quipped, making the two of us crack up completely.

Tyrone and Jason had come as Edward and Jacob from *Twilight*. Their costumes were pretty good matches, aside from the fact that Jason wasn't deathly pale – although he put in a pair of plastic fangs.

It was surreal, looking around the party. Ninjas and sailors were playing pool with Count Dracula and Rocky Balboa. Mermaids and fairies were making out with firemen and GI Joes.

I hadn't seen Noah yet, though. And believe me, if he'd been there, I'd have known.

I did feel a little left out – all the couples were making out, and then people were randomly hooking up in the party spirit.

But I was okay. I was chatting with people and laughing and joking around. A few of the girls asked me where Noah was, but everyone was too busy talking about the costumes to be that bothered about the latest couple to grace the social scene.

I did want to know where he was . . . But honestly? I was having so much fun, I barely gave myself time to wonder why he wasn't here with me.

'Doesn't Faith look so pretty in the Grecian dress? I heard it was her grandma's.'

'Oh my God, have you seen that thing Tammy's wearing? I mean, what's she even supposed to be? A Victoria's Secret model?'

'Joel looks so hot in that sailor outfit, don't you think? Oh my God – I think he just looked over here. Is he looking? Oh my God, no, don't look! Not so obviously! Oh God, he just saw me. Quick – pretend to say something funny.'

That kept most of the girls busy, if they weren't making out or flirting with guys.

And the boys? They certainly didn't want to hear all about how things were going with Noah and how great a kisser he was.

I wandered out to the back yard and found Dixon hanging out with some of the guys by the pool. He was pretty tipsy and singing, 'Yo ho, yo ho, a pirate's life for me!' at the top of his lungs.

I laughed. 'And here I was, wondering where all the rum had got to.'

Then, all of a sudden, arms curled around me from behind and I felt warm breath in my ear. 'Hey, birthday girl.'

I turned around and pushed up the hat so it didn't conceal his face. Not that I needed to see his face to know who it was. 'So you finally decided to show your face, then?'

He chuckled. 'Yes, ma'am.'

He was wearing a charcoal-gray pinstripe suit with shoulder pads, a white shirt and black tie, extremely shiny shoes that would probably show your reflection, and one of those ivory 1920s hats with a black ribbon sewn around it.

'Al Capone?' I smiled. 'You look—'

He cut me off before I could finish – cut me off by smashing his lips to mine, if only for a brief second. 'Don't. Say. That. Word.'

I giggled. I wasn't even aware that everyone was looking at us. Aside from the end of the Summer Dance, nobody had really seen us together much. But I didn't even register that practically everybody we knew was here, at our party, looking at me and Noah.

'It is, though.'

'Don't.'

'Why do you hate it?'

'I'm the toughest guy in school. I drive a motorbike, I get in fights. And you're calling me *that*? Of all the adjectives out there, you pick that one?'

'I'm sorry. But it's so appropriate!'

He gave a chuckle, and tweaked my nose. I grimaced, but it only made him laugh more.

'Having fun, then, birthday girl?'

'Hmm, not just yet.'

He cocked an eyebrow, his head tilting to the side, like a curious dog. I smiled in response to his unspoken question before going up on my toes to whisper in his ear, 'I haven't had my birthday kiss yet.'

He just looked at me for a long moment. I felt my pulse pick up; maybe I couldn't really pull off sexy or seductive. It was a stupid thing to do . . .

He leaned forward a little, his lips barely brushing mine, let alone kissing me.

With his lips like that, he said, 'What happened to the sweet, naïve, innocent little Elle Evans I thought I had to keep safe from a horde of hormonal teenage guys?'

'The kissing booth happened?'

He chuckled again; I felt the sound reverberating through his chest where my hand was resting.

'I guess so.'

'So do I get my kiss now?' I asked, pulling away from him to pout. I wasn't sure if my puppy-dog expression only worked on Lee and my dad, but it seemed worth a shot.

'You do know it's not actually your birthday yet?'

'So? What's your point?'

He rolled his eyes, but gave me a peck on the cheek

before pulling my arms away and starting to walk off. I didn't move, I didn't even blink – I was too stunned. A peck on the cheek? That was all?

'Hey,' I called after him. For some reason I wanted to laugh, probably because we both knew he was teasing me – but I kept my expression calm, controlled. 'You think I'm letting you get away with that?'

'I'm Al Capone,' he replied, cool as a cucumber. 'I can get away with anything.'

'Very funny.'

'I thought so,' he said. His mouth curled up in his trademark smirk, yet his eyes were glimmering with amusement.

I couldn't help what I did next.

I pulled a face at him, even sticking my tongue out, like a little child.

All Noah did then was laugh – a proper laugh; the hearty kind; the kind where your eyes water and your mouth stretches into a smile so wide that your cheeks cramp up and your stomach aches after thirty seconds.

'God, I love you, Shelly,' he said quietly, the laughter still in his voice and his eyes and his face.

Maybe it was the way he was holding me, or the look on his face, or the laugh, I don't know – but whatever it was, I practically swooned. No kidding – I knew what all those cheesy romance books meant when they talked about your knees going weak and feeling like you just wanted to melt. And if Noah hadn't been holding my shoulders, I was sure my legs would've buckled under me.

I felt my own mouth mirror his smile and he said, 'I'll catch you in a little bit. Go party, birthday girl.'

'Wow. Who'd have thought I'd see the day when overprotective, violence-junkie best friend's brother would tell me to "go party"?' I teased. 'And not tell me to watch what I drink or who I talk to, or make a comment about how I'm dressed.'

I expected him to roll his eyes, or laugh at me, or make a witty comment back. But actually, he gave me a sheepish smile, looking kind of . . . guilty.

'I didn't mean it in a bad way,' I told him.

'I know. Don't worry. I am sorry for that, though. You know – being all . . .'

'Overprotective? Controlling? A jerk-face?'

He laughed. 'Yeah. That. But just for the record . . . You look extremely hot tonight.'

I grinned and blushed all at once, making him smirk.

'Now go party, Elle, and I'll find you in a bit.'

'All right,' I said brightly, giving him a kiss on the cheek as I breezed past. All of a sudden I could feel dozens of pairs of eyes on me.

So I braced myself and grabbed a can of Coke from the fridge, turning around to face all the swarming girls who were cooing about how cute we were as a couple, and how jealous they felt; how hot Flynn looked, and how lucky I was; and then again how cute a couple we made.

'I wish I had what you had,' Tamara told me with a wan smile.

'What? A hot bad-boy?' I frowned in confusion.

She laughed. 'No. A fairy-tale ending.'

Chapter 30

I wish it could've been a fairy-tale ending.

The party ended too quickly. The hours blurred by until it was one o'clock and the house was empty, save for me and Noah, Lee and Rachel. The house wasn't too much of a mess since there hadn't actually been much drinking. We swept some trash into bags and left them out on the sidewalk, and by two a.m. Rachel was passed out in Lee's arms on the couch, and his head started drooping too.

I lay on the other couch, my head in Noah's lap. I wanted to stay awake, spend more time with him. I might've been able to keep my eyes open had he not been running his fingers through my hair. It was more soothing than any lullaby.

'Noah,' I said, but it came out as a sleepy murmur.

'Mm.' He sounded just as half conscious as I felt. Maybe he was. My eyes were shut and I was past the stage where I had the willpower to open them again.

'What are you thinking about?'

He hesitated before replying. 'Us. College.' I waited patiently for him to develop that answer. 'I don't—' He broke off with a yawn, and had to repeat himself. 'I don't want you to be hanging around for me to come back for holidays and not having a life. I know that sounds weird coming from me, after I tried protecting you all this time, but . . . I don't know. It just doesn't seem – seem fair to you,' he said, yawning again, 'to have to wait around on me . . . I'm tired. I'm no good with this stuff anyway.'

I gave a sleepy laugh, a half-smile on my lips. 'The "emotional crap", you mean?'

'Yeah. I don't know. We'll give it our best shot and hope for the best. That's all we can do, right?'

'I'm going to miss you,' I said, shrugging, still thinking. He squeezed my arm.

We sat in silence for a few moments. I knew he wasn't asleep since he carried on running his fingers through my hair. I heard a jerking snore that broke the silence before it petered out into even breathing again. Lee. He was asleep, then.

Noah moved, jostling me around. I squeezed my eyes shut tighter, making a small grumbling noise in protest, but then he was still, lying along the couch beside me and keeping me tucked against him. I smiled. I wanted to roll so I was facing him, but it took a moment to actually do that because I was so sleepy.

'Elle,' he said then, in that ominous kind of tone that told me he wanted to actually talk about something serious. I was too tired for talking now . . .

'What?' I whispered back drowsily into the darkness.

'I love you.' He kissed my forehead. I snuggled closer, burying my head into the crook of his neck as his arms tightened around me.

I was asleep in seconds.

None of us woke up when Lee's parents got in. None of us woke up when they pottered around the kitchen, making brunch, or cleaning up the rest of the house.

It was almost two in the afternoon when I eventually opened my eyes.

I'd slept most of the day away, and the afternoon was spent playing video games with Lee. Noah had disappeared to a scrap yard somewhere to get parts for his bike. His text hadn't been clear since there was no part of me that spoke mechanic; I had to guess what he was doing.

And then it was my birthday.

Just like that I'd turned seventeen.

I'd stayed up until midnight to text Lee, but it only really hit me now that I was really wide awake and

403

staring at my ceiling and the shapes the morning sun played on it.

It felt like I'd suddenly grown up in the last year.

And to be totally honest, I kind of hated it.

Mostly, it was the fact that growing up meant making the big decisions. Like college next year. I'd have to think about college. Hell, I didn't even have a clue what I wanted to do as a career! I just went with the flow. I didn't think about things like that much. I just *didn't know*..

Sure, growing up meant all the good things, like having boyfriends and driving and finding out who you were, yadda, yadda, blah-blah-blah.

But was it really so bad that a little part of me wished things could stay the same forever? That I could run home and have my daddy put a Band-Aid on my knee when I tripped, that I could cannonball into Lee's pool with him and not give a damn about anything else other than making a bigger splash than him.

Then my door burst open.

'Happy birthday, troll!'

I sat up, throwing a pillow at Brad, but he shut the door on it before it went careering into his face. He opened the door back up and said, 'Get up already!'

'Why? It's, like, eight in the morning!'

'If I'm up, you're up!' I noticed then that he was

already dressed, and rolled my eyes. It was kind of true – Brad felt the need to have everybody in the house up once he was up. I imagined he'd already dragged Dad out of bed to reach him a cereal bowl down from the cupboard so he could have breakfast.

'I'm up, I'm up. Jeez!'

'I said happy birthday, though, didn't I?' he said.

I sighed. 'Yes. Thank you, Brad.'

'Just hurry up, all right?'

I didn't see what his rush was, but he threw the pillow back onto my bed and shut the door before crashing down the stairs with as much grace as a hurricane. I rolled my eyes but smiled anyway, before opening my closet to find something to wear.

We were going out for lunch, but I'd change later. I pulled on a pair of denim shorts and a T-shirt for now. We went out every year, and it was always a family affair. Lee and I, his parents and my dad – my mom too, when she was alive – and Brad and Noah. A couple of years, if our grandparents had been in town, they'd tag along as well.

I couldn't be bothered to do much with my hair for now, so I just twisted it into a ponytail and went downstairs.

'Finally,' Brad muttered as he heard me come to the kitchen.

'Happy birthday, bud!' Dad said, beaming hugely. He was stood behind the kitchen table, which had a massive cake on it. It was chocolate, with strawberry frosting and white icing that said *Happy 17th* in messy writing.

'Is that my breakfast?' I joked hopefully.

'Not quite. But me and Brad were up extra early to bake it. I'm making pancakes.'

'Yeah, and he won't make them till we're all here,' Brad grumbled. His stomach growled in response, like a caged tiger teased with meat. Dad and I both laughed. 'He said it was silly to make them twice.'

'That's why you were telling me to get up, grumpy guts,' I said, ruffling his hair as I went around to give my dad a hug.

'How was the party? You didn't get much chance to tell me about it yesterday.'

'Sorry.'

'That's all right. You were at Lee's all day; I thought maybe you had a killer hangover and were avoiding facing your father.'

I laughed. 'Not quite. Nobody was drinking much anyway, really. We're just so much fun we don't need it, I guess.' It was a joke but, in Dad-mode now, he just pulled a face that broadcast, *You don't need to be drunk to have fun anyway.*

The rest of the morning passed pretty quickly, and by half twelve we were pulling up outside some fancy restaurant whose name I couldn't even pronounce. I'd changed into a cute summery dress, dark blue with yellow floral patterns on. I'd just thrown on some sandals and jewelry, leaving my hair as it was.

We walked in just after the Flynn family arrived. The waiter said, 'Ah, you're all here. I'll show you to your table.'

I heard June ask my brother how soccer was going, and our dads chatting too.

My eyes instantly found Noah, and he smiled at me, but before I had the chance to respond, Lee fell into step beside me. I tore my gaze away from Noah to give my best friend my full attention.

'Happy birthday!' we said in unison, identical grins on our faces. Lee laughed and flicked my ponytail so that it swung around like helicopter blades. I shoved my shoulder into his and gave him a big hug. He hugged me tightly, leaning back so I was tipped off my feet for a second.

'How's your day then?' he asked me before we followed our families.

'Same as when I talked to you earlier – good. You?'

'Do I need to bother repeating your answer?'

'No,' I laughed.

'Well, actually, I did get to see Rachel,' he said. 'Only for about an hour, before we left for here.'

'Aw. Did she give you a big birthday kiss?' I pulled a face and made loud kissy noises.

'Well . . .'

'You guys are so cute together. It's like . . . like Spider-Man and Mary-Jane. I'd have said Batman and someone, but I don't know who Batman dated.'

Lee just laughed. 'What does that make you then? Beauty and the Beast? You being the Beast, of course. Noah and I share the same gene pool, and I'm definitely not from the same gene pool as the Beast. I mean, just look at me.'

I did, and pulled a face. 'Gross.'

He laughed again and we took seats next to each other at the center of the table. Noah was opposite me, for once. It made a nice change from Brad, kicking me and complaining he didn't have enough leg room with my 'thunder-thighs and cankles'.

'Happy birthday, Elle,' he said with a soft smile.

I grinned back. 'Thanks.'

'So what did you get for your birthday, Lee?' my dad asked.

'I don't know yet. I was waiting for Shelly.'

'How about you, Elle?' Matthew asked me.

'I was waiting for Lee,' I said, laughing sheepishly.

The waiter came up to take our drinks orders and handed out menus. Noah stood his menu up, and hunched over the table a little so that I couldn't see anything more than his elbows and the top of his head.

I was scanning the menu I see at least once a year here, and wondering if I should be daring and try something different, or if I should just have the chicken breast with parmesan and barbecue sauce, roasted vegetables and fries.

Next thing I knew, my cell phone trilled briefly, signaling I had a new text. I thought it might be Warren or someone, texting me happy birthday.

It wasn't Warren.

You look really pretty.

I looked up, but he was engrossed in his menu, seemingly oblivious to me. I blinked a few times before looking down at my phone and hitting REPLY.

Thanks. I didn't know what else to say, really, so I just left it at that – short and sweet.

What are you doing later?

I don't know. When's later?

After cake. I've got something in mind for the birthday girl. There was a winking face at the end as well. I looked at the text for a moment, wondering if there was any innuendo there. Knowing him, he probably had something cheesy planned that he knew I'd love.

'Elle, stop texting at the table,' my dad admonished me.

'Sorry.'

I saw Noah smirking at his menu, still not looking at me. I thought about texting back asking what he had in mind, but he was probably waiting for me to ask so that he could carry on teasing me – telling me it was a surprise just to bug me. So I didn't give him the satisfaction. I just put my phone back in my purse.

'Thank you,' Dad said pointedly.

'Are you all ready to order?'

We went back to the Flynns' house afterward, as always, so we could open our presents and gorge ourselves on the massive cake my dad and brother had made that morning.

Lee's parents had got him some CDs and clothes. Noah got him a new stereo for his car – he said that's why he'd been down the scrap yard, to get some extra parts. Lee had kind of guessed what CD I got him already – it would've been hard not to after I'd told him he wasn't allowed to download it on his computer a couple of days ago but refused to tell him why.

He liked the wallet too, and then opened the T-shirt. It was blue, and read, I'M WITH STUPID, and had an arrow pointing down.

He burst out laughing, then grabbed one of my presents and tossed it at me. 'Thanks, Elle. Open that one now.'

'Is it from you?'

'Duh. Now open it already!'

I did. And it took me a full minute to stop laughing. He'd bought me a yellow T-shirt – from the same store too – and it said I'M WITH STUPID, and had an arrow pointing up. It was like the female version of the one I'd got him.

Talk about freaky.

'What did you do, coordinate?' his dad joked as I held the top up in front of me.

'No,' we chorused, laughing.

Lee said, 'We're just telepathic like that.'

He also got me a couple of books – vampire-themed ones, since he knew I had a soft spot for them – and then there was something small, wrapped up tightly and covered in so much tape I had to tear it open with my teeth.

'What is it?' Brad asked impatiently, while I was still gnawing at the tape.

'I don't know, it's still wrapped up!'

'I'm not telling!' Lee teased. There was something evil in his smile; something that made me a little scared to open it . . .

Finally the tape snapped free and I could rip the paper off. It was like pass the parcel or something; whatever it was had a long strip of the paper wrapped around it, like, a billion times over.

'What is it?' Brad asked, trying to see.

When I saw what it was, my cheeks flamed instantly, and I dropped it like a live bomb. 'Lee!'

'What? I don't want to be an uncle yet – I'm not old enough!'

'What, and you couldn't have given me that when we're not around people?' He knew what I really meant – why in front of my *dad?* And his *parents!*

'And your boyfriend, let's not forget.'

I willed my cheeks to cool down, but they just wouldn't. Dad had already started making hasty small talk with June and Matthew, all of them determinedly ignoring the packet of condoms I'd just picked up.

Noah reached down from his spot on the sofa, plucking them out of my hands. 'Thanks, Lee. I'll keep them handy for later.'

I didn't think it was possible, but I went even redder. I buried my face in my hands. June coughed, and I knew that there was no way our parents had missed that comment.

Lee didn't seem too bothered, though. He just

reached over to pat my hand, saying, 'I just want you to be careful, Shelly. I'm looking out for you here.'

'I can't see,' my semi-innocent ten-year-old brother complained. 'What is it?'

'Grown-up stuff,' I said.

'Tampons,' Lee told him.

I smacked him across the head that time – not hard, though. 'You, my friend, are just intolerable.'

'I know,' he grinned, and I had to laugh. I just *had* to.

The parents seemed to notice that the condoms weren't in the limelight any more, and my dad said, 'Here you go, Elle.' He handed me a box. It was a long, black velvet one, like a jewelry case.

I took it hesitantly. 'What is it?'

'Well, it was actually, um . . . it was your mom's. She always said she wanted you to have it though. And I meant to give it to you last year, but I'd forgotten all about it. I know seventeen's a bit of a random age for this, but . . . I didn't want to risk forgetting next year too.' He gave a guilty laugh and smiled sadly.

We'd kept all my mom's jewelry, of course we had. It wasn't the kind of thing you threw out. I had a few pairs of earrings of hers I'd always liked when I was a little girl, and there was a gold chain I wore sometimes too. But whatever this was, it was obviously not just everyday jewelry.

I undid the gold clasp on the front of the case and opened it.

I'd thought maybe it was a necklace – some fancy string of pearls or something. But it wasn't. It was a watch – a shiny silver one with tiny topaz gems around the face. The second hand ticked away, a slim silver line against the black face. I picked it up carefully. The blue gems looked pretty authentic, and I was sure it had been incredibly expensive.

'The stones are real,' Dad told me, as if reading my thoughts.

'It's beautiful,' June commented with a motherly smile.

I thought maybe I'd cry. That was what they all expected. I could practically see them all just waiting to see me break down in tears and cry and say I missed my mom.

And I *did* miss my mom. I really did. I wished she was still around; that she was there, pottering about in the kitchen, or sat watching a crappy soap on TV, or getting ready for work.

But there was nothing I could do about the fact she was gone; I'd accepted that years ago. I could miss her and want her back so bad it hurt, but I couldn't actually do anything about it. And I got that. There was no use in crying over her when crying wouldn't bring her back.

But I was sure they were shocked when I grinned and clipped the watch around my left wrist. It was cold and heavy, and it hung kind of loose, but I loved it.

'Thanks, Dad.'

He smiled, his face showing a mixture of emotions. The sadness in his eyes; the happiness in his smile; the relief wiping away the small frown on his brow. But then he took something else out of his pocket – another small black velvet box. It was different to the one the watch had been in: there was no gold clasp and the hinges weren't visible either.

'Is this the matching earrings?' I joked.

'No – that's this year's present. Technically the watch is overdue . . .' He laughed, shaking his head as if trying to banish the sadness. I smiled and took it.

And actually, I did half expect matching earrings.

It was the right shape for them, after all.

But it wasn't earrings. It wasn't any kind of jewelry.

'You got me a . . . key?' I picked it up, dangling the keychain off my fingertip and frowning at it. Then it clicked. 'Ohmigosh! You got me a car!'

Everyone laughed, obviously knowing beforehand or, in Lee's case, getting it before I did. I leaped up, tackling my dad with a massive hug.

'Thank you thank you thank you thank you!'

He laughed. 'You haven't even seen it yet.'

'Yeah, it could be some crappy, beat-up piece of junk that stalls every time you hit a stop sign,' Noah joked.

'It's parked in the garage,' June told me. 'We had to hide it somewhere you wouldn't see it, didn't we?'

I ran outside, heaving up the garage door with a grunt.

Behind me I heard them all filtering out of the house. The garage was kind of dark; the floor was stained with oil, and Noah's tools were scattered around everywhere. Lee's bicycle was propped against the wall. There were footballs and soccer balls, and random pieces of old or broken furniture.

And right in the middle of it all was my birthday present.

It was a second-hand Ford Escort. It was midnight blue, and there was even a pair of neon-pink fuzzy dice hanging from the rearview mirror.

'The dice were my idea,' Lee's dad said. 'Just for the record.'

I laughed, giddy, leaning in the open window on the driver's side. The inside smelled of pine and old leather. It didn't look like it would run like a dream, with a silent purring engine, and I wouldn't be shocked to find myself waiting on roadside service at some point.

But I loved it instantly.

I didn't expect my dad to get me a brand-spanking new car. I didn't want one, either. I wanted something I wouldn't be afraid to drive. I was never the best driver. But I finally had my own car!

'I won't have to bug you for a ride all the time now, Lee,' I told him.

'Well, I'm not riding with you,' he quipped, his voice grave. 'I value my life too much, thank you very much.'

I laughed and went to give my dad another hug. 'Thank you, I love it!'

'I know she's not the best, but you can start off with this old girl. She'll take a few knocks and dents, no problem.'

'Does *nobody* trust my driving skills?'

Everyone laughed at that, and then Brad said, 'All right, all right. Is it time for cake now?'

As if on cue, mine and Lee's stomachs rumbled in tandem, and we said, 'Most definitely,' before racing each other inside.

Chapter 31

'So what exactly have you got in mind?' I asked Noah. He was putting plates in the dishwasher when I brought in a few empty glasses. Lee was outside in his car, fiddling with his new stereo. Brad was watching TV, the parents all talking about . . . well, whatever it was they talk about. I'd been waiting for the opportunity to talk to Noah alone.

He looked up, twisting his head to look under his arm, which was leaning on the counter as he bent to load the dishwasher.

'Earlier,' I explained, 'your texts said you had something in mind for later for me.'

'Oh, that.'

'Yeah, that. So are you going to tell me what it is?'

'Telling you would defeat the whole point of it being a "surprise", you know.'

'I had a feeling you'd say that,' I groaned, passing

him the glasses. He put them in, then stood up and kicked the dishwasher closed.

Pulling me into his arms, he breathed in my ear, 'If I told you it involved Lee's present for you . . .' His lips brushed over my jaw.

I didn't know how to reply to that – but I couldn't have done so anyway; I seemed to have suddenly lost my voice.

Noah gave a quiet chuckle. 'That wasn't what I had planned, though,' he said, pulling back to give me that devilish smirk. 'I was going to take you somewhere. I know you'll love it. But it's got to be a surprise.'

'Right . . .' I racked my brain. I knew it couldn't be going to see the sunset or fireworks again; it had to be something different . . . but Noah seemed so full of surprises now, it could be anything.

'Although,' he said thoughtfully, 'if you do want to put Lee's present to use later on . . .'

I blushed, burying my face in his shoulder so he didn't see my blush. But he laughed and kissed the top of my head, his arms tight around me.

Ignoring his comment, I hugged him back. 'I love you.' The words were out of my mouth like a reflex, rolling off my tongue like they were the most natural three words in the world to say to my best friend's big brother.

He kissed the top of my head again and said, 'I love you more.' I shook my head into his shoulder.

We didn't say anything else. Just stood there in each other's arms, in our own little bubble.

'Oh! Sorry – don't mind me, just grabbing a drink!'

We pulled apart a little, and I saw June grabbing a glass of water. When she turned around, she gave us a smile – it wasn't one that said 'caught red-handed'; it was more like 'you kids are adorable'.

At least we hadn't been making out or anything.

Now, that would've been just plain awkward.

Noah's mom went back into the lounge and I looked back at him. 'So when are we going to this surprise place?'

'Now, if you want. It won't take too long.'

'Now? Really?'

He shrugged. 'If you want to go now, then sure.'

I grinned suddenly. 'Can I drive?'

'Drive to a place you have no idea about . . . Because that's such a smart idea, isn't it, Elle?'

'Well – you can tell me where to drive, right? Please, please, please?' I gave him my best, biggest grin, so excited at the prospect of taking my new car for a spin.

'All right, fine! But you can't blame me if you guess where we're going and it spoils the surprise, all right?'

I giggled. 'What is it with you and surprises, anyway?'

He shrugged. 'I thought it was more romantic than saying, "Hey, Elle, I'm going to take you to . . . to see the sunset and a firework display," and you've always loved those corny romance movies.'

'Well . . .' I bit my lip sheepishly. 'Okay, okay, I see your point. Let's go.'

'Impatient, much?'

'Okay, just take a left here . . . then second right. There should be a parking space there.'

I followed his directions, and wished I hadn't asked to drive here. I was so focused on not scratching the car that I had to keep my eyes on the road. I couldn't let my eyes roam around the streets and try to figure out where we were headed. I didn't recognize any of these roads – I didn't have any clue where he was leading me, and even less of a clue as to what this surprise was.

I found a space to park and got out of the car, hearing Noah's door slam shut too.

'All right, then,' I said, unable to rein in a grin. 'Lead the way.'

He smirked, and grabbed my hand as he stepped up onto the sidewalk beside me, linking our fingers together. Our arms swung like a pendulum as we walked back in the direction we'd come from.

Looking around, I realized we were no longer in the city, or even a town. Some of the houses seemed to have been converted – the ground floor occupied by a florist's shop, or a baker's. I still had no idea where we were, but it looked nice. There were a few trees planted on random squares of grass, and flowers blooming on the windowsills. There were a few people milling around, one or two dog-walkers amongst them, and the occasional car driving past.

It was a quaint little village. I heard church bells peal somewhere off in the distance, as if to echo my thought.

I turned back to Noah, who caught my eye and gave me that half-smile, half-smirk, like he thought keeping me in the dark about where we were going was funny.

I smiled back, squeezing his hand.

'Here we are.' He stopped, and I took a step back, letting him lead me into the shop we stopped outside. There was a dark green awning over the doorway, casting a shadow over Noah's face as he pushed open the door. A bell tinkled – it was a cute kind of sound, reminding me of the fairy in *Peter Pan*.

Then it hit me. The smell.

It was a gorgeous aroma: sweet vanilla, strong cocoa, the hazy sweetness of melted sugar, and the all-round stomach-rumbling, mouth-watering scent of chocolate.

It drifted out of the shop the second Noah opened the door, blasting me full-force and making me gasp.

I stepped inside ahead of Noah, who held the door open for me. Only a few months ago, I remembered going into his house behind him to see Lee. He knew I was there, but didn't even think of holding the door for me – just let it swing shut for me to catch on the way in. He didn't do it out of spite: it was just Noah Flynn being typical Noah Flynn.

But I didn't miss the way he held the door for me now. It seemed so trivial, so unimportant, but I shot him a smile nonetheless.

Then I let the smell of the chocolate wash over me again. The shop was lit by warm, firelight-yellow lamps. On the floor was a dark, mahogany-colored carpet, and the walls were a soft cream color. There was a counter with a cash register on it – some childish part of me was delighted to see that it was a really old cash register, the kind that had buttons like an ancient typewriter and made a loud ring when you opened the drawer.

The shop looked as sweet as it smelled, and as I turned in a slow circle, my mouth forming an O and my eyes widening in sheer awe, I saw all the chocolates.

I didn't know what to do – where to look first; what to say to Noah.

'Hello, dears!' trilled a voice. It was the sort of voice you knew belonged to an old person, and when I looked up from the pralines lined up on the glass counter, I saw a woman who was in her sixties or seventies. She was just the kind of person you could picture owning a candy store.

She was plump, with really rosy cheeks, and dark gray hair pulled back into a bun, wispy strands escaping around her face. She wore jeans and a white cotton blouse, with a bright pink apron tied that was stained with chocolate and sugar and cream, icing and syrup and fudge. Some of it looked almost decades old, like it was a part of the apron itself, but some had clearly been slopped down her that morning.

'Hi,' Noah said, strolling past me. 'I called ahead, earlier? My name's Flynn.'

'Oh, of course, of course! I remember. I've got it right here for you, dear! Just give me two seconds!' The woman gave a motherly smile, before bustling backwards, knocking over a stack of cardboard boxes as she did so. Luckily, it sounded like they were all empty.

'Whoops-a-daisy!' She shoved them back into place, laughing at her own clumsiness. As she retreated out of sight, I heard her humming tunelessly to herself in the back of the shop.

'You called ahead?' I asked, and Noah turned to look at me. I felt a smile tugging at the corners of my mouth. 'How'd you even know about this place, anyway?'

'I, um . . .' He cleared his throat and scratched the back of his neck. 'Remember when – no, you probably don't – but when we were really little, I read that book, *Charlie and the Chocolate Factory*, and I kind of got it in my head that I wanted to go to Willy Wonka's chocolate factory, and my mom – and your mom, I remember, she tagged along too – my mom brought me here because she said it was close enough. I remembered about it a couple of years back and took a bus up here to find it again.'

It took a minute to sink in. For one thing, it was so un-Flynn-like for him to disclose a personal memory like that; for another, thinking of him as such a cute little kid wanting to visit Willy Wonka made me want to giggle. Not in a mean way – in a cute way.

Though I didn't think he'd appreciate me mentioning the cuteness.

So instead I said, 'I remember. I wanted the book for a school project. There were no copies left in the library, and Lee told me you had one so there was no point in buying it, and you wouldn't let me have it.'

'Oh, yeah.' He laughed and bit his lip, looking a little sheepish. 'What was my excuse again?'

'You didn't have one,' I said after a moment. 'You just wouldn't let me.'

He nodded. 'That sounds about right.'

'You really wanted to go to Willy Wonka's chocolate factory?' A little teasing note had crept into my voice, my smile spreading wider again.

'I was like, eight, okay? Give me a break.'

We both laughed, just as the woman came back holding a big, flat white box with a purple ribbon around it. 'Here you are!'

Noah clasped his hands behind his back, rocking back and forth briefly on his heels.

I got the message, and jolted. 'They're for me?'

'What, did you think I really forgot to get my girl-friend a birthday present?' He gave me a devilishly handsome grin, and the old woman laughed kindly.

'Well, it – it just didn't occur to me earlier.'

'Shelly. I have *always* got you a birthday present.'

'You got me a whoopee cushion one year.'

'It was still a present. And I was a twelve-year-old boy that year, if I remember. Did you expect me to buy you something nice or meaningful?'

I laughed. 'Well, no.'

'And you really think I just forgot you, this year especially?'

I shrugged sheepishly. When he hadn't given me a

present earlier, I didn't exactly ask him where it was. For one thing, it would've been incredibly rude. But when he said in his text that he had 'something in mind for the birthday girl', I thought maybe he'd take me out somewhere, even if only to make out, instead.

I took the box from the lady. 'Thanks.'

'One of everything in there,' she said. 'Well, as much as I could fit in two layers. But I made sure you got the nicest things. You're not allergic to nuts, are you, dear?'

'N-no.' I only stammered because she spoke pretty darn fast – with an excitement that seemed to be part of her warm personality.

She smiled. 'Good, good, good! Well, feel free to have a look around – unless you're not stopping. In which case, I'll ring up that order for you right now.'

'Uh . . .' I looked at Noah. I had no idea if we were just here to pick this up, or if he had any other plans. I mean, he was full of surprises these days.

He put up his hands and shook his head, giving me a small smile. 'You've got the car keys.'

I bounced around on my toes at that, beaming brightly. 'Oh yeah!'

'Tell you what's really good,' the lady said, pottering over to one cabinet. She pulled open a drawer and lifted out a tray; I'd drifted after her, Noah half a step behind me.

It was a tray of tiny squares of chocolate, each one labeled with tiny handwriting, so loopy it was practically illegible. They looked like tiny cuts off larger slabs, and the scent wafting up to my nostrils and settling on my taste buds was enough to make me drool.

'This one' – she pointed – 'has that popping candy in it. Strangest sensation in the world, popping candy! And this one's mango-flavored. I've got a few fruit-flavored ones like that.'

'How about orange?' Noah asked, and I felt his body press against my back, a hand resting on my forearm as he leaned over me to look at the tray.

'Ah-ha, here we are!' She picked one square up and handed it to Noah. He took it and popped it in his mouth.

'This is my taster tray,' she told me, seemingly reading my mind. 'Go ahead, dear, help yourself!'

With that, she pushed the tray into my hands and left me to peruse it at my leisure.

The bell tinkled again, and I glanced over my shoulder to see a woman walk in. 'Hey, Mabel,' she said to the shop owner. I turned back to the tray.

Noah reached over me and plucked out another square at random. He made a choking noise, and when I looked at him, his face was scrunched up in disgust, but he swallowed hard. 'Coconut.'

I laughed. 'Oh, right. Well, you should've read the label, idiot.'

'I tried,' he muttered in my ear.

I stifled a laugh, and hesitated, my fingers drumming the air as I tried to decide which one to try. White chocolate? Dark chocolate? One with sprinkles? A coffee one, a fruity one, a solid chocolate one?

The cursive scrawl of *Honeycomb* caught my eye, and I picked that one out. I was half glad of the old lady's writing being so hard to read. If I knew what all these flavors were, I'd want to try them all.

We picked out a couple more and went over to the cash register.

'So how long have you kids been together?' the woman, Mabel, asked.

'Um . . .'

'Couple of months,' Noah answered. 'But we've known each other practically our whole lives.'

'Well, now, that's just sweet as apple pie! Always see young couples coming in here, you know, and let me tell you, if I had a wall of fame with them all on, you two would be right there near the top.'

I laughed. 'We're that cute together, huh?'

I noticed Noah's grimace at the word, but he didn't say anything, instead taking out his wallet and handing over the cash. As we bundled our purchases into a bag, the woman handed us over a box of fudge.

'You can have these ones on the house,' she said, smiling.

'Oh, no, it's—'

'It's your birthday, right?' I nodded. 'Well, happy birthday then!'

I smiled. 'Thank you.'

One of Noah's arms snaked around my waist. I automatically leaned back, my head fitting into that spot between his neck and his shoulder. Again, the clichéd romantic in me wondered how we seemed to fit so perfectly, two pieces of a jigsaw, and have such different, clashing personalities. Noah planted a kiss on the side of my forehead, and right then, I didn't care how bad we were for each other or that he'd be off to college soon; I just remembered that I was in love with him.

Chapter 32

The days flew by. I did some dog-walking for the neighbors – not for the cash, but more for something to occupy me. Sometimes Noah came with me.

Since Dad was in work, he bribed me to taxi Brad and his friends around in my new car – to the park; to the soccer pitch; to the movies; out for a milkshake.

I would've refused, but Dad had said, 'Bud, do you want me to be that dad who gives you a curfew when you go on dates, or has strict rules about your boyfriend? Because I'll do it.'

'You're going to ransom me Noah to take Brad places?'

He nodded. 'I'm still not entirely happy about you two, Elle. I don't think you know just how lenient I'm being here.'

So I let it drop.

Plus, I did tend to get back late – spending the day lounging around the Flynns' pool, usually with the guys; watching a movie with Noah in the evening, Lee and Rachel on the other couch; and then, later, losing track of time, too taken up with Noah.

One day, the Monday before we were due to go to the beach house, we were lounging around by the pool. Some of the girls were there too – Lisa, who was still dating Cam, and Rachel, and May. Noah was out with some of the guys from the football team.

Lee's dad was cooking a barbecue for us all while his mom sat on the decking reading a book. The smoky scent of summer at Lee's house filled my nostrils.

'Girls' day out tomorrow,' Lisa announced from her sun lounger. I was about to get in the pool, T-shirt halfway over my head, and I paused.

'Cool,' Rachel said.

I finished tugging it off, and dropped it on the lounger, pulling off my sunglasses too.

'Elle, you coming?'

'Oh, come on! It'll be fun!' Lisa said brightly.

'What'll be fun?' Cam asked, suddenly appearing out of the pool. He shook his hair like a dog and, dripping wet, gave Lisa a kiss on the cheek before standing up again. 'Ah, Elle, don't tell me you've got some wild prank in mind.'

I laughed. 'No.'

'We're going shopping,' May told him.

'Without Lee,' Lisa added.

'What's happening without me? Shelly? Rachel? What're you ditching me for now?'

'Shopping,' Rachel and I answered, and we laughed.

'You? Shopping? Without *me*, your personal stylist?' Lee looked horrified. 'Will you still get me a milk-shake?'

I laughed. 'Fine.'

'So that's a yes, then?' Lisa said.

'Sure.' I was actually kind of flattered to be included in something that didn't involve Lee. But I was just a little worried I'd feel out of place, since I didn't usually go on girlie outings.

'Oh, Elle, it won't be that bad,' Dixon said, heaving himself up onto his elbows on the side of the pool. 'You can buy some sexy lingerie for Flynn.'

I didn't know how to react to that – laugh or blush. I did both.

Then Lee splashed him right in the face. Dixon must've swallowed half a gallon of water, and flopped back into the pool, spluttering, while we all laughed.

'Dude, that's my Shelly you're talking about!' Lee protested dramatically. He said 'my Shelly' like another guy would say 'my little sister'. But then he said, 'Talk about disgusting,' and shuddered.

'Oh, yeah?' I challenged him.

'Oh, yeah!'

I stood, blinked innocently at him, and yelled, *'Cannonball!'*

As it turned out, shopping was fun. It was kind of weird, in a way, to be going shopping with 'the girls' instead of my best friend, but I enjoyed it all the same.

The day after that was spent packing and repacking, and then upturning my case to pack it all over again. I always had trouble packing for the beach house. In the end, though, I took the same things I always did. We'd gone to the Flynns' beach house every summer for years now.

I wanted things to be exactly the same as always – but I knew they wouldn't. Noah and his dad were leaving two days earlier than the rest of us, to check out the campus at Harvard. Rachel came for a couple of days too – not that I minded: I actually enjoyed having some female company other than June for once.

And even if the beach house seemed the same as ever – sandy floors, a little too cramped to fit all of us, the peeling paint and creaky floors and mismatched furniture we loved so much – it was different. At first, I thought everything was just as it always had been.

The first night Rachel was there we all went out to dinner, and Noah and I were acting like a real couple;

once he made me dinner when everyone else was out, and we walked along the beach together. And times like that, I remembered just how much everything really had changed, and how nothing was going to stay the same.

Not even my relationship with Noah.

I didn't know how things would work out when he finally left. I didn't want to think about it. I didn't want it to put a dark cloud over the time we had left together. I kept telling myself we'd cross that bridge when we came to it, but . . .

I didn't know if we'd even cross it then, to be honest.

It was weird, trying to split my time between my best friend and my boyfriend. I was thankful that Lee had Rachel; I didn't feel so bad about spending so much time with Noah then.

He'd take me to movies, and it was so nice just being a regular couple after all the time we'd spent sneaking around. I still couldn't believe how much he'd changed in the past few months.

Although once, when I was dropping Brad at the park to play soccer with his friends, I saw Noah getting in a fight with some guy he was playing football with, while the rest of the team egged them on.

For all I'd managed to change him, he was still the bad-ass guy I'd grown up with. I kind of liked that, though. It was comforting, in a way, to know he hadn't totally lost the rough edges I'd ended up falling for.

The bike, on the other hand . . . He kept trying to get me to ride it, saying it was easier to park than his car, and faster; he even wanted to teach me to ride it for myself. But I remained adamant: I hated the bike.

And then we were at the airport, the tannoy overhead announcing that the eight-oh-five to Boston was now boarding at Gate Five, if all passengers could please make their way to . . .

I stood up with Noah and felt his hand tighten on mine. He slung his rucksack over his shoulder with his free hand.

'Guess this is it,' Lee said. I let go of Noah's hand as the two brothers gave each other one of those brusque guy-hugs, slapping each other's backs. 'Good luck.'

'Try not to get in too many fights, son,' Matthew told him, slapping his back but with authority in his voice. Noah just nodded but we all knew he wasn't really paying any attention.

'Call us when you get there,' June said, hugging him. She was beaming proudly, but her eyes were mournful to see her little boy growing up and moving across the country for college, leaving the nest. She swallowed, like she was trying not to cry.

And hell, she wasn't the only one.

I didn't want to lose him. I still didn't want him to go; but it wasn't my choice to make. I knew that there was a chance this might not work out between us.

And you know what?

I was okay with that.

Not every relationship is going to last for ever, not outside of fairy tales. I might fall in love a hundred times before I found the one I'd want to spend the rest of my life with, and maybe that one would be Noah, maybe it wouldn't. I knew things might have to end, and I didn't want them to – but if they did, I'd deal with it.

Maybe I'd be the one to get my heart broken, waiting for some other guy to come piece it back together; but until then, I was happy to stay in love with Noah even if he was all the way over in Boston. I was living in the present.

I *wanted* it to last for ever, though; the hopeless romantic in me hadn't died out just yet.

I walked up to the gate with Noah. A small queue of people filtered smoothly past the woman checking their boarding documents. He squeezed my hand and then turned to face me.

'It'll work out,' he told me. 'Somehow.'

'Now who's being the silly romantic?' I teased.

'I'll see you in a few weeks,' he told me. After a pause he said, 'I'll miss you.'

'I'm going to miss you too.' I went up on my toes to give him a kiss, before dropping back down. 'We're trying it at least. They can't say we didn't try.'

'Ever the pessimist, aren't we, Shelly?' he joked, tweaking my nose. 'I'll call you when I get there.'

'You better call your mom first,' I told him. 'She'll be mad if you don't tell her you landed safe.'

'I think you're right,' he laughed, and his arms wrapped around my waist.

'Final call for all passengers boarding the eight-oh-five to Boston . . .'

I sighed and hugged him tight, breathing in his scent. I knew it so well, but now I was trying to fix it into my senses permanently. He hugged me back, and I tried to memorize that feeling too – his arms around me, his face in my hair.

'I love you,' he breathed in my ear.

'I love you,' I replied, all of a sudden trying to hold back the tears that pricked behind my eyes. 'So much.'

'We'll try,' he told me, kissing me now, his lips soft and sweet on mine. He tasted like cotton candy, just like when we'd first kissed: he'd bought some from a candy stand in the airport – 'For old times' sake.'

My fingers played with the hair at the nape of his

neck, and the familiar sparks danced through me as we kissed. It was like all the happiness, all the sadness, all the hopes and fears – everything we had went into that kiss. What seemed like decades later, we broke apart, his forehead resting against mine.

'I have to go,' he murmured.

'I'll talk to you later. Good luck.'

He gave me his infamous smirk as he walked backward toward the gate. 'Luck? Shelly, you forget – this is Flynn you're talking to. I don't need luck.'

I laughed, and wasn't entirely shocked when a tear splashed down my cheek; I felt the salty taste on the corner of my mouth, where the memory of Noah's kisses lingered. 'Stupid violence junkie.'

He winked, laughing, and disappeared through the gate, out of sight.

A few minutes later, I stood by the windows, watching the plane roll down the runway, and I felt someone at my side, putting an arm around me. I leaned my head on Lee's shoulder. He didn't say anything, but he didn't have to. He was there for me, just like he always would be.

As Noah's plane built up speed and eased up into the air and the wheels left the ground, I felt myself smiling a little – a sad smile.

Maybe things really would work out with Noah. I

hoped they did. I had my fingers crossed tightly by my side. Maybe things wouldn't work out with Noah – we'd meet other people, or we'd drift apart, or a long-distance relationship just wouldn't suit us. But whatever happened, I knew there was part of me that was always going to belong to Noah Flynn, the school bad-ass; a little piece of my heart that was always going to be his.

Whatever happens, I told myself, staring after Noah's plane, *things are going to be okay*.

'Just think,' Lee said then, 'all this, just from the kissing booth.'

I laughed, pushing him slightly, and he laughed too, squeezing me tight for a second before we turned away from the view of the empty runway, where the plane was lost somewhere in the cloudy sky, and walked off.

Acknowledgements

Firstly, a huge thank you to the team at Random House – particularly to my fantastic editor, Lauren, who's been brilliant. Also a big thanks to the Wattpad team, and all the people who followed me. You've all helped me to find my feet as a writer, and I'm so grateful to all of you. I wouldn't have come this far without you.

Thank you to my A Level teachers and my Head of Year for allowing me the indulgence of such a big distraction. Your constant support and encouragement has been invaluable.

To everyone in the Fishbowl (or, as some call it, the school common room), I'm lucky to have you guys. You've inspired me and supported me so much, even if you didn't know it. Amy, Caroline, Kate, Abi – I don't know where I'd be without you all. Thank you James, for encouraging me to never give up. And Aimee J, thank you for the endless laughter you've brought into my life.

Thank you to my family. You've all been incredibly supportive of my rather time-consuming hobby and my (hopefully!) new career path.

And, last but not least, a big thank you to my GCSE English teacher, Mr Maughan. Your enthusiastic teaching and interest in my writing was a huge motivation.